Stories
From
Way Out West

Stories
From
Way Out West

Bill Fearnow

Full Court Press   Tubac, Arizona

To contact the author, write to us at
P.O. Box 4710, Tubac, AZ 85646

Cover design by
William D. Fearnow

ISBN: 978-1-7338800-0-8

Library of Congress Control Number: 2019909739

Published in the United States of America
First Print Edition: April, 2020

Contents

To my wife

The Flyboy's Daughter

I flew out into space like flying off a swing, but headfirst. And it took much longer than going off a swing. I landed face down. I don't think I bounced, but I may have. The soil must have been soft.

I'd jumped from a stack of hay bales the size of a barn. I don't remember how I got there. I must have climbed. It was pitch dark. Before things grew up around the farm, there were hardly any lights, even on the horizon. I was wearing my favorite dress, the one I'm wearing in the picture of me standing next to the swings in the back yard on my eighth birthday.

It hurt, and I knew I was hurt. I kept still. But once I'd concluded I was still alive, there was nothing to do but get up, walk back to the house, bang open the back door, barge through the kitchen into the living room and cough up blood all over my dress and my mother's rug.

Mom was not happy. There was blood all over her rug. As far as she was concerned, everything in the house was hers and no one else's. My sisters, Doreen and Ellen, weren't happy either. They had to clean up the blood, or at least try to. All they talked about three weeks later when I came home from the hospital was that when she'd come home later that night, Mom had woken them up, screamed at them and made them clean up the rug. I suppose she had to yell at someone. Maybe she felt something.

Mom picked me up, carried me to the car and laid me on the front seat on an old horse blanket she pulled out of the trunk. Even in an emergency, she wouldn't risk bloodying the front seat of one of the brand-new cars she got every year.

They took one look at me at the emergency room and rushed me into surgery. I'd ruptured my spleen. Dad arrived once I was in recovery. It must have been about two in the morning. No one else from the family was around. Dad didn't say a thing. We stared at each other. When I woke up later in my hospital room, he was gone.

Dad kept a landing strip on the farm, not far from the house, so his Marine pilot buddies from the war could fly in anytime. He used most of the farm buildings as shops and hangars. My Grandma Jean, Dad's mother, said the grass on the landing strip was the only crop Dad ever cared about.

Dad and his friends flew experimental airplanes or modified, surplus fighters. Dad spent most of his time working on whatever plane he was interested in at the time. He'd take them up to test them over the farm. We'd be sitting at the kitchen table having dinner and hear his engine quit. We'd hold our breath. Sometimes he'd get the engine started and we'd go back to eating dinner. But if he didn't, we'd get into my mother's car and drive around the farm looking for him. Which aggravated my mother primarily because her car would get dusty, or muddy, or both. Although one was always around, she wouldn't have been caught dead driving a farm truck, even if it was pitch black and we were on our own property where no one could have seen us, even in broad daylight.

Dad usually managed to land without wrecking his planes. We'd drive up, he'd get in the car and drive us back to the house while my mother yelled at him. My sisters and I would ride back to the plane with Dad in the pickup he'd hot-rodded, which was more fun than any ride at the county fair. He was always in a hurry. He'd slide the truck around corners, get airborne going over bumps, and bottom the springs out on the landings. We loved it.

If the plane could roll, he'd tell us where to crawl and where to tie a rope to the landing gear. Then he'd tow it back to the shop with one or two of us in the cockpit to work the brakes to steer. If he'd had a hard landing, we'd go out with a loader and a farm wagon. After he'd lifted the plane onto the wagon, he'd place us on the parts to keep them from falling off and pull the wagon back to the hanger while we'd act like the dead weight we were supposed to be.

Even on good nights, Dad didn't come in until after we'd been put to bed. Mom would sit in the house and smoke cigarettes and nurse her iced tea. The night of one of Dad's crashes I woke up and heard Mom, through the walls, accusing Dad of not caring about her, her children, or her farm. She asked him, repeatedly, what would she do if he killed himself. He didn't say much but finally, he exploded:

"Care about the kids? If you cared about the kids, or me, half as much as you care about that God-damned, idiot brother of yours, it would be like God-damned heaven on earth around here."

My sisters and I heard the front door slam, followed by Dad's pickup roaring out of the front yard. We all acted as if we were asleep.

All Dad's friends flew in on the last Thursday night of every month. Friday morning, dozens of airplanes would be parked on the edge of the strip. My mother's yard, which she insisted Dad irrigate and plant in grass and fill with citrus and shade trees, would be strewn with adults and their children sleeping beneath the trees in blankets or Army surplus sleeping bags.

All weekend, the men flew and tinkered with their planes, drank, and told stories. The mothers fixed and served food. They also chatted, mixed cocktails, and got tipsy. The dads drank their liquor from flasks they kept in their old flight suits. The kids roamed all over the farm, or as far as we could get on foot, which wasn't far because most of the time it was hot and dry. I'm pretty sure it was a Friday or Saturday night of a fly-in I decided to jump off the hay bales.

I think Dad was angry that night at the hospital. It would have been hard to tell. He rarely became angry and when he did his face hardly changed. I used to think he'd been mad at me, but I don't think he was. I think he knew what had happened.

Except for my father that one time, and my mother, my Grandma Jean was the only one who came to see me in the hospital. She came every day, like clockwork, morning and afternoon, and sat in a chair beyond the foot of my bed, out of the nurses' way. I don't remember her saying much. She wasn't the comforting type. She acted almost as if she was keeping a close eye on me. I doubt she knew about Darrell, but she may have had her suspicions.

Although Uncle Darrell didn't live with us, he was almost always around the farm. Even though he's not all that much younger than she is and about six feet, four inches tall, my mother still calls Darrell her "baby brother." He must have been about twenty-two when I was eight.

My mother would drive Darrell out to our farm from their parents' house downtown. He never had a car because he usually didn't have a job. Darrell's being on the farm drove Dad crazy. Darrell would stand around the shop with his hands in his pockets and ask Dad questions. Not that Dad could trust Darrell to do anything. I think Darrell had long ago fouled up enough things so Dad wouldn't dare ask him to help. After a while, Darrell would go into the swamp-cooled or air-conditioned house, and sit around with my mother while they both smoked cigarettes and drank iced tea.

Darrell isn't as dumb as he's made out to be. He acts like some caricature of an eighty-year-old farmer even though he's not very old and he's never farmed a day in his life. His act didn't work on the detectives, but it must have fooled the county attorney.

My mother had to have known all along. It's one of the things that make me so angry. It must have been why she told hardly anyone about my accident, or even that I was in the hospital. She told Doreen and Ellen I'd "gone to Grandma Jean's." They assumed I was somewhere getting something they weren't.

I don't think my Grandma Jean was any more fond of my mother than she was of Dad. Maybe she thought anyone who'd marry Dad was suspect. Except when Dad was away for the War, he and my Mom had been together their entire lives. They grew up next door to each other and went to school together from kindergarten through high school. When my grandfather died while the War was going on, the government sent Dad home so he could keep the farm going, growing cotton. By that time, he'd flown so many missions they'd had to put him out to pasture as an instructor over at Yuma. That's when my parents got married and started our family.

They were childhood sweethearts who probably had no business getting married. But once he decided to do something, Dad did it. He would call her "Doll Baby" when they were both in a good mood. When she wanted to, she could play up to him.

Back then, I had beautiful, dark, thick hair like Dad's and my grandfather's. It was my pride and joy. But one school day, after I came home from the hospital, during second grade art class, I took those little round-tipped scissors and began lopping off entire chunks of my hair. I have no idea how I did it. You can hardly cut construction paper with those scissors. But before the teacher had noticed, there was a pile of hair on the floor around my chair and my head looked as if a rat had been nesting in it. Absolutely panicked, my teacher scooped me up and carried me to the principal's office as if I'd broken my leg, or fainted.

Everyone in the principal's office tried to act as if having half your hair missing when you're eight years old is perfectly normal. About twenty minutes later, my mother charged in, as angry as could be, grabbed my arm, yanked me out of the room, and pulled me all the way to the car.

Once we were in the car, she screamed, "So! You think you can cut your hair? Huh? All by yourself?" I didn't say a word. "You don't like having the most beautiful hair in the family? The most beautiful hair in this filthy little town? That's not good enough for you?" I didn't say anything, but I did look at her. If I had looked away, she'd have screamed: "Look at me when I'm talking to you!" Not that looking at her helped. "You want to make yourself look like you're a little boy?" she asked. "Instead of a beautiful, precious, little girl?" I looked at the floor. "Fine then."

She drove me to the barber shop and had them cut off all my hair. I don't think the barbers were very enthusiastic about doing it, but I doubt they wanted to cross my mother. As soon as the barber started, Mom stormed out. When he was all done, I was left there with him and the two other barbers. There were no other customers that morning, so while they talked about the weather, the price of cotton, and whether the alfalfa would be any good that year, I stared at my now completely fuzzy, gray head, front and back, reflected into infinity in the mirrors hanging on the opposite walls of the shop. My eyes, which are just like my dad's, looked larger, and darker, than ever.

Dad arrived just as the barbers were closing up for lunch. He tried to pay and even tip them for my hair cut, but they all just smiled, looked down at the floor, and shook their heads. Everybody in town loved Dad. As far as they were concerned, there wasn't anything he couldn't do. Before becoming an ace in the War, he'd been the star on all the high school teams. He'd maintained and drove the school bus. He was the drum major of the band. He could play every instrument. He even repaired them if they broke. He'd always been able to fix anything mechanical.

But about the same time I began cutting my hair, Dad started drinking at bars and having girlfriends. He also worked less on his planes. After dinner, instead of going back to his shop, he'd shower, shave, dress up and leave the house, saying he had a meeting. I can still remember the smell of his aftershave hanging in the air after he'd headed out the door.

We acted as if we were still a family. The fly-ins continued, and Dad still did his air shows. He was famous for doing very low-altitude maneuvers in his little experimental planes. We'd pile in the car with my mother and drive to his shows. We were watching Dad with the rest of the crowd at one show. He was right over the runway and his engine was running fine. He was going through all his stunts, one after the other, as effortlessly as rolling off a log. The crowd loved it. Then his engine quit. It didn't sputter and it didn't backfire. There was just silence. You could have heard a pin drop.

Everyone in the stands sat with their mouths wide open for what seemed like a minute. Doreen and Ellen and I thought we knew how things were supposed to turn out: Dad would either get the engine to start or he wouldn't. If he didn't, he'd manage to land. We'd get in the car, drive out, pick him and the plane up, and drive home.

But this time when his engine quit Dad was only fifty or a hundred feet off the ground, and upside down. He tried to roll over and gain some altitude, but he crashed in a cloud of dust and dirt just beyond the end of the runway.

Mom jumped out of the stands like a horse bolting from its stall and took off down the runway in her heels. Her purse was in one hand and she was holding her hat down on top of her hairdo with the other. My sisters and I stood in the stands while the fire trucks and the ambulances roared past. They pulled Dad out of the wreckage, put him in the ambulance and drove off with the siren screaming. Mom went with him. The organizers cancelled the rest of the show and the spectators began to wander off.

We three girls sat there. Eventually, one of the organizers took us to the ticket trailer and gave us some unsold popcorn and cotton candy. Eventually, somebody came and took us home. I don't remember who.

Although he broke his back, Dad was flying again in three months. When it came to flying, he had more lives than a cat, which was one of the things that made it so hard to believe he died in a plane crash.

By then I was in college. He'd called me from California, woke me up around five or six in the morning. He didn't sound good. He said he wanted to hear my voice. He told me "goodbye" and that he "loved me," something he never said.

Later, we found out that after having been out all night, he'd been dropped off before sunrise that morning at the little airport he'd flown into the day before. The airport wasn't open when he got there, so he climbed over a chain link fence and walked nearly half a mile to his plane.

By then Dad had been disinherited. My Grandma Jean had died and left the farm to my sisters and me. All Dad had been left under her will were a few shares in the power company my grandfather had helped form and a salary for running the farm for us, which he could hardly live on, particularly once his drinking and dating floozies became so expensive. The bank had re-possessed his car and the loan on his plane was just about to be called, as I found out when I settled his estate, what there was left of it. At least the bank had made him keep the plane insured.

I knew he'd called for some reason other than just to check in, as he'd been doing before longer flights. At least no one else was in the plane. No matter how bad things had gotten for him, he wouldn't have allowed himself to kill anyone in a plane crash. He never took any of us up in his experimental planes. He always kept a factory-built airplane for flying people around. But the girl he'd flown over with the day before had decided to spend the night with someone else. I can't help thinking if she'd stayed with Dad a few more hours, he might still be alive.

When the phone finally rang later that day, I knew it wasn't going to be good. It had been hours since Dad should have called to check in. I hadn't gone to any of my classes. I'd stayed in bed. I hadn't eaten a thing, and I hadn't gotten dressed.

All I could hear was Mom sobbing. The FAA had called her after the highway patrol found Dad's plane crashed halfway to Tucson, about twenty-five degrees off course and eighty miles past where he should have landed. There hadn't been any fire. The investigators concluded Dad set the plane on autopilot and went to sleep. The plane ran out of fuel, stalled and fell out of the sky.

When they flew in for the wake and funeral, Dad's friends had to use the airport because by then the strip at the farm had long since been grown in with cotton. My mother had divorced Dad and re-married and my sisters and I were all grown. None of us lived on the farm. The house was vacant and nearly derelict.

My dad's friends were respectful, a little more so to me, I think, because they considered me a pilot. I'd been flying quite a while by then. I could do the stunts and aerobatics Dad had taught me. And even though he'd died in a plane crash, and even though they got themselves completely drunk, none of them said anything bad about Dad's flying. They knew him well enough to know it hadn't been an accident.

We buried Dad next to my Grandma Jean and my grandfather in the family mausoleum my grandfather had had built in the pioneers' graveyard in the middle of our little downtown. Four big old F-4s from Yuma flew the missing man formation over the graveyard. They came in so low people in town must have thought the East Valley was being used for bombing practice. When they were right overhead, one of them went ballistic and flew straight up and out of sight. It was worse than watching Dad crash at the air show.

Then the bugler played "Taps" and they fired a twenty-one-gun salute. There I was trying to stop crying while they're firing their rifles. They folded up the American flag from on top of Dad's casket and gave it to Mom, even though she was remarried by then. She cried on our stepfather's shoulder behind the veil she had carefully pinned to a new, black hat.

Although our inheriting the farm was probably the straw that broke Dad's back, I doubt he blamed anyone other than himself. He was too smart about too many things. He had to know he had an adrenalin problem. I asked him once why he flew so close to the ground in his air shows, and he said otherwise flying was "unexciting." He'd taught himself to water ski by getting his friends to drag him down irrigation canals behind one of his hot rods. Fortunately for me, by the time I was old enough to learn to ski, he'd dug us a lake on the farm.

When my mother told him she wanted her divorce, Dad had agreed to see a psychiatrist. They went to a retired Air Force flight surgeon. According to my mother, the flight surgeon cracked open a bottle of whiskey he kept in his desk drawer. Then, after she'd declined their offer of a drink, he and my father filled two tumblers with a few fingers of whiskey and sipped on their drinks and asked my mother, as politely as two men could, exactly what she thought the problem was. I have no idea how much she was exaggerating.

Although Mom only lasted that session, Dad kept seeing the flight surgeon even after Mom had given up and filed for divorce. Dad thought the flight surgeon was intelligent, and nearly everybody enjoyed Dad's company. Dad admitted the flight surgeon told him, more than once, he had to stop drinking, stop smoking, stop driving my mother crazy, and stop doing so many dangerous things. "Sounds like a life sentence, don't ya' think?" Dad said. He laughed and I laughed, even though I wasn't sure he was kidding.

The flight surgeon even put Dad on medication, although Dad said the pills were for his heart, which he said my mother "had broken." Another time, Dad told me the flight surgeon had told him he was "nuts."

Not that I've had much luck with psychiatrists, either. I'm willing to sit and listen to them once a week, but that doesn't mean I'm happy about it. It's not just the cost. The pills make me feel worse. They're too strong. Sometimes I think the psychiatrists are trying to kill me. One day the girl running the register for the pharmacist looked at my prescription and said, "Wow, these are really strong! These are anti-psychotics!" Why that psychiatrist had me on anti-psychotics is beyond me. They were supposed to just be anti-depressants.

It went on with Darrell from the night I jumped off the hay bales until I went away to college. I was never a great student but college did get me away from home, and Darrell. And I met my husband there. Gil and I married right after we graduated. We had our family, and then we started having our problems.

I'd never told anyone about Darrell until I was in my late thirties. And even then, it was almost by accident. Gil and I were separated by then. I was on a date, having dinner at a restaurant with a friend, Stewart. While he was buttering a dinner roll, without looking at me, Stewart asked, "So, did something happen to you, when you were younger?" I nearly fell out of my chair. Although we'd gone to grade school together, at the time I hardly knew Stewart. But somehow, he knew.

"How'd you know?" I gasped. He never really answered. He told me he knew something about "this sort of thing." Stewart's a reader. He told me I should get professional help or things would gradually get worse. You'll notice he didn't say things would get better, but I thought about it.

Things weren't going well for me then. More often than not, I was fighting with Doreen and Ellen, and my marriage to Gil was shaky. Our kids were all right, but that's about all you could say. My mother was as much a problem as ever, but at least Darrell was married and leaving me alone.

If I had it to do over again though, I would just deny it.

Not long after the dinner with Stewart, I was in a marriage counseling session. Gil had skipped, of course, so I brought it up with the counselor. Without even being shocked, he told me I had to tell Gil, which was a terrible mistake. He didn't really say anything at the counselor's office during the session when I told him, but once we were home, Gil grabbed his hunting rifle and was nearly out the door before I could stop him. I almost had to tackle him. Darrell dead, and Gil in jail was the last thing I needed.

I should never have told Gil. By then, I hadn't told him for all the years we'd been together. Another fifteen or twenty wouldn't have made things any worse. I was able to calm Gil down enough that day that he didn't murder anybody. Next session I told the counselor what happened with Gil, and he told me I had to confront my mother and sisters. Fool me once, shame on you. Fool me twice, shame on me. But I did what the counselor said. Dumb.

My mother screamed at me and called me a liar. We were in her kitchen. I thought she was going to grab a knife off the counter and come at me. "Get out!" she screamed. Unbelievably, the next day she took her "little brother" Darrell to a psychologist "to make sure he was all right." She called me and told me first, that nothing I'd said was true, and second, if it was, it was all my fault, and third, that Darrell was going to be fine, despite the fact I was trying to ruin him.

Doreen and Ellen were furious. My mother had warned them I was going to talk to them. She'd convinced them I was trying to kill her. The counselor had told me odds were that if Darrell had done what he'd done to me he'd done the same thing to Doreen, or Ellen, or both of them. I hadn't really expected them to bake me a cake or think I was a hero, but I hadn't expected them to pretty much stop talking to me.

Then I went to the police. The detectives had me talk to Darrell on a telephone call they recorded. Basically, Darrell confessed. He apologized, actually. He even broke down and cried. I almost felt sorry for him. When the detectives interviewed Darrell in person, he admitted everything to them. Then he changed his mind and denied everything. Then he said he couldn't remember because he had Alzheimer's. He even apologized to them for not being able to "be of more assistance, officers." Those were his words. The detectives interviewed me again, and then forwarded their report to the county attorney.

The detectives called me once a month to give me updates. But after nearly a year, the county attorney decided not to prosecute. I have no idea why. Gil insisted it was because the county attorney and Darrell belong to the same church. The detectives told me it didn't help it had happened so long ago. They also said they supposed Darrell wasn't a threat any more. How they knew that, I have no way of knowing, any more than I know how it had anything to do with what he'd done to me.

His wife hates me now, but Darrell's as fine as can be. My mother decided she had Alzheimer's too. Maybe it runs in families. She moved herself into an assisted living facility and began acting as if she can hardly speak. Doreen and Ellen only talk to me when they need something.

I went through the trauma, sleepless nights, worry, and pulling my hair out. I lost my family. For what? Nothing. Everything was supposed to have gotten better, but instead things got worse.

Things even got worse with Gil's family. Not that they'd ever been terrific. Although I didn't meet Gil until we were away at college in Flagstaff, Gil was raised on a farm too. Although we were from different towns, the valley's not very big when it comes to farm families. Gil's grandfather and my grandfather had done business and sat on boards together. I don't think Gil's dad, Mr. Gardner, had ever been thrilled about me and Gil, but he kept it to himself most of the time. I think Gil's mother used to see to that. Most of the time Mr. Gardner's very smooth, very polished. He's a good businessman, farmer, and politician. He was even mayor when their town was smaller. But he has a mean streak.

When Gil's mother was in the hospital, dying from cancer, I was there almost non-stop, making sure the nurses were doing what they were supposed to, sitting with Gil's mother and trying to calm down Gil's sister. I wore myself out. But after the funeral, Mr. Gardner got drunk and told me in front of the whole family and nearly everybody else we all knew, I'd "single-handedly destroyed his son's life" and "absolutely ruined" his son's children, or as he referred to them, "his grandchildren."

I left right away, but it was a big scene. I drove straight home, went to bed, and didn't come out for a week. I realized Mr. Gardner blamed me for, among everything else, Gil not being successful and powerful, at least in his eyes. He also thinks our kids have a hard time because of everything that's happened to me.

Gilly, or Gil Junior, our son, can't sit still for more than two minutes. Our daughter Genevieve has problems too. But Gil's no genius. He'd as soon ride a tractor all day as prepare a financial statement to get a bank loan. I do those things. I even did them for Gil's family's farm when we were divorced and were hardly seeing each other. We're still divorced, even though sometimes I think we spend so much time together we might as well be remarried. But Gil lives at his farm, and I live alone in my own house. The psychiatrists aren't happy about it, but I do. Gil and I haven't lived in the same house since we first separated and I was living with Stewart.

When I moved away from Gil and the kids to be with Stewart, I thought I could be happy. Other people are. And Stewart was so nice. He was nice about us being together, back East where he works as an engineer, and he was nice about me having to leave him and move back home. Why aren't there nice people in my life? Gil's nice but he's not the most sensitive person in the world. He forgets things and he's always late. But he is reliable and he's sane. But there's so much he doesn't understand. I try to explain things to him, and he says, "Now Leanne, it's probably not that bad." But it usually is. Stewart was nicer. Maybe "considerate" is the word. Of course, compared to my family, maybe all he had to do was not be mean.

And things are just as terrible with my family. Like I said, Doreen and Ellen have hardly spoken to me since I reported Darrell to the police. But by then we were fighting over what to do with the farm. They wanted to sell it as quickly as possible to whichever developer was willing to close as quickly as possible, regardless of what they were willing to pay. I wanted to keep farming so we could pay the taxes and take our time to wait for the right deal, or try to develop some of it ourselves to keep more of the money for the kids. I didn't care if we had to wait for years. But all their husbands wanted was cash. Immediately. Maybe it makes sense. Doreen and Ellen and their husbands have gone through everything else they've gotten. I don't know how they live with the possibility of their money running out. It's sure one of the things that keeps me up nights.

They also blame me for Mom being in assisted living, which is expensive. And even though they think there's something wrong with me, when something has to be decided, they turn to me. Then, once I come up with a solution after doing a lot of work, they do the exact opposite of what I recommend.

Doreen and Ellen have always done a good job of acting normal. They think I should have kept quiet about Darrell and not ruined things for everybody. Maybe I should have just kept trying to act normal. I couldn't live the way they do, but it seems to agree with them. They've never jumped off haystacks. They don't cut their hair. They don't get divorced and then spend most of their time with their ex-husbands. They can go outside whenever they want.

I still cut my hair. But now, once I come to my senses, I put on a baseball cap, go to a salon and have them try to do something with whatever's left. It's a condition. It has a name and it must be where the expression "pulling your hair out" comes from. Not that I don't have plenty of reasons to pull my hair out.

But when I'd moved away to be with Stewart, I was living happily in beautiful, leafy Connecticut. I might as well have been living in a magazine. I was even on the verge of buying a house. It was wonderful. Then Gil called to tell me Genevieve was having problems. I thought to myself: problems? What could possibly have been wrong in her life? She'd had a great childhood, a father who was there, a mother who loved her and took care of her. She'd had dance lessons, piano lessons, her own bedroom in a nice, new home in a subdivision that wasn't in the middle of a cotton farm. We'd even bought her a horse. What child could possibly be unhappy if her parents bought her a horse?

But Genevieve had decided she didn't want to go to school any more. I asked Gil, "What kid has ever wanted to go to school?" But I could tell it was over. Genevieve wouldn't even come out of her room. Gil said the school psychologist had told him she was clinically depressed. I thought to myself, clinically depressed about what? Shouldn't it have been me getting that kind of attention? At least I hadn't bought a house in Connecticut, but that was the end of my having a life of my own.

Then, once we got Genevieve into therapy, on medication, and back in school, and with a nice, smart boyfriend even, Gilly began having problems. He decided to drop out of his senior year of high school. Not that he had been the greatest student. He just stopped talking. We sent Gilly to every specialist in the valley, with my money. Eventually, we just gave up and Gilly managed to pass his equivalency exams and get his diploma, two years after he should have graduated from high school. He's driving a long-haul truck and he's happier than I've ever seen him.

All of which is a big hit with Mr. Gardner. So much for the next generation of Gil's family becoming important.

But at least the kids are healthy. They haven't come down with the cancer that seems to run in Gil's family. Sometimes I think if I had cancer, maybe people would feel sorry for me. I'd have a disease. I'd lose my hair because of chemotherapy. People wouldn't ask me, "What's wrong, Leanne?" or say, "You'll get over it," or, "It's all in your head."

Eventually, the psychiatrists talked me into checking into an expensive clinic. It's in Tucson and it's almost like a resort. I was there a month. I stayed in at night and did all my assignments. I kept the journal they told us to keep. I made all the art projects they seem to find so important. While I was doing all my homework, the other patients were all having the times of their lives. The sex addicts were running around with each other in the bushes. The alcoholics were out on the lawn, drinking. The prescription drug addicts were gobbling their pills and the potheads were puffing up a storm. It was as if they were on all-expenses-paid vacations. Most of them had been there before. They're constantly in and out of jails, or they're trying to kill themselves or otherwise costing their families a fortune. They don't care, but I cared. I'd paid thirty thousand dollars of my own money. I still don't know why I was there with all those crazy people.

My last day was "Family Day," a Sunday. It's supposed to give the staff a chance to tell everyone how well you've done, explain the things you're going to be dealing with, and lay out all the things the families should do to help ease you back into the "real world." None of my family came. Not Gil, and neither of the kids. They couldn't make it. They were too busy. There I was in the facility's elegant dining room, all alone at a big round table, just myself and name cards for all four of us. I didn't try to invite my sisters or my mother. I guess I'd learned that much. But I had changed into a dress and put on make-up.

A lot of the time I wonder what these so-called experts are thinking. If I had a real family, would I have needed to be in a place like that to begin with? I go to all the trouble and expense to get myself straightened out, and my family can't spend an afternoon driving down to Tucson and back?

I don't expect anything from them anymore. I guess I still do from Gil. He tries, most of the time. But the kids are just kids and they always will be. They don't realize it, but it's true. My sisters? They're too busy watching out for themselves. My mother? She's always hated me. Mr. Gardner? I guess I should just be happy he doesn't insult me in public anymore. He's happily married to his secretary and doesn't have much time for any of us these days, anyway.

But the psychiatrists seem to think my family, the cause of all my problems, is going to cure me. Just like they told me I would get better by having the police put Darrell in jail, that I would feel better once society punished him. But I was the only one who got punished.

I asked the psychiatrists why I'm so affected by things. The ones at the clinic said what happened to me permanently damaged my nervous system because I was so young when it started happening. I'm not so sure about that. Others tell me all I need to do is take my medicine. They say the drugs will even things out and I won't end up like my dad. But I'm not like Dad. Why do they bring him into the conversation? I ask them, "If I take these drugs, I'll feel terrible all the time? That will be better?" The drugs are so powerful they'll kill me. I can't trust psychiatrists. I can't trust my family. So, who can I trust?

And with everything that's happened to me, not just Darrell, everything, what happens if I do end up like Dad? It wasn't fair, what happened to him, any more than what's happened to me. Maybe I should worry about that too.

But thanks to me, the only family I had is gone. Not that it was much of one, but it was the only one I had. They were. They just were. And now they're gone. Not just Dad, all of them.

Way Out West

Sunlight forced its way around the edges of the shade blacking out the window. The air conditioner ground away in the flimsy front wall. Someone was knocking on the door.

"Just a minute!" Evan shouted, jumping out of bed and stumbling to the door, nearly tripping over his shoes.

Evan's head was not clear. He'd slept poorly, waking up more than once in darkness. Finally, he'd checked his watch, which had read four o'clock in the morning, before staring at the ceiling until he'd fallen asleep. Now it felt as if it were midday.

Opening the door to the blinding sunlight, Evan found himself face to face with the Quaker Oats Quaker sporting a white, polyester mesh ball cap with "Prescott Concrete" in green letters above a green bill. Close-set blue eyes sparkled above large pink cheeks separated by an almost regal nose. A smile revealed a set of perfect, pearly white teeth, out of place in an at least seventy-year-old face. Aside from the incongruous hat, the man wore regulation country western star clothes: a red-checked shirt stretched over a barrel-like torso bulging over the silver buckle of a tooled leather belt supporting pressed blue jeans tapering down to pointy cowboy boots.

"Mornin'!" the man bellowed, toasting Evan with the coffee mug he held in his left hand.

"Mr. Breen?" Evan asked, still squinting against the sunlight.

"Yes sir!" the man enthused, extending his right hand. "We all ready to go?"

Shaking Mr. Breen's hand and gathering his wits about him, Evan asked, "Do you want to come in? I need to take a shower."

"I'll just wait here," Mr. Breen chuckled.

"Okay. I'll be right out." Evan closed the door. Making his way back through the darkened room to the watch he'd set three hours ahead upon landing in Phoenix last night, Evan turned on the light on the stand. His watch read seven o'clock, ten o'clock on the East coast. No wonder he was mixed up. He made his way to the bathroom, stripped, turned on the shower and stepped in.

Evan's father had died earlier that summer, leaving Evan, his father's "only son and heir," as Mr. Jones, his father's lawyer, called Evan, "the proceeds of a few small life insurance policies" and, "much to everyone's surprise, some not insubstantial southwestern real estate holdings." In other words, some land in Arizona. Which they'd found out about only because while he was in the hospital dying, Evan's father had received a letter from a company in Arizona asking whether the land was for sale.

"How did they find out about my," Evan's father paused, "condition?" He shook his head and winced. "Those guys," he wheezed. "I thought they wanted to make me rich." He paused to catch his breath. "Big mistake. That and thinking I'd have time to retire," he concluded before erupting into a coughing fit. Evan called the nurse, who increased his father's intravenous pain medication and sedative, giving Evan the opportunity to end his last visit with his father, who died in his sleep later that night.

A few days after the funeral, Evan had been summoned to Mr. Jones' office. The company in Arizona was still in contact. It turned out Evan's father owned almost two thousand acres. Although Evan's father had seemed discouraged about the property, Mr. Jones said, "Two thousand acres. That's a lot of land. Let's see. If it's only worth a thousand dollars an acre, which would seem ridiculously inexpensive, that would be two million dollars. I do remember your dad saying something about some land in Arizona that was supposed to be 'primed for development.' It should be worth a lot more, don't you think?" Mr. Jones seemed more excited than Evan, but before long Evan was intrigued.

Evan had never really seen much of his father. Just out of engineering school, his father had started with a New York City-based international construction firm. Within a month or two, the firm sent Evan's father overseas and, for all practical purposes, he never came back. All Evan and Evan's mother, a receptionist at the construction firm whom his father had courted, married and impregnated over the course of the week he'd been "home" to celebrate his fortieth birthday and "settle down," knew was he traveled the world supervising big construction projects, in more recent years as the owner of his own one-man consulting firm.

Evan's father and mother got along, but they were rarely together. His father had taken good care of Evan and his mother, and even after Evan's mother divorced his father when Evan was in junior high school and married Evan's Manhattan banker stepfather, Evan's father continued supporting Evan generously and without complaint.

At times Evan's mind raced with the possibility of having inherited over two million dollars. Although he wasn't greedy, approaching his last academic year as a college English major, Evan had begun wondering how he was going to support himself. Although he was pretty good at school and thought he'd make a decent high school teacher, Evan wasn't sure teaching would be all that interesting. And although teaching college might be more interesting, graduate school sounded like a lot of work. He also wondered whether he could support himself on even a professor's salary.

Evan's stepfather made lots of money. Evan and his mother moved into his stepfather's big, beautiful house after his mother and stepfather were married. Evan had no idea what his stepfather did in the City to make all that money, but he did know he, Evan, couldn't do whatever his stepfather did having studied English in college. He'd begun to wonder whether he should have studied something more practical, even though math and economics hadn't interested him and, unlike his father, he had no head for math and science.

But having had a savings account and a few savings bonds since childhood, Evan knew if you put money in a bank or gave it to the government, they'd pay you interest. And even Evan could calculate that just five percent interest on two million dollars equaled a hundred thousand dollars. A year. With that kind of money, even an English major could live pretty well, maybe even in Europe. Although he'd never been there, based on what he'd heard in college, living in Europe sounded pretty neat. And maybe his property was worth more than two million dollars. Mr. Jones seemed to consider a thousand dollars an acre a conservative estimate. Maybe his father had been busy all that time making Evan rich. Although he tried not to think that way, it was possible. Wouldn't that be something?

The people at the company in Arizona, called Intercontinental Holdings, and Mr. Jones thought it would be good if Evan went to Arizona and saw the land before deciding whether he should sell it or "hold onto it as an investment," as Mr. Jones said. "Unfortunately," Mr. Jones tried to explain to Evan, "there could be estate taxes and back taxes," whatever those were. And there would be "additional, ongoing, real estate taxes to pay in the future, and because the property evidently doesn't throw off any income, any kind of taxes aren't anything you can pay if you retain the property, electing not to liquidate is most likely not a viable alternative." Evan took this to mean that being in college, he couldn't afford to keep the property, which was fine with him. Although he hadn't told his mother or his stepfather, or Mr. Jones, Evan wanted to just take the money, particularly if there was a lot of it.

Evan's stepfather wanted some time to check into Intercontinental Holdings and even send one of his younger associates along with Evan to evaluate the situation, but he was in the middle of some big deals and Evan didn't want to wait. He only had a week before he was due back on campus. Intercontinental Holdings had agreed to reimburse Evan for his airfare and motel room when he sold them the land. They'd also arranged to have Mr. Breen, the man at the door, who, it turned out, was an old friend of Evan's father, show Evan the property and introduce him to the lawyer for the company, Mr. Kurtz, Jr., also an old friend of Evan's father. Mr. Breen would also take Evan to meet the president of Intercontinental Holdings, who would take Evan out for dinner. "Dining on the old corporate expense account. They're rolling out the red carpet," Mr. Jones almost bragged to Evan. "They must be anxious to tie that property up. Be sure not to sign anything while you're out there, though. We don't want to give the property away, do we? We'll string them out a little. Once you get back here, and you've had a chance to sleep on it, we'll talk, and you can make a decision. Basic 'Negotiation 101,' right? Do they teach that at your college?" Mr. Jones laughed and so did Evan, without being sure exactly why.

Evan's stepfather didn't think much of Mr. Jones. He even said something about Evan's father probably having hired Mr. Jones, a local lawyer in their town, rather than a lawyer in the City, to save money. He seemed dubious of the whole thing but ultimately told Evan to go ahead and take the trip if he was in a hurry. "There's no hurry. We can figure this all out when I've got the time." Which was good enough for Evan.

So, on a late summer afternoon, Evan packed a change of clothes in his backpack, took a cab to Newark airport and flew out on an early evening flight that deposited him in Phoenix on an incredibly oven-like, super-hot night. Taking a cab to a motel near the airport, Evan had what he guessed was almost a mild panic attack wondering what his father had gotten him into. But he had a meal at the McDonalds across the motel's parking lot and then watched a movie on the T.V. in his room before falling into the fitful sleep from which he'd been startled awake by Mr. Breen's knock.

Finishing his shower, Evan toweled off, dressed, threw his things into his backpack, and exited the motel room. He was booked back to Newark that night on the red-eye. He'd land at seven o'clock tomorrow and head back to college the following day to begin his senior year. Although he was anxious to get started, because what they had planned shouldn't take more than a couple hours, Evan was worried about filling the entire day.

Mr. Breen took Evan's bag and tossed it in the back seat of his big, new, crew-cab pickup truck with an open trailer full of crates and boxes hitched behind it. The diesel engine idled noisily.

"Taking some things to the boys. Hate burning all this fuel without hauling a respectable load," Mr. Breen shouted from the other side of the truck before jumping in and slamming his door shut. Evan scrambled in. "Came out to see what your dad left you," Mr. Breen shouted as they pulled out of the parking lot. Evan nodded. "Atta boy!"

Although Evan's motel had been fairly new, within a few blocks they were driving down a street lined with run-down motels and shuttered businesses. Groups of unattractive women in awful clothes congregated here and there along the sidewalk.

"The old main drag through town," Mr. Breen announced. "Built these motels after the War and on into the 'fifties and 'sixties. Good business, motels. Until the interstate came through." Mr. Breen stopped speaking until Evan looked toward him. "Only customers now are the girls working the morning commute."

Prostitutes? In a place like Phoenix? The truck turned onto a ramp leading to an elevated highway. Although Evan hadn't expected Phoenix to be endless golf courses surrounding gleaming office buildings and resort hotels, he had expected something a little more elegant. A boyhood friend had escaped one New Jersey January at a Phoenix resort, mailing Evan a postcard depicting three massive swimming pools and telling Evan of frolicking in the pool between signing for hot-dogs and soft drinks. The Phoenix they were driving through reminded Evan of the uglier parts of New Jersey. Not having much time to get his questions answered, Evan figured he'd better jump right in.

"So, how much is the property, my property, worth?"

Mr. Breen chuckled.

"Well, that depends on how much somebody's willing to pay."

Perhaps Evan had posed the question incorrectly.

"What's it worth an acre?"

"Can't really sell it in acres. Unless you subdivide it. But that's expensive. The least you can sell is 'forties.'" Evan must have looked puzzled. "Thirty-six acre parcels. I'm not really sure what the number would be, per acre."

Thirty-six acres make forty acres? Either way, that was a lot of land, at least in New Jersey where it would be a farm or a couple of shopping centers or office parks, at least. Evan wasn't sure what to think. Could people in Arizona afford to live on such big pieces of land? Evan decided to keep his mouth shut and wait. They'd be at the property soon enough. Maybe then it would make sense.

After half an hour driving on expressways, they seemed to be out of town. The compass feature on the truck's digital screen indicated they were heading north. The houses and businesses had thinned out. Because the property was supposed to be near Phoenix and ready for turning into houses, Evan assumed they were almost there, which was good. Mr. Breen was a talker.

"The old Prescott stage road," he announced, pointing at a dirt road paralleling the highway. Rolling hills led up to good-sized mountains in the distance. The vegetation was scrubby but plentiful and the soil was the color of baseball diamond dirt. A four-wheeled all-terrain vehicle sped along the dirt trail, spewing a rooster tail of orange dust.

"Tough business, stagecoaches. Not sure they ever turned a profit. Lasted only about ten years before they ran the railroad up north and killed the stagecoaches." Mr. Breen shook his head. "Used to be a station house there. Big, wooden buildings. Double doors on both ends. When they were being chased by Indians, they'd drive the coaches in the front at a full gallop, the station attendants would close the doors behind the stage, and the drivers would put on the brakes and slide clear out the other end before they could stop. Then they'd back into the station and close the doors on the other end. Dug arrowheads out of those doors when we were kids."

How could a building, or a dirt road, last in the middle of nowhere for a hundred and fifty or so years? Indians with bows and arrows sounded like something out of the movies. And why didn't one group of Indians just wait in back, close the doors as soon as the coach slid out and attack then? It just sounded fishy. The truck began climbing up some steep grades.

Evan was growing impatient. He didn't want to sound stupid or seem rude, but he was having a hard time holding himself in check.

"Are we getting any closer to my dad's property?"

"Sure," was all Mr. Breen said, which emboldened Evan.

"Where is it, exactly?"

"On up ahead."

"Is it near here?"

"Probably not as near as you might think." Which went without saying. "I think your dad had the same, what would you say, 'misconception?' He probably thought the land was close to Phoenix. But it's not, really."

Evan wasn't sure he should be alarmed or relieved at Mr. Breen's being so forthcoming. He looked around at the mountains. Mr. Breen resumed his narration.

"Hauled a lot of gold out of these hills." Gold? "When they built the interstate, they kept a crew of miners on call. Every time the road builders blasted into a vein of quartz, they'd call the miners in. Once they got out the quartz, the road builders would go back to building the road. Took eighteen million dollars out of these hills. The only road the government ever built at a profit."

Eighteen million dollars-worth of quartz? Evan's childhood rock collection had included four or five sugar-cube-sized chunks of various shades of quartz carefully glued into a little cardboard box.

"Quartz?"

"Sure. That's where they keep the gold!"

"I thought gold came in nuggets."

"Only in the movies, mostly. What you do is you find a vein of quartz, pull it out, crush it to powder, soak it with acid. Gold drains right out like magic. Big business, gold mining. But you can lose your shirt in a hurry." Evan was still a little dubious.

"Is there any gold on my property?" he asked.

"Not that anybody's found."

As far as they'd driven, Evan was beginning to suspect something was amiss.

"So, my father's land isn't really ready for development, like he thought?"

"Oh, no. It's perfect for developing," Mr. Breen enthused. "Into forties. Your dad has three sections. Six hundred and forty acres each, give or take. A square mile. So that would be forty-eight forties, or fifty-one thirty-six acre lots. That's a lot of lots you've got to sell. Say fifty, for ease of calculation."

Just fifty lots in two thousand acres? Evan's stepfather's house was an estate and it was two-and-a-half acres. Most really nice neighborhoods in New Jersey only had acre lots.

"They must be worth a lot?"

"They can start at five, eight, ten thousand dollars and then go on up, maybe." Evan did the math and became alarmed.

"So, just five hundred thousand dollars?"

Mr. Breen shook and chuckled.

"Might be the number. But you have to spend some time and money before you get to that point. Have to survey, build roads, get permits, do title work, so on and so forth. Takes time. And money. None of which your dad was really interested in doing, at least here in the U.S. And not on his own account, of course."

Two hundred fifty dollars an acre? Evan wasn't sure what to make of this. After a few silent minutes Mr. Breen waved both his hands deliberately from side to side in front of the windshield and over the steering wheel.

"Dad owned all this," he said. Evan perked up.

"My dad?"

"No," Mr. Breen said, shaking and chuckling, "mine. Bought this ranch from the government. During the War."

"Everything we can see?" Evan asked.

"No," Mr. Breen chuckled. "But close to it. Paid half a million dollars for a million acres." Evan panicked.

"Fifty cents?" he nearly shouted, "an acre?" Mr. Breen chuckled and nodded.

"Sure. People thought he was crazy. But the government had priced the land on how many cows they thought were on the property. In two years we hauled out, and sold back to the government, enough wild cows to recoup the half a million, and then some. Beef was pricey during the War." Evan looked blankly at Mr. Breen. "A 'wild cow's' a cow that's born to a herd. Usually, you don't even know they're there. By the time we were done selling wild cows, we still had all the cows the government thought was there when they sold it to us. Heck of a deal."

Maybe there was another way to approach the question.

"What did my dad pay for his land?"

"Depends on who you talk to," Mr. Breen answered, which struck Evan as a non-answer. "Your dad traded into his land as part of some work he'd done for the Libyan government."

"Libya? In North Africa? Next to Egypt?" Mr. Breen nodded.

"And if your dad thought he was getting some valuable land, the sellers must have thought they were getting something valuable too, don't you think?"

Evan wasn't sure what this meant. He felt almost woozy. He'd never known where in the world his father worked. For some reason, his mother never told Evan, nor did his father. It was as if it just never came up. But Libya? The grandparents of one of Evan's grade school classmates had been killed in the Pan Am bombing over Scotland. His father had been doing business with a terrorist regime? Hadn't that been illegal? Evan decided to change the subject. Assuming as old as Mr. Breen was, his father must be dead, Evan gestured out the window, asking, "So you own all this?"

"Oh, no. Dad sold out to John Wayne."

"John Wayne? The movie actor?"

"And he was tickled to get it for three million."

"Dollars?" Evan blurted.

"Yes sir."

"Six dollars an acre?"

"Yes sir. It was quite a scene when he signed the papers in the law office to buy the land. They let the secretaries come to the door, one at a time, and take a peek. He had quite a bit of ranch land by the time he died, but his family didn't really want to graze cattle. So, Dad bought them out," Mr. Breen winked at Evan, "for a bit of a discount."

Although Evan wanted to nod his head in agreement, all he could do was move his head in a circle.

"Saw John Wayne one other time over in Los Angeles. Walt Disney was trying to get some folks here in Arizona to help him start Disneyland. They sent me over to scout it out. I came back and said I didn't think it would catch on." Mr. Breen paused and looked over at Evan before laughing and shaking. "Guess I was wrong on that one, huh? Can't ever tell how things are going to turn out. Might as well just flip a coin."

John Wayne? Walt Disney? With this guy? Give me a break.

"That was before jets. I flew over to L.A. and back to see John Wayne and Walt Disney in a nice Beechcraft twin. During the 'sixties, the bank repossessed a farm just across the Colorado that had one of the first Learjets. As long as the bank owned the farm, and the Learjet, they'd have me fly over in the dark, check on everything there as the sun came up, then fly back, all in time for breakfast. One hotrod of an airplane. Didn't need a pilot's license back then. Pretty much taught myself how to fly it."

When could anybody fly a private jet without a license? Didn't even people like Charles Lindbergh and Amelia Earhart have pilots' licenses? Was this guy B.S.-ing him?

Evan looked away, concerned his frown might be showing. And anyway, where were they going? Evan felt himself getting angry. He looked at his watch. They'd been out of sight of Phoenix for over an hour. Evan's mother had taught him to count to ten when he was angry. Most times it worked. Evan caught a glimpse of a farm field in a valley off to his left as his anger subsided to irritation. If his property wasn't ready for building houses, maybe it could be farmed.

"Can you farm on my property?" Evan asked.

"Funny you should ask." Evan had no idea what was funny. "When they first ran the railroad through up there, grass was waist-high from horizon to horizon. All anybody had to do was turn some calves loose, let them grow into cows, round 'em up, load 'em onto rail cars, ship 'em back east, and count your money." Mr. Breen chuckled. "Only problem was, once the cattle ate the grass, it didn't grow back." Another chuckle and shake of the head. "Never has."

Mr. Breen fell quiet for nearly the first time during the trip. What am I doing here, Evan asked himself. Stuck in a truck with what? A compulsive liar? The village idiot? Having flown three quarters of the way across the country on a charge to his stepfather's credit card he feared he'd have no way of repaying, Evan was beginning to feel trapped in a bad dream where money was pouring out of his pockets and he couldn't do anything about it. Since his property had already dropped from two million dollars to half a million dollars, Evan had already lost a million and a half dollars, and he hadn't even see his property.

They exited the interstate onto a two-lane highway leading into scattered subdivisions around a town Mr. Breen declared to be "Prescott, Arizona. My home town and headquarters. An Indian fighting post, then the territorial capital, then not much of anything, and now," pointing past Evan's nose, "the Indians are using that casino right there to get even, one quarter at a time."

Evan recognized the huge video sign and the hotel looming behind it as an Indian casino like the ones on the East Coast. "Good business, casinos," Mr. Breen bellowed, almost angrily. "If you're an Indian, or one of the mobsters they hire to run them."

Driving further into town, they turned into the gravel, fenced yard of a huge concrete plant which seemed, inexplicably, to be right in the middle of the town. Mr. Breen jumped out and bounded into a small office. Two guys wearing ball caps like Mr. Breen's appeared from behind the office, unhitched the trailer from the pickup and walked back behind the office. Mr. Breen emerged from the office, scampered back to the truck more energetically than a man half his age and climbed in. Driving out of the lot, they headed down the street to a large car dealer's sales lot which seemed to comprise most of the rest of the town. A lanky, young salesman wearing a white shirt and skinny black tie and black dress pants ran to greet them.

"How do you like the truck, Mr. Breen?" the salesman gushed.

"Pretty nice," Mr. Breen cooed and nodded. "Yes sir."

"How many will you need for the plant?"

"Not sure, yet. Maybe just this one, maybe a whole fleet." The salesman jumped from foot to foot. "You don't mind if I drive her around town for another day? To get a better feel?" Mr. Breen asked.

"No sir! Not at all! Take your time!"

"You got yourself a deal, partner," Mr. Breen said, shaking hands with the salesman through the window. "Adios!"

Mr. Breen returned to his narrative as they drove out of town through more scattered subdivisions.

"See that steel tank next to the railroad?" A large, peeling, black tank stood on a scrub-covered hill, looking as if it should have been in a tank farm back home. "Dad had it built back East. Brought it out here in pieces by rail, had it put together and ran a pipe to an artesian well on the other side of that hill. Used to fill tank cars and haul water up to the Grand Canyon."

"We're almost to the Grand Canyon?" Evan blurted.

"No," Mr. Breen chuckled. "The Canyon's about a hundred miles on up the road. They needed water because the hotel wells were running dry. Later on, Dad ran a pipe from that tank to the Grand Canyon and sold the whole operation to the hotel folks before he had some oil boys drill some deep wells up at the Canyon. Tank just sits there now. Water's hard to get out of the ground and it's hard to pipe long distances."

Unless you have an artesian well or you pipe it a hundred miles, Evan thought. Of course, those weren't the only things that weren't adding up. Something was definitely wrong. Maybe "just outside" had a different meaning in Arizona since it was clear Evan's father's land wasn't "just outside" much of anywhere, never mind Phoenix. Mr. Breen babbled on.

"Dad grazed cattle on the ranch next to yours back during the '52 snow storm. Snowed the cows in. Ten feet of snow. Got cold and stayed cold. Dad had the Governor get the National Guard to fly hay in so the cows wouldn't starve. Flew open-backed C-119 Flying Boxcars up there full of hay. Me and some of the boys flew with 'em. Showed 'em where the cows were." Mr. Breen shook and chuckled.

"We were making our last run late one afternoon and the load jammed. Couldn't get it out of the plane. Couldn't get it back in the plane. Hell of a situation. Some baling wire had got caught on the wall of the plane. So, I crawled back there, unhitched the wire, and sure enough, the load started moving, out the door. Faster than I could make it to the front of the plane, of course. All I could do was hang on." He almost cackled. "Out we went—whoosh—me and the hay." Mr. Breen chuckled and shook before regaining his composure. "As you might have guessed since I'm here telling you this, I just rode that hay down to the ground. Landed pretty soft. Between ten feet of snow, eight feet of hay, and not much altitude, there I was."

Flying out the back of a plane? Without a parachute? Without being killed? Wouldn't the hay come apart, or tumble?

"It was cold and quiet, but I could hear the cows, and they sounded hungry. I didn't have much to do, so I figured which direction they were in and started tunneling through the snow. Popped out into a kind of roomful of cows. When they clump up, cows can throw off a lot of heat. The ground around them was bare. They'd melted all the snow. So, I went back through my tunnel and got them some hay. Made a bed for myself once they were fed. I have to say, it was kind of pleasant and peaceful out there, me and those cows," Mr. Breen concluded wistfully. Evan envied the cows.

"At daybreak, the planes came back and dropped some supplies, and food, and a newspaper, but it was a few days before they could get me out. They brought the snow cat from the ski hill outside Flagstaff to get me out."

Wouldn't you freeze to death overnight, Evan wondered? And how could they drop supplies close enough that he could find them in ten feet of snow? Ten feet? A hundred and twenty inches? Mr. Breen rattled on.

"Always have loved to drive. Dad volunteered me to trailer some quarter horses over to New Mexico. Big quarter horse races there. Nice drive. Long day each way. Some of the boys gave me a suitcase of cash and a list of horses to bet on, in which races. Darned if they didn't all come in."

Evan wondered whether he was in Arizona or some third world country. Besides feeling as if his fortune was dwindling by the moment and being annoyed by all the preposterous local color, Evan was beginning to wonder whether he'd been kidnapped. Were they going to drive forever? Would he make his plane? He'd be trapped in this wilderness. The countryside was vast. You could see forever in every direction. There wasn't a cloud in the pale-blue sky. "God-forsaken" and "desolate" both came to mind.

Turning onto another interstate highway, they headed west. The signs showed a few hundred miles to Los Angeles. This was not good. Were they going to California? Soon, Mr. Breen turned off at an exit sign for a town, although there was no town in sight.

"Seligman, Arizona," Mr. Breen announced. "Just outside your property. Named after a railroad man from your neck of the woods. Built a big meatpacking house here. Lost a lot of money." Mr. Breen shook his head sadly from side to side. "Just an old railroad town now. Railroad's down there in a gully. You can see the telegraph poles running next to it. Built towns every forty miles, as far as a steam engine could get on a load of water. The crews went forty miles one way, stopped for lunch, got into a train headed the other way, and were home for dinner. Now, most of these railroad towns are obsolete. Diesels go a long way." They were driving past motels, like the ones they'd driven past in Phoenix, that appeared to be serving as run-down apartments.

"Like I said, tough business, motels," Mr. Breen said. Until now, Evan had not realized the American West was nothing more than one business disaster after another. Mr. Breen slowed down and pointed to the small houses along one side of the street. "Built by the railroad. Shotgun houses. You can shoot a shotgun from the front door, through the house, and out the back door and not hit anything." Was this a good thing?

The houses stood shoulder to shoulder, surrounded by a variety of hand-made fences, their small yards filled with miscellaneous junk, faded plastic children's toys, and rusted cars and trucks. Soon, ramshackle restaurants and burger joints lined the other side of the street. Evan noticed people sitting in lawn chairs on the sidewalks who, since their truck was the only vehicle on the road, seemed to be waiting for Evan and Mr. Breen. In another minute, a line of pickup trucks appeared in the opposite lane, heading slowly toward them. Teenagers sat calmly on the hoods and roofs of trucks, festooned with paper streamers and messages painted on the windshields and windows. It was a parade.

Mr. Breen slowed down as the trucks crept by. Girls in ball gowns and wearing tiaras atop their piled-up hair waved grimy, white-gloved hands. A boy wearing a white tuxedo and a crown waved enthusiastically. Next, boys wearing large cowboy hats, football jerseys, jeans and cowboy boots sat on the hoods and roofs or stood in the beds of more pickup trucks, alternately looking fierce, and smiling and waving to their cheering families. A pickup truck with its stereo wired into large living room-type speakers perched on its rooftop brought up the rear blaring festive, Mexican-sounding music.

"Homecoming here at the high school in Seligman," Mr. Breen concluded, before accelerating out of town.

Evan was hungry but there were no more restaurants in sight. After driving along a two-lane road paralleling the railroad for about fifteen minutes, Mr. Breen slowed, made a left turn, crossed over the tracks, and headed onto a dirt road winding into a huge field. Although Mr. Breen continued his narration and the surroundings were discouraging, Evan couldn't help feeling a little relieved that at least maybe they were there.

"Anybody who develops your land may have to build a tunnel there," Mr. Breen said, jerking his thumb back over his shoulder. "The railroad doesn't much care for people crossing over their tracks these days. Too dangerous. That's something you might want to think about in deciding whether to sell or not."

Traffic? There wasn't another car or truck in sight, never mind a train.

"Was hauling a bulldozer out of here one summer when we were chaining out trees. Got hung up on those tracks. Had to get out of the truck so I could back the 'dozer off the trailer so the trailer would clear the tracks. Sure enough, here's a freight train bearing down on us, so I had to hurry. Of course, that 'dozer's engine wouldn't catch. By this time, I could see the engineer was beginning to get nervous. I got the 'dozer started and went right off the back of the trailer, which I figured was an improvement. At least the train could just blow through that trailer. Then I thought that wouldn't set real well with the trailer and tractor truck, not to mention my dad. Figured there was time to push the trailer and tractor truck clear to the other side. So, I did," he chuckled. "Except once I was done, there I was on the 'dozer, on the tracks, all over again. And, as you probably guessed, the engine stalled. It'd been doing that all summer. By then the engineer was about ready to jump. But I got the 'dozer cranked and backed it out of the way, just as the train blew through. The engineer tooted his horn. Once all the cars had gone past, the conductor waved from the caboose."

Was Mr. Breen pulling Evan's leg? He'd been required to read some so-called frontier humor and tall tales in one of his less interesting American literature classes. Had Mr. Breen gone to college? Was he some sort of poor man's Mark Twain, or Will Rogers, or something?

They drove on, through the huge, dusty plain, passing a big, drying mud puddle with a few cows, the only cows Evan had actually seen, drinking from what little water remained. Winding along the dirt road, they came upon a travel trailer and pickup truck. Four or five old people, sitting on lawn chairs and grilling food and drinking cans of beer and pop, waved. Mr. Breen waved back.

"Retired mailman. Talked to him last time I was up here. Comes down from Montana. Likes it here. It's cheap. Says he can live like a king out here." A king? Of what? Mr. Breen pointed to Evan's right, almost putting his hand into Evan's nose. "That piece right there, that's one of your sections. From the water tank over to the gate and on up that rise."

Although he'd been suspecting something like this for a while, Evan was stunned. This was it? A dusty piece of ground, in the middle of nowhere? This was his inheritance? His future? Evan felt the blood flushing his face as Mr. Breen looked toward him.

"Confused, huh," Mr. Breen said, consolingly. "Out here, a 'tank's' what you might call a 'watering hole,'" Mr. Breen explained. "Maybe what you'd call a pond, back East. Mostly dry right now, though."

"DISASTER" was the only thought in Evan's mind. No wonder his father had been so down on "those guys." Mr. Jones had no idea what he was talking about. A pang of aloneness swept over Evan. Like his father, he'd been duped. He wasn't rich, he was a sucker. This was the worst day of his life.

"So, you've got a section here. A square mile. You've got three of them," Mr. Breen said, evidently trying to cheer up Evan. Evan wasn't at all sure having three times as much of this land was much consolation. "I wanted you to see for yourself. These are the forties down here that would be worth five, maybe eight thousand a piece. But remember, you've got to survey, build roads, and plat and so forth. And you never know what the market for forties is going to do. Could go up, could go away entirely. Like grazing cattle or running motels or stagecoaches. And your sections are checker-boarded. You've got to get butterflies if you want to be able to get around up here."

"Butterflies?" Evan almost barked in frustration.

"Sure," Mr. Breen chuckled, "not the bugs, more like bandages. You need right-of-ways to get around. Can't just drive anywhere, at least not legally." Evan couldn't believe anybody cared where anybody went in this wilderness. "You see, 'checker-boarded' means you've got a private section given to the railroad back in the old days, and then a section still owned by the state, then private, then state, and so on." Mr. Breen let go of the steering wheel and held his hands straight up, crossing and uncrossing them. "If the private sections are red, state land is black. Looks like a checker board, on a map." Mr. Breen was becoming almost animated. "To get from one private section to another, legally, you have to get easements at the corners. To cross over from one red to another red. The easement's small but it connects two big pieces, like those bandages they use to close up cuts," Mr. Breen concluded triumphantly. "That's 'butterflies!'"

"Oh," Evan said.

"The State doesn't charge for 'em, but they take time to get, and time's money, right? And knowing who to talk to. And there's always conversation down in Phoenix about stopping people from developing forties. Some folks think they junk up the countryside. Me, I don't see it that way. People like owning a piece of the West, you know? But,"

Mr. Breen waved his hand above the dashboard, "if the boys out at the legislature do that, your land won't be worth much."

"You think they'd do that?" Evan almost gasped. It was one thing for Evan to think his property was nearly worthless, but it was another thing to have Mr. Breen confirm his fear.

"Never know, do you? But if they did, all this land would be good for is grazing a few head of cattle. Of course, somebody else already owns the grazing rights. And somebody else owns the water and the mineral rights." Evan had only an inkling of what this meant, but it sounded bad. He shook his head back and forth slightly and just looked away, out his window. They drove on, bouncing over little more than a path in the scrawny vegetation, and began to climb into higher ground covered with shrubby trees that gradually grew larger and more dense as they climbed.

"Pinon pines," Mr. Breen announced. "Get thick as hedges. The damn things grew up in the pastures and made it hard for grass to grow. So, we'd hook both ends of an anchor chain onto the backs of two bulldozers and head in. The chain tore the trees out of the ground. Pushed 'em into piles, let 'em dry out, and had some bonfires. Good for grass. What's good for the grass is good for cows. Nowadays, folks seem to like trees on their property. Anyway, that's what I meant when I said we were chaining trees."

Evan was struck by how much pleasure Mr. Breen seemed to take in destroying things. They drove onto higher ground covered with taller trees.

"This is another one of your sections," Mr. Breen said. "The third one's over there, down the slope to that big plain." Mr. Breen pointed out the windshield to an expansive vista to the west as he drove along a ridge. Evan could see large rectangles outlined in the scrub, stretching to the distant horizon. "Those ranchettes out there were about the first ones done. Back in the 'sixties. That's what the salesmen call forties: 'ranchettes.' French word. That's another expense." Evan wondered whether you had to pay a fee to the *Academie Francais* to use French words. "Got to hire salesmen to haul people up here to see what they're buying." They drove along the ridge then down through a steep little canyon.

"The state will make you put a bridge in here." There was no water in sight as they drove across the sandy bottom of the little canyon and headed up the steep other side. "This is a creek bed." Evan was dubious.

"A bridge?"

"Yes sir."

"How much does that cost?"

"A bridge like what you'd need here will set you back, oh, about a million."

"Dollars?" Evan gasped.

"Yes sir." Mr. Breen shook and chuckled.

After a few more minutes, they parked the truck and got out so Evan could, as Mr. Breen said, "walk his property and feel what it's like." Evan's head ached but he felt a little better once he was out of the truck. He stretched his legs and arms. The wind was strong but the air was cool and clear. Evan vacillated between wanting to think there was something to this land, and thinking this was all a terrible waste of time. Although they were in the middle of nowhere, it was pleasantly peaceful. Evan was even thinking it would be a perfect spot for a Sunday afternoon picnic when a guy in a huge cowboy hat roared up in a big, old, beat-up Buick and skidded to a halt, enveloping Evan and Mr. Breen in a cloud of dust. The guy leaned on his horn to get Mr. Breen to get back in the truck and move it, even though the guy could easily have driven around the truck. Once Mr. Breen pulled the truck off the "road," the guy roared off in a spray of gravel, giving Mr. Breen and Evan the finger. Evan climbed back into the truck.

They drove past a small rusted, tin shed on the side of the road.

"That's the well we dug a while back. Didn't hit water until five thousand feet or so. Almost a mile."

"What do people do up here for water?" Evan asked.

"Mostly haul it in on trailers," Mr. Breen said.

"They haul water in?" For some reason, of all the things he'd heard so far, this struck Evan as the most preposterous.

"A few companies do it for hire, but most people put a tank on a trailer and go to town once a week and fill 'er up. Guess you don't have to do that back home, huh? Anyhow, five thousand feet, that's a lot of drilling, and casing, and pipe, which are all expensive. And it takes a lot of electricity to pull water up from that far."

"Are there any artesian wells up here?

"Nooooo," Mr. Breen brayed, shaking his head vehemently, as if artesian wells were a figment of Evan's imagination, punctuating his observation with a final "No sir" before going on. "You'll find getting water where it needs to be is a big part of most anything, as it turns out. And of course, power's an issue too."

"So how do you get electricity out here?" Evan asked.

"Power lines are here and there, but none too near here. Some people use windmills and batteries, but generators are your best bet. Even though the wind's strong enough most of the time to drive you kind of crazy, it's not what you'd call real reliable."

"Couldn't you pipe water in, like your dad did, to the Grand Canyon?"

"Piping water long distances creates all sorts of problems. Static electricity, and so forth." Which made no sense to Evan since Mr. Breen's father had purportedly piped water over a hundred miles to the Grand Canyon. "But you know," Mr. Breen announced, scanning the horizon, "there's nothing like this land. Nothing."

Evan was unsure what to say, and surely didn't know what to think. Two thousand acres was a lot of land, but there was just so much. Land went everywhere, as far as the eye could see. But Mr. Breen wouldn't be wasting a whole day if the land was worthless, would he? They rode on in a reverential silence for a few minutes before Mr. Breen, apparently reading Evan's mind, asked, "You seen enough?" Evan looked around before nodding. "What you say we head back to town and have lunch?" Mr. Breen asked, leaning over and slapping Evan on his knee.

"Sure."

They lunched at "Seligman's Own Famous Snow Cap Café," whose interior walls were covered with shelves of knickknacks and "Route 66" paraphernalia for sale. On Mr. Breen's enthusiastic recommendation, Evan joined him in ordering "Our Famous Open Face Turkey Sandwich." Almost instantly, plates appeared before them bearing two untoasted pieces of white bread topped with sliced, processed turkey peeking from beneath scoops of instant mashed potatoes coated with a glutinous, semi-transparent, yellow liquid. Mr. Breen ate his and then finished most of Evan's after Evan told him he could have the rest. Needing to put something in his stomach, Evan joined Mr. Breen in ordering and eating a slice of "Our Famous Homemaid Cherry Pie," wondering who could think the industrial strength pastry had been "maid" anywhere other than a factory. Thankfully, Mr. Breen hardly said a word, eating slowly, squinting his eyes, seemingly isolating and inventorying each and every unpalatable ingredient.

Back in the truck, Evan was beginning to think the day would never end. It was nearly two o'clock, nearing dinner time back home. They headed south, toward Phoenix. Mr. Breen was silent, content to concentrate on digesting his food, Evan guessed. Having had at least a bit of food, he felt a little more clear-headed and wondered what his dad had been thinking buying some of this awful land. Had he staged a posthumous gag by leaving Evan a crank time capsule he was supposed to open so those springy clown snakes would pop out and startle him and amuse everyone else? But, as awful as the land was, Even figured it had to be worth at least half a million dollars. Maybe that wasn't so bad. It wasn't two million, but it was still a lot of money.

As reluctant as he was to break the wonderful silence, Evan felt compelled to ask Mr. Breen whether there was some rational explanation for how his father had become involved with so much odd real estate in the middle of remote Arizona.

"So exactly how did my dad end up with the land?"

"Well," Mr. Breen began excitedly, "that's a real good story." Evan figured as much. "Like I said, your dad did some work in Libya, built airbases and harbors and such, back when they were on our side, in the nineteen-sixties. Then, things got a little less smooth between us and the Libyans. The Libyans have a lot of oil, but they have a hard time keeping themselves fed. Their desert's not like ours over here. There's is pretty much just sand. But there is a ton, I mean a ton, of groundwater. And it's right below the surface. Putting a pipe in the ground is like putting a straw in a drink. And there's lots of sun. You plant something in Libya, water it, it'll grow.

"Just for example, during WW Two, Colonel Kurtz, the father of the lawyer you're going to see, was over there with the Army Air Corps. That's why they called him 'Colonel.' They were having a heck of a time landing and maintaining airplanes in all the Libyan dirt and dust. Being from Arizona, Colonel Kurtz came up with the idea of growing grass airstrips. They covered the desert sand with bermudagrass seed he flew in from Arizona, watered it to beat hell, and in two weeks' time they were landing B-24s on bermudagrass runways."

Another tall tale, Evan thought.

"Anyway, the Libyans were long on water and soil and sun, and so they came up with the idea of building a big old farm out in the middle of their desert. But they're short on know-how. It's a military dictatorship, you know. So, the generals got hold of Colonel Kurtz, in a kind of roundabout way, and he called your dad because he knew your dad and knew he could get big things done in strange places. They'd been together in Libya back when Colonel Kurtz was the U.S. ambassador there. Mr. Kurtz, Jr., the son, worked in the embassy for his dad. The Kurtzes were not only good at growing things in the desert but they could also provide the financing, through the bank. That's how I got to know your dad. The bank sent me over there to keep an eye on things.

"We shipped over construction equipment, dug wells, leveled thousands of acres of land, installed irrigation sprinklers, brought in farm machinery and seed, fertilizer, the whole thing. In just a year, they had thousands of acres of high quality durum wheat. They like pasta. The bank got repaid all the money they fronted and the Kurtzes got their share. Everybody was happy as can be. Huge success, on our end.

"But there was a catch. What I didn't tell you is the real good Libyan groundwater's about eight hundred or so miles from anywhere people live. Your dad wanted the Libyans to build a canal or a pipeline to move the water to where the people were, but the Libyans kind of run the place by committee and they're always in a hurry. Bottom line, they didn't want to spend the money for what your dad had recommended. And they didn't even want to build a road, which was your dad's third choice. Long story short, there was no way to get that wheat we grew to where the people are on the coast. After we harvested the wheat, the Libyans piled it in piles two and three stories high, and left it there. That wheat's just sitting there, to this day. Too hot for any rats, or bugs, or mildew out there. Like an oven. It's still good."

Mr. Breen was chuckling and shaking, evidently having concluded yet another preposterous story that seemed to have nothing to do with Evan's land.

"So, like I said, everybody on this end got paid, in advance or with letters of credit, but your dad was kind of trusting. A Grade 'A' engineer, but not what you'd call a great business man. Because the Libyans blamed your dad for the farm, or the water, take your pick, being in the wrong place, the generals didn't want to pay him. Like I said, you'll find getting water where it needs to be is a big part of most anything. Eventually, the Libyans paid your dad with the couple hundred thousand dollars in Libyan government bonds. Of course, getting a group of fella's like those Libyans to pay was a different story all together. Mr. Kurtz, Jr. had a big law firm in New York try to collect on those bonds in a lawsuit for your dad, but all that did was run up legal fees your dad had to pay."

"But wasn't it illegal to do business with Libya?" Evan couldn't help asking. Mr. Breen chuckled.

"I suppose the boys in Washington could have stopped us if they'd wanted to. Lord knows they stopped your dad's lawsuit. Eventually, he traded the bonds for your land, sight unseen, to the company that supplied the equipment for the project in Libya. And I'll be the first one to admit, when your father got a chance to come through Arizona and check on things, there was more than a little, uh, confusion about where the land was supposed to be, and what it was supposed to be worth." Mr. Breen looked at Evan. "But I guess you could say the same thing about those bonds."

Which didn't make all that much sense to Evan. Maybe Mr. Kurtz, Jr., his dad's other lawyer and friend would explain it to Evan at the next stop. They drove on. Sooner than Evan expected, they were back in the town where they'd dropped off the trailer at the concrete plant.

"Here we are," Mr. Breen said, pulling up in front of a non-descript single-story building on the far side of the concrete plant's yard. "They're expecting you. I'll get the trailer hooked up and wait for you here."

Evan exited the truck and walked down a few steps into a small covered porch along the front of the building. A piece of cardboard nailed to the painted brick wall was marked with a double-ended arrow between a hand-lettered "CHURCH" on the left and "LAWYER OFFICE" on the right. Evan walked to the right. Opening a carved wooden door, Evan entered into a waiting room. Evan's eyes adjusted to the darkness. Tired carpeting appeared on the floor, heavy drapes covered the windows, and an assortment of chairs lined three of the walls. The air reeked of tobacco smoke. A woman about Evan's father's age sat behind a reception desk typing index cards on a typewriter squeezed between two bulky, old computer monitors. She didn't look up from her work until Evan was standing in front of her desk, at which point her eyes grew as large as saucers.

"Evan? Is that you?" she asked, as if waking from a dream, and jumped out of her chair, ran around the big desk and threw herself at Evan, pressing her entire body against his for what seemed an unnaturally long time. She pushed Evan away, holding him at arms' length. "You look just like your father!" she almost squealed. "Come with me," she said, shivering with excitement. Taking Evan by the hand, she whispered, "He's waiting for you. We've been waiting for you for what feels like almost our whole lives."

The receptionist led Evan down a short hallway to an open door and stepped to the side, waving Evan into the room, whispering "you go ahead." Evan entered a large, clubby office resembling an office furniture showroom. Everything was perfectly in place and the only papers in the room were stacked neatly in front of the man sitting behind the large, glass-topped desk in a huge, leather chair. "Guess who this is!" the receptionist squealed.

Mr. Kurtz, Jr. was Mr. Breen's opposite. He was well dressed in a starched, buttoned-down shirt and silk tie beneath a brown tweed sports coat. He was so lean his skin seemed almost transparent. His thinning hair was dark and stringy and plastered back over his bony head. He held a cigarette in his left hand. He must have been so lean because he was a smoker. His eyes glistened and watered behind horn-rimmed glasses, as if he had a fever. The whites of his eyes were blood-shot. Evan marveled anyone this old could be called "Junior."

"Evan," Mr. Kurtz, Jr. said matter-of-factly, knocking the ash off his cigarette and pointing to the chair in front of the desk without getting up. The receptionist nodded enthusiastically, backed out of the room, and closed the door.

"You willing to sell?" Mr. Kurtz, Jr. asked, before Evan had sat down, turning around the stack of papers in front of him and pushing them toward Evan, reminding him of Mr. Jones's admonition about "sleeping on it."

"What do you think I should do?" Evan asked, surprising himself by adding a "Sir?"

"Can't really say," Mr. Kurtz, Jr. said, looking at his wrist watch and drawing deeply again on his cigarette. Evan was surprised, and disappointed, which must have shown. "You see," Mr. Kurtz, Jr. said, "I do some legal work for the buyer, so I can't really help you," he exhaled a cloud of cigarette smoke up into the air between them before concluding, "ethically."

Mr. Kurtz, Jr. put his cigarette in the already-full ashtray on his glass-topped desk. Taking a handkerchief from his pants pocket, he pulled his glasses from his face, and wiped the lenses before holding them up to ceiling light and squinting to see if they were any cleaner.

"But personally, I don't have any idea why you'd want to keep that property." He cleared his throat and put his glasses back on. "You know what the people who deal in that sort of property call it?" Evan shook his head. "'Junk land.'" Evan felt himself blush from a combination of embarrassment and confusion. "But to tell you the truth," Mr. Kurtz, Jr. continued, almost earnestly, "I don't think it's such a bad deal for you."

"How much do you think the land is worth, sir?" Evan asked timidly.

"I already told you, I can't say." Mr. Kurtz, Jr. seemed annoyed. "But the buyers are willing to pay you a hundred and eighty thousand dollars." Evan's heart sank. "Net of real property taxes, commissions and fees, you should clear almost a hundred and fifty thousand." Evan felt dizzy and wondered if he was going to throw up. "The best thing to be said for your dad dying is you get a stepped-up tax basis in the land so you won't owe any income taxes." Evan had no idea what this meant, but it sounded like a mean thing to say. "That's a lot of money for a college boy, don't you think?" Mr. Kurtz, Jr. concluded, making a slight smile by exposing his teeth before taking a long drag on his cigarette, then blowing out the smoke between them. "I know it would be back when I was in college."

Evan's head was spinning. He'd lost another fortune. First Mr. Breen had told him the property was worth a quarter of what Evan had hoped.

Now he'd been told it was worth what, a quarter of that amount? For the first time since his father had died, a deep wave of sadness nearly overwhelmed him.

"But," Evan whined, almost breaking into tears, "Mr. Breen said it was worth at least a half a million." Mr. Kurtz, Jr. was silent.

"He's not authorized to talk price," Mr. Kurtz, Jr. finally said. "Your father didn't give you a heads-up on all this?" Evan shook his head, fighting off tears. "Well look, if it hadn't been for a lot of effort by a lot of folks, your father could have spent years in a federal prison for dragging a bunch of people over there under the impression that that Libyan caper he cooked up was legitimate, never mind his fraudulently obtaining your land for some worthless paper issued by a bunch of international terrorists." Mr. Kurtz, Jr. sounded angry. Evan actually began crying. He couldn't believe it. He sobbed once before regaining a little control. Mr. Kurtz, Jr. lowered his voice to a less threatening volume.

"Look here, son. If I were you I'd take the money and run." Evan wiped the tears from his eyes and cheeks with his hands. He'd never been so embarrassed in his life, or felt so terrible. "It takes a lot of time and more money than you have to dress that property up and find buyers dumb enough to think they want to own their own little piece of paradise. You've seen it." Evan looked up to see Mr. Kurtz, Jr. take another drag on his cigarette. "I'd take this deal in a heartbeat," he concluded before exhaling the smoke. Even though he was now completely demoralized and more than a little scared by Mr. Kurtz, Jr., Evan managed to nod in agreement.

"Okay then," Mr. Kurtz, Jr. said, suddenly upbeat, "here's what we can do. You sign this contract and I'll give you this check for five thousand dollars earnest money."

"What's 'earnest money?'" Evan asked, wondering whether that was the term for the money he was supposed to get to pay for his airfare and motel.

"It's a deposit," Mr. Kurtz, Jr. almost snarled, evidently amazed Evan didn't know what the term meant. "You sign the contract and I'll hold it here. You can even sign the closing documents. Once your father's lawyer's got the property in your name, all the buyers will have to do out here on this end is send the rest of the money, right into your bank account. Now, doesn't that make sense to you?"

Evan nodded. He was tempted to just sign the papers. After all, the property was in the middle of nowhere. It was going to cost a fortune to do anything with it, and fixing it up would be complicated and wasn't anything Evan knew how to do, or had any interest in learning how to do. Although it all sounded reasonable and Mr. Kurtz, Jr. was probably just trying to help him out of a bad situation, Evan was still uncomfortable signing anything against Mr. Jones's and his stepfather's advice.

"Can I just take the papers with me?" Evan heard himself ask. "I'm not supposed to sign anything."

"You don't want to sign?" Mr. Kurtz, Jr. almost shouted.

"I don't think so," Evan heard himself say.

"Well, son," Mr. Kurtz, Jr. said, crushing his cigarette out in the full ashtray before gathering up the papers and dropping them into a drawer in his desk, which he slammed shut. "I'm sorry to hear that. Real sorry." He extended his hand across the desk toward Evan without getting up. Evan jumped up so he could shake hands. "I'll do what I can to hold the buyers still, but I can't promise you anything." Mr. Kurtz, Jr. waved his hand toward the door before brushing his sports coat back and pulling a cigarette out of a pack in his shirt pocket. "You know the way out."

Evan finished wiping the moisture from his face as he walked toward the front of the building. Mr. Breen was out in front leaning against the truck, talking to the receptionist who was smoking a cigarette. She ran toward Evan and gave him another big, unsettling hug and a lipsticky kiss on his cheek, which she wiped off with a tissue she pulled out of her blouse. Evan and Mr. Breen climbed back into the truck, Mr. Breen honked the horn, the receptionist waved her cigarette at them on tiptoe, and off they went.

"So," Mr. Breen said conspiratorially, "you made the deal?"

Evan couldn't imagine how the meeting could have gone any worse. What little money he might have gotten was now probably at risk since, following Mr. Jones' instructions, Evan had probably lost the deal with Intercontinental Holdings. And now that the meeting was over, Evan realized he must have thought, or hoped, he'd have gotten some information about his father, or even some fatherly advice, from Mr. Kurtz, Jr., even if he wasn't going to be able to sell the land for a whole lot of money. Instead, Evan felt as if Mr. Kurtz, Jr. had punched him in the stomach and threatened to throw him in jail for not signing the papers. Was he in shock? And when was he going to get a check, or something, to cover his plane ticket and motel room?

"No," Evan mumbled, almost beginning to cry again, which was incredibly embarrassing.

"You didn't?" Mr. Breen spun in his seat and for the first time the entire day actually looked directly at Evan before slipping back behind his merry Quaker Oats Quaker visage.

"I guess the buyers don't want to pay very much," Evan almost squeaked, suppressing a sob. Mr. Breen was quiet.

"Well?" Mr. Breen finally asked, lifting his ball cap and scratching the top of his head, "how much will they pay?"

"A hundred and eighty thousand. That's all."

"A hundred and eighty thousand?" Mr. Breen shouted, almost rising out of his seat. "Dollars?" he squeaked. "I'd take that in a heartbeat!" Evan was floored.

"You would?"

"Heck of a price." Mr. Breen shook and chuckled. "If you don't want that deal, I'll take it. I've still got a few sections laying around I wouldn't mind unloading. I'm surprised at you holding out. I thought you'd been paying attention."

Evan was recovering enough of his composure to feel like a dope. Was it too late to tell Mr. Breen to turn around? But Evan had to meet with the man from the company for dinner in Phoenix and then catch his plane. Or would that meeting be cancelled because of what had happened with Mr. Kurtz, Jr? Although Evan knew he wasn't supposed to sign anything, he was less and less sure why. What was going to change between today and tomorrow? Was the land going to move closer to anywhere? Was it going to grow streets and sidewalks and power and water lines? Evan shook his head, resting it in his hand, his elbow propped on the rest in the door of the truck. Despite the endless, bright sunlight outside, Evan felt in a very, very dark place.

Mr. Breen drove on through a forested area. Before too short a time, he was back at it.

"After I got that 'dozer back on the trailer, I was driving down this road right here. All of a sudden, traffic backed up and then stopped dead. You could see smoke up ahead and fire engines and police cars were heading south down the empty northbound lane. After I'd sat there a few minutes, a policeman drove up and said, 'follow me.' At first, I thought I was getting my own private escort, but you know what? We'd been commandeered, me and the 'dozer. The policeman led me down to where all the fire fighters were staging. They told me to take the 'dozer into the forest and help them build the fire break they were working on. In we went and worked a couple hours, knocking down trees and brush and such." Mr. Breen's favorite thing to do. "Things were going pretty well until the wind shifted. That fire headed right toward us, at a gallop. I tried to back out, away from the fire, but, you guessed it, the engine stalled. Had to jump off and high tail it. Got into a shelter the firefighters had made and darned if that fire didn't blow right over us. We were fine, but the 'dozer wasn't. The government ended up paying us the cost of a brand new one. Made out all right. Didn't even ask us whether it stalled or not. And we got to keep the old one, and sell it for scrap!"

Unlike Evan and his dad, evidently, not only did Mr. Breen have nine lives, no matter what happened, Mr. Breen and his dad never failed to make a profit.

An hour and a half later, they pulled into the parking lot of a non-descript, single story office building near downtown Phoenix. Evan guessed it didn't matter that his meeting with Mr. Kurtz, Jr. had gone so badly.

"Here we are, Intercontinental Holdings HQ." Mr. Breen got out of the truck, took Evan's back pack out of the back seat and placed it at the front door of the building. It was unspeakably hot. They shook hands. "You'll find your man right inside. Adios, Señor." Mr. Breen turned and walked to the truck, waiving his cap above his head without looking back at Evan.

Evan opened the Spanish-styled, carved-wood door bearing an engraved plastic sign reading "Schreiner Land & Cattle Co." above another one reading "Intercontinental Holdings" and another reading "Exotic Entertainments Unlimited." Inside, the room was meat-locker cold. Chairs lined the dark, paneled walls and large plastic plants filled the corners. A large map of Arizona peppered with colored push-pins hung on the wall. The room reminded Evan of his dentist's office before it had been remodeled. There was no one anywhere.

"Hello?" Evan asked in a low shout. Eventually, a young man not much older than Evan but sporting an expensive haircut, a white silk shirt, elegant black trousers and Italian loafers walked into the room, pulling his cell phone away from his ear.

"Hey, Evan, right? I've been waiting for you," the man said, extending his right hand to shake Evan's. "Call me 'Rick.'" Returning to his phone conversation, Rick waved Evan to follow him down the hallway and into an office at the back. Once in the office, Rick pointed at a chair in front of a desk. Evan put his back pack on the floor and took a seat while Rick walked behind the desk, opened the top desk drawer, pulled out a set of keys and closed the drawer. Evan sat while Rick finished his call, closed his phone, placed it in his shirt pocket, waved his right arm at Evan as if to signal a cavalry charge and walked out of the office and down the hallway, away from the reception area. Evan grabbed his back pack and scrambled behind.

Popping out a back door into the still incredibly bright light and oven-like heat, they walked to the only car in the building's small, covered parking lot: a brand new, metallic black Bentley convertible. He was pretty sure that color was called "anthracite." Evan liked cars. This was one of the finest, most popular ultra-luxury sedans on the market. "Throw your things in there," Rick said, waving his hand to indicate Evan should place his things behind the seat, which he did. "It's not locked. Hop in."

Once in the car, Evan realized something was horribly wrong: The Bentley was dirty. Evan couldn't believe a car costing nearly a quarter of a million dollars needed to be vacuumed. Worse yet, used paper coffee cups filled the cup holders and smudges filmed the windshield.

"Long trip, up there and back, huh?" Rick almost shouted, starting the car and heading out of the parking lot, without seeming to want an answer. They drove a few blocks through what felt like a blast furnace in the moving, open car, even though the air conditioner was on max fan, to a concrete block building on a corner. Its parking lot and the surrounding streets were filled with an odd assortment of parked sports cars, luxury sedans and pickup trucks. The building itself was painted in loud, clashing colors. Plastic car lot pennants ran from the building to light poles and signs in the parking lot. Cartoon-like paintings of scantily-clad girls awkwardly dodging shrapnel and the sign reading "Bombshells! A Gentlemen's Club" confirmed where Evan and Rick were heading: a strip joint. Rick parked right next to the front door, leaving the top down.

"Don't worry about your stuff," Rick instructed, "they'll keep an eye on it." A valet approached Rick saying, "Mr. Schreiner," with his hand out to accept the key to the car. Rick held his right hand out with his index finger extended and wagged it like a metronome. The valet laughed and veered off toward his station. Evan followed Rick into the dark, noisy, concrete-floored building which seemed to be little more than a neighborhood dive bar. At least it was air conditioned. A hostess in high heels and a really tight, really tiny bikini emerged from the darkness to give Rick a kiss on the cheek and show them to what Evan guessed was Rick's regular table. As they sat down, two beers were delivered to the table by a girl wearing nice underwear. Rick turned toward Evan, toasting him with one of the beers.

"So, you're not going to sell your land after all."

Shaking his head, all Evan could muster was, "I'm not sure."

"After a whole day trapped in a pickup with Breen? That's hard time."

"I suppose, yes," Evan ventured, looking at Rick, who laughed.

"Just so you know, if those guys had been trying to sell you a big chunk of ranch land and, let's say you were from Switzerland, they'd have met you at the airport, put you in a jet chopper and had you up and back in less than an hour." He laughed almost to himself. "People make the mistake of thinking all Arizona property is created equal." He laughed again and took another swig. "So, what do you think of Breen?"

"Kind of an interesting guy," Evan answered carefully, taking a drink himself. The beer tasted good. Maybe Rick was someone to whom Evan could relate, or at least talk to.

"He's a boob." Evan almost spit out his beer. "But his father was sharp as a fucking tack. He invented the whole business, he and my grandfather. Here's how it works. You've got these old ranching families with all this acreage they've owned and grazed cattle on forever, but can't do anything else with. They've owned their places for generations. Probably got 'em for free from the government a hundred or so years ago. Then there's usually a bunch of clueless grandkids and great-grandkids, not to mention wives, and ex-wives, and girlfriends, hell, even boyfriends, standing around with their hands out. I come in and tell them they can keep grazing their cattle and I'll sell their land to dopes here in Phoenix who think they need to own their own personal piece of the wild, wild west. Which they'll never see more than once or twice, never mind use, or live on. We reserve any mineral rights, and water rights, and grazing rights, and anything else that's valuable, and sell them to somebody else. If I'd thought of this business, I'd consider myself a genius." Rick finished his beer and signaled for another, before continuing. "They say real estate's always a good investment and how they aren't making any more of it." Evan nodded. "They're right. They aren't making any more of it. But let me tell you, when they were making it, they made a TON."

The girl brought both of them another beer, even though Evan had hardly gotten started on his first one.

"I've got more of these ranch people begging me to sell land like yours than I know what to do with." Rick took a big swallow of his second beer and wiped his mouth with the back of his hand. "Of course, unlike the Breens and Kurtzes of the world, most of them don't have the cash to front the development costs. So, I'm always happy to do business with Breen and Kurtz, Jr. even on little deals like your property." He took another swig of beer. "But running out of property, and people who want me to develop and sell property like yours doesn't keep me up nights." Evan was getting nervous again.

"You mean Mr. Breen, and Mr. Kurtz, Jr. are the ones who want to buy my property?"

"Kurtz Jr.'s church. Or his old man's, the Colonel's, bank. Or their title and trust company. Can you believe a guy that old still goes by 'Junior?' They do almost all their deals through that goofy church. Some sort of tax dodge. Christ, I guess I should look into it myself. 'Good business, churches,' is what Breen would say, right?" Rick laughed but Evan was unable to respond. His head was spinning again and it wasn't the beer, the loud music or the flashing lights.

"They didn't tell you that, huh," Rick said. Evan shook his head.

"Ooops!" Rick shrugged his shoulders and looked at the girls. "I just don't have the attention span those guys have. Must be some sort of generational thing. You much like your father?"

"No, not really, I guess," Evan muttered, before admitting. "I'm not sure."

"For some reason, Breen and Kurtz, Jr. are obsessed with getting back that land they traded to your dad. Me, I just don't get it. Those guys made a ton of money sticking the Libyans with all that used equipment and doing a little farming over there. Amazing." Rick shook his head. Everyone in Arizona seemed to know more about his father than Evan did. Maybe Rick could answer some of Evan's questions.

"But wasn't it really illegal to do business in Libya?" Evan asked. "If you were an American?"

"Kinda makes a feller wonder, don't it?" Rick replied, imitating Mr. Breen and smiling and winking at Evan before almost shouting, "Hell yes it was! And now the Libyans are trying to get back on the reservation, Breen and Kurtz, Jr. think they can cash in those bonds. You know Kurtz, Jr.'s father, Colonel Kurtz? He was over in Libya during World War Two and then he was the U.S. ambassador." Evan nodded carefully. "That was years ago. But get this. They've been flying him over to Libya and back and forth between here and Washington D.C. and the Libyans are probably going to get their arms twisted into paying on those bonds. Kurtz Jr.'s father's old, but there he is being carted half way around the world like a case of canned tomatoes, grubbing for money. Maybe it really is all about staying power. I don't know about you, but I hope I have something better to do by the time I'm as old as that guy. I mean, do you want to even live to be ninety-five?" Evan shook his head. "Me either. Maybe it's just as well your dad died. It would have killed me. At a million bucks face amount, with fifteen percent interest, those bonds are now worth something north of three million dollars. At least that's what Kurtz, Jr. is telling the people they're getting if they buy into those bonds. Too bad your Dad wasn't able to hold on. You'd have been one rich son of a bitch."

Evan was definitely in shock. He wasn't sure he could take any more getting, and losing, colossal amounts of money. He stared at the bubbles in his beer glass. Was this some sort of a dream, or nightmare? Should he try waking up?

Evan wasn't sure how much time had passed before he realized Rick was looking at him. Embarrassed, Evan decided he needed to say something. Rick seemed almost kind of normal. Maybe he could help Evan figure out whether any of what had gone on during the day made sense.

"Are Mr. Breen's stories true?" Evan asked. "Stagecoaches and Indians, John Wayne, Walt Disney, falling out of airplanes, near train wrecks, forest fires, scamming the government?" Or, Evan thought to himself, bombers landing on grass grown on sand, mountains of crops in the middle of the Sahara, Libyan bonds, people wanting to buy land that's absolutely useless. Rick just shrugged and grimaced before slapping his hand on his thigh and almost shouting above the noise,

"Well, enough of this business stuff, huh? Before you know it, I'll have to get you out to the airport. After seeing about a quarter of God damned Arizona, what do you say we enjoy some nicer scenery, of the female variety?" Evan saw no option other than to agree with Rick and look around.

It was a wonderland. Beautiful, beautiful girls strolled around in nothing but really high heels, sequined bathing suit bottoms, make-up, hair spray and jewelry. They were all busty and friendly and wanted to get close to you, if you paid them. Girls at college only wanted meaningful relationships. A girl came up to their table and plopped herself down on Rick's lap.

"What can I get you today, Honey?" Rick asked.

"A job where I can wear clothes?" she asked, slumping her shoulders and affecting an exaggerated pout. Rick just laughed.

"This is Mr. Evans, Honey," Rick said, pointing and nodding toward Evan. "He's a land baron." The girl looked at Evan in a way no girl had ever looked at him. Rick laughed and shooed the girl away. "Go on, we're conducting business." She got up and walked away, acting as if she was hurt. Rick laughed again. "Nothing sexier than a fat wallet. To hear these girls talk, they're all working their way through medical school. Trust me, they're not," he said, completely draining his beer before continuing. "Well, let me know what you want to do. You can sell the land to Breen and Kurtz, Jr. and they'll throw it in with me. If you can wait for your money, you could throw it in with me. I'll take care of Breen and Kurtz, Jr. with some part of the deal. But either way, you'll make some money."

"Should I just hold onto it? Maybe it would be worth a lot more someday? With some more time?" Evan had been thinking maybe he needed to be patient with his land, like all these business people were.

"Not anything I'd recommend. Junk land's not like wine or cheese. It doesn't get any better with age." Rick reached over and slapped Evan on the knee and winked before looking around the room. "You seen enough?" Evan nodded. It was clear Rick wanted to leave. "Let's get you to the airport. You can grab a bite there."

As he and Evan got into the Bentley, Rick extended a twenty-dollar bill to the attendant, then pulled it away. Rick and the attendant both laughed. It was still hot as blazes. Mercifully, Rick put the top and the dirty windows up so the air conditioning could actually work. They were at the airport terminal in ten minutes. Rick pulled the Bentley up to the curb, Evan pulled his back pack out from behind the front seat and climbed out while Rick remained seated but extended his hand to Evan who leaned in to shake it.

"If you want to sell, I could go another ten thousand a section." Rick held onto Evan's hand. "Seventy thousand a section. It's about what I have to pay. Two hundred and ten thousand. But don't take long. There's a lot of that stuff out there." He let go of Evan's hand and waved saying, "So long." Evan stood up, and swung the heavy door shut. The elegant car pulled away from the curb, then sped off, squealing its tires slightly.

Walking into the cool, well-lit airport terminal, Evan checked in at the ticket counter, made his way through security, headed to a sports bar, and ordered a hamburger, fries and a beer. Once the food arrived and Evan began eating, he felt a sense of relief. Looking around, he couldn't help feeling as if he'd made it back to civilization. The airport was modern, well maintained and, what, typical? Normal? Evan sat in relative silence, blessedly alone.

At least it was over and he was eating some real food. Evan chewed his burger and mulled things over. He'd started the day thinking he was going to get a check for two million dollars. That had all but disappeared. Then to top it all off, he found out if his father had held on for a while, Evan would have inherited over three million dollars cash. But maybe two hundred thousand dollars was nothing to sneeze at. Feeling flip, Evan wondered whether he should blow the whole wad on a Bentley like Rick's. At least he'd keep his clean. A little less upbeat, Evan reverted to feeling he'd lost a fortune. Feeling worse, he couldn't help thinking once again his dad hadn't really let him down so much as he just wasn't there. And hadn't ever been.

Although two hundred thousand was one tenth of what he'd hoped for, Evan had to admit it was probably more than he was entitled to have expected to get from his dad. But five percent of two hundred thousand was only ten thousand a year. Evan couldn't live on less than a thousand dollars a month. Europe was out of the picture. But with the benefit of a full stomach, looking on the bright side, Evan realized at least he wouldn't ever have to make this trip again. He ordered another beer.

By the time Evan's flight took off from Phoenix, it was already two o'clock in the morning on the East Coast. He was crammed into a crowded airplane, exhausted and a little too buzzed from all the beers he'd had at the strip joint and then in the airport sports bar. His meal-induced euphoria having abandoned him, Evan flew into the middle of the night wondering how he was going to repay his stepfather for his airfare and motel room, not to mention his hamburger and fries and all those beers.

When Evan was awakened by the engines slowing as the plane began its descent, the sky outside was turning pink. People in the cabin were moving around and getting ready for landing. The plane dropped into a solid cloud cover then emerged into a cloudy, wet, and rainy early morning. Although the sky was slowly brightening, the street lights below were still glowing and strangely visible. At only seven o'clock the section of the Jersey Turnpike they passed over next to the airport was already jammed with cars and trucks. The plane thumped down onto the runway and the world outside gradually came to a halt. It felt good to be home and awake, back on the East coast, back to what – reality?

Regrets Only

Jane was packing her things into her rental car to drive to the Tucson airport when her father called and told her her brother Grant had killed himself the night before in Phoenix. Stunned and shocked, rather than driving to the airport and flying home to Chicago, Jane began the two-hour drive from Tucson to Phoenix.

Before she'd even made it to the interstate, Jane's husband called. Working on a case in New York for his Chicago law firm, Ed said he was sorry for Jane and offered to fly to Phoenix, saying he could be there that evening. Jane thanked Ed but declined his offer. His being around would only make things harder. She told Ed they would stay in touch by phone, and went back to trying to concentrate on the tedious drive.

Cars lined both sides of the street as Jane drove up to the house where Grant had been living for the past year with his girlfriend Libby. Walking back to the house from where she'd had to park, and making her way up the walkway to the front of the house, a near roar of conversation poured from the wide-open and unattended front door. Surrounded by a bevy of girlfriends, presumably co-workers from the law firm where she worked as a paralegal, Libby stood in the center of the living room. Mostly women, but a few men, stood everywhere else in the living room and adjoining rooms, comprising as large a group as Jane had ever seen at any party. Upon seeing her, Libby made a show of Jane's being there, throwing herself at Jane, shouting her name, burying her face in Jane's shoulder, and sobbing "Why?" Jane patted Libby on her back. The girlfriends dabbed their eyes with Kleenex, shaking their heads and echoing Libby's "Why?"

"I'm so glad you're here," Libby blubbered, stretching out the 'so.' "You're such an angel! I know how much you like your coffee. It's in the kitchen. Please, Janie, help yourself." Jane drank tea and no one except Grant ever called her 'Janie.' Almost shoving Jane toward the kitchen, Libby returned to her coterie and their "Whys?" which sounded to Jane as if they were primarily bemoaning the fact Libby would have to cancel the elaborate June wedding she'd been planning.

In the center of the kitchen, more youngish women hovered over a box of donuts on the large island while a Hispanic woman washed dishes at the sink behind them. Grant's best friend Dan sat on a stool at the island, his head down, almost touching the counter, holding his cell phone to his ear, nodding his head before saying, "Okay, thanks," and hanging up. Upon wiping his hand across his face and opening his eyes and seeing Jane, Dan ran to her and gave her a long hug.

"God, I loved him," Dan nearly sobbed, unsettlingly, before hurriedly adding, "That crazy guy."

Dan explained he'd been on the phone with a Phoenix police detective in Dan and Grant's informal running group. According to the police, the night before Grant had driven to an indoor shooting range on the near west side of Phoenix, rented their most powerful pistol, a so-called "44 Magnum," proceeded to his assigned shooting station, fired wildly toward the target a few times, alarming the attendants and nearby shooters with both his wild laughter and gross incompetence, before placing the gun beneath his jaw and pulling the trigger.

According to the police, Grant had signed, and notarized himself (which caused Dan to almost chuckle, or sob, Jane wasn't sure which) a document directing the police to allow Dan, rather than Libby or any family members, to identify his body if they felt that was necessary, "notwithstanding the fact that" (the document stated) he'd placed the envelope containing the affidavit, together with his driver's license, passport, bar association card, and Junior Scientist Club membership card issued to him by the Museum of Science and Industry when he was six, on the floor where he'd assumed he would fall.

If it was acceptable to Jane, Dan would swing by the morgue on his way back to his office and identify Grant's body. Jane thought that would be fine and told Dan her father would be out from Chicago later in the day and, although she had no idea how these things worked, she guessed they would have Grant's body shipped to Illinois for burial. Dan nodded and gave Jane a long hug before slipping unhindered through the crowded living room and out the front door.

Ignored by everyone, Jane wandered into the bedroom end of Libby's home. Frilly and reeking of perfume, the master bedroom was obviously Libby's. One of the smaller bedrooms belonged to Libby's son Connell. Not fond of teenagers, Jane considered Connell insufferable and, for no reason Jane could see, full of himself. His bedroom's black walls were plastered with creepy fantasy and science fiction posters. Clothes were strewn everywhere.

As monastic and anonymous as a motel room, the third bedroom must have been Grant's study. A photo of Grant's running group assembled on a mountain overlook shared the top of a nearly empty book case with a photo of Grant and Dan sitting next to each other at a banquet table in formal wear, their arms around each other. Massive, unlit cigars planted uncharacteristically but jauntily in their grinning mouths, Grant and Dan mugged goofily for the camera as Libby and Dan's girlfriend, Lois, sulked in the wings. The picture brought tears to Jane's eyes as she walked back to the living room.

Seeing no point in staying, and wary of trying to work her way to Libby to say goodbye, Jane slipped around the edges of the living room and out the front door. Wiping her cheeks, she walked down the street, climbed into her car, and cried. Once the tears and sobs subsided, she drove away.

Checking into a nearby business hotel, Jane made a phone call to her secretary, Karen, at the offices of the University of Illinois-led astronomy consortium Jane managed. More her best friend and cheerleader, Karen, and presumably the rest of the campus, had heard about Grant.

"Oh my God, Jane," Karen gasped. "I'm so sorry. Poor Grant. Poor you! Will you be all right? Don't worry about work. We'll take care of everything. How's your father going to take this?" Too overwhelmed to say much, Jane thanked Karen and hung up, remembering having asked Karen how she was able to always say, and do, the right thing in any circumstance. Karen answered cheerfully, "I'm a secretary. I have time for these sorts of things. You're a boss. You do the hard work. I do the easy stuff!"

Since there wasn't anything new to report and he would be busy, Jane decided not to call Ed. Exhausted and unsure what to do next, Jane reclined on her hotel room's bed and closed her eyes.

Jane was awakened from a strangely deep sleep by a phone call from Dan. Apologetic, Dan told Jane Libby had had Grant's body claimed from the morgue and taken to a local mortuary to be prepared for a wake to be held there the following night. After a funeral service at Libby's boss's country club the morning after the wake, Grant would be buried in Phoenix in a grave Libby's boss was making available. Too groggy to fully comprehend what Dan was saying, never mind respond, Jane listened as Dan closed by saying, in his mind, "this would be the best thing, all things considered," before saying "goodbye" and hanging up.

Waking up, Jane didn't think she'd been out of line assuming her father was coming to Arizona to return Grant's body to Illinois. Although never articulated, Jane suspected the whole family, and perhaps even Grant, had considered his being in Arizona something temporary, a sabbatical, or even a lark.

Six years younger than Jane, Grant had always been a little unconventional, probably because he was so bright. An academic's son, he was the valedictorian of his high school class. Rather than going somewhere more prestigious for who knows what reason other than he could be shy and, surprisingly, he didn't seem to mind living at home, Grant stayed in Champagne-Urbana, graduating from the University of Illinois with highest honors and, like his father, Phi Beta Kappa. But rather than going to graduate school in history at Harvard, as had their father (and as their father had wanted Grant to do), Grant had done very well at the law school at the University of Chicago, which university, according to Grant, was where, if he were ever to admit it, their father had always wanted desperately to teach and base his academic career.

Instead of starting with a downtown Chicago (or New York, or Washington D.C.) law firm, Grant took a job in Phoenix with a, for Phoenix, large and in Grant's words, grinning slyly, "purportedly prestigious" law firm. Their father scoffed, pronouncing Arizona "the frontier" and Phoenix "a cow town." Recounting the exchange, Grant concluded,

"He called Phoenix a 'cow town,'" chuckling, "unlike Chicago."

Grant told Jane he wanted to "try someplace new, maybe find myself, strike out on my own." Having been enthusiastic but hitless in little league, Grant added, "Maybe that's not the right term." As it had maddened him that Grant had no qualms about being terrible at baseball, it had irritated their father that Grant was content to wander off to an "undistinguished, third rate, lower middle-class watering hole" to pursue what should have been doubtless, in his mind, Grant's inevitably brilliant legal career. To which Grant responded when recounting their father's comment afterwards to Jane, "Hey, at least I'm not moving to Vegas!"

Grant flew off to Phoenix, bought a new car and rented a spacious apartment in a new apartment complex. As he'd done in Chicago, Grant shared the apartment with Dan, who'd graduated from the John Marshall Law School and taken a job with the Phoenix public defender's office. Best friends since grade school and both good looking (Dan more than Grant) and smart (Grant more than Dan), because for some reason neither of them had ever been comfortable or successful with girls, they'd spent a lot of their time in high school studying, listening to music, following sports, and reading. Although Grant had had friends who were girls, he hadn't had any girlfriends.

Even though it didn't offer the cultural and social benefits of Chicago, and even though it was "hotter than Hades" as Grant reported, shaking his jowls to impersonate their father, Grant could run year-round in Phoenix without worrying about snow or ice, adding cheerfully, "or, for that matter, rain." Grant loved to run. Wearing out a pair of running shoes every month as he'd been doing since junior high school, Grant began running with a group of good looking, young, obviously athletic guys, including Dan. Lawyers, accountants and insurance and real estate brokers, they ran out of the downtown Phoenix YMCA in the early mornings, at lunch, after work, or sometimes, in Grant's case, all three.

Phoenix agreed with Grant in other ways. He scored the highest grade on the Arizona bar exam. (Their father's reaction: "Isn't Arizona still a territory?") He even acquired his first steady girlfriend, meeting Libby at his first law firm. When Dan moved out of the apartment he shared with Grant to move in with Lois, Grant moved in with Libby and Connell. Things had seemed to be going well for Grant.

Although mystified by why Grant killed himself, Jane had a theory about how he'd done so. Jane suspected Grant had decided, somewhat perversely, to make a final statement on guns. Grant and their father, a historian, archivist and university professor who'd never come close to owning, never mind using a gun, had argued about guns since Grant had first been able to carry on a conversation, which, given his precocity, had been early on. Grant was opposed to guns and gun rights while, having specialized in the Civil War and American and Illinois State history, their father always took the position that, for good or ill, individual freedoms and gun violence had made the United States the country it was.

"Grant," their father would plead, "notwithstanding their inherent viciousness, guns are just too much of this country's fabric to ever be outlawed."

"That's the problem, not the solution," Grant would counter.

"You can't take guns out of American culture," their father would respond sternly, whereupon Grant would whisper as an aside to Jane, "There's an oxymoron."

"Do anti-gun-rights people really believe anyone can bloodlessly root out an entire people's love of guns?" their father would continue, raising his voice, "just because it might, I repeat, might be a good idea?" Grant would shake his head earnestly as if attending one of their father's lectures. Their father would begin shaking. Grant would grin broadly.

Nor could Jane help recalling that as a teenager Grant had become obsessed with a goofy movie called "Joe Versus the Volcano," which only he found amusing, telling Jane he had decided to title the movie depicting his life "Grant Versus the Volcano."

Reluctant to recall any more memories of Grant, Jane looked at her watch and realized it was past time for her to pick up her father at the airport.

Once in the car, Jane's father asked her what had taken her so long. Before she could answer, he told her to watch out for a truck pulling into their lane. Eventually, Jane managed to advise her father of Libby's plans for Grant's funeral.

"The hell, you say," he shouted, in the quaint Nineteenth Century parlance he often fell into, having spent his career compiling, editing and publishing the correspondence of Ulysses S. Grant in thirty-one, and counting, volumes. "My son's not going to be buried in this God-forsaken, remote," he huffed, "desert."

Despite the verbal fireworks in the car, upon arriving at Libby's, Jane's father gave Libby an uncharacteristic hug and patted her comfortingly on her back, saying "now, now," repeatedly and soothingly. As far as contesting Libby's plans for Grant's burial was concerned, that was that. After sitting in the nearly empty living room for a while and being introduced to the only work friend of Libby's still on duty at her house, Jane and her father excused themselves and drove to the hotel in silence. Jane's father retired to his room for the night. Jane went to her room, kicked off her shoes, collapsed onto the bed and phoned Ed.

Ed's thinking Grant's becoming a lawyer was a bad idea had been, at least in Jane's mind, a bone of contention between Ed and her. Ed had thought Grant was more than bright enough, but even when Grant was applying to law schools, Ed had encouraged him to pursue a career in legal academia or the judiciary. Ed thought Grant was "too creative" to practice law for a living. For Ed, practicing law was a very mundane business; challenging in its pace and intensity, but not engaging intellectually, and somewhat, for lack of a better word, nasty. Although Jane admitted Grant didn't have a mean bone in his body, she was unwilling to believe the law was as stultifying as Ed made it out to be. Jane was certain Ed had some other reason for disapproving of Grant's career choice, which reason Jane suspected was unfair to Grant. Although Jane had never pushed Ed on this point, and Ed had let it drop, Jane was fearful Ed would take an "I told you so" approach and attribute Grant's suicide to an unwise career choice.

But Ed was a gentleman and concerned only about Jane's wellbeing. Jane admitted to Ed that she had no idea what she was feeling. It was all so strange and foreign. She told Ed she was okay, but she thought she was probably in shock, and she felt as if she'd been beaten all over her body with rubber hammers. Again, Ed offered to fly out and again Jane declined. Wanting to change the topic and make small talk, Jane asked Ed what was new on his end. He replied his law firm had just told him they wanted him to move to New York to open their office there.

Although she couldn't be too surprised, the news struck Jane as another blow. During the last year, Ed had been spending most of his time in New York. Very good at what he did, Ed was highly regarded at his firm. Thinking it was the appropriate thing to do, Jane congratulated Ed. He insisted it wasn't an honor and told Jane they could discuss it later once things settled down. Although his partners were in a hurry, as usual, they could be made to wait. Ed asked Jane how her father was.

"As irascible as ever? Isn't that what you'd say?" Jane answered, attempting to head off any further discussion of her father. All Ed said was, "I suppose we all grieve in our own way."

With little left to say, they said "good night" and hung up, whereupon Jane fell into a deep sleep. Waking in the middle of the night fully clothed and on top of the bedcovers, Jane got up, changed into her pajamas, climbed under the covers, turned out the light, and went back to sleep.

The next morning, Jane was awakened by a phone call from Dan. Per Libby's request, Jane and her parents had been scheduled to meet a little later that morning with the funeral director to go over the arrangements for Grant's funeral, which struck Jane as a little odd in so far as Libby seemed to have taken control of such matters. In the early afternoon, they were to go to Grant's office to remove Grant's personal effects. After silently downing cold cereal in the hotel's breakfast room, Jane and her father met her mother at the airport. Because she never flew, Jane's mother hadn't known to pack only a carry-on bag, causing Jane's father to erupt at having to wait in baggage claim for, in her father's words, "the other bag," justifying his bad behavior by insisting they were now late for their appointment at the mortuary.

"Mortuary?" Jane's mother exclaimed, looking from Jane to her father and back. "Aren't we here to bring Grant home?"

"Of course, Grant's being buried here," Jane's father shouted. "It's all been arranged, by Libby. What are you thinking?" Except for looking briefly at Jane, her mother made no response.

Thankfully, there wasn't much to do or see at the mortuary. The funeral director explained that the proceedings would be closed casket without going into any details as to why. There would be a wake that evening and then "a celebration of Grant's life" the next morning, followed by an interment at the nearby cemetery. The funeral director then showed them the very expensive casket Libby had selected before leading them into his office.

"All told, including the two burial plots and the headstone," the funeral director concluded, pushing an invoice across his desk toward Jane's father, "it comes to twenty-five thousand dollars." Jane and her mother gasped. "Your daughter-in-law has very good taste," the funeral director added.

"Two burial plots?" Jane's mother asked.

"Typically, no fewer than two plots can be conveyed at one time."

Holding up his hand to prevent any discussion, Jane's father pulled his checkbook from his suit coat's inside pocket and asked, "Will a personal check be satisfactory?"

"Certainly," the funeral director responded.

Following a morose chain restaurant lunch, Jane and her parents drove to the offices of Grant's firm, which was not the one Grant had joined out of law school. Grant's first firm, the firm for which Libby still worked, took up many of the highest floors in a, for Phoenix, tall office building and, according to Ed, had a national reputation. Jane recalled their offices being very elegant. Although Grant's second firm occupied the top two floors of a downtown building, the building was relatively squat and surrounded by a sprawling outdoor city bus station, a parking lot, an eight-story parking garage, and the tired-looking, brick YMCA frequented by Grant and his running group. The building's lobby was unattended and opened into a now-closed and vacant bank branch on one side and a closed restaurant on the other. The elevator arrived half a minute or so after Jane's father had begun incessantly pushing the call button.

As the family came off the elevator, the receptionist and telephone operator Jane knew as "Tina" from having called to speak to Grant, rushed from behind her desk and gave each of them big, teary hugs before dabbing her eyes with a tissue and summoning an underling to attend to the reception desk and the phones. Tina then escorted them down an unattractive internal circular staircase to Grant's office on the floor below.

All the secretaries in the work area outside Grant's office stood at their desks looking uncomfortable, some dabbing their eyes with tissues.

"So, this is where our little Grant played lawyer," Jane's father announced. The secretaries nodded and looked more uncomfortable. Everyone was introduced to everyone. "Let's see Grant's office," her father merrily proposed. The secretaries seemed to groan.

Grant's office was furnished with an old desk and an equally old, but unmatched, credenza, two uncomfortable looking client chairs and a large, black Naugahyde executive chair behind the desk, patched with peeling, silver duct tape. Grant's things were packed into two cardboard boxes on the desk. The window stared out at the parking garage across an alley. Emitting a large "Well!" Jane's father turned and led Jane and her mother back out of the room. As Tina led them down the hall to meet Jim Byrnes, Grant's immediate supervisor, they came upon a line of secretaries filing into a conference room.

"Oh," Tina enthused, "this might be something worth your joining," cutting them ahead of the line, leading them into the room and seating them at the conference table. Jane concluded the room was nearly filled with secretaries and paralegals, assuming the secretaries were middle-aged or older women and the paralegals were younger women. Once all the seats at the table were filled, a dapper, well-groomed, rosy-cheeked man in a crisp white shirt, a colorfully bright bowtie, a light blue seersucker sports coat and tan trousers entered the room, shut the door, and strode to the head of the table.

"This is grief counseling," he announced. "You're probably wondering why a young man would take his own life." He paused. Some of the attendees nodded while others simply looked around. "Let me save you some time. There's no rational answer. Suicide is not, I repeat, not a rational action." He paused, held up the palms of his hands and shook his head slightly from side to side. "Only the mentally ill take their own lives." The attendees looked at Jane's father who flinched but otherwise showed no emotion. "Just as only people with heart disease have heart attacks," the grief counselor continued. "And there should be no more moral baggage associated with suicide than there is with having a heart attack. There's no one to blame." He flashed a big grin. "So, don't ask yourselves what you could have done to prevent this. The answer is –" here he raised the pitch of his voice as if soliciting an answer, before concluding, "– absolutely nothing." Jane's father nodded.

Pleased at making his way through his speech uninterrupted, the grief counselor resumed, "If there are no questions, you're best advised to get back to work, to the extent you can. Feel bad, if you have to. There's nothing wrong with that. But please, please don't blame yourselves."

The paralegals and secretaries filed out, Jane's father waiting for the women to exit first, at which point he shook the grief counselor's hand and exited the room ahead of Jane and her mother. Tina escorted them to Mr. Byrnes' office, stepped to the side of the open door and waived them in.

Telling them to call him "Jim," Byrnes struck Jane as pleasant and genuinely upset. He graciously welcomed Jane and her parents into his bland but typical looking lawyer's office. Once he'd settled Jane and her parents into client chairs facing his desk, he sat down behind his desk, his left arm across his mid-section, supporting his right arm and hand, with which he cupped his chin. His face was a little doughy and he looked as if he hadn't slept.

"You're wondering what happened," Byrnes began. "And I don't know how much you know."

"Nothing," Jane's father interjected loudly, adding another "nothing" less loudly. Byrnes nodded.

"Grant was helping me with a suit on a personal guarantee." He stopped and sighed, wiping his face with his hand before continuing. "He missed a filing date and the judge dismissed the case, with prejudice." Although Jane knew this was bad, her parents didn't know enough to say anything. "I've already filed a motion to get the case reinstated, and I think we'll prevail, and I told Grant that." Here Byrnes paused before continuing. "But I think that's what caused him, Grant, to, you know...." Byrnes's voice trailed off and he looked down at the floor.

"So," Jane's father bellowed, "Grant screwed up?"

"Well," Byrnes said, tilting his head and sitting up straighter and holding his palms turned up before folding his arms back over his chest and sitting back in his chair. "I told Grant, we all ...." Byrnes tilted his head and blinked. "But, for some reason...." He stopped, then began again. "Grant could be such a funny, happy-go-lucky guy. I was stunned when I heard. He was such a good lawyer. He was too organized to let something like that happen. It's the kind of mistake I'd make," Byrnes joked, or at least Jane assumed he had. Jane's father nodded. There didn't seem to be anything else to say. They stood and Byrnes ushered them out.

Tina led them upstairs to the office of the law firm's head, Mr. Steiner. As they were shown into his corner office featuring floor to ceiling windows overlooking the city and the distant mountains, Mr. Steiner closed the laptop computer on the credenza behind his desk on which, Jane noticed, he'd been playing solitaire. He stood up behind his desk, cleared his throat but said nothing, extending his hand to each of Jane's father, her mother and Jane without making the effort to come around the desk.

"So," Jane's father began after settling onto the edge of one of the four client chairs facing the desk and the windows beyond, "Mr. Steiner, our Grant screwed up?"

"Well," Mr. Steiner managed before Jane's father held up his hand.

"Say no more. Well I know Grant. I, we, the whole family, thank you for employing him. On Grant's behalf, we apologize." Jane's father stood up. Hardly settled in their seats, Jane and her mother followed suit. "We won't take any more of your time. I hope your Mr. Byrnes, can get things straightened out. Will we see you at the funeral tomorrow?"

"Why–" Mr. Steiner mumbled. Struggling to get out of his chair and seemingly surprised to learn there was going to be a funeral, he emitted a startled "Yes!"

"Very well," Jane's father shouted, shaking Mr. Steiner's hand violently before turning and shooing Jane and her mother from the room, commenting as they hurried out, "We'll get out of your hair. Surely you've more important things to do."

The wake that evening was awkward. Although a great number of people showed up, other than Dan and a few of Grant and Dan's running friends, no one seemed very well acquainted with Grant or knew, or cared, Grant had any family other than Libby. By contrast, most everyone seemed intimate with Libby. Jane and her parents sat in a small parlor off the main room. Dan shuttled between them, Grant's casket, a few of the runners as they came and went, and the activity surrounding Libby. As time passed and the main room emptied, Jane and her parents excused themselves, begging off the offer of extravagant amounts of food "laid out," in her words, at Libby's house.

Jane and her parents ate dinner at a fast food restaurant across the street from their hotel. As had been their other meals together, other than proper table manners and a flair-up by her father, nothing was said, making Jane realize that, in the past, whenever they'd all been together, it had fallen to Grant to either initiate conversation or stir up controversy. When she felt up to it, Jane could make small talk with her parents, but she didn't feel up to it. The flair-up had occurred when her mother, who could stay silent for days, or babble incessantly about nothing, had gone on about how wonderful their hotel was, at which point Jane's father shouted "Elaine!" silencing her mother. "Please," her father pleaded, almost apologetically, as both he and Grant did, closing his eyelids over his rolling eyes and shaking his head. Thinking perhaps Grant had been too much like their father, Jane wondered whether she was too much like her mother.

They returned to the hotel, going to their separate rooms without even having the energy to say "good night." Although he had called and left a message on her phone, Jane didn't feel up to checking in with Ed, and went to bed.

As a startlingly large crowd settled into the rows and rows of white event chairs arrayed in the dining room of Libby's boss's country club the next morning, Jane wondered how so many people had deemed it necessary to take time off from work to attend Grant's funeral. They couldn't have all been close friends. Grant could be personable and fun to be around, but there were tons of people. Jane concluded the well-dressed guys in suits, accompanied by well turned-out women, were Libby's friends.

Dan sat in front, leaning forward, holding his head in his hands. His girlfriend Lois was nowhere to be seen. Jane recognized a few of the secretaries from Grant's firm. Mr. Steiner and Jim Byrnes sat next to each other toward the rear of the room, their arms folded, talking.

The audience quieted as Libby strode to a lectern cradling, almost erotically Jane thought, a cordless microphone in her overly manicured hands. Decked out in a tight, short, and strapless white satin number, Libby resembled a trade show hostess. Jane resisted thinking Libby had settled on her dress because, first, she didn't have anything more appropriate to wear and, second, she hadn't wanted to waste money buying anything appropriate.

Again, Jane was struck by how much Libby differed from the few girls Grant had associated with, mostly brainy, soon-to-be academics like their faculty parents. Although some had been a little pretty, Libby was, for lack of a better word, stylish. She'd bleached highlights into her hair to the point it was almost entirely blond. Her makeup was not subtle and she plucked her eyebrows to within an inch of their lives. She dressed in the latest fashions and colors, regardless of whether they suited her build or complexion. And she had a full-chested figure which Ed suggested had been surgically augmented, making Jane wonder that he noticed such things. Ed had also theorized that the raccoon-like dark patches beneath Libby's eyes, which she tried to hide with heavy make-up, indicated her perfect, thin, turned-up nose was the work of a plastic surgeon. Jane had to admit she suspected Libby was older than she let on and much older than Grant. When she wasn't keyed up, as she was for the funeral, or otherwise putting on a show, Libby could look tired. She'd struck Ed as being "very experienced for her age."

Although a game show-like placard perched on an easel next to the lectern declared the funeral "A Celebration of Grant's Life," as promised by the funeral director, Jane would rather have attended a funeral. What followed was the worst ceremony Jane had ever witnessed. Foregoing a minister, Libby acted, essentially, as the master of ceremonies. As the minutes dragged on, Jane could only compare the proceedings to those horrible "roasts" celebrities humorlessly inflicted upon each other.

Eliciting a much smaller laugh from the audience than she must have anticipated, Libby opened by stating how much Grant hated golf. Looking past Libby through the two-stories-high window wall at the brilliant green golf course stretching beyond, Jane couldn't help wondering why Libby had decided to have Grant's funeral at a country club. Although as he'd grown into adulthood he'd learned to suppress it, Grant had a very strong egalitarian (Ed preferred "Marxist") streak. He despised the idle rich. And even though he was terrible at it, golf was their father's favorite, and only, athletic endeavor.

"But without further ado," (Libby's exact words) "my son, Connell!"

Wearing an un-pressed black shirt and black, loosely-tied necktie over baggy black jeans barely held up by a too-long belt, their cuffs bulging over black, unlaced sneakers, Connell shuffled to the lectern. His head down, his long, unkempt, dark hair draped over his head and face like a mop, Connell cleared his throat loudly then began reading from a crumpled piece of paper.

"Most people think I hated Grant," Connell mumbled into the microphone before clearing his throat again. The crowd tittered nervously. Jane considered herself firmly in the "most people" category, having worried at times that Grant may have been little more than Libby's no-cost, live-in, teenager-sitting service. Constantly on assignment with her boss, Libby too often left Grant home alone with the surly Connell. "But it's not true," Connell continued sweetly as the crowd relaxed a little. "I loved Grant," he said. "Grant sucked at playing video games." The crowd became uncomfortable. "I could beat him like a rented mule." A few people laughed. "Any time. So, I'll miss Grant a lot," Connell concluded, looking up and showing his face to the crowd for the first time, before smiling and adding, "more than you'll ever know."

Jumping from her seat, Libby led the audience in a round of applause before giving Connell a hug. Connell sat down to spend the rest of the ceremony playing a video game on his hand-held electronic game thing, snorting, shrugging or chortling in response to almost everything said during the ceremony, without once looking up.

Jane felt bad for her father who was making the chewing motion he, as had Grant, made when he was agitated. Jane remembered the night Grant had used "sucked" in front of their parents, incensing their father who demanded, "And when did a colloquial euphemism for *fellatio* become acceptable, in polite company?" which more mystified than shamed then eight-year-old Grant into silence.

Dan stepped to the podium and began reading from a yellow legal pad, sniffling as if he had a cold.

"As most of you know, among many other things, Grant was a runner. He wasn't a good runner, he was slow. But he loved running. And very unfortunately, Grant didn't like running alone. Any time, day or night, you could get a call from Grant. He wouldn't identify himself. He'd just say, 'so let's go,' or 'it's only a hundred and eighteen out,' or, 'it's two in the morning, why aren't we running?' He was insistent, but always jovial." Dan stopped and blew his nose before resuming.

"Grant said he ran the high hurdles in high school." Laughter roiled through the audience. "Because nobody else would. According to Grant, he ran the hurdles with a pole." The crowd laughed a little and Dan shook his head and sniffled.

Jane could tell her father was becoming irritated. He'd never approved of Grant's self-deprecating and admittedly silly sense of humor. "Where did that come from?" their father demanded in exasperation one night after Grant had unleashed a string of corny jokes at the dinner table. Grant lifted his eyebrows and nodded first toward their father and then toward the tall stand of corn in the field visible through their dining room window.

"When he'd finally make it to the end of a hurdles race," Dan continued, "Grant said they had to dust him off to read the number pinned on his uniform." The crowd laughed politely. "If it was still there."

The most memorable example of Grant's sense of humor had come at their father's expense. Invited to appear on a live public television broadcast from Grant's tomb in New York City celebrating a Ulysses S. Grant anniversary, their father was ecstatic to have a national audience. Upon hearing about the upcoming broadcast, Grant opined that the only thing he and their father shared was "a face for radio."

Their father was having the time of his life during the broadcast. Even the final ten-minute segment, reserved for "open phones," was going well until the host announced the professor might know their next caller, "Grant from Phoenix." Although he managed a smile, her father's panic was evident to Jane and Ed watching the broadcast in their Chicago apartment.

"Hi Dad," Grant chirped, "this is Grant." Their father nodded stiffly as the host smiled and nodded enthusiastically. "I'll ask my question and then hang up so I can listen to your answer on the television." Their father and the host nodded again. Ed said, "This isn't going to end well."

"My question," Grant said cheerily, "is: Who lives in Grant's Tomb?"

The television host thought it was cute and laughed politely. Even though he managed to contain himself by twitching and watching the host wrap up, Jane's father was apoplectic. Although it had never been discussed, Jane was certain their father had never forgiven Grant, who thought it was hilarious.

"Of course," Dan continued, "none of Grant's stories were true. He made them up, 'out of whole cloth,' he admitted once, adding, 'polyester, actually.'" Dan stopped, dropped his notes to his side and looked away before continuing, "There were lots of things about Grant people didn't know. People have no idea how," here Dan paused, "creative Grant was. He could have done stand-up comedy, or written it." Dan took a moment to gather himself. "But Grant tried to practice law, which, in the long run, didn't turn out so well. Of course, as Grant said, over and over, 'In the long run, we're all dead.'" Almost shaking off Libby's attempt at delivering a big, theatrical hug, Dan returned to his seat.

Although a number of other people spoke, judging from how they spoke of him, none of them seemed to have known Grant. They spoke mostly about Libby. Jim Byrnes and Mr. Steiner did not speak.

The interment was equally dismal. Although it was never supposed to rain in Phoenix, as Jane drove her parents to the cemetery, the skies darkened ominously. The weather grew more threatening until finally, as they lowered the casket into the grave, the wind howled and the skies unleashed a cold rain. Everyone huddled beneath the canvas awning which had doubtless been rolled into place to shade everyone from the absent sun. The rain stopped as suddenly as it had begun.

As if generously opening up the reception following a wedding, Libby invited everyone to a buffet at her house. Although Jane and her parents thought they should make an appearance, failing to find a parking space anywhere near Libby's house, they returned to their hotel for the rest of the afternoon.

Dan had invited Jane's family to dinner at Lois's house that night. Although somber and less forced than the funeral, the evening was not as comfortable as Jane thought it would be. Lois served everyone drinks and snacks once they were seated in the living room, refilling the drinks as soon as they were finished. She had dinner on the table before round two had been completed. As soon as everyone finished eating, Lois cleared the table, loudly placed all the dishes in the dishwasher in the kitchen and turned it on before excusing herself saying she had an early morning the next day and going to bed.

"You probably want to know what happened," Dan asked once they were alone.

Jane nodded earnestly and her father opened his mouth as if to say something then closed it. Her mother shook her head, looking down at her hands folded before her on the table. The question still plagued Jane. She didn't agree with the grief counselor that only the mentally ill committed suicide. Was it that simple? Didn't you need to know Grant and the surrounding facts? How could the psychologist be so sure?

"I think it's pretty simple," Dan began. "Steiner doesn't work, which in most firms is fine. He's a rainmaker. But to justify paying himself much more than anyone else, he thinks he has to bill more hours than anybody." Jane's father nodded. Almost sighing, Dan continued. "So, Steiner holds onto his files, thinking he's going to do the work so he can record a bunch of hours on his time sheet. But the files usually sit on his desk until he summons somebody to his office, tells them to drop whatever they're doing, and get his work done. It's always the other lawyer's fault the work is overdue.

"Grant was working on a bunch of things when Steiner gave him a suit on a five-million-dollar personal guarantee. I'm guessing Grant didn't get a chance to look at it for a couple of days because he already had all sorts of things going on. When he found out the time to file had passed, Grant asked the other side for an extension, but they ran in and got the judge to dismiss the case." Jane gasped and Dan nodded.

"Although Jim Byrnes thinks he can get the suit reinstated, Steiner screamed at Grant, saying it was all Grant's fault. The day after everything came out, they cancelled Grant's parking garage access. He was returning to the office after lunch and he had to back his car up the ramp and park on the street. When he finally made it up to his office, they'd stacked all his books out in the hall. They locked the door and changed the key. So, he goes back down to the street and discovers his car has been towed because he hadn't had any change for the meter." Dan paused and shook his head. "He laughed. He said he thought he'd fallen into a Charlie Chaplin movie. He said his books being piled at his office door was a surprisingly funny gag, 'for that place.'"

Jane's father broke the silence.

"Weren't they within their rights? To fire Grant? Wasn't it his fault?"

Dan looked at Jane before responding.

"Libby says Grant told her the time to file the response had already run by the time Steiner gave him the file. She thinks the firm blamed Grant to protect Steiner. She thinks Steiner caused Grant to kill himself and he's liable to her in damages. She's going to sue Steiner." Jane's father straightened up in his chair, puffed out his cheeks and raised his eyebrows. "Ironically," Dan continued, "Grant wanted to move out of Libby's and, uh, have us move back in together. But I couldn't do that," Dan concluded, closing his eyes and rubbing his forehead. Jane was about to ask if it wasn't his fault, why Grant would have taken the blame, when her father erupted.

"No!" he shouted, pounding his fist on the table. "That opportunistic little tramp isn't going to drag Mr. Steiner's name through the mud just for some, some," here he searched for the correct word, "lucre!" He pointed at Jane and her mother for emphasis. "Our family will not, I repeat not, be party to any such thing!" ending the conversation, and the evening.

Jane and her parents returned to Illinois, Jane to Chicago, her parents to Champagne-Urbana, and the routines of their lives. Although Jane couldn't say she felt better about Grant, when she thought of him, as she did within moments of waking, the pain gradually became a little less acute. Although Ed was resisting his partners' urgings to move to New York City, he was there almost full-time. Jane and Ed saw each other on weekends in Chicago and when Jane's travel otherwise allowed, in New York. Although at times this arrangement made her feel estranged from Ed, more often Jane appreciated having the time alone to recover from Grant's death and as well as think about some other things.

Jane was beginning to wonder whether she was really suited for what she'd thought was her life's work. She worried she'd become obsolete. At some point during her career, universities had changed. In the past, universities provided money to scholars in return for scholarship and prestige. Now, scholars seemed to be expected to provide scholarship, prestige, *and* money *to* universities. Just recently, during another trip to Tucson and Kitt Peak, the astronomers there had informed Jane they'd obtained a grant with which they were all going to leave Jane and the University of Illinois and the consortium, and align themselves instead with Stanford University.

Of course, astronomy, never mind administration, hadn't been Jane's first choice. As a star high school student, Jane had wanted to become a mathematician. But advanced college mathematics quickly exceeded her capabilities. Unfortunately, her second choice, astronomy, quickly turned into very abstruse physics, chemistry and, again, mathematics. Jane took her undergraduate degree in the history of science (Her father's comment at the time: "That's a field of study?") And although her graduate degree in administration had allowed Jane to work in science without having to do any science, now that administration was turning into fundraising, Jane wasn't comfortable. Although she was sure fundraising wasn't her forte, she'd come to realize she wasn't sure what her forte was.

Also, haunted by how thoroughly her father dominated her mother, Jane had begun wondering whether her relationship with Ed was any more balanced. She and Ed had never really seen that much of each other. When they met in graduate management school, they were busy studying. Upon graduating, Jane began work for the astronomy consortium and Ed went to law school. Following law school, Ed clerked for a federal judge in Washington D.C. before joining his large Chicago law firm's bankruptcy department, working seemingly around the clock. Although they shared their downtown Chicago apartment, Jane spent much of her time traveling to visit her astronomers at their observatories, or meeting with the administrators of other astronomical institutions, literally around the world.

Jane and Ed were not just physically separate. At Jane's suggestion, but with Ed's concurrence, they maintained separate finances. And although Jane was unsure how they'd come to the decision, they had not had children. For the first time, with Grant's passing, Jane had become concerned her family would die out. She wondered whether, but for the influence of Ed's over-powering presence, she would have pursued such an all-consuming career. Practicing law was all Ed did and all he wanted to do. In contrast, Jane wondered whether she'd been duped into letting Ed lay out her life as disastrously as her mother had let her father lay out her life.

Jane also had less abstract concerns. Her father had changed. Usually meticulously polite and ingratiating ("Obsequious," Grant said.)

to colleagues, staff, students and supporters of the Ulysses S. Grant Foundation ("… i.e., anyone not in our immediate family," according to Grant), Jane's father had begun almost literally screaming at everyone. Both the secretaries at the Foundation had filed complaints with the University alleging extreme verbal abuse. Previously a very popular history department professor whose History of the Civil War and Illinois State History courses had always been over-subscribed ("Because they're guaranteed As," Grant opined), stories of students being berated and belittled during her father's lectures circulated throughout the campus. A number of otherwise stellar students who'd received Cs and Ds and even failing grades from her father had lodged formal complaints with the dean of the faculty.

No one had been able to deter Jane's father from what Ed termed his "relentless self-destruction." The University had been forced to threaten terminating its relationship with the Grant Foundation and evicting it from its offices on the campus. And although her father couldn't be fired because of tenure, the University was intent on placing him on probation and limiting him to teaching a single graduate seminar after serving his probation, all of which only further infuriated him. At the University's request, her father and mother's childhood schoolmate and recently widowed longtime friend who was the Chief Justice of the Illinois Supreme Court and chairman of the Grant Foundation's advisory board, had been brought in to try to negotiate a truce.

As her father's continued belligerence was causing discussions between the University and Justice Cameron to go as badly as possible, at Libby's request, Dan called Jane's father and asked him to consider filing a bar complaint against Mr. Steiner and Jim Byrnes while she was putting the finishing touches on her wrongful death lawsuit against them and their firm.

"What will the bar complaint allege?" her father asked Dan during the conference call he'd taken in Justice Cameron's office in Springfield, which her father insisted Jane attend. During his battle with the University, Jane's father had become increasingly conversant with legal terms and concepts, becoming, in Ed's words, "a bit of a jailhouse lawyer."

"That's a good question," Dan responded, troubling Jane but pleasing her father who took it as a compliment. "I suspect they're hoping the bar complaint will pressure them into settling with Libby and paying her something."

Justice Cameron nodded and grimaced for a moment before speaking to Jane's father.

"John, although I suspect these fellows would stipulate they may have been mean to Grant, I doubt they've violated any ethical rules. Unfortunately, if that's the right word, no one killed Grant, except Grant." Which was exactly the same thing Ed had said to Jane.

"I'm in, Dan," Jane's father enthused. "Just send me the form and tell me where to send the complaint. I'll draft it." And that was the end of the conference call.

A week later, Jane's father insisted Jane read the completed ethics complaint. Replete with "reprehensibles," "indefensibles," and "unconscionables," the letter assumed all the mistakes on the lawsuit had been made by Mr. Steiner and concluded Grant had been "scapegoated, tarred, feathered, and summarily run out of town on a rail." Jane nodded and handed the complaint back to her father who beamed the way Grant did after making a pun.

A few weeks later, much to everyone's other than his surprise, her father received a letter informing him a date had been set for a hearing on his complaint at the Arizona bar association's Phoenix offices. "I've booked our tickets," her father gushed, meaning Jane would be accompanying him to the hearing. During the weeks leading up to the hearing, Jane's father reverted to his formerly jovial professional self, allowing Justice Cameron to finalize a settlement with the University that would, in time, fully restore the old order.

Things had not gone as well for Jane. When they were together, she and Ed were not getting along as well as Jane thought they should. Things came to a head one evening when Ed, apparently tired of Jane obsessing about Grant, came right out with what he was thinking.

"Look Jane, in a perfect world, I'm just not sure somebody like Grant should have ever been a lawyer."

"What do you mean?" Jane had cried. "He was smart, and witty and incredibly creative." Ed responded cautiously.

"Yes, but, I'm just not sure those attributes help in being a lawyer," and let it drop.

Upon recounting the scene to her secretary Karen, Jane guessed she hadn't explained how much these and the other things Ed said about Grant upset Jane, at which point Karen replied, "I guess that's not the worst thing Ed could have said, is it?"

Even though Jane's father was anxious to proceed without a lawyer (*"pro se,"* being the correct Latin legal term he used), Dan engaged a legal ethics lawyer in Phoenix to represent her father at the hearing. Jane and her father met Dan and the lawyer, Roger, in Phoenix the night before the hearing at a dinner Libby and her boss had arranged and were supposed to attend but backed out of at the last moment. Lois was also a no show. As it had on Jane and her father, Grant's death seemed to have taken its toll on Dan. He'd moved out of Lois's a few weeks after Grant died and moved in with a running buddy.

Roger struck Jane as rough around the edges. His wavy, thinning brown hair was uncombed, his suit was rumpled, and his tie was loosened to a few inches below his unbuttoned shirt collar. He also talked when his mouth was full, which was just as well because otherwise he could not have said a thing. For a short time, Roger had worked for the lawyer who would be representing Mr. Steiner and Jim Byrnes at the hearing.

"Don Gordon. Big deal in the bar association. He's old, but still powerful." Roger paused and chewed for a while before continuing. "But hiring him for this?" Roger paused to swallow and held both his hands with their palms up, before reaching for another dinner roll. "Like using a howitzer to kill a gnat." Jane's father nodded intently. Roger continued after taking a large gulp of iced tea.

"The guy who's conducting the hearing used to work for Gordon," Roger chuckled. "Gordon put together a conference call the other day and tried to get him, Steve King is his name, to recuse himself. Steve laughs and says, 'Don, if all the lawyers in Arizona who've worked for you recused themselves, would there be any lawyers, or judges, to choose from?'" Roger snorted. "It's to our benefit. I'm guessing Steve can't stand Gordon." Roger chuckled again, reaching for another dinner roll. "A funny story: Steve flunks the bar exam the first time he takes it. When he comes back to his office, Gordon has somebody pile his things in the hallway, lock the door and re-key the lock."

"Why," Jane's father gasped while Roger chewed on his food, "the same thing happened to Grant!"

"That's what they say," Roger said, nodding and chewing. "You know, sometimes I wonder whether those stories aren't apocryphal." Jane's father grew quiet. Roger ate before Jane broke the silence.

"What do you think our chances are, you know, of winning, tomorrow?" Roger chewed. Thinking perhaps Roger had not heard what she'd asked, Jane was about to repeat the question when he answered.

"Can't say," he managed before swallowing and taking another gulp of tea. "Can't predict the future. Might just as well flip a coin." Even Jane was disappointed. "But I'm going to make an exception for you," Roger said, lifting Jane's spirits. "We don't stand a snowball's chance in hell."

"But their conduct was absolutely reprehensible," Jane's father pronounced indignantly, as angry at Roger as at his opinion. Jane frowned but kept quiet. Unfazed, Roger responded.

"By any normal standard, yes. But we're dealing with lawyers here. The conduct has to be unethical." Roger returned to chewing. Having assumed, of all people, lawyers would know the difference between right and wrong, Jane remembered her surprise at learning from Ed years ago that lawyers had their own set of ethical rules. Not knowing any better, her father plowed ahead.

"Aren't lawyers held to a higher standard?" he asked.

"You'd think so," Roger answered before wiping his mouth, getting up from the table and shaking everyone's hand. "It's not something non-lawyers really understand. Thanks for dinner. See you tomorrow."

Jane awoke the next morning fearing the hearing would be nothing more than an exercise. In contrast, her father bustled through breakfast as if he were about to be awarded the Nobel Prize. But for its horrible postscript, Jane would have simply remembered the hearing as the non-event it was.

The lethargic receptionist at the bar association ushered Jane and her father into a window-less conference room. Surveying the three folding tables arranged in a triangle in the center of the room, metal folding chairs lining the outer sides of the tables, Jane realized she had expected something more formal, perhaps a small court room.

Roger arrived and sat next to Jane's father. Mr. Steiner and Jim

Byrnes arrived next with their lawyer. Mr. Gordon was an imposing, John Wayne-like, but nearly elderly, man with a hair weave. After shaking hands uncomfortably, they sat down at the table comprising another side of the triangle. Dan arrived, embarrassing Jane's father by giving him and Jane each a big hug before shaking hands with everyone else and taking a seat in one of the folding chairs along the wall. Emerging from a door in a far corner of the conference room, Mr. King took a seat on the third side of the triangle. He greeted everyone individually by name with a nod and a small waive, then read a newspaper as they awaited Libby's arrival. Five minutes later, Libby breezed in and sat down in a chair against the wall, folding her arms. Libby's boss, whom Jane recognized from Grant's funeral, shook hands all around congenially and took a seat next to Roger, at which point Mr. King folded his newspaper and opened the file folder he'd brought in. Jane recognized one of the only two pieces of paper in the file as her father's complaint.

"I've reviewed the file," Mr. King began, smiling slightly. "Are we ready to proceed?"

Mr. Gordon stood up deliberately, unwinding his body as if it were a jack knife.

"As you can see from our responsive pleading," he almost mumbled, pointing at the other piece of paper in the file with the reading glasses he held in his large hands, "we object to this proceeding." Mr. King held up his hand.

"Your objection is duly noted, Don. But I think we need to give the professor a chance to be heard, don't you?"

"No," Mr. Gordon answered, a small smirk crossing his face, "not really." Mr. King ignored Mr. Gordon and spoke to Jane's father.

"Professor, welcome to Arizona. I am sorry for your loss. Would you care to elaborate upon your complaint?"

"Thank you, your honor," Jane's father almost shouted, hurrying to his feet.

"Please professor, I'm not a judge. It's Mr. King, or Steve."

"My apologies." Jane's father bowed, clearing his throat nervously, his voice quavering. Raising his arm and pointing at Mr. Steiner and Jim Byrnes, he began loudly, "These two men murdered my son." Mr. Gordon, who was no closer to sitting down than bending over slightly, stood erect, raised his reading glasses as if requesting permission to speak. Mr. King raised his hand and Jane's father continued, oblivious to Mr. Gordon's and Mr. King's pantomime. "My son would still be alive if these two had not conspired to drive my son to kill himself, out of heartbreak, over a mistake, not of his making, toiling for these two." Here Jane's father stammered before blurting, "imposters posing as colleagues and," more stammering, "professionals." Jane's father paused as if gathering his thoughts. "Like my dear son, I thought the law was a noble profession." Jane's father's voice began to quaver again and his hands began to shake. "If you do not purge these men from your ranks, membership in your ancient guild will be reduced to nothing more than a license not just to steal, but to kill." Shaking even more, Jane's father took his seat.

"Thank you, Professor. Don? Er, Mr. Gordon?" Mr. Gordon stood erect, putting on, then taking off, his reading glasses and scratching his head with a quizzical look, shifting his weight slightly from foot to foot, and then scratching his cheek.

"You know, Steve," he began deliberately, emphasizing the inappropriately familiar 'Steve,' "I can't find an ethical violation anywhere here." He shrugged before continuing. "I just don't think it's unethical to pay good money to an associate who decides to blow his brains out." Jane gasped. "We shouldn't even be here." Mr. Gordon sat down and Jane's father stood upright.

"What they did was at the very least immoral," Jane's father blurted. "And, if morality should inform the law, it should certainly inform legal ethics, a subset of the law!" No one said anything. Mr. King finally spoke.

"Anything further?" he asked, looking at Mr. Gordon and then her father. Her father shook his head meekly. Both Roger and Mr. Gordon stood and said "no." Mr. King closed the file before him.

"Professor, I probably shouldn't have held this hearing. But I felt you deserved to be heard. Unfortunately, there's really nothing I can do for you. No one's violated any ethical rules. This is the wrong forum. I'm not even sure there is a right one." Libby jumped from her seat and ran from the room, followed by her boss. "Again, I can say I'm truly sorry about what happened to your son. It's a tragedy." Jane and her father both nodded reflexively. "But, if there's nothing further, I'm afraid we're done here."

Mr. King stood up, as did everyone else other than Jane's father. Even after Mr. King had walked from the room, Jane's father remained seated, staring ahead. Everyone else shook hands civilly, and Mr. Gordon, Mr. Steiner and Jim Byrnes walked quietly, if a little triumphantly, or so it seemed to Jane, from the room. Roger said goodbye to Jane and Dan, shook their hands, patted Jane's father on his shoulder, and departed. Jane and Dan waited, giving her father some time to regain his composure. Eventually, he struggled to his feet and headed unevenly toward the door. Walking next to him, Dan offered his elbow for support but her father brushed it away petulantly. Making their way out of the building, across the driveway and into the parking lot, Jane's father pulled away from them in a hurried shuffle Jane had never seen before, at which point everything went wrong.

Jane's father failed to negotiate the few steps leading from one level of the parking lot to the other. Falling awkwardly and not bracing his fall, his head struck the concrete with a rifle-shot-like crack. By the time Jane and Dan reached him, her father was rolling onto his side, blood dripping from his forehead, his eyes blinking and his mouth opening and closing, guppy-like, as he and Grant did when deep in thought.

An ambulance arrived within minutes and took Jane's father to a nearby hospital emergency room. Miraculously, within a few hours, Jane's father had largely recovered. He'd been stitched and bandaged and admitted to the hospital. A brain scan was performed that afternoon which confirmed the doctors' suspicion that he had most likely suffered a mini-stroke, although there was another more precise medical term for it. Early that evening, a neurologist urged Jane's father to allow them to do a fairly simple procedure during which they would insert a small screen in the artery sending blood to his brain to prevent another more serious stroke, but he shook his head resolutely, saying, "No," which made Jane wonder whether he was thinking clearly. Other than keeping him in the hospital overnight for observation, there was nothing more the doctors could do.

Having received a definitive diagnosis, Jane called home for the first time. When Jane finished explaining the situation, her mother's non-response made Jane think the connection had been lost.

"Mom?" Jane asked.

"Yes?" her mother responded as if answering the phone for the first time.

"Did you hear me?" Again, no response. "Mom?"

"Is there anything you need me to do?" her mother asked.

"No," Jane answered.

"Let me know when you're coming home," her mother said and hung up.

A week or so after he'd returned home, it was clear Jane's father had changed. Although no longer irritable, he'd retreated beyond his old geniality to total lethargy. He said little or nothing to anyone. Allowed to return to his office at the Foundation, he sat behind his closed door from nine in the morning until four in the afternoon. At home, he sat in his study doing nothing. Total inattention replaced erratic behavior.

Her father's condition haunted Jane. She couldn't help recalling how frail and helpless he looked, bloodied and sprawled in the parking lot. Ed hadn't helped much. After describing her reaction to him, Ed said, "I suppose having our own mortality stare us in the face is disconcerting," which had struck Jane as unnecessarily cold and hurtful.

Then one weekday afternoon, the secretaries at the Foundation heard a large crash inside her father's office. He'd fallen from his desk chair to the floor, turning the chair over his prone body. Unconscious, he was rushed to the hospital in an ambulance. One of the secretaries called Jane and then Jane's mother, and then Justice Cameron. Making it from Chicago as quickly as she could, Jane was at the hospital in a few hours.

As the day passed, it became evident that this time there would be no miracle recovery. Jane's father had suffered a major stroke rendering him totally incapacitated and nearly vegetative. As the shock wore off that night and into the following days, Jane kept thinking her mother would want to come to the hospital to be with her gravely ill husband. But she never did.

Declining gradually over the course of a week and never regaining consciousness, Jane's father died in his sleep early in the morning following his, and Jane's, sixth night in the hospital. Other than Karen, who came to the hospital regularly to look after Jane, only the retired, former head of the University's history department, a contemporary of

Jane's father, and Justice Cameron, had visited. Ed had wanted to visit, but Jane fought off his attempts to do so.

Although Jane had assumed her father would be buried in Champagne-Urbana, her mother insisted Jane arrange to have her father's body shipped to Phoenix and buried in the cemetery plot next to Grant, saying, "He wouldn't want Grant left alone. Besides, we had to pay for both of those plots."

"What about a funeral?" Jane asked, stunned.

"For whom? There's just you and me left."

"But Dad was important, to his friends, the University, the Foundation."

"They can do whatever they want."

Ed's comment: "We all grieve in our own way."

A week after Jane's father's body was shipped to Arizona, Jane flew to Phoenix alone. Other than the cemetery workers who'd dug the grave and waited quietly nearby to cover up the coffin, Jane, Dan and Dan's roommate, were the only attendees to her father's interment. Dan showed little emotion, which was understandable. Except for during the run-up to the disastrous ethics hearing, Dan and her father had never been on very good terms. Dan's roommate stood next to Dan and squeezed his shoulder before all three of them walked away from the grave. The hug Dan gave Jane when they said goodbye struck Jane as desultory. The hug Dan's roommate gave her seemed more heartfelt. Able to get a seat on a late afternoon flight out of Phoenix, Jane arrived in Chicago in time to get to her and Ed's downtown apartment a little before one in the morning. Ed was in New York.

The next morning, Jane locked up the Chicago apartment and made the drive to Champagne-Urbana. Jane had concluded it made little sense for her to be in Chicago. And even though he was hardly ever in Chicago, Jane had decided she needed a break from Ed. But before making any sort of definitive decision about her relationship with Ed, and thinking her mother would appreciate her company, Jane was considering moving back into the family house.

"Don't do it!" Karen had urged when Jane broached the subject with her. "Don't make any sudden moves, Jane. You've been through two traumas. Grant kills himself, who knows why. Then your father turns into a maniac. Then he dies. No one in their right mind wants to be in Champagne-Urbana unless they have to. Besides, Ed's a doll."

It rained the whole way to Champagne-Urbana. When she arrived at the house in the late morning, it was so dark it might as well have been early evening. Turning off her car, Jane looked at the house her parents had built years ago on what was still the edge of town, the house in which they'd raised Jane and Grant and spent their married life. As the rain poured down, Jane thought how much had changed since the intensely bright morning in Arizona her father had told her Grant had shot himself. Perhaps being home again would help settle things down. Even though she feared her long-married and loyal mother would disapprove of her not being with Ed, Jane hoped she and her mother, the family's sole survivors, could re-connect.

Or so Jane was thinking when a terrific bump jolted her car. Startled, Jane looked in the rearview mirror. Inexplicably, another car had struck the rear of her car and the woman driving the car looked like her mother, who'd never driven a car in her life. More strangely, the man in the car's front passenger seat looked just like Justice Cameron.

Jane climbed out of her car into the rain and walked back to her mother, who rolled down the window once she'd located the switch.

"Mom? What are you doing?"

"Driving?" her mother said, tentatively.

"But you don't know how."

"I went to a driving school?"

"Whose car is this?" Jane looked at Justice Cameron and then at the price sticker on the rear window.

"Mine?" Justice Cameron looked uncomfortable.

"What about Dad?" Jane blurted, before catching herself and adding, "Dad's car?"

"Traded it in?"

"But you were married–" Jane's lips trembled, and her tears were mixing with the rain dripping onto her face, "– for fifty-three years!"

"Yes." Her mother tapped the back of Jane's hand softly, looking briefly at Justice Cameron before turning back toward Jane. "It's perfectly legal, dear. Don't you know? This is the 'until death us do part' part!"

The Critic's Choice

Mark sat a little nervously in his car in front of the light brown tract home standing shoulder-to-shoulder with the other houses in the newer Glendale neighborhood that already looked a little tired. The driveway was only a single car-length deep, just like all the other driveways running down both sides of the straight, two-blocks-long street. Although he'd just spoken to Mr. Mientkiewicz on his cell phone and been told to wait in his car, Mark wasn't positive he was in front of the right house since they all looked the same.

The dusty, brown, double garage door of the house next door on Mark's right slowly lifted to reveal a single car nearly buried among books and other things, from which an old man walked determinedly wearing a shirt buttoned at the throat, a sweater with buttons, and brown polyester pants. Mr. Mientkiewicz was even older than Mark had expected.

Before Mark could unbuckle his seatbelt, Mr. Mientkiewicz made his way across the tan gravel yard, opened the car door, climbed in and extended his hand to Mark, nodding and saying, "How do you do?" formally.

"I'm fine, Mr. Mientkiewicz," Mark responded, nodding awkwardly and shaking Mr. Mientkiewicz's hand, which had a very, very strong grip.

"It's 'Felix,' as in 'happy.'" He fished the seatbelt from behind his shoulder and snapped it in place. "And it's 'Man-KAY-vitch,' not 'MAN-k-o-witz.' And you are Mark."

"Yes," Mark nodded, beginning to add his last name "Powell" before being cut off by Mr. Mientkiewicz.

"And you have the misfortune of transporting a modern-day Methu-selah across the better part of Maricopa County while interrogating, or, interviewing him, who would be me, for a student newspaper piece?" Mark nodded. Although Mr. Mientkiewicz was smiling, he stared at Mark. "Fine and dandy. Drive on." He waved his right hand in the air before touching Mark on his right thigh. "Only in reverse, at first, please." Mark nodded and looked at his watch before backing his car into the street.

"Worried we'll be late?" Mark shook his head even though he was a little concerned about how long the day was going to take. Mark had a light class schedule on Thursdays, and no classes at all on Friday. It was spring and the weather was beautiful. Mark and his house mates were scheduled to head out to some parties later and he didn't want to miss anything. "Currently, I am in a constant state of lateness. As with Beethoven, where you have the early, middle, and late Beethoven, today you see before you the late, or at least, fortunately for me, the later, Felix Mientkiewicz."

A retired, classical music critic for *The Arizona Republic*, Mr. Mient-kiewicz was the guest speaker at an Arizona State University School of Journalism "brown bag" luncheon. In his third year at ASU (although only a sophomore, as Mark explained to his mother, not because he didn't do well in his classes, not that he'd done that great, honestly, but because it was kind of chaotic at ASU trying to get into the classes you needed to, when you needed to) and in his first undergraduate journalism class, Mark wasn't sure whether the teaching assistant running Mark's discussion section had picked him to drive Mr. Mientkiewicz because he considered Mark a good student, or because he was the only student who raised his hand both times when the class was asked who had a car and who was from the far west side of Phoenix.

"Maybe you can write an article on how he became a journalist," the TA suggested, handing Mark two crisp twenty dollar bills for gas money. "I'm told he's led a pretty interesting life. I wanted to drive him, but, I've got a, a scheduling conflict."

"You are a journalist or a musician?" Mr. Mientkiewicz asked before they'd made it to the end of the street.

"A journalism student. But I like music." Which was kind of true.

Mark's mother listened to classical CDs. She even remembered Mr. Mientkiewicz's name from the paper. "Don't do, or say, anything dumb, okay?" she'd said when he'd mentioned his driving assignment on the phone last night. "I'm sure he's a very, very erudite, and cultured, man."

"You have an expense account?" Mark nodded but wondered why having an expense account was the first thing a real journalist would want to talk about with a journalism student. Because Mark was required to write an article and submit it to the ASU newspaper for his journalism course, and because he was having a hard time coming up with a topic, Mark would have taken the driving assignment for free, and driving around for half a day should be a fairly painless way to gain some points with the TA.

"Good! Expense accounts are important. And a good retirement package. The paper gave me a very nice retirement." Mark hadn't even graduated from college, never mind gotten a job, and he was supposed to be worried about retiring?

"I am assuming the deal is that you drive me to and from this extravaganza in return for which I give you my biography?" Mark nodded. Maybe Mr. Mientkiewicz was a little with it after all. "I'll give you the sweetened, condensed, version, like the canned milk used for making confections." Maybe Mr. Mientkiewicz would conduct the interview himself. Mark hadn't had time to think up questions like he probably should have. Mr. Mientkiewicz tapped Mark on his thigh, saying quietly, "You're driving so fast, that's all we'll have time for."

Mark slowed down to the speed limit. He decided he'd call Mr. Mientkiewicz "Mr. M." Not to his face or out loud, just mentally. He didn't seem like the kind of guy who'd like being called a nick-name.

"My parents were from Odessa." Mark nodded. "You know Odessa?" Mark shook his head. "Not in west Texas, in Russia, or Ukraine." Mark found it hard to believe anyone in Arizona had parents from the Soviet Union. "But my brother and I were born in Berlin." Mark was surprised Mr. M was so willing to talk.

"You're German?" Mark asked. "You sound so American."

"I've been speaking American English at least three times longer than you have." Mark worried he'd pissed off Mr. M. "Slavs have an ear for languages. And music. But I'm an American." To Mark's relief, Mr. M continued without Mark having to say anything that might annoy him.

"Berlin was a beautiful city between the wars." Which wars? Mark wondered. "My father was the concertmaster for the Berlin Opera's orchestra. You know the concertmaster?" Mark shook his head. "The best violinist, the chief musician, in the orchestra." Mark nodded.

"My mother played the 'cello and taught 'cello and piano. In addition to the violin, my father played, and taught, the viola. We had a large, elegant apartment. Not one, but two Bechstein grand pianos sat side by side in the parlor." Mark nodded "You know Bechstein pianos?" Mark shook his head. "The preferred piano in Germany, before World War Two." Those wars, Mark thought. "A Mercedes to Steinway's Cadillac. But after the war Bechstein suffered because during the war Therese Bechstein became a little too close to Hitler, if you know what I mean." Mark had no idea what Mr. M meant, but kept his head still.

"Our apartment looked like pictures you see of Leschetitzky's apartment in Vienna." Mark nodded, so he wouldn't crack up at the funny name. "You know Leschetitzky?" Mark shook his head. Obviously, Mr. M didn't need any encouragement to talk. "A very famous piano teacher. You wouldn't know him. And yes, his name was 'Lesch-a-*popular-slang-name-for-women's-breasts*-kee." Mark had no idea how to react. "Man, these names," he thought to himself. Fortunately, Mr. M plowed right ahead. "Leschetitzky lived in the nineteenth and twentieth centuries. And here we are in the twenty-first. You're getting this down?"

Mark had wondered how he was going to drive and take notes. A good-looking girl in his class had offered to lend him her dual microphone, digital recorder set-up, but Mark declined her offer saying he had the same set-up.

"You're young. You'll remember the important things. I never took notes; too distracting. And rude. I kept it up here." He tapped his temple with his forefinger. "There was always music, beautiful, serious, live music, in the house. My father took my brother and me to rehearsals, and performances, at the opera, and when he would substitute for friends in the Berlin Philharmonic. We'd sit in the balcony. If the operas were sold out, we'd sit in the orchestra pit. It was heaven on earth."

They'd driven through the middle of the nice, shady, resort part of Litchfield Park. During the summers, Mark and his grade school friends would sneak onto the golf courses, cool off in the sprinklers, or just goof around. They were approaching the entrance to the interstate in the newer parts of Litchfield Park where Mark's family lived in a subdivision not as new as, but a lot nicer than, Mr. M's. "You need to turn left here," Mr. M commanded. Mark nodded and turned onto the interstate heading east toward Phoenix and Tempe.

"Then we moved to Luxembourg, which is also a beautiful city, and a beautiful little country. My father played in the Royal Luxembourg Orchestra while my mother taught. They also played chamber music with lawyers and doctors, wealthy dilettantes who paid good money for good players who were willing, and able, to carry them. My brother studied the 'cello with my mother. He was very serious. My father taught me the viola because it's easier to get a decent tone out of a viola than a violin, and violists are always in demand. Everyone wants their children to grow up to be little Heifetzes, so there are always lots of violinists." Mr. M. chuckled. "You know Jascha Heifetz?"

"A violinist?"

"The most famous violinist of my father's generation. They grew up, and played, together. You know any famous violists?" Mark shook his head. "There aren't any!" Mr. M roared. Mark laughed, relieved it was a joke rather than an unanswerable question. To Mark and his buddies there was nothing worse than guys who told bad jokes and thought they were funny. "At the beginning of World War Two, during high school, my brother and I went to Paris. I was eighteen, about your age."

"I'm twenty," Mark interjected. "Almost twenty-one, actually."

"Yes, *about* your age. Eventually, my parents ended up in Marseilles. I enlisted in the French Army. They sent me to North Africa with a bunch of other recruits and marched us around with wooden rifles. Lucky for me, when they found out I could play clarinet and viola, they put me in the marching band and the orchestra. It's no fun trying to play clarinet while trying to march, but it beat walking around on rocky dirt with a wooden gun.

"It was delightful, really. For the only time in my life, I was a full-time, professional musician. I was paid to practice and play. We played for dignitaries, and the military brass, and at dances and concerts for the officers and local bigwigs. But when I joined the Free French Army, they didn't have much time for music. They taught me how to drive an anti-tank truck. My musical career was over," Mr. M chuckled and tapped Mark on his thigh, "but I do know how to drive.

"Then they sent us to Italy. I drove up and down the boot, from Naples, to Siena, and back. I spent some time in Rome, visiting family friends." Mr. M's war sounded like a family vacation. "The girls in Rome were wonderful, as were the ones in Naples. They were very, how should I say, appreciative of us having chased the Germans away. Then we were shipped to Toulon, in the South of France. When we landed, we found an excellent, large, wine cellar. Our entire regiment was incapacitated for three days. It was a good thing the Germans had already retreated. Had they attacked us, we would have been too drunk to even surrender competently."

Mr. M was way too short, and old, of course, to seem like a soldier.

"We made our way up through southeastern France to Grenoble, where I was re-united with my mother. She'd been living in the Alps, above Grenoble, with a friend." He was silent for a while and watched the traffic around them. "Look out for that truck," he said, pointing to a truck that seemed to be weaving.

"After the war, I got a job with a large manufacturing concern in Paris. They made heating and cooling machinery. I was a secretary because I could carry on their business correspondence in all the languages they needed: German, French, of course, English, and even some Spanish and Italian. I dated, and then married, the owner's daughter, a beautiful girl. Not bad for being a male secretary, eh?" Which was exactly what Mark had been thinking.

"Then, we made the big move to Los Angeles. In those days everyone wanted to go to America. They really thought the streets were paved with gold." Mark was always amazed to hear about people who wanted to leave a cool place like Europe to come to a boring place like the United States, never mind Phoenix. "I made it to Los Angeles." At least Mr. M got to go to a place like L.A.

"I was fortunate enough to live among many of the artists who'd gone there before the War: Rachmaninoff, Isaac Stern, the most famous violinist of my generation, Eric Korngold, the famous Viennese composer of movie music. I had an aunt living there among all those

people. I even got work in a movie about the French Foreign Legion."
Mark nodded.

"You know '*Beau Geste*?'" Mark shook his head. He had to stop giving
Mr. M chances to scold him. "The studio placed an ad in the paper for
anyone who'd been in the French Foreign Legion. They dressed us up
in uniforms. I certainly looked the part," Mr. M chuckled. All of which
seemed a little unbelievable to Mark.

"I also worked in the business office of an import and export company. Remember, I could correspond in various languages. Eventually, I
found my true calling." Mark thought Mr. M was finally going to get to
the journalism stuff Mark could use. "I sold lingerie," Mr. M laughed.
Did he really mean he sold women's underwear? "I drove the Southwest
in my R.V. selling women's underwear wholesale, listening to recordings
of opera." Which, except for the opera part and the selling underwear
part, didn't sound so bad.

"A friend in Phoenix told me *The Republic* was looking for a music
critic. So, I applied. They bought me a ticket to a concert, I wrote them
a review, they liked it, ran it, and hired me. And the rest, as they say, is
history. I even suppose you could say I *am* history." Mr. M chuckled.

"I've been considering what to say today," Mr. M resumed. "Should
I recommend your colleagues begin their newspaper careers by selling
women's underwear?" Mark thought Mr. M was serious until he punched
Mark in the shoulder and laughed. Mark's shoulder hurt. For the rest
of the trip they rode in silence. Mr. M even dozed, snoring a little.
That's it? Mark wondered, panicking a little. Mr. M only worked for
one newspaper? When he was already old? He never studied journalism?
He never even went to college? How was any of this going to be useful
to a journalism student, or anyone Mark's age?

Minutes before the luncheon was scheduled to begin, Mark drove up
to the main entrance of the classroom building where the full professor
who taught Mark's journalism course was waiting with the good-looking
woman professor who assisted him and taught writing technique (one
of Mark's least favorite subjects – and teachers), and another man.

"It's Robert Hansen," Mr. M almost shouted. "Every sentence he
writes is beautiful, and effortless."

Before Mark had come to a complete stop, Mr. M popped off his seatbelt, opened the door and nearly bounded toward Mr. Hansen, shaking his hand enthusiastically. Mark's full professor nodded at Mark before being introduced to Mr. M. The writing professor seemed out of sorts, as usual. Mark drove to his assigned parking lot, parked, and then headed back to the luncheon on foot, wondering how he was going to make an article about anything out of what Mr. M had told him. It was one of those beautiful, perfect, spring days. The sky was blue, the air was cool but not cold, and the light was bright but not blinding. If he could have gotten away with it, Mark would have skipped the luncheon and lecture.

By the time Mark had made his way inside to the auditorium, Mr. M and Mr. Hansen were seated down front behind a table next to a lectern from which the dean of the school of journalism was welcoming everybody and describing the other luncheons scheduled for the rest of the semester. Mark took a seat far over in the last row. The room was nearly full since attendance was required for all the students in Introduction to Journalism. A few professors and other adults were sitting in the back, most of whom Mark didn't recognize other than two of the music professors who taught the easy music appreciation course he'd taken. The auditorium had no windows, the air conditioning was on and the seats were comfortable. It reminded Mark of a movie theater. He was tempted to take a nap.

The important people down in front were already working their way through box lunches. Most of the people in the auditorium seemed to have already finished their lunches and drinks. Mark finished the energy bar he'd thought to stuff in his shirt pocket earlier that morning. Mr. M was devouring a cookie as Mr. Hansen stepped to the lectern.

"Unlike so many of us journalists, my good friend, Mr. Felix (he pronounced it correctly Mientkiewicz"), in addition to reporting upon things other people do, has actually done things. And despite enduring all manner of tragedies, large and small, Mr. Mientkiewicz has retained his upbeat outlook, his sense of equanimity, and his relentless, if at times, downright raunchy, sense of humor. Mr. Hansen looked at Mr. M who tilted his head sideways and nodded. The audience sort of laughed. Mr. Hansen must not have been on a university campus recently where, at least in the classrooms, macho guys weren't very popular.

"Felix is certainly the most interesting character I've ever met. He speaks French in German." There was a slight laugh. "Not to mention Russian. And Felix is such a good writer he wrote his biography himself." There was a little laugh from the audience but most people seemed a little puzzled.

"Without further ado, I present to you the distinguished honoree for today's luncheon, the retired, but certainly not forgotten, classical music critic for *The Arizona Republic*, Mr. Felix Mientkiewicz." The audience clapped politely as Mr. M made his way to the lectern, shaking Mr. Hansen's hand and patting him on the back as they passed each other. Mr. M pulled down the microphone to his height, cleared his throat loudly, and began.

"Why is a viola more valuable than a violin?" he asked, pointing at a student in the first row who shook her head. No one raised their hand to answer. Mr. Hansen doubled over in his chair, laughing. "When used as firewood, the viola burns longer." There were a few chuckles. Mark didn't think the joke was funny, but he did find the whole situation a little amusing.

"But seriously, writing is important." Mr. M spoke strongly, right into the microphone, as if he'd received an injection of energy. He seemed younger. He raised his right hand with his index finger extended and shook his arm. "Educate your reader. I always strove to teach my reader about music. But also entertain, whenever possible. And protect the English language from abuse and carelessness. If we writers don't, who will?" The students in the audience were sitting up straight, as if they were being scolded.

"A violist and a 'cellist are standing on a sinking ship, 'Help!' cries the 'cellist, 'I can't swim,'" Mr. M squealed, impersonating a woman before dropping his voice to a lower tone. "'Don't worry,' says the violist, 'No problem. Do like I always do. Just fake it.'" A few of the music professors laughed harder than the other attendees, who seemed to be laughing mostly out of politeness. Mr. M sounded like Seinfeld, but wasn't as funny.

"Language is how humans communicate. Without language, there is no communication. And without communication, we risk becoming inhuman. Music is also important. Music must be protected from malfeasance, by musicians, and by critics." Lowering the tone of his voice, he pulled away from the microphone slightly.

"Fortunately, music was protected from me." He paused, as if expecting a laugh which didn't come. "Even though my parents were great, professional musicians, as was my brother, as a musician, I was a joke." He paused. "I played the viola." A few people laughed. Mr. M took a handkerchief from his pants pocket and wiped his forehead.

"I had the greatest job in the world. For more than two decades, I was paid to listen to the best music. Maybe some of you can be so lucky to have such a job. Unfortunately, I am here, eating a free lunch, under false pretenses." Mr. M looked at the dean and the others on the stage before turning back toward the audience. "I can't tell you how to go about getting my old job. Before becoming a music critic, what did I do?" Mr. Hansen rubbed his hand over his face and laughed.

"I sold women's lingerie." The audience squirmed. "Wholesale!" Mr. M almost shouted. "And wholesale lingerie buyers are generally not the kind of women one wants to see too much of." Mr. Hansen was now hiding his face. "Fortunately, as part of the purchasing process, they don't try on the wares."

The dean and the other people sitting on the stage seemed a little nervous, and Mr. Hansen was shaking his head. Not many professors tried to tell jokes in lectures.

"When the young violist first took his seat in the orchestra, a 'cellist came up to him and asked him how old he was. 'Nineteen,' he answered. 'My God,' the 'cellist exclaimed." Mr. M covered his mouth and opened his eyes wide before gasping, "'and already a violist?'" Mr. M took a drink from the bottle of water on the lectern.

"I've heard it said, rather foolishly, if you ask me, but they are asking me, aren't they, Robert?" Mr. M turned to Mr. Hansen, who laughed and nodded. "They say 'writing about music is like dancing about architecture.'" The music professors broke into applause and most of the audience turned around to see who was clapping. Mr. M was unfazed.

"But I disagree. I know nothing about architecture and I can't dance, but I wrote about music, and my editor kept paying me for over twenty years. Generally, people don't make the same mistake for twenty years." Mr. M looked at Mr. Hansen who laughed. "Except me, when it came to wives. I was married four times," Mr. M confessed, "but to only three women. I married one twice." Mr. Hansen was the only one who laughed. "But I'm here as a music critic, not a marriage expert." Mark thought being married four times wasn't anything to brag about.

"Why do violists stand outside people's houses for long periods of time?" The audience didn't respond. "They cannot find the key, and don't know when to come in." The music professors and a few others in the audience laughed.

"At this time, perhaps you in the audience would like to ask some questions?" Mr. M asked.

"Who was your favorite composer?" a student toward the front asked.

"Ask me my religion," Mr. M responded, almost belligerently. After an awkward pause, the student asked, "What's your religion?"

"Gustav Mahler. His work embodies all human existence, as near as I have been able to determine. So far." Mr. M looked around for the next questioner.

"What's your opinion of Wagner?" the student who'd asked the first question asked. "Wasn't he an anti-Semite?"

"Rick-hard Vohg-nair," Mr. M said slowly, before looking down, sighing and shaking his head. "A horrible, horrible man, but," Mr. M held up his finger, "a tremendous, extremely significant composer. Unparalleled artistry, a lasting influence. Single-handedly changed the course of music. As with Mahler, I like composers because of their music, not because of what they think or how they treat their wives. Mahler married a beautiful, wealthy soprano, the toast of Vienna. She remained devoted to him until the day she died, almost fifty years after he died, even though he was terribly, terribly mean to her. But," lifting his finger again, "if we wait for artists to behave like saints, or even like ordinary people" — here he dropped his voice down really low — "such as ourselves" — before continuing in his normal voice — "we will live in an artless society, a fate I consider worse than death." Mr. M took a drink from the water bottle.

"Take Picasso," he paused to place the cap back on the bottle before adding, "please." Mr. Hansen guffawed. "Perhaps the greatest painter of the Twentieth Century. He discarded his wives, and his mistresses, like so much dirty laundry. Jascha Heifetz stiffed my uncle on a car he'd agreed to buy from him in Berlin. Isaac Stern, also a not so perfect man. But they both considered themselves the greatest violinist of the Twentieth Century." Mr. M held both his hands up, palms raised. Mr. Hansen laughed.

"But these are geniuses." Mr. M shrugged his shoulders. The questioner nodded her head and the student next to her asked a question.

"Is Wagner actually better than he sounds?" The crowd laughed a little.

"Samuel Clemens. A great wit but maybe not such a great music critic, no? I was never flip about music. It was my job to make my readers understand great music. Wagner's music is great music." There was a moment of awkward silence. "What's the definition of perfect pitch?" Mr. M pointed at the music professors in the back of the room, one of whom shouted: "Being able to identify a tone by name upon hearing it."

"Thank you, but the answer I prefer is 'throwing a viola into a dumpster without hitting the rim.'" Mr. Hansen laughed. The audience was quiet for a moment before one of the music professors shouted:

"Have you ever conducted anything? Chamber music? Small ensembles? A symphony orchestra?"

"Yes." Mr. Hansen laughed out loud. "Briefly. In high school, I was to conduct the school's student symphony in its performance of Beethoven's Third Symphony, 'The Eroica.' As you know, rhythmically, the Eroica begins, '*Boomp*, two, three. *Boomp*, two, three. Ya dee-dah, dee-yah dee-dee-dah, de-dum," Mr. M sort of sang, moving his hands and arms as if he was a conductor, then lifted them above his shoulders before dropping them to his side and letting his shoulders slump. "Yes?" People in the audience nodded in agreement.

"I never got past the first two measures. I tried a few times, and the teacher tried a few times to get me to count it out correctly, but he failed, and I failed. He snatched the baton from my hands. It was the alpha, and the omega, of my conducting career." The students in the audience seemed to find the anecdote entertaining, but the music professors seemed annoyed.

"What's the difference between a viola and an onion? No one cries when you chop up a viola. And so how can you tell when a violist is playing out of tune? His bow is moving," The audience laughed politely then fell silent.

"What qualifications do you think a music critic should have?" one of the music professors shouted. The audience pulled in their breath.

"A music critic must have an extremely," he dragged this word out and then repeated it, "extremely difficult to spell, and to pronounce, last name." Most of the audience laughed except the music professors. No one seemed willing to ask a question.

"Maybe some of you play in orchestras. A conductor and a violist are standing in the middle of the road. Which one do you run over first. And why. Answer: The conductor. Business before pleasure."

"What do you look for in a concert?" Mr. Hansen asked as if to distract from the scene the music professors were making. Mr. M turned to the audience and, covering his mouth with his left hand, said in a low voice, "In the interview business, this is called 'tossing a softball?'" Mr. Hansen laughed, and the audience seemed to relax.

"Robert, I went to concerts to see, and hear, geniuses. You know what a genius is? A genius is someone who can do the impossible. That's what we go to concerts for. And we go to concerts to fall in love. We want to fall in love with the performers and the performance. You want to have in any concert, a divine moment of pure beauty, perfection, you might say. I call it," Mark noticed Mr. Hansen covering his face, "having a musical orgasm." The audience either laughed or groaned. Mr. M pointed at Mr. Hansen.

"After he'd attended a concert, I would always inquire, 'Robert, did you have your musical orgasm?' If Robert said 'yes,' I knew the concert had been worthwhile, if not…." Mr. M shrugged. The audience seemed stunned, or offended, into silence.

"But this shouldn't devolve into me telling a bunch of war stories, should it Robert?" Mr. Hansen, his face still covered, shook his head. "I have those too, but I'd rather tell jokes. Why is it violists don't play hide and seek?" Mr. M took a drink from his water bottle. "No one will look for them."

"What famous people have you interviewed, and what is important about interviewing famous people," asked a serious girl journalism student Mark recognized.

"Many, but a few come to mind. Anna-Sophie Muter, a tremendous violinist of our time. I was to have only fifteen minutes, but we ended up spending two glorious hours together. She loved being able to converse in her native Berlin German. So, I would say, always be able to speak famous people's language. It's very helpful." Mr. Hansen was the only one who laughed, although Mark also thought it was kind of funny.

"Also Herbert Von Karajan. I was at a luncheon in Berlin, a little like this one. But maybe just a little more elegant. The public relations man for the Berlin Philharmonic set it up. I'm sitting at the table with a few other journalists when in breezes Von Karajan, but more like a blizzard." Mr. M stood up straight and stiff and affected a stern, "Hogan's Heroes-type" German accent. "He sits down and he demands, 'With whom am I seated?' The PR man goes around the table introducing us, one after the other. Karajan sniffs, nods, announces he has a headache, and leaves." The audience gasped.

"So, when interviewing famous conductors, always bring very fast acting aspirin." Quite a few people laughed and a few even clapped.

"Wasn't Von Karajan a Nazi?" the student who had asked whether Wagner was anti-Semitic asked.

"I don't think so, no. There are no politics in music. No one gets murdered by music. It was very dangerous not to like the Nazis, and Hitler liked a number of conductors. I refuse to believe just because Von Karajan was Hitler's favorite conductor he was a Nazi."

"Is it true your only appearance as a musician was as a kazoo soloist?" one of the music professors shouted out.

"No. Playing the kazoo was not my only appearance. I also played the toy trumpet." Mr. Hansen and a number of people in the audience actually laughed. "And I played both of them quite well, if I do say so myself. And, of course, I did say that in the reviews I wrote of my performances, which, considering my mastery of both those instruments, was a position I felt perfectly justified taking." At which point the music professors stood up as one and walked noisily out of the auditorium.

"Is my time up?" Mr. M asked the audience and then the people sitting on the stage.

"It's up to you, Felix," Mr. Hansen answered.

"You must stand for something," Mr. M said, turning to the audience. "You don't have to write about music. I never wrote about architecture, or dance, but they are of course important. Write about important things. Be serious. Use correct English. It's a wonderful language." People were getting ready to gather their things and head out. "What do a viola and a lawsuit have in common? Everyone is happy when the case is closed." People laughed and a few clapped. "For the moment," Mr. M concluded, "I am out of jokes."

Mark pulled his car up to where he'd dropped off Mr. M. He was standing with Mr. Hansen and the writing professor. Mr. M and Mr. Hansen were laughing but the professor didn't seem happy. Mr. Hansen tried to give Mr. M a hug, which Mr. M avoided by shaking Mr. Hansen's hand and bowing to him. Mr. Hansen laughed and bowed back. Mark leaned over and opened the passenger door. Mr. M was holding the professor's hand after having shaken it.

"Can I bring her with me?" Mr. M asked Mr. Hansen and even looked at Mark for approval. Mr. Hansen cracked up and kind of guided Mr. M into the car. The woman professor looked even less happy. Mark drove off.

"Ah," Mr. M sighed loudly. "The trip back home. In sonata form, the return to the first theme. Sometimes a little depressing, as in Chopin. It's as if he's returning, not home, but back to sad thoughts. You know Chopin?" Mark shook his head. Mr. M shrugged.

"I'm tired, Mark. Even at my age I get keyed up before performances, and deflated after." Mr. M looked around before shaking his head as if to clear it. He seemed tired. He closed his eyes and rested his forehead on his right hand's fingertips, his elbow propped on the passenger side door. They drove in silence. Mark checked his watch.

"Worried about being late?" Mr. M asked, startling Mark. Mark shook his head although he had been trying to figure out by what time he'd be able to make it back to Tempe and his friends. "Don't worry about me being late. Soon I'll be '*the* late Felix Mientkiewicz.'" Mark was kind of surprised to find old people actually talked about dying.

"I was tipped off the music department would be waiting for me. They all think a critic needs to have a degree in music performance, or theory, or preferably both. I never went to college. Worse, I reviewed one of their faculty recitals. It was dreadful. I considered it my duty to warn the public against bad performances. Music teachers don't have time to prepare. A concert pianist needs to practice seven or eight hours each day. For a musician, having to teach at a university is a recipe for disaster." Mr. M rested his forehead on his fingers.

"They were there to embarrass me. They were defending their own. Admirable, if misguided. Only because they don't have time to practice, we are inevitably at odds. But giving bad reviews is part of the job." Which struck Mark as kind of harsh.

Wanting to avoid the unusually bad traffic on the main road he was on, Mark decided to cut through some of the older Tempe neighborhoods to get to another main street that would get them onto the interstate heading west.

"Those ditches," Mr. M said, pointing to the irrigation ditches still running along the streets in front of the old wooden and brick houses in the old part of Tempe, "remind me of my escape from Luxembourg: a two-day bike race to Paris. The ditches on each side of the roads were filled from the German air force, the Luftwaffe, strafing. There were cars, trucks, dead people and dead horses, lots of dead horses, in those ditches." Horses being killed in wars had never occurred to Mark. It was kind of creepy. "Truth isn't the first casualty of war, horses are." Mr. M's story was getting kind of grim.

"On the second day, my brother and I became separated in the chaos. I had no idea what had become of him until after the war. He joined the French resistance, and fought with them, and survived. He was good on the 'cello. He caught on with an orchestra in Argentina. Then he was recruited by Fidel Castro to play in Cuba's national symphony orchestra. He played for them for the rest of his career."

Cuba, Mark thought. Wasn't it illegal to go there?

"Died of cancer a few years ago. Too many fine cigars, I fear. My brother loved them. Probably the primary reason he went to Cuba. That and a reliable pay check. He wasn't a Communist, that's for sure. Musicians can't afford to be political.

"In Paris, I stayed with family friends we used to visit during our summer vacations. I wanted to do something about the Germans, but they don't let just anyone join the French Army, even as a volunteer. You must be a French citizen. The recruiting officer told me to go around the corner to the Foreign Legion. 'They'll take anybody,' he told me. You'd have thought I was applying for welfare rather than volunteering to defend France against the Germans.

"The French Foreign Legion was not as romantic as in '*Beau Geste*.' The only 'romantic'" — here Mr. M paused to make imaginary quotation marks with his hands —"experience I had was one long, terrible night spent in a tent fending off an old, ugly, homosexual sergeant." This guy is definitely not politically correct, Mark thought to himself.

"I did however, lose my virginity, in Rome, to an older woman. It was very strange. We accomplished our objective, in the dark, standing up, in a phone booth, of all places. She cried the entire time. I never saw her again." Things seemed to be going from bad to worse.

"That was after I'd joined the Free French Army. You know anything about the French in World War Two?" Mark shook his head. "They surrendered to the Germans because they didn't want their country destroyed by the Germans. Are you lost," Mr. M asked Mark, who shook his head even though he had to admit he was wandering in the neighborhood a little.

"Although I had no desire to be in what had become a branch of the German Army, I had to get to the Free French lines without getting shot as an approaching enemy by the Free French, never mind getting shot in the back as a deserter by the collaborationist Vichy French. I spent three days wandering in the North African desert. Quite Biblical, except for the machine guns, and barbed wire." Mark still had a hard time picturing Mr. M in any army.

"While I was in North Africa, my parents made their way to France, ending up in Marseilles." Mark nodded. "You know Marseilles?" Mark shook his head. "Not the kind of place my parents would ever have chosen. But they thought they were safe there."

Mark finally succeeded in making his way onto the interstate and headed past the airport toward downtown Phoenix. Traffic was horrible. At times, they came to a complete stop. Since it was too early to be rush hour, Mark assumed an accident was causing traffic to back up so badly. Mark was getting discouraged and a little frustrated. He was beginning to think he'd never make it out to Litchfield Park and back to Tempe. He wondered whether he could get paid overtime, or something. Mr.

M started up again.

"We were in France, chasing the Germans as they retreated north. I was in my anti-tank truck, which I commanded from the top where I had a machine gun. We were parked, resting along the side of the road when, around the corner comes a German army truck. The driver's shouting and waiving at us. I assumed we were under attack so I shot, and killed, the driver. The truck crashed harmlessly in front of us." Mr. M waved his hand in the air and shook his head.

"Unfortunately," Mr. M took in a large breath, "the dead driver was," he paused, "my best friend. I hadn't told you I had a best friend in the army." Mark shook his head and then nodded. "We had absolutely no idea how he'd gotten out in front of us." Mr. M shook both his hands in front of his face. "And what on earth was he doing in a German Army truck? I loved him dearly, and I killed him."

Mr. M was quiet for a while. Mark had no idea what to say. They were heading through downtown Phoenix toward the west side of town. Traffic was moving, but slowly. Mr. M waived his hand.

"Then, I injured my shoulder. Well," he chuckled, "I didn't injure my shoulder, a German soldier injured my shoulder. One night we came upon a farmhouse and were told to go see whether there were any Germans in there. I made the mistake of poking my head into an open window. Not too surprisingly, the German soldier inside had a rifle, the butt of which he used to render me completely unconscious." Mr. M shook his head.

"My buddies killed him and the other Germans in there, but my shoulder was broken. I was transported to the hospital in Lyon. It was such a bad injury the head surgeon, the director of the hospital, took on the job as a challenge, 'a great honor,' he called it. I was not as en-thusiastic."

"Was he able to fix it?"

"Oh yes, he did a splendid job. He was very pleased with himself."

"Is your shoulder okay?"

"It's fine. No problem." Mr. M lifted his right arm a few times. "But for me, that was the end of the war." He looked out the window as if he was looking for something in particular. "After they released me from the hospital, I was able to visit my mother. She'd hidden in the Alps above Grenoble with her resistance fighter friend. By that time, he'd returned to his home, in Austria. My mother nearly fainted when she saw me because, of all things, my arm was in a sling." Mr. M laughed and shook his head. "Very ironic." He laughed and looked out his window. "I could just as well have been dead, and there she was upset about my arm being temporarily in a sling." Mr. M's parents must have divorced during the War. Maybe that was why he'd been married so many times.

Mr. M started dozing and the traffic cleared allowing Mark to make good time. Mr. M didn't wake up until they'd turned off the interstate into the newer part of Litchfield Park. Mr. M pointed at a young, transplanted tree among older trees in the landscaped area next to the road.

"That's the tree they planted to replace the one I drove my car into when I had my first stroke. I never lost consciousness but it was as if everything was in slow motion." He shook his head. "That was the end of my driving career. They tell me the odds are good I'll have another stroke and it will most likely kill me. I guess it's good to know what will kill you." Mark wasn't sure he agreed.

"So, I guess I don't have much time left." Mr. M seemed to want some sort of agreement. Mark nodded. "For me, being able to write about music was a gift from heaven. I never suffered the ignominy of having to write about ninety-year-old, washed-up, music critics." Mr. M nudged Mark on his shoulder. "You know what they do with a second chair violist once he dies?"

"Uh, no," Mark said, knowing a goofy punch line was coming.

"Move him back to third chair," Mr. M said, chuckling and nudging Mark's thigh. Mark thought maybe he should try something to get Mr. M onto a happier subject.

"Do you have children, and grandchildren?" Mark asked.

"Yes, but they haven't been the panacea they're purported to be. My children and grandchildren are all good people, but I find my solace in music. Without being able to listen to music, I'm not sure I could go on living." Things were getting kind of grim again. "But yes, certainly, I've had more luck with my children than their mothers and my other wives. My first wife was, how should I say, unhappy. A beautiful girl, but mentally unstable. She was unhappy when we were in France, primarily because she was in France." Mr. M shrugged his shoulders and tilted his head to the side. "After we managed to move to Los Angeles, as she wished, she was unhappy because she wasn't in France. Her psychiatrist said maybe it would be a good idea if she went back home for a visit so she could see it wasn't her location that was the problem. So, she did, and never returned. We were divorced. Within a few years she had drunk herself to death." Mr. M shrugged his shoulders. "Very sad." So much for cheering up Mr. M.

"But I got my son from that marriage. Wife number one, his mother, was the one Isaac Stern tried to steal from me. A great violinist, but not such a great man. He propositioned her, made a pass at her, one night, right in our house.

"But there I was, in the United States, mostly because of her. People from all over the world want to come to the United States. Certainly, in Europe after the end of the war, they did. They really thought that in America the streets were paved with gold. The people who were already here told us that." It wasn't a good sign that Mr. M was beginning to repeat his stories.

"But you know, Americans misunderstand that saying. Do you know the rest of it?" Mark shook his head. "It doesn't mean Americans are so wealthy and extravagant they gold-plate the roads, like bathroom fixtures. The rest of the saying is: 'and all you have to do is pick it up and put it in your pocket.' You see," Mr. M chuckled, "in much of the world, if things, even cobblestones, aren't glued down, they get stolen.

"But for me, it wasn't so easy. For it to be easy, I think you have to know how to make money. If you're a businessman, it's easier over here than in Europe. I wasn't a businessman, I was a secretary. And over here, that's a woman's job." Mark nodded.

"Of course, it didn't help the man I worked for in Los Angeles was an imposter. He was the ne'er-do-well husband of a very, very wealthy woman who gave him an allowance to play at business during the day. He never closed a deal. It took me too many months of working for free to figure that out.

"And I lost my job selling lingerie after fifteen years because the man I assumed was my partner replaced me with his son-in-law. What can you do?" Mark didn't know. "I was out of work for a while, which spelled the end of my marriage to wife number two. I did get my daughter from that marriage, though. Wife number two wasn't a bad woman but she wanted to stay in LA when I came up with the brilliant idea of moving to Phoenix. And what do you do when you move to Phoenix?" Mark tilted his head and grimaced trying to figure out a punchline that would involve a viola. "You become a realtor!" Mr. M crowed. "Selling houses in Phoenix has to be about as easy as stealing golden cobblestones, right?" Relieved, Mark nodded.

"Wrong!" Mr. M shouted. "You're looking at the only realtor in history who has never made a penny selling houses in Arizona. Never sold a single one. I was terrible at it!" Mr. M laughed. "But perhaps that shouldn't have come as a surprise. When I started selling underwear, I wasn't good either. One buyer told me she'd only ordered anything from me the first time because I looked so miserable, and I was such a bad salesman she felt sorry for me. If I hadn't caught on with *The Republic*, I'd have been the first realtor in Arizona to starve to death."

Mr. M. laughed then grew silent, which was fine with Mark. So much of the stuff Mr. M insisted on telling Mark was just depressing and had nothing to do with being a journalist. Mark's story's summary would read: "Mr. M is kind of a crazy old guy who did lots of stuff before he lucked into getting a job as a music critic, although the jury's still out on whether he was any good."

As they drove through the nice part of old Litchfield Park, one then another fighter jet screamed overhead as they took off from Luke Air Force Base, just over the hill in the desert adjoining the road. The car shook.

"They teach German pilots to fly there." Mark nodded. "I was savoring breakfast one morning in a restaurant when five or six big, young, blond, blue-eyed, uniformed Luftwaffe pilots strutted in and sat down at the table next to mine. I hadn't seen those uniforms since the morning they landed their gliders out the kitchen window of our house in Luxembourg. I was terrified. Turn here," Mr. M commanded even though Mark was already making the turn onto the street that led into Mr. M's subdivision.

"In German, I told them it was the second time in my life they'd ruined my breakfast and that the last time had been over sixty years ago. They smiled and nodded, and seemed surprised to hear good German so far from home. They had no idea what I was talking about."

Mark pulled his car into what he thought was Mr. M's driveway, but he was even further off target than he'd been when he'd picked up Mr. M.

"You missed by three houses this time. It's over there. A common mistake in this neighborhood. I had a beautiful condominium of my own, but since stroke number one and my slaughtering that tree, I have been required to live with my daughter and my two grand-daughters. Her husband has left her, and his children, for another woman, a drug addict. Now all of my daughter's money goes to her lawyer. Her husband is a terrible man, as it turns out.

"Not unlike the resistance fighter my mother lived with above Grenoble. After the war, my mother lived in Germany, near the Austrian border. The German government provided her an apartment and a stipend. She also taught 'cello and piano. She wanted to be there because she knew I would come back to Austria and Germany every summer for the music festivals, and she was right. She looked up her resistance fighter in Austria years later, only to find him living, as man and wife, with one of his daughters. My mother lived quite a while longer, but I don't think she ever recovered from that." Mark maneuvered his car out of the wrong driveway, up the street and into the right one. "But here, in my daughter's house, I miss my things, and my old life. So?" Mr. M asked, laughing and shaking Mark's hand, "did you get that all down?"

"I, uh, think so. You should write a book, Mr. Mientkiewicz."

"You're by no means the first person to tell me that," Mr. M said, getting out of the car and opening the garage door with a clicker he'd had with him. He disappeared into the garage, but before Mark had begun to back out of the driveway, he reappeared with a paperback book held high above his head, like a sword. He made his was to Mark's side of the car and motioned for Mark to lower the window.

"I want to give you a copy of my book." He held the book with its cover toward Mark.

"Why, thank you, thank you very much, Mr. Mientkiewicz." Mark looked at the photo on the cover of a man who looked a lot like Mr. M but was half Mr. M's age. He was smiling and seemed less grumpy than Mr. M. He held either a violin, or a viola, under his chin. The title across the top of the cover read: "My Father's Son."

"A photograph of my father."

"Of course," Mark said, "Is he playing a violin or a viola?"

"What difference does it make? They put him on a train from Marseilles to Auschwitz. We never heard from him again. I went to Auschwitz years ago. They couldn't find any record of him ever having been there. He may have died on the train." Mark didn't know what to do.

"You know, they mailed me a questionnaire when I was in North Africa, about my parents. I never responded." He paused. "Perhaps, had I filled out that form, perhaps things would have turned out differently, for all of us." He shook the book in his hand, saying, "I have yet to understand how anyone could find it necessary to murder such a beautiful man." He handed Mark the book.

"Thanks, Mr. Mientkiewicz. I'll return it once I've read it."

"That's not necessary. I have plenty," he said, turning and walking into the garage, disappearing into the cluttered dimness as the door lowered down to the driveway.

Mark fanned the book's pages to the pictures. Among others, there was a photo of a much younger Mr. M standing next to a pretty cool looking woman wearing pointy, really dark sunglasses, a hat and gloves, a very stylish, tight fitting dress and high heels. She must have been wife number one. Mr. M stood next to her looking sharp in a suit with big lapels on the jacket and pleats on the pretty baggy pants. On the facing page, a younger Mr. M stared at Mark in what the caption said was a French Foreign Legion uniform. He was wearing one of those funny French hats that looked like a small hat box with a bill on the front. Mr. M didn't look happy. The credit below the picture said it was from Warner Brothers. It must have been a publicity shot for the movie he'd been in.

"Wild," Mark thought, closing the book and tossing it onto the passenger seat. Maybe he should have asked Mr. M more about being in the movies in old-time Hollywood. That would have made a good article.

Scherzando

Mickey

He was bathed in sweat. He blinked to make sure his eyes were open rather than closed. The dream part of yesterday must have ended and the awake part of today must be beginning. What would he see? There'd be more heat than he could remember. Would he see any neighbors? What condition would they be in? He'd gone to bed convinced today would be the day he'd take action.

The arms on the clock next to his soaked mattress said four-thirty, but that couldn't be right. The sun was clearly up. He couldn't have slept through most of the day. The power must be off. He'd seen the bright pink and purple glow to the northwest yesterday evening. The nuclear plant near Phoenix must have melted down.

He scratched his itchy scalp and face. Surprisingly, his matted, moist hair and beard seemed to be growing. He'd shave his beard and hair to show solidarity with those who were losing their hair. He'd need electricity. He didn't trust razor blades.

The bomb's electro-magnetic discharge had disabled the grid. Or maybe all the power lines were melting and snapping from the un-precedented heat. Anything was possible. Maybe he could place solar collectors on the roof. He'd studied up on solar power. Or maybe he could use power lines that had been knocked down by the blast to run power from a dead neighbor's existing solar set-up.

The far-away buzzing of a military plane distracted him. Every morning since the bomb had dropped he noticed the big gray plane flying deliberately over what had been downtown Tucson, and then his location in the foothills north of Tucson, before heading off to the north. They must be collecting scientific data. Tucson and its surviving inhabitants were clearly lab rats in an experiment. By the time he scrambled outside, the plane was out of sight. Soon it was out of earshot. Silence returned.

The fires were bound to start again. Dark fire clouds were already visible, rising to the south and east. The bomb must have created whirlwinds and firestorms of its own. The macro-climate had been changed forever. Or did he mean micro-climate? It might never rain again.

But just figuring things out wasn't enough. He had to do something. Fortunately, he felt up to the task. His senses heightened, things appeared brighter, clearer, more defined. He felt the way he felt as a kid setting off on a trip in the family car, anticipating the things to come. He felt like the boy who, although he'd seen a tornado spawned by the bomb, wasn't afraid. Like the boy, he considered everything since the bomb had fallen an adventure, a camping trip.

Even though his mind was clear, "as sharp as a tack," as his father would have said, his body was stiff. The mattress he'd laid out in the shed was more like a Japanese-style mat, which was probably what was making him have such science fiction-like dreams. He didn't like science fiction.

Why hadn't the government surrendered instead of fighting to the death? The military-industrial complex must be calling the shots. Had Phoenix been bombed as well? If Phoenix hadn't been bombed, why weren't people there concerned about Tucson? Shouldn't they send help? Tucson would have helped Phoenix.

But having surveyed the neighborhood, he wasn't sure anyone was still alive to care about anything. Although most of the nearby houses had somehow miraculously survived the night's firestorms, no inhabitants were visible. Had it been a neutron bomb whose radiation had somehow not killed him?

As if in answer, the old man next door appeared, walking around the shed at the back of his house, which was just like the shed he'd been forced to take shelter in. The old man's head was bandaged in clean, bright white gauze, as if he was wearing a ski hat. How had he found such a big, clean bandage? Maybe he had a first aid kit. The old man seemed to be walking fine. He wasn't using a cane or a crutch.

He had to find out what the old man knew that he didn't. He headed through the desert toward the old man but didn't make it very far. The blast had evidently torn his shoes from his feet. A few steps into his walk, he stepped on a cactus spine. It didn't go far into his skin and it came right out when he pulled it, but he would have to be more careful. He slowly picked the rest of the way through the destroyed desert.

He edged his way around to the door of the old man's shed and spied him holed up there. He had suspended a Geiger counter from a cabinet and was typing on his computer, taking notes on what the Geiger counter was registering on an oscilloscope he had on his bench. It hit him like a ton of bricks: the old man was a scientific operative collecting data for the scientists who'd had the bomb dropped to study its effect on humans, animals, the environment, the entire ecosystem. The old man was in on it, one of them. Before he could escape, the old man spotted him and came to the door.

"Old man," he said, "What are you doing?"

"Good Afternoon," the old man said. He must be acting crazy as a disguise. "Come in, come in, young man."

Entering the old man's laboratory would give him a closer look at the instruments. The old man was hiding his sensing instruments under a camouflage of woodworking tools, wood scraps, and shavings. There was even sawdust sprinkled around on all the work surfaces, even on the floor. The old man was evasive. He insisted all he was doing was making "instruments" and conducting harmless experiments.

Because the old man wasn't going to cooperate, he'd have to take care of the situation as best he could. On his way out of the shed, he saw a can of kerosene in the old man's carport. It gave him an idea. He grabbed the can and picked his way back home.

Back in his own shed, he didn't feel well and there was a sore on his forearm he had no idea how he'd gotten. And it wasn't healing. Radiation sickness. He lay down on his mattress. Looking around, he inventoried the few clothes he had hanging from nails. Like the woman who was down to only a single kimono, maybe he should give most of them away. He lay still on the mattress to stay cool. Like the Catholic priest, he knew all of the uneasiness – all of the temptation to lose spirit and be depressed – and of then starting again to see if he can do his job. If he ever met the priest, he too could say, "I experienced the atom bomb" – and from then on, the conversation would change. They would both understand each other's feelings and nothing would have to be said.

The silence returned. There was no traffic noise from the roads below because there was no longer any traffic. He was tired. It had to be the A-Bomb disease. He'd been awake for days now. He fell asleep remembering that people died by the thousands, tens of thousands, maybe a hundred thousand. But they'd all died alone, like he would.

John

As much as he hated admitting it, maybe Marilyn was right about the youngest Slattery boy. Anyone who was beginning to look like a street person and came walking through the desert in his bare feet to stare into John's workshop at five in the afternoon on a hotter than hell July day wasn't all that well.

"Mickey, what are you doing?" John asked.

"What's wrong with your head?" he answered sullenly, avoiding making eye-contact. John had been to the dermatologist earlier in the day to have some spots removed from his scalp. Even though his bandage made him look like a Hollywood movie zombie, the wounds were minor. He only had to wear the gauze wrapped around his head for the rest of the day.

"My dermatologist. It's nothing serious."

"What are you doing?" Mickey lifted his head to face John, his eyes genuinely sad, as if someone had killed his dog, which, John recalled, was exactly what Mickey's father had done. Convinced the family dog was carrying a disease that had infected one of his then small children, Jack Slattery, thoroughly drunk, had dragged the family dog out behind the house by the collar, yelping horribly, and shot it dead with a pistol before anyone could get to him and calm him down. The kids only stopped screaming when their father turned back toward the house, menacingly, gun in hand.

As were all the Slattery children, Mickey had been an intelligent, thoughtful and talented kid, perhaps the most intelligent of them all. He'd gone off to an Ivy League school on a scholarship, but returned sometime during his first year and never went back to any school, as far as John knew. He read a great deal and traded in rare books. He rode his father's rickety, old bike all over Tucson scrounging for books at yard sales and second-hand stores.

As usual, Mickey was carrying his tattered copy of John Hersey's *Hiroshima*. Although John admired Mickey's being a voracious reader, he wished Mickey would read something more along the lines of *The Power of Positive Thinking*. For too long he'd been reading *Hiroshima* as if it were a breviary. Although John readily admitted *Hiroshima* was a beautifully written and important book, he feared it had led Mickey more than a little astray, certainly in his understanding of the early days of John's career.

Along with nearly every other freshly-minted physics graduate in the early 1950s, John had been dragooned into working on the hydrogen bomb for the Department of Defense. John had used early computers to do thermodynamic modeling. All of which John had explained to Mickey every time he asked. But each time, Mickey seemed less happy about what John was doing in his workshop. Since retiring from teaching physics at the University of Arizona, John spent most of his days building violins, using an electronic set up of his own design to guide him in selecting the pieces of spruce best suited for serving as the faces of his violins, and in carving them to the proper shapes and widths, trying to determine whether he could build a better violin with modern technology unavailable to a Stradivari, or a Guarneri, or even a contemporary builder using traditional techniques. Could he electronically replicate an expert violin builder's ear using readily available, off-the-shelf science and technology?

He'd had some success in competitions, and Marilyn thought very highly of the instruments he'd built, which was significant. Unlike John, who had no ear or ability for music, Marilyn was a very accomplished player and even acted as a judge in some of the instrument builders association's annual competitions.

While John couldn't think of a more harmless use of science than making better-sounding violins, Mickey had convinced himself John was engaged in something nefarious. But unlike Marilyn, John didn't think this was a valid reason to steer clear of him. John thought interaction with other humans was probably good for Mickey in his current state, whatever state that was.

"Today is August seventh," Mickey intoned, "A day that will live in infamy."

"No, Mickey. Today is July seventh. And you're confusing Pearl Harbor Day with another day." The day John didn't want to mention was the anniversary of the day they'd dropped the atomic bomb on Hiroshima. Mickey didn't respond.

John had repeatedly had "The Conversation" with Mickey. As did most everyone, Mickey had asked John whether he and the other scientists who'd worked on the bomb in the early days of the Cold War had been ethically conflicted about what they were doing. In Mickey's words, "Using science to kill people in numbers unimagined even by Hitler." As he always did, John responded, "No, it wasn't an ethical problem. We were in a war with the Soviets. We were insuring the survival of the human race. People forget that. I slept like a baby then. I still do."

How old was Mickey? With his unkempt hair and beard obscuring so much of his tanned and sunburned skin, Mickey could have passed for forty-five in a police line-up. Was he that old? He should only be about twenty-five or so. John could remember being in his twenties and having a career, or at least work, stretching out interminably before him. Anything seemed possible. Almost everything was interesting. Why didn't Mickey see things that way?

"How old are you, Mickey? And tell me again what exactly you're doing these days. Still finding rare books at garage sales?" Mickey frowned at John and glared like an unhappy four-year-old.

"I'm reading books now," he said defiantly, cracking open his *Hiroshima*. "And what about you, are you still building A-bombs and making observations on radiation levels, rather than providing aid to the suffering?"

Everyone assumed John worked on the atomic bomb even though he was only fifteen in 1945. He called himself a retired computer professor. When he used to try to reason with people, he'd say, "Nothing I did ever hurt a soul. It may have saved countless lives. Who knows?"

Mickey was shaking his book at John like a Jehovah's Witness pounding home his point, uninvited, on John's doorstep.

"Scientists showed up in Hiroshima to study the survivors," he shouted.

"That's what scientists do, Mickey, they study things."

"They didn't help the survivors. They didn't reduce their suffering. They just left once they were done with their research."

"They weren't medical doctors, were they? I don't know how to treat a sunburn, never mind radiation sickness. It's just not something physicists do." Mickey was having none of it. "Look, the world just went mad for a while there. I was part of a team working on a very small part of the over-all hydrogen bomb program. We were doing computer modeling of the heat signature of various devices. Not that that made me any less involved or responsible, if you're looking for a participant." Mickey had turned to a page in the book and was reading from it.

"When the war crime trials were going on in Tokyo, the German priest said, 'I think they ought to try the men who decided to use the bomb and hang them all.'" Mickey looked up before continuing. "The people of Hiroshima considered themselves to have been part of a laboratory experiment." John knew he shouldn't get drawn into another argument, but he couldn't resist.

"Have you read the 1985 edition of your book there, Mickey? The Soviets hi-jacked the so-called 'Peace Movement.' They made us the bad guys and them the good guys. We didn't start World War Two. We didn't start the Cold War." Mickey had a funny way of shutting his eyes when he was hearing something he didn't want to hear. "It was us or them. I had nothing to do with Hiroshima, or Nagasaki. I was a kid in junior high school then. In the 1950s, we were in a race with the Russians, not the Germans or the Japanese. My job was to help make sure our bombs would work so they wouldn't use theirs against us." John lost a little control of his temper, which he didn't like doing. He knew he shouldn't make his arguments personal. "And who would that include, Mickey? That would be your parents and people like you and your brothers and sister. Wasn't your father in the Pacific as a young man? I think he was." Mickey just read from the book, flipping quickly among favorite passages.

"Father Cieslik said, 'I started to bring my books along, and then I thought, this is no time for books.'" Here Mickey added his own aside, "Who's going to want to read books now that we're under attack? Why should I worry about collectible books?" He returned to the book. "Mr. Fukai ran back to immolate himself in the flames. They never saw him again. Dr. Sasaki worked for three days with only one hour's sleep. 'If your God is so good and kind, how can he let people suffer like this?' 'My child,' the priest said, 'Man is not now in the condition God intended. He has fallen from grace through sin.' And he went on to explain the reasons for everything." Mickey fumbled with the book, looking for his next selection. John jumped in.

"Listen to me. Hiroshima, and even the 'fifties, and the 'sixties, and the H-bomb were all a long time ago, Mickey. They're history. They're buried. They're past. They're THE past." John couldn't help sounding exasperated. "What can anyone do about them? They're over. I don't build bombs. I never did. I build violins. What's wrong with that?"

"But the atomic bomb…" John cut Mickey off.

"Different bomb, different war. They projected occupying Japan would kill a million American soldiers. A million teenagers and twenty-year-olds. Have you ever read about Okinawa? The Japanese scared their people into committing mass suicide rather than being subjected to the alleged brutality of the invading Americans. Was that ethical? A hundred and eighty thousand people died just in the taking of a little island like Okinawa. And you don't think the Japanese were warned?" Mickey wasn't paying attention. John knew it was pointless, but he was exercised.

"I don't do physics any more, except to make violins. And that's just fairly simple sonic analysis."

"You mean you don't build bombs in here?" Maybe John was getting through to Mickey.

"Of course not. I never even built bombs when I worked at Lawrence Livermore. I did computer modeling. For thermo-dynamic analysis. Hydrogen bombs generate massive amounts of heat."

"'Thermo' means heat. Like a thermos bottle."

"Yes."

"Those bombs burned people."

"'Incinerated' would be more accurate, yes."

"The people who survived thought the scientists in America considered them nothing more than guinea pigs in their little private laboratory experiment." So much for getting through to Mickey.

"I don't know that."

"Eighty thousand people were killed in Hiroshima alone. By the military-industrial complex."

"Eighty thousand? What about all the people the Japanese murdered in the Philippines? And in China, and Korea, and Indonesia? What about the Japanese military? You want a military-industrial complex? There's one."

It was frustrating that Mickey wasn't hearing anything John was saying. Mickey was more interested in constructing his own personal reality than historical accuracy. There was no point in talking any further. John would just build violins.

"Do you need electricity to do your work?" Mickey asked.

"Of course." John was settling down. Maybe Mickey could be engaged in some normal conversation. "My sonic instruments require electricity. That's the fun part, the scientific part. I carve by hand, so I can do that work without electricity." Mickey turned and left.

John sat down on his stool and took a deep breath. He shouldn't have gotten so exercised. He was too old. And what did what he thought matter? He returned to his work, which was soothing.

Time passed until john remembered Marilyn had a house concert planned. She'd probably need some help getting the house ready. He noticed storm clouds surrounding Tucson to the south and east. Maybe the monsoon would finally break the tremendous heat and dryness that was beginning to wear on even someone who loved the desert as much as John did.

Marilyn

Marilyn desperately wanted her piano to go to a good home. To have it owned, and played, by an honest-to-goodness, world-class player who'd grown up in the neighborhood would be icing on a wonderful cake. And, as far as Marilyn was concerned, Linda Slattery needed the piano as much as the piano needed Linda. But Marilyn couldn't tell whether Linda was being polite and merely considered the piano an acceptable instrument, or whether she considered it a serious instrument she wanted to own. In any event, Marilyn was going to have to talk price tonight, which worried her.

John scolded Marilyn for worrying, but was she not supposed to worry about finding a home for a nearly one-hundred-year-old, seven feet long, Steinway & Sons grand piano? Was she just supposed to die some day and have her daughter give the piano to a grade school, or a church, or sell it to a piano dealer who'd sell it to someone who'd put it in their living room to display rows of family photographs in expensive frames? And shouldn't John worry about selling his violins?

John's violins were wonderful instruments. Many were outstanding. But for some reason, John had no interest in getting them into the hands of players who would appreciate them. "I'm not into marketing," he'd say, or "I'm content leaving behind some buried treasure." Marilyn had no idea where he'd come up with his "buried treasure" crack. She had no intention of leaving anything, particularly anything even resembling treasure, buried. She feared even things left in plain sight would be squandered.

But Marilyn also worried she'd paid too much for the piano. Although it had been in her and John's house for years, she'd had to buy it from her stepsisters when their father's, her stepfather's, estate had been settled, for its then appraised value of thirty-five thousand dollars. With the recession, piano prices, even of Steinways, had fallen. Which wasn't supposed to happen. When she'd visited the Steinway dealer in Tucson, who'd since gone out of business, while buying the piano, they'd given her a brochure detailing what Steinway piano prices had done over the entire twentieth century compared to the stock market. Of course, the stock market had also been cut in half by the recession, but Marilyn was still stunned she might have to take a loss on the piano. It might only be worth as little as twenty-five or twenty thousand dollars, which was a shock. Some days, when it was closed, the long, polished piano looked to Marilyn to be little more than an elegant, over-priced coffin.

The fact Linda hadn't jumped at the chance to buy the piano when Marilyn had proposed it was even more upsetting. Whenever she played the piano, Linda told Marilyn it was "beautiful." She'd pretend to give the piano a big hug. Sitting at the keyboard, she'd stretch her arms out to hold both sides, lay her head on the music rack and say, "Oooooh," which Marilyn found silly, but cute. The piano came alive when Linda played it. There was no other way to describe it. It took Marilyn's breath away.

And Linda should have been able to afford it. She was the assistant music director at a good church in town, had a large stable of private students, taught music and choir at a number of schools, and was in demand for local recitals. In addition, her partner was a psychologist with a private practice as well as a very prestigious position at an institute at the university.

Of course, Marilyn didn't know everything about Linda, and some of the things she did know were not all sweetness and light. Why Linda didn't play more seriously, with the symphony and the like, or take a position at the university, was beyond Marilyn. In any event, Linda was a serious, serious pianist who, at least in Marilyn's opinion, needed a serious instrument, of her own. And Marilyn had a serious instrument she needed to dispose of. As a result, Marilyn was hosting a soiree at which Linda would play. Marilyn had invited a good-sized audience which would be so enthusiastic about Linda's playing on Marilyn's Steinway that Linda would absolutely have to buy it for whatever she could afford. At least that was the plan.

Marilyn headed out to John's work shop to see whether he would help her get the house picked up, but found him spending time with Linda's troubled younger brother, Mickey. What Marilyn knew about Linda and Mickey's family history was terribly sad. Although John had dubbed the Slatterys' house "The Crisis Center," Marilyn had never found the Slatterys at all funny.

Sue and Jack Slattery had been good Catholics. They'd had four children as well as any number of miscarriages. Linda was the oldest, twin boys were next, and Mickey was the youngest. Looking back, it was obvious Sue had suffered from severe post-partum depression. The mother of only one daughter, Marilyn thought if she'd been forced to bear four children and lose a number of other pregnancies, she'd have been depressed too.

And before he drank himself to death, Jack, the former head of engineering for Tucson's power company, had been reduced to riding his bicycle down the hill to a bar to drink until the wee hours before calling Sue or the boys for a ride home, which invariably ended with things breaking and voices shouting inside the house that could be heard all over the neighborhood.

But the four children had survived. Linda had attended the University of Arizona before heading off to New York for her graduate piano studies. The twins had obtained scholarships and degrees from schools in California before marrying and settling in different cities on the West Coast.

Things had not turned out well for Mickey. Probably the brightest of the Slattery children, Mickey had won a full scholarship to Princeton, but dropped out after only a semester and returned to Tucson to start, in his words, "a landscaping business." More accurately, he began supporting himself, his drug habit, and soon, his young wife and baby daughter who moved with him into his parents' house, doing yard work. Terrified by his increasingly violent tendencies, Mickey's wife and daughter soon ran away from Mickey, who also departed the scene. For years, Mickey lived beneath a bridge in South Tucson. When Linda returned to Tucson after her parents had died, she somehow got Mickey into a program for street people where he was diagnosed as a full-blown paranoid schizophrenic.

Mickey had been on and off, but mostly off, his medication ever since. When he was good, he "bartered in books" because he "didn't believe in money," currency being just one of the many ways "*they* control *us*." He rode his father's bike all over Tucson to yard sales in search of first editions and other collectible books he'd trade to the two rare book dealers in town for various necessities he made them purchase. When Marilyn asked Mickey how he identified valuable books, he said they "emitted an aura."

Just as John wasn't concerned about Marilyn's being able to get Linda to buy her piano, he didn't think Mickey was a problem, which worried Marilyn, more about John's well-being than Mickey's. Although Marilyn considered Mickey beyond help, she feared he had the potential to harm John, or even Marilyn herself, if John wasn't more careful around him and less indulgent of his, as John called them, "idiosyncrasies," which Marilyn considered Mickey's dangerously unpredictable insanity.

Nor was John supportive of Marilyn's selling the piano, to Linda or anyone. Although he didn't play, John admired the Steinway as "a significant piece of woodworking," almost an art treasure. "It's an heirloom," he said. "I like having it around." But their daughter had no interest in the piano. What good was a 'loom' when you had no interested 'heirs?'

And a piano should be, needs to be, played. And Linda could play, even though John always made a point of reminding Marilyn that their tuner, Dean, had seen Linda's current piano and politely refused to work on it because it was in such terrible shape. According to Dean, but for the fact it was a Steinway, it would have been a candidate for the scrap heap. The pin block was no longer able to hold a tune and the action was worn beyond repair. The case had been sunburned and cigarette burned and otherwise abused. The ivory key tops were cracked, yellowed and grimy. Dean had warned Marilyn, "If that piano was a horse, they'd shoot it."

But Marilyn knew enough about playing and instruments to know it took hours and hours of repetitive practice to acquire and maintain proper technique and a large repertoire. And powerful players, like Linda, were hard on pianos. And maybe Linda wasn't good with things. Maybe she was like Marilyn's daughter who was just hard on things, accusing Marilyn of liking her things more than she liked people, or at least her.

When Marilyn mentioned to Linda that Dean tuned and maintained Marilyn's piano, Linda had volunteered, "He seems a little strange. He wouldn't even tune my piano, never mind voice it and regulate it, like I asked him to. Maybe it was something I said?" And then there was the story Linda told about being back east and renting an apartment above a bar during a summer break. When she'd had to move out in the fall and take her piano with her, she went downstairs to the bar and announced she needed help moving her grand piano out of her apartment. Whereupon a bunch of presumably inebriated but muscular volunteers, with Linda's direction and assistance, proceeded to carry her Steinway out the apartment's window, down a rickety fire escape and into the back of a borrowed pick-up truck. But even Marilyn herself had had her Bohemian phase. In any event, she'd resigned herself to bearing the expense of having the piano properly moved to Linda's house once she agreed to buy it.

Marilyn vacuumed the entire house, stripped the beds and washed the sheets. She washed all the towels and bath mats in all the bathrooms, put out the guest hand towels in the powder room and dusted everywhere. She did the laundry and watered all the houseplants and the potted plants out on the patios. She swept the patios, not that anyone would go out on them since they were too hot this time of year, but they'd see them. She even vacuumed and dusted the inside of the piano and cleaned the keys with alcohol on cotton cleaning balls as she'd been instructed by Dean because water loosens the glue holding the thin ivory tops in place. She baked a coffee cake and some cookies, her standard party fare. She also baked a loaf of bread because realtors baked bread in houses they were holding open because the smell of fresh-baked bread made people want to buy houses. Maybe it also made pianists want to buy pianos.

Although Marilyn had told John about the soiree, when he got involved in his violin building, he could disappear for long periods of time, which was good in some respects, but it could also be annoying. She was probably right not to count on his helping get the house ready. It wasn't cooling off but at least it was getting a little less bright out. There appeared to be a dust storm heading their way from the south. Maybe it would be followed by a rainstorm and the heat would break a little.

Marilyn felt tired and nervous. She didn't mind hosting evenings at which her amateur string quartet or other players performed serious music, but she was uncomfortable attending random, pointless parties. She felt like a turkey at a turkey shoot. She disliked having no control over who came up to her and wanted to talk, or, more often, who would not stop talking to her. She always seemed to end up being talked to by one fairly boring person for most of the night. She didn't know how to disengage. "Just walk away," John insisted, but that would be impolite.

And she was getting more worried about negotiating with Linda. Although she didn't want to put Linda off by asking too much, she didn't want to lose too much money either. She really wanted Linda to have the piano, but she didn't want to be unfair to herself. Marilyn thought honesty was the best policy and preferred just asking for the price she wanted.

"Great theory, Marilyn," John said. "One problem: it doesn't work. People want to bargain. It's how the game's played." Marilyn didn't like playing games. All she wanted was to get her piano sold to someone who could, and would, appreciate it.

Marilyn washed up, put on a dress and straightened her hair. She rarely drank, but felt she needed a drink. She helped herself to a glass of the white wine she'd had John lay in for the party. It was cold and tasted good. After finishing the wine, she stared out the rear patio doors of the house and relaxed, at which point she noticed Mickey lurking around in his back yard carrying one of John's cans of something or other. Marilyn hoped Mickey wasn't up to one of his projects. As a boy, intent on clearing a play area in the desert between their houses, Mickey had chopped down a stand of ancient creosote bushes and then poisoned them. Marilyn brought the tragic destruction to the attention of Jack Slattery who snorted, snarled "Good for him! Maybe he's going to be a real estate developer," and returned to his high ball.

Mickey had been hanging around his family's former house, which had been effectively abandoned since the recession had started two years before. Marilyn hated the recession. Even their very nice neighborhood had been affected. Three or four houses had been foreclosed upon just on their street. Two had simply been abandoned. And these were nice houses, family homes owned by well-to-do, professional people. Marilyn and John weren't in danger, but the recession was taking too great a toll on too many younger families.

John was less sympathetic. When she'd mentioned the recession's effect upon the Slatterys and their abandoned house, John said, "They lost that house years ago, and not for economic or financial reasons, unless you call being too drunk to stay awake and go to work during working hours a financial problem." That was the end of that conversation.

But Marilyn felt bad for the Slattery children having lost both their parents and then their childhood home, which just sat there, unsold, uninhabited (except lately by Mickey) and derelict. It seemed unimaginable there'd be such financial devastation in Marilyn's lifetime. Her parents had survived the Depression which had affected them greatly. Marilyn never expected she'd experience anything even remotely similar during her lifetime.

And it was unsettling that a person as unstable as Mickey was living in the wreck of their home. Who'd have thought Marilyn would live to see a squatter in the foothills above Tucson, and such a scary one? Mickey had been reduced almost to something out of a childhood fairy tale. He could pass for a troll beneath a bridge. And John thought nothing of it. But she'd have to leave that for another day. People would begin showing up soon.

Mickey

The light was dim, and the sky looked almost yellow. He made his way to the door of his shed and looked outside. It was the worst-case scenario: a cloud of radioactive dust particles loomed overhead, engulfing the entire city. Visibility was little more than fifty feet. He couldn't even see the neighboring houses. Did they still exist? The air was hot and windy. The fires must be raging once again. He remembered what he'd resolved to do. Individually, it wouldn't mean much, but if like-minded people were able to act, they would have an effect. At least he had to try to stop the old man's dastardly work.

He headed to his father's garden shed with the can of kerosene he'd found at the old man's house. The gods were with him. What his father called his "weed and bug sprayer" was still hanging on the wall of the old tin garden shed. He poured in the kerosene and fiddled with the controls. It wasn't working and he needed to find some way to ignite it. The sky was getting darker. The flames of the fires weren't visible but they were being reflected off the bottoms of the atomic dust clouds snarling overhead. Without power, the old man wouldn't be able to continue his experiments. Mickey was ready. His days of just thinking about what had happened and what to do were over. Finally, he'd be fighting fire with fire. Literally. All he had to do was find some matches and get the sprayer working.

Marilyn

The pre-recital drinking and conversation went as well as could be expected. As John was fond of saying, "at least there weren't any fist fights." Of course, like most university gatherings, unless there was a great deal of alcohol involved, the party was a pretty homogeneous affair. John again: "In their superior, collective wisdom, most university people tend to agree on most everything."

People even paid attention to the music. They were almost rapt. Linda played beautifully, but a little wildly and inaccurately at times, which was something Marilyn couldn't remember ever seeing before. It was almost as if Linda wasn't being careful, or was playing so recklessly she didn't care about being accurate. Maybe she wasn't practicing enough, one more reason Linda needed to have Marilyn's piano.

Marilyn enjoyed another glass of wine while Linda played all her show pieces: a fiendishly fast Scarlatti Sonata; Marilyn's favorite Schubert Impromptu, the E flat; and the E major Chopin Etude that begins so serenely before going into what Marilyn believed mental health professionals would call a "psychotic break." All those horrible, dissonant chords crashing into each other as if they are falling down a set of stairs or drowning in the surf, before the serene first theme re-appears. Finally, Linda played the Liszt *Mephisto*, which she always preceded with an explanation of the piece's programmatic aspects, including musical snippets illustrating the various characters and their themes including Faust, the Devil, and Gretchen, the beautiful young woman Faust woos before being dragged into, of course, the flames of hell.

For her encore, Linda played the Rachmaninoff C Minor Prelude, the only Rachmaninoff people ever really knew or cared to hear. A very depressing piece of course, written to express the impending doom Rachmaninoff felt in the face of the Russian revolution. Even though Marilyn was feeling a bit of impending doom given the impending negotiations, it made a perfect encore. Everyone clapped enthusiastically before heading *en masse* to the dining room and kitchen for more food and drink.

Linda wandered among the crowd receiving their accolades while Marilyn served food and knocked down another glass of wine. As the crowd thinned, unable to put it off any further, Marilyn approached Linda.

"Your playing seems more freed up, if that's the right way to say it."

"Yes, it is," Linda almost gushed. "I've decided not to worry about knowing all the notes. You can't. Or at least I can't. I remember how the piece goes, structurally, so if I don't remember everything I still know where it's going and how to get to the end. Other than judges at competitions, who knows I'm filling in the blanks? Why worry?" Linda grabbed a wine glass and held it out for Marilyn to fill. "And anyway, I'm no good at competitions."

Was Linda giving up her career? If so, she wouldn't need the piano. Marilyn changed the subject.

"How's Mickey doing?" Linda almost spit her wine.

"My brother? I haven't seen him. Have you?"

"He's right out back." Marilyn pointed out the rear patio doors which were now almost entirely black since the sun had set and the dust storm that had blown up during the recital was winding down. "He's living at your house."

"My house?" Linda took another drink. "He's not supposed to be doing that. We don't own the house any more. That's been the case for quite a while. They've shut off the power, and the water, and everything. It's supposed to be locked up, secured, with plywood." Linda's voice trailed off before concluding: "But Mickey's not big on following rules, is he?" Marilyn couldn't help herself.

"I worry about Mickey."

"Hah!" Linda laughed. "I can't any more. Things aren't going to turn out well for Mickey, any more than they did for you-know-who." Marilyn shook her head. "My father. Mickey's headed down a different road but it ends in the same place. I used to think we were lucky that at least Mickey didn't drink." Linda looked around the room as if she wanted to have a conversation with someone else. "I just hope he doesn't take any of us with him."

"That's what I've been trying to tell John," Marilyn almost blurted. "Good."

"But he doesn't listen." Marilyn sounded as if she was whining.

"He should. But Mickey can be so damned charming at times. He's my little brother. But as Andrea says, 'you can lead a horse to water but you can't make him take his medication.' Not that I can always keep myself from caring. You know, Mickey has wads of cash. He's not poor like I am. He doesn't barter, he sells for cash. He has no expenses and he collects a fair amount of benefits, here and there, from the state and from shelters. He's not dumb." Marilyn was surprised to hear Linda speaking so unflatteringly of her brother. With her free hand, Linda grabbed Marilyn firmly by one shoulder.

"I'm sorry Marilyn. I'm not going to be able to buy your piano."

"Why?" Marilyn almost moaned surprised it was Linda who'd brought the subject up. "Is it the action? It can be fixed, or adjusted, or even replaced with a new one, can't it?" Marilyn nodded urgently. "Is it the tone? I thought you loved the tone." Marilyn was crestfallen.

"I love the tone."

"Is it the finish? It could be rubbed to make it more satin-like."

"The finish is fine."

"It's the price."

"We haven't discussed price."

Before Marilyn could blurt, "Then what on earth is it?" Linda let go of Marilyn's shoulder and said, "The color, Marilyn. It's brown, not black."

Marilyn nearly fell over. Until they'd decided to have it restored, the piano had been covered in a dull, crackled, funereal, black varnish. They got a call from the restorer one morning saying, "You'd better come down here and see what you've got." They drove down to his shop. He'd removed a patch of the old finish to reveal the beautiful flame mahogany beneath. "This was their top of the line cabinet," the restorer said. "Steinway put the less expensive veneers on the pianos they painted black. In the early twentieth century, everyone wanted fine, wooden furniture. I don't think it was until after the war people wanted concert hall-style pianos as a status symbol. I can leave it black but I think the wood should really be shown to its best advantage." So, they'd had the piano refinished to its original, natural, mahogany grandeur.

Even at the time, Marilyn had had second thoughts. Perhaps she was an artistic snob. A black satin finish did seem more serious, more professional. And now, her decision, or her failure to fight for what she'd really wanted, had come back to haunt her. She felt a little light-headed, as if she needed to sit down. Linda was talking.

"I've had a brown piano all my life. I've realized I want a real piano, a black one, a serious one, one you'd see on stage, in a recital setting. I know it's silly, but...."

"It used to be black," Marilyn managed. "Then we uncovered this beautiful flame mahogany." Linda nodded, then shrugged.

"I'm sorry Marilyn. I'm sure someone will want it." Linda smiled and shook Marilyn's left hand, the one that wasn't holding a glass of wine. "I've got to get Andrea home." At which point Marilyn's ear burst or a blood vessel in her brain burst and everything went black and she was about to die.

Linda

Linda knew Marilyn would be disappointed she wasn't going to buy her piano, but what could she do? As Andrea constantly told her, she had to learn to face the fact she wasn't the solution to Marilyn's problem and she wasn't put on earth to solve every problem of every person she happened to meet. Although Linda didn't think she went that far overboard about other peoples' problems, she agreed with Andrea that some of her own problems could definitely use her attention.

Such as, now that the chances of her ever being a touring, highly-compensated, concert and recording pianist were non-existent, what was she going to do with her life? Playing for little or for free at house concerts wasn't going to cut it. Had the twenty-five years of her life she'd spent learning the piano simply gone down the drain? Was she going to be a burden on Andrea? What kind of life would that be? But poor, sweet Marilyn.

As Linda launched into the Scarlatti for a group of appreciative, mostly university people, of whom there were only so many in Tucson, Linda couldn't help wondering why she'd come back. Nothing had been happening for her in New York career-wise, or otherwise, for that matter. But Tucson? It was her hometown and she and Andrea had met and gotten together there since she'd returned from New York. But Tucson was, for lack of a better word, a cow town. Outside the university, Tucson had next to nothing going for it musically. There were tiny pockets like Marilyn's soirees, and the symphony, and, she supposed, the music school, but there just was not enough culture in Tucson to support someone like Linda. It was a desert.

And what was so great about Tucson being her hometown? Both

her parents were dead. Her childhood home was a derelict owned by a bank. Her twin brothers, whom Andrea called "the normal ones," had fled Arizona for college and never returned. The only one still in Tucson was her baby brother Mickey, whom Andrea called "Oh," as in "Oh brother!" But Mickey was little more than a ghost from the past. The person, her little brother Mickey, had been gone for years.

And although Andrea was Linda's main tie to Tucson, there were times Linda even worried whether Andrea was serious about their relationship. Among so many other things, Andrea could be flippant about people. She could categorize, characterize and dismiss them with a word or a phrase. Would Andrea effortlessly dismiss Linda with a few choice words some day? Maybe their relationship was nothing more than a fling, or worse, a research project. Andrea insisted a person could never be sure of anyone else's true desires or intentions. What if Andrea was as right about that as she was about people?

But when Linda was growing up in her chaotic home, Marilyn's house, like Marilyn, was always calm. And Linda had always loved playing Marilyn's piano. Compared to the clunky upright at her house, playing Marilyn's piano had been like swimming in a pool of sound. And it still was. Linda couldn't help noticing the piano sounded tremendous playing the Scarlatti. Of course, it sounded tremendous playing most anything. And the action was so nice. It made playing the Scarlatti almost like being in a dream.

Not that much of Linda's so-called concert career had been a dream. Playing at a restaurant's ancient fern bar while completing her PhD dissertation had been a nightmare. It was when she most often recalled how when he was getting drunk, as if posing an algebra problem, her father would ask: "If a dream deferred is a dream denied, what's a dream denied?"

Linda's mother had insisted her father drank because even though he was its smartest electrical engineer, he wasn't named president of the power company. But according to Andrea, a psychology PhD, people didn't become alcoholics because bad things happened to them during their careers. She said people became alcoholics because of a genetic predisposition, severe trauma at an early age, or some combination of both. And maybe Andrea was right. Even though her life had been filled with disappointment, Linda didn't drink. And Mickey, to whom nothing bad had ever happened, was a mess.

Linda moved on to the Schubert, one of what Andrea called her "war horses." As Andrea had been urging her, Linda played it as fast as possible, ignoring her various teachers' strictures about accuracy and clarity. "People go to piano recitals for the same reason they go to car races: to see a wreck," Andrea counseled. The audience seemed to be eating it up. Maybe it was time for Linda to break away from all her piano pedagogy, as well as her past and her family. What did she have to lose? But doing either wasn't easy.

Besides her alcoholic father and her little brother, there was her mother. Why, after enduring paralyzing depressions (which Linda had identified in retrospect with Andrea's help) after every pregnancy, had she had so many? And why had she had Mickey? Didn't she know any better before number four? Not to mention the three miscarriages no one ever talked about? When her mother fell into another depression and her father would have to drive her up to Phoenix, he'd announce their mother was going on another "vacation" at a "posh resort." Of course, the "resort" was the state-run women's mental asylum, next door to the women's prison. Other times he'd say she'd been awarded a fellowship to do "psychiatric research." The "fellowship" comment was a swipe at what her father considered her mother's inferior intellect. Her father valued people, his wife and children included, by their academic credentials and what he considered their intelligence, or lack thereof. Linda's mother had never gone to college, unlike Marilyn's physics professor John, whom Linda's father considered a very big deal.

"Those guys who worked on the bomb were heroes," he'd roar. "They were Gods!" He'd waive his drink for emphasis. "The Gods of the Twentieth Century. All the work, or thought, of every God-damned western philosopher who'd ever lived was reduced to mere speculation by those guys. They unlocked all the secrets of the universe, in just a few years, in the middle of a God-damned war. And beat the Krauts to it. And defeated the Japs! With nothing more than brains and slide rules."

Which was funny because John always discounted what he'd done. All he ever said he'd done was early work with computers. He called it "computational grunt work."

"And it even cost many of them their lives," her father would go on. "They made a pact with the devil. And our neighbor John worked with those kinds of guys. No matter what anyone says, that John over there, he's okay with me." Of course, Linda never remembered anyone saying anything bad about John.

The Chopin went well. The *Mephisto* was next. Again, Linda played it as fast as she possibly could, mistakes be damned. "Don't worry," Andrea urged. "People wouldn't know a mistake if it came up and bit them on the leg." Although Linda was a little uncomfortable with this concept, it did seem to free up her playing. The audience seemed to be eating it up. "What the hell," Linda thought to herself, almost laughing.

Although Linda was happy being with Andrea and together they'd put a lot of the things from Linda's earlier life behind her, Linda was troubled by Andrea's decision to have a baby. She was due in two months. Although Linda wasn't exactly positive having a child was going to be hell on earth, Linda had never wanted to have a family or be a mother. All Linda had ever wanted in life was to be an artist. How had she ended up facing the terrible responsibility of raising a child? None of which worried Andrea.

"You'll be a great mother. You're the maternal one," Andrea said. And what if their child was a problem, like Mickey?

"I'm a child psychologist?" Andrea answered. And what did they know about the sperm donor father?

"A hell of a lot more than I'd know about some guy I met in a bar. Like, oh, say, your mother did about your father?" Linda's parents had met in the bar her parents, Linda's grandparents, owned and her mother had worked in.

All of which was true. But even when he was little, Mickey had been a problem. He challenged everyone and everything. He was always in trouble, but was never punished because he was so smart. And as far as their father was concerned, Mickey could do no wrong. Whenever Mickey got into trouble, their father would brag, "That's my boy!"

Which only applied to Mickey. On the rare occasions the twins had gotten into trouble, they were left to their own devices, or worse, spanked by their father. Nor did the phrase apply to Linda for at least a few reasons. She never got into trouble, and for some reason, she didn't matter to her father. Nor did her twin brothers. Linda once asked the twins whether they were upset by how their father doted on Mickey and ignored them. "You think we want to be *his* 'boy?'" they answered, one finishing the other's thought, "Mickey can have that."

If anyone said "white," Mickey said "black." And he was never wrong. Which meant Linda, and nearly everyone else, were always wrong. He was impossible to argue with. He could always pull some fact out of thin air to win any argument. A voracious reader, which he got from their mother, and a whiz at math, which he got from his father, Mickey never got anything less than an A in school, except for conduct. He aced the SATs without even breaking a sweat.

But he'd always wanted to be the bad guy, the outlaw, which tickled their father, but unsettled Linda. Mickey had displayed his perverse streak from an early age. He'd insisted on having a black cowboy hat and cowboy suit. Things got progressively worse as Mickey grew until at some point he simply became bad, or evil, or possessed, or something. Linda couldn't talk to him, no one could. He brooked no opposition. He'd gone off completely into his own world.

Mickey considered paying taxes immoral, so he didn't pay taxes. Which Linda thought was crazy, not to mention illegal and wrong. According to Mickey, tax laws were man-made, not natural law. Mickey was big on natural law, whatever that was. Mickey also said he bartered for everything and never dealt in cash. He said money was the root of all evil, man's most deadly invention. Linda agreed that money wasn't always the greatest thing but she, at least, needed some to live her life. And whenever he needed it, Mickey always seemed to have a wad of cash he could pull out. If Andrea's child was even half as difficult as Mickey, how on earth would Linda handle it? To which Andrea would respond:

"Why assume you're going to re-live your childhood? Does everything have to end in failure and defeat? When you play, do you always assume you're going to crash and burn?" Until she'd finally tried Andrea's "play like a wild woman" theory of piano performance, Linda would have answered "yes." Maybe she just wasn't as smart as Andrea.

She finished the *Mephisto* with a flourish, which garnered a lot of enthusiastic applause. She moved on to the Rachmaninoff as an encore.

The recital was a success. Sure, she'd made, for her, a relative ton of mistakes, but the audience seemed to like her playing more than usual. Had it been as properly correct as one of her teachers would have wanted it? No. Would it have satisfied a judge? No. But maybe this was the way to go. She'd been a little less stressed than she usually was before and during a recital.

By comparison, she feared telling Marilyn she wasn't going to be able to buy her piano was going to be difficult and downright unpleasant. Linda was too embarrassed to admit she couldn't afford the piano, no matter what Marilyn was willing to take. A piano like Marilyn's would be put on the Steinway store's floor for forty or fifty thousand dollars. But considering her dead-end performing career, her lack of income, and having a child to care for soon, owning such a majestic instrument would be like buying an expensive grave stone to mark the death of her artistic career. Fortunately, she'd come up with the "it's the wrong color" excuse, which wasn't a total lie. It even sounded plausible as Linda spelled it out. Unfortunately, Marilyn didn't take it well.

At which point there was a tremendous explosion and all the lights went dark. Before Linda's eyes could adjust to the darkness, everything seemed to be lit with a strange, eerie, green, then orange glow. A fire was burning in John and Marilyn's back yard. Linda was one of the first guests to make her way to the sliding glass door leading onto the patio out back. Stranger still, some maniac was out there shooting flames into the air with – Oh Christ Almighty, it was Mickey!

The big electrical box between John and Marilyn's house and Linda's family's old house was on fire. There was also lightening in the air and the smell of ozone. Mickey was setting the desert on fire with one of their father's favorite toys, a military flame thrower. Mickey was spraying a rope of flame on each side of him as he made his way toward John and Marilyn's house.

"It's Mickey!" Linda screamed to Andrea, who'd been sitting outside on the patio in a near dust storm rather than sit through another of Linda's recitals. "What's he doing?"

"Setting the desert on fire with a flame thrower? Heck of an explosion, huh?"

"Mickey!" Linda screamed, "What are you doing?" Andrea pointed toward the far end of John and Marilyn's house, getting up out of her chair.

"If you ask me, I'd guess he's going to set this house on fire next."

Officer Al

The fire guys' call to dispatch said they were being held off containing a transformer fire by "Jesus wielding a flame thrower." Responding to the call, once he'd gotten within a block of the address, Al Abrera realized the address was the Slattery twins' house. The last time he'd been there had been ten or so years ago to attend, not respond to and break up, a high school drinking party.

The Slattery twins were unusual. They were really, really smart and really, really good football players. Most smart guys knew enough not to play football. But the Slatterys had been starting linebackers and the hardest hitters on the team all three years of high school. Everyone tried to stay away from them during practice. Although the twins were basically normal guys, their mother was crazy and their father was an old-fashioned, falling-down drunk, wet-his-pants, alchy. And although they could have played serious college football on athletic scholarships, they took academic scholarships to Cal Tech, or Stanford, or some other very good schools in California and, as far as anyone knew, had never been seen around Tucson since.

They'd had a party at their house their senior year to celebrate the end of football season. Everyone in town was invited, or at least that's how many kids showed up. It was probably the most memorable high school party ever held in Tucson. Old man Slattery put the entire house and yard on tap. If a parent did something like that now, their mug shots would be on the front page of the newspaper the next Monday.

As Al pulled up in his cruiser, he was confronted by a bizarre standoff. The fire department guys were standing next to their truck. One was spraying water on the scrubby desert they had in what people called "The Foothills" neighborhood of Tucson, while some others watched a transformer fire burn. Another had a big hose pointed at a guy who did look like Jesus with a big contraption on his back attached by a hose to a metal pipe with a gun stock on it and a pretty damned good-sized flame burning at the end of it. The fire guys had evidently put out a fire around the transformer but were just letting the transformer fire burn itself out. It was quite a scene.

One of the high points of that party had been when old man Slattery went into a shed behind the house and come out with an honest-to-God, Government Issue, military flame thrower strapped to his back and started launching massive bursts of bright orange flames into the air, supposedly to clear the area of bugs, but more likely to entertain and amaze the crowd of high school kids. It was usually either too cold or too hot for bugs in Tucson. Everyone cheered, and Mr. Slattery insisted everyone have more to drink. Al was pretty sure that was the same flame thrower Jesus was sporting. Al climbed out of his cruiser and approached the fire guys.

"What we got, boys?"

"That guy's got a flame thrower."

"I can see that," Al nodded. "You going to soak him and put out his flame?"

"We put out fires. You guys deal with nut jobs."

At which point, the guy with the flame thrower shot a huge plume of fire into the air. Al and the fire department guys drew back reflexively.

"You going to shoot him?" the fireman asked.

At which point a woman came running through the desert, waiving her hands above her head. Audience participation was never a good idea in these sorts of situations.

"Mickey! Mickey! What are you doing? Stop! Stop! Stop!" the woman shouted. The flame thrower guy responded by firing his flame thrower up in the air. Al was beginning to think he was having a flashback. The woman must be the twins' older sister. She'd been good looking but all she ever did was play the piano. The guy with the flame thrower must be Mickey Slattery.

Two years younger than Al and his twin brothers, Mickey had been the smartest Slattery. Rumor had it he was the smartest guy who'd ever graduated from their high school. But he'd also been a know-it-all pain in the ass. He hadn't played sports and he'd gone off to a school back east before going completely nuts. It had been a while, but the last Al knew, Slattery was living under a bridge or an overpass somewhere in

South Tucson. Mickey turned to face his sister and adjusted a knob as if he was about to fire up the flame thrower and roast his sister.

"Linda," Al shouted, "Get away before you get hurt." She stood in her tracks.

"Mickey!" Al shouted and began walking. "Put down the flame thrower before someone gets hurt." Al unbuttoned his firearm but left it holstered. He approached with his hands in front of him, palms facing forward.

"Abrera?" Mickey bellowed, wheeling toward Al. "Is that you?"

"That's right."

"You're a cop?"

"That's right, Slattery. It's me, and I'm a police officer. Put down the flame thrower." Al couldn't believe he was actually saying that. "I have a gun, Mickey. A gun versus a flame thrower isn't a fair fight. Bullets are faster than flames. You're the smartest guy here, so you know that." As early as kindergarten, Al had learned the best way to deal with people who thought they were smarter than he was was to come right out and tell them they were smarter. After that, things went more smoothly, unless you were dealing with a nut case. But Al suspected that deep down, the same obnoxious, big-shot Mickey Slattery was still in there, somewhere. "You ready to take a ride in my cruiser?"

"I don't ride in cars." Mickey bellowed, sounding like a defiant little kid.

"I know that." Mickey was well known among the patrol officers for riding his bicycle all over hell and back. He could be spotted almost anywhere in the county, never mind the City of Tucson. "Maybe you can make an exception for me."

Al was getting closer, well within the flame thrower's range. Maybe he should have called for backup and just waited with the fire guys.

"You're not going to help me?" Mickey whined.

"Help you do what, Mickey?"

"We need to stop the guy in that house, over there." Mickey whipped the flame thrower's wand past Al to point at the house next door. The sudden movement made Al reach for his weapon.

"Why's that, Mickey?"

"He's building bombs!" Al tilted his head toward the house.

"In there?"

"That's right."

"What kind of bombs, Mickey?" Al couldn't dismiss this out of hand even if he was talking to a lunatic. There was more dynamite and other explosives in the hands of amateurs in Tucson than you'd think.

"Atomic bombs. Or hydrogen bombs. One or the other. Maybe both." At least Al was just dealing with a lunatic rather than with a lunatic on the trail of an explosives aficionado.

"That's a problem, Mickey. We need to do something about that, don't we?" Mickey made another burst of flame with his wand, which was more than enough for Al. He stopped walking, pointed his gun directly at Mickey and knelt down on one knee. "Drop it Mickey." Thankfully, Mickey put the flamethrower wand down and raised both his hands.

"If we don't stop him he's going to vaporize the entire country, Abrera, not just Tucson."

"We'll get to that, but first let's get that rig off your back. Then I want you to lie down. Now. Then I'm going to have to cuff you, Mickey. Once you're in the car, we can do whatever we need to do about your mad bomber buddy."

Once Slattery was in the back seat of Al's cruiser, the entire neighborhood seemed to come out of hiding. The neighbor Slattery had been trying to kill came and spoke to Al, as did Slattery's sister, whom the neighbor had been restraining from getting herself hurt.

"So," Al asked the guy from the house next door, "what are you doing in your workshop that Mickey Slattery would want to burn it down, probably with you in it?

"Building violins?" the man answered. Al couldn't help chuckling.

"Why do you suppose he wants to stop you from making violins?"

"I suspect he thinks I'm working on nuclear weapons."

"So I've heard. Maybe I should come over and take a look." Al had to check out even a crazy guy's allegation of bomb building in a residential neighborhood. They walked over toward the house.

"You make a living building violins?"

"It's just a hobby. I retired years ago from teaching, at the university."

Al's retired policeman father pretty much hated college-educated people. Although Al had gone into police work right out of high school, he'd obtained a two-year degree to help get more promotions. His father had never gone to college. One of his father's favorite things to do while working in Tucson had been to ask people what the degree abbreviation "B.S." stood for. "Bullshit!" he'd crow when he'd gotten someone to bite. "And you know what 'M.S.' stands for?" He'd shout. "'More shit!' And you know what 'PhD' stands for? 'Piled higher and deeper!'"

Although Al wasn't as bad as his father, policing a university town had made him a little leery of people who worked at the U of A. A person could honestly say they tended to think they knew better than most people, certainly policemen. Plus, more well-to-do people lived in the Foothills, so you had people with brains and money. It was where Al's wife wanted to have a house, which was unlikely unless they won the lottery.

Al looked around in the workshop and didn't see anything suspicious. He'd mention it in his report and someone else could decide whether to investigate further. Al made his way back toward the cruiser. The transformer was still burning, but less intensely. Al approached the senior fire guy.

"So, did he come after you guys once he set the transformer on fire?"

"We were just trying to put out the fires either he or the transformer fire started in the brush, and he just appears out of nowhere. Who knows what set off the transformer? It could have been a lightning strike. It was dust storming for a while. Could have been a power surge. Or it could have just gotten old and gone up all by itself. They can have a mind of their own."

Linda Slattery reappeared.

"Are you going to arrest him, officer? Please?"

Used to families providing flimsy alibis for their favorite perp, Al didn't know what to make of Linda's request. She was almost shouting and nearly hysterical.

"You'll have to arrest him, right? Thank God! Finally, someone will do something about him. We used to think he was just eccentric, and smart. But he's ill, mentally ill. He's paranoid and schizophrenic. God, I don't know. He's been diagnosed as everything from that to clinically depressed to hyperactive to being a genius to being ill-mannered. But nobody's been able to do a thing for him. He won't take his medicine.

He thinks the pills are poison and we want to kill him with them. Thank God he's committed a crime. Now they'll keep him somewhere, even if it's in a jail. Right? Maybe they can make him take his medicines. I can't even care any longer. I'm done." At which point Linda turned and ran back toward the bomb builder's house, shaking her hands above her head.

None of which helped Al. If he took Mickey to the psych ward for an involuntary hold, he'd be back out on the street in two or three days, which seemed pointless. But was the county jail really a good place for somebody like Mickey? Jail time for criminal destruction of property, arson and assault with a deadly weapon probably wasn't a great place to begin getting mental health treatments. Just last month, a guy who'd been an Eagle Scout and a nearly Olympic track star who'd gotten into methamphetamine had been accidentally killed while in custody at the jail. He'd been very violent and strong and then improperly restrained. Mickey couldn't help wondering why the guy's wealthy and big-shot parents hadn't done more to help their son instead of immediately filing a multi-million-dollar lawsuit against the county.

But Al had never heard of Mickey Slattery being violent, and he seemed pretty tame sitting in the back of the cruiser, his head down, almost between his knees. If Mickey hadn't set the transformer on fire, a person, certainly a lawyer, could make a case for his not having done much of anything.

Al retrieved the flame thrower. To the extent he could, he made sure it was off and wasn't going to leak anything flammable as he put it in the trunk of his cruiser. They'd need the flame thrower if they were going charge aggravated assault. At a minimum, they could get Mickey to surrender the flame thrower so it couldn't do any more harm.

There were days when Al wished he was a policeman during an earlier time. A patrol officer as well as a community outreach officer who was famously known to every elementary school kid in town as "Officer Al, the kiddie's pal," his father would have probably run the flamethrower over with his cruiser a few times, scared the hell out of Mickey, and sent him on his way, which was probably what Al should do.

"Can I have my bike?" came from the back of his cruiser in the voice of what sounded like Al's five-year-old son. "How else can I get home?" Al almost felt bad for Slattery. His cruiser had a bike rack for officers who patrolled downtown. Maybe seizing his bike would keep Slattery off the streets a while longer.

"Where is it?"

"In the carport?" Again, the five-year-old voice. "Of my house?"

Al went to the abandoned house, picked up the beat-up old bike, carried it to his cruiser and lashed it onto the bike rack before getting back into the cruiser.

"Okay, we're set, Slattery. We've got your flame thrower, your bike, and you, all on board. Away we go."

"Where to, Officer Al?" the little voice asked.

Al laughed. Aside from being amused by being called his father's name, he remembered one of the good, serious teachers in high school saying, "smart people know the answers, brilliant people know the questions," which Al never really understood. Al tended to think about things that puzzled him, which got him into trouble. More than once, his football coach had yelled at him: "Do us both a favor, Abrera. Just do what you're told and stop thinking."

"Good question, Slattery," Al answered, turning his cruiser around and heading down the street toward town. "Good question."

Advanced Placement

Huge red velvet curtains opened revealing a shiny floor, tall walls and long, white drapes. Everything was gold and marble. Two singers snuggled on a couch and sang. The camera zoomed in. Yikes! They were both women!

"As far as Strauss was concerned, you couldn't have too many sopranos. *Der Rozenkavalier* has three," said Mrs. Huston, as if that explained anything. "The one on the left is really a young man." Carly's eyes must have bugged out. "No, no. The soprano's a woman, but she's playing a seventeen-year-old boy named Octavian."

At the end of their junior year, Dr. Reed had given each soon-to-be senior who'd be taking his advanced placement humanities class next year a DVD of an opera, of all things. They had to watch the DVD and then, if they wanted extra credit, write an essay discussing "Whether Opera is Relevant to Contemporary Life." Carly had had a busy summer and put off doing the assignment for such a long time she was beginning to think she'd just watch the DVD some night and skip writing the essay. Dr. Reed directed the school's choir and its theatrical and musical productions. He really liked Carly because she sang in the choir and accompanied the choir and any musicals on piano. Realistically, she doubted she'd need any extra credit.

Then, while doing her college application volunteering every Friday afternoon at a nursing home, Carly had been switched to a lady who, according to Carly's mother, had been an important cultural person in Phoenix and was just staying in the nursing home until she could go back east to stay with her daughter. As well as being in charge of training the guides at the art museums in town, Mrs. Huston had reviewed books and plays for the paper and the public TV station. She'd also done luncheon book reviews for women's groups, more than one of which her mother had attended.

"She can explain the opera to you while you're volunteering. You'll kill two birds with one stone," Carly's mother insisted. Even Mrs. Huston seemed to think it was a good idea.

"Oh goody," she said, clapping her hands, "we'll explore the essential question of comedic drama: will the heroine marry well, or will she marry *badly*?" Mrs. Huston was kind of funny. She rubbed her hands as if she wanted the heroine to marry badly.

So, surprisingly, Carly was finally getting around to watching *Der Rosenkavalier* with Mrs. Huston. Which was good. She'd likely have time, and ideas, for doing the extra credit essay. The two singers were singing, and acting, as if they were love birds.

"They've just spent the night together." So much for their just being love birds. "Oh, for God's sake!" Mrs. Huston moved herself around in her bed. "They're supposed to be in bed, not on a couch. This scene was the height of scandal in the early Twentieth Century. Von Karajan is being silly insisting they appear to be innocently sitting on their parent's living room sofa."

If Carly had just made out with Don on the living room sofa, things would still be fine.

The bigger woman sang lots of high notes. Her singing sounded kind of beautiful, but Carly couldn't understand the words, and the language she was singing in, German Carly guessed, didn't sound nice. The two women hugged and kissed before the supposedly guy one hid in a closet because a little blond girl in a turban, a silk outfit and curled up, pointed, silk shoes shuffled across the stage and put a tea tray on a table. Her face was covered with what looked like brown shoe polish. They must have wanted her to look like a little Indian or Arab kid, but she just looked creepy. She shuffled back off stage, and the two women got back together and sang some more.

"He's seventeen and she's thirty-two."

"At least Don isn't thirty-two," sounded like what Carly's best friend

Sally Ann would tell Carly to say when she finally told her mother. Don was four years older than Carly.

"They're having an affair."

Which was what Sally Ann squealed when Carly told her what had happened. Not that Carly had planned anything, or had particularly wanted it to happen. It just had.

Don had come over three Fridays before while Carly's parents were out having dinner. Friday was Carly's one night off from doing homework or practicing piano or going to choir practice or a swim meet or all the other things she had to do in the evenings. It was baking hot and Carly was in the swimming pool, which by the middle of the summer was so warm it felt like a bath. Don walked his motorcycle down the alley and let himself in through the gate in the backyard wall. Since he wasn't wearing swimming trunks, he took off all his clothes except his boxers and joined Carly in the pool. They swam around a while, then started kind of hugging. Carly got out of the pool and turned off the pool light, the only light on outside. It was pretty dark, even though the sky was still a little blue and pink. Don sat on the steps and Carly got back in and sat on Don's lap.

"The Marshalin, the blond soprano, is worried she's too old. Thirty-two's pretty old, huh?" Carly nodded. "No, it's not!" Mrs. Huston waived her hand at Carly. "She's young, but she thinks she's old. I'm old, but most times I think I'm young. Hah!" Mrs. Huston had a way of kind of cackling.

Don began feeling Carly up, and for no reason she'd been able to determine, she took off her bikini bottom and sat down on Don's lap. He was inside her and done in what seemed like an instant. They climbed out of the pool. Carly put her bottom back on and wrapped herself in a towel and Don got dressed and left through the gate to the alley. They hadn't said a word.

"Someone's coming," Mrs. Huston said, "Maybe it's the Field Marshall, the Marshalin's husband, home from his hunting trip."

Although at the time she'd been nervous she and Don would get caught, either by her little brother who was inside the house or her parents, now Carly wished they had been caught, in time at least. She'd have gotten into major trouble, probably grounded for like a semester or something, and her mother would have been mad and really disappointed, but eventually everyone would have gotten over it. Now Carly might be facing a problem that would last the rest of her life.

The supposedly older soprano hid the supposedly younger soprano in another closet, reminding Carly of the "Three Stooges" movies her little brother thought were funny.

"It's her cousin, not her husband. Nobles called each other 'cousin,' which they may have been. There was a lot of intermarriage, which wasn't good for having healthy children, of which he may be one. He's named Ochs, 'O-C-H-S.' He's an 'ox,' as in 'dumb as one.' Definitely not what you'd call a catch."

Carly's mother didn't consider Don a catch. She thought Carly was selling herself short even dating Don. He'd gone into the Air Force instead of going to college. He worked as a mechanic at the Air Force base and lived with his divorced father who worked out of town almost all the time. Don and his father were more like roommates than father and son. Carly had met Don the summer before. They'd dated off and on, as much as she could date anyone since she had so little free time and her mother was basically opposed to her dating anyone, never mind somebody like Don.

 The other soprano emerged from the closet in a maid's outfit. So that made her a woman, playing a man, who was playing a maid, just the kind of thing that made Carly wonder about opera.

A big man in a white wig, with a super deep voice, strutted on stage. He flirted really stupidly with the "maid" and then began talking to the other soprano.

Don was pretty much the exact opposite of everything Carly's mother thought was important. He had no interest in going to college and was just an enlisted man in the Air Force. Worst of all, his parents were divorced. All of which may have been part of Carly's attraction to him. But now that he was more than just a rebellion thing, Carly, whose entire reputation revolved around everyone thinking she was talented and smart, felt kind of dumb.

"Ochs has an appetite for servant girls. He's entitled." Mrs. Huston laughed. "His soon-to-be father-in-law owns twelve palaces in Vienna. Ochs plans to get the palaces, and the money, once the father dies. He's a gold-digger, but he's distracted by the maid. He asks her to come to his hotel room."

Don hadn't pressured Carly into doing anything. They'd kissed and made out before, and she'd let him feel her up before. But he'd never gone farther than Carly had wanted, and anyway, Carly had been the one who'd taken off her bikini bottom. She wasn't supposed to make those kinds of mistakes. Why had she done that?

Nor did she see a money thing with Don. Carly's mother seemed to think every boy who looked at Carly was out to get her parents' money or the money Carly would make as soon as she was a doctor, a concert pianist, a college professor, a lawyer or a business person, which were the sorts of things Carly was expected to be.

"But every opera needs a villain. Who else is going to sing the bass parts?"

Carly knew there were bad boys. Some of the rich boys the rich girls at school liked were pretty bad. Then there were the boys her mother wanted her to like, boys in her youth orchestra, or the choir, or the brainy guys. Don wasn't a bad person. The real problem was, personality-wise, Don wasn't much of anything.

"Ochs wants the Marshalin to recommend a young nobleman to deliver a silver rose to his fiancé. 'Rosenkavalier' means a gentleman rose deliverer, literally, a 'rose deliverer rich enough to own a horse,' which was that time's car."

Carly hadn't been formally introduced to Don by anyone, certainly not a relative. She first met Don at the roller rink she and Sally Ann went to mostly in order to meet boys. Don worked there part-time as an assistant manager. She and Sally Ann nicknamed him 'the lifeguard guy' because his job was to skate around and keep an eye on things. Because he'd grown up in Canada playing hockey, and he could skate better backwards than most people, certainly any of the boys they knew, could skate forwards, all the girls thought Don was pretty neat.

"What good are boys who don't have cars?"

Don's motorcycle was another problem. Carly's mother had forbidden Carly from going anywhere with Don on his motorcycle, so most of the time Don could only come over to the house and sort of hang around. But even having them where she could keep an eye on them hadn't made her mother happy. She just didn't like Don.

And if they'd been able to go out in a car like normal people, maybe Carly wouldn't have felt obligated to sneak Don into the backyard while her parents were away. Maybe things wouldn't have turned out the way they had. Being hit by a car while riding on Don's motorcycle probably wouldn't have been half as bad as what happened.

"Ochs wants the Marshalin to pay her lawyer to draft his wedding contract."

Carly had always assumed she would fall in love before she got married. Now, she might have to marry Don. If she felt anything for Don, Carly probably felt bad for him. He was good looking and wasn't mean, or dumb, or any of the things her mother thought he was. He liked Carly and she didn't dislike him. But he just wasn't interesting and she sure wasn't in love with him. Honestly, the possibility of having to spend the rest of her life with Don terrified her.

"Like lots of wealthy people, Ochs is cheap."

While Ochs was trying to put his hands all over the maid, the Marshalin had her butler send in her lawyer, who was standing outside her bedroom door first thing on a Sunday morning. That was weird. Carly's father was a lawyer and worked long hours and even weekends sometimes, but she doubted he'd ever go to his clients' bedrooms on Sunday mornings, or that her mother would go for that.

"Ochs is a fifty-year-old bachelor. Why would such an old man be interested in such a young woman?"

Which was pretty much what Carly's mother wondered about Don.

"Octavian's a teenager, the kind of boy your mother would want you to date."

Carly blushed. Her mother probably didn't want her dating anyone.

"Ochs is bragging about his conquests. Octavian's offended but the Marshalin is amused. Octavian considers Ochs unromantic. The rich can afford to be unromantic."

Don wasn't rich and he didn't brag, but he hardly said anything.

"So Ochs can recognize the Rosenkavalier, the Marshalin has Octavian bring her the locket he's just given her with his picture in it." Mrs. Huston shook her head. "Would you give away a picture locket your boyfriend just gave you, right in front of him?"

Don had given Carly a charm bracelet she didn't much care for and didn't really wear. What would Don say if she was pregnant? Would he say anything?

"The Marshalin and Ochs joke about the picture in the locket looking like the maid. Ochs assumes the maid's an illegitimate daughter of someone in the Rosenkavalier's family." Tons of people began crowding into the Marshalin's bedroom. "Peddlers, beggars, and a lawyer."

What was Carly's father going to think? Would he do something or would he just stay out of her mother's way?

"And a rumormonger, or rumor seller; the Eighteenth Century's grocery store checkout-line newspapers."

An effeminate actor waltzed on stage and began primping the Marshalin's hair. Carly figured it meant hair dressers were gay. Next a singer with a high, beautiful voice appeared and sang in a language not as clunky as German, probably Italian.

"Strauss had had enough of Italian opera. He didn't want tenors in his operas." Mrs. Huston thrust her fist into the air and shook her head. "Strauss wanted German opera, true opera."

Carly liked the song, more than the rest of the singing, which sounded kind of flat and aimless most of the time. But the Italian song ended and a bunch of grungy servants ran onto the stage. The one who stood right next to Ochs looked like a younger, skinnier, dirty version of Ochs.

"That's Ochs' illegitimate son, most likely by a maid or a servant girl."

If Carly had the baby, and kept it, and didn't marry Don, would that be Carly, and her baby? Carly had heard some girls had babies and then had their parents raise them, but she doubted her mother would go for that. And how strange would it be keeping a baby around without admitting it was hers? She'd be the baby's sister? Instead of its mother?

"Ochs is telling the lawyer what to put in the marriage contract. The lawyer says Ochs wants everything for nothing, but Ochs won't hear it. Rules are for little people."

When a rich senior got pregnant last year, her parents flew her away on their jet to their Utah ski home for most of the year. She had her baby, gave it away, and flew back to Phoenix in time to take her finals and graduate. She even went to the prom. The story was she was training for the Olympic ski team, which no one believed. Flying away on a private jet wasn't an option for Carly.

The tenor sang another love song while the lawyer and Ochs argued. Ochs threw a fit and the tenor got scared and ran off the stage.

"Business trumps romance," Mrs. Huston said, shaking her head.

Carly had no idea what to think about romance any more. How could she have had sex with, and gotten pregnant by, a guy she was hardly interested in, never mind in love with, even a little bit? What could be less romantic? The Marshalin was having a fit.

"She's accusing her hairdresser of making her look old. She's only thirty-two. How much older can your hair make you look when you're thirty-two?"

The Marshalin's hair didn't look all that great to Carly and thirty-two did sound old. When she was thirty-two, her child would be fifteen, a sophomore in high school, two years younger than Carly. Ugh.

"The rumormonger talks Ochs into hiring him and his woman partner to help him get the maid into bed. The rumormonger's the anti-Rosenkavalier, the bearer of falsehoods, rather than the bearer of the most wonderful message you can have in a comic, romantic opera."

What if Don wanted to marry Carly?

"The Marshalin agrees to have Octavian deliver the silver rose to Ochs's fiancé." The Marshalin was left on the stage all alone.

"She's singing what a bad person Ochs is. She was forced to marry a nobleman she didn't love, which made her wealthy, but unhappy."

If Carly had to marry Don, she'd be poor. She'd have to live in Air Force base housing or with Don's father. She'd have to take care of the baby, and cook meals, and do laundry, and grocery shop, and clean the house. They wouldn't be able to afford a car. She'd be one of those people who use grocery carts to take their groceries home and then leave the carts on the sidewalk. None of her friends would have anything to do with her. They'd go off to college, and she'd be an idiot her entire life.

"She thinks she's old. She sings, 'I'm old but I'm still the same. Why does God let this happen? It's a mystery.'" Why had God let this happen to Carly? "Which is beautiful poetry. Sometimes I wonder the same thing."

But what did Mrs. Huston expect? She'd lived a long time. She'd had a husband and kids and everything. Carly would be stuck being a mother and a wife before she was able to do any of the things she wanted to do. Having to be old once you were old seemed fair.

The soprano playing Octavian appeared in tight, white satin pants, a blue satin coat, a flouncy tie and clunky, buckled, high heels. She and the Marshalin got into a fight.

Some girls at school said they liked to get into fights with their boyfriends so they could make up. But fighting was foreign to Carly. Her parents never fought. They hardly ever even disagreed. Since Don hardly said anything, it was impossible to disagree with him, never mind get into a fight.

"The Marshalin's convinced things will turn out badly. She fears Octavian will turn into a boor like her husband and Ochs." Which was how Carly felt.

"She says, 'everything we seek vanishes, like mists and dreams.' Octavian thinks she doesn't love him anymore. He's hurt and angry, but the Marshalin wants him to be sensible. She knows he'll leave her because of their differing ages. 'Who makes you talk like that?' he demands. She says time is a strange thing we hardly notice when we live from day to day, but suddenly, all we feel is time. Time shows in our faces, it throbs in our temples. Sometimes she can hear the time flying by relentlessly."

Over the last few days, time seemed to have stopped for Carly.

"Beautiful poetry, isn't it? She says, 'one shouldn't be afraid of time because even time is the work of God, the creator of us all.' The Marshalin's very religious."

Which was another problem. Carly went to the main Catholic girls' high school in Phoenix because, according to her father, it was the best school they could afford. Her father was Catholic but didn't go to church. Carly and her mother weren't religious but they belonged to the main Episcopal church in Phoenix because Carly sang in their choir on Sundays with a lot of the other girls from Phoenix's Girls' Choir, and because Carly's mother wanted to be able to have Carly's wedding there. Her mother was a planner.

But for the nuns and priests who ran her school, abortion was murder. If Carly had an abortion, and someone from her school found out, would she be thrown in jail? If the nuns just found out she'd had sex, they'd probably kick her out. How could she put getting kicked out of school on her college application? She'd be ruined.

"But Octavian doesn't care about philosophizing. He's angry. And he's hurt. He can't believe the Marshalin thinks he'll leave her for someone younger. He can't believe she's pushing him away. 'Today or tomorrow, or the day after,' the Marshalin sings. 'We should take things lightly. If we don't, life will punish us. God will show us no mercy.' More beautiful poetry with more than a bit of truth to it. Hofmannsthal, the man who wrote all of Strauss's best librettos, was a tremendous poet."

Carly had no idea how to take things lightly. Sally Ann always said Carly was too serious. And here she was already being punished for having sex and by probably being pregnant. What would the punishment be for killing the baby? Were poetry, and opera, supposed to be good if they made life even more depressing and scarier than it was?

"'You should leave me,' the Marshalin says. She's going to church before having lunch with her old, invalid uncle to atone for her sins. Kind of like you coming here to visit us old people, huh?" Mrs. Huston must have seen Carly's eyes get big. "Sweetie, you're too young to have done anything requiring atonement." Carly felt herself blush. "You deserve a big, gold star for sitting around with us old folks."

Mrs. Huston didn't seem to notice Carly was panicked. She just went on about the DVD.

"The Marshalin tells Octavian maybe they can meet in the park where the nobility conduct clandestine affairs in their carriages." Mrs. Huston laughed. "From whence the illegitimate children flowed, no doubt. Telling a boy he's just a fling is mean, don't you think?"

Carly had no idea what Don thought. Could he be in love with her?

"Octavian's not happy but he agrees to do as he's told and leaves. The Marshalin has a fit because she didn't kiss Octavian goodbye." The weird little servant with shoe polish on her face came back on stage. "The Marshalin tells her page to take the silver rose to Octavian. She says he'll know what to do. Which is true because he's a nice boy."

Carly had no idea whether Don was nice. Maybe harmless was the right word. But then again, maybe not. The Marshalin looked at herself in her mirror then covered it with her hand. The huge curtain came down.

"End of Act One." Carly's watch said a quarter to five. "Opera intermissions are long. The singers need time to catch their breath. In Germany, the audiences break for entire meals. I have to nap before they bring me dinner. We'll watch Act Two next time, sweetie." Mrs. Huston waived her hand and rolled over to face the window looking out over the parking lot. Carly shut off the DVD player and the television, put the remote on the stand next to Mrs. Huston's bed and, kind of like the weird little page, quietly left the room.

That night, Sally Ann came over once Carly's parents left for their usual Friday night dinner out. She and Carly walked to the drugstore and bought a pregnancy test kit. Carly hadn't wanted to, but Sally Ann insisted.

"You can't just ignore this, Carly. Anyway, it'll be fun. My sisters do it all the time."

Back at the house, they took the package into the bathroom. Carly thought they should read the instructions but Sally Ann ripped the package open and said, "All you have to do is pee on this paper stick thing." Carly sat on the toilet and did as she was told. "Now we wait," said Sally Ann. After a minute or so, the stick turned bright red. "Uh-oh," said Sally Ann, "I'd better be leaving."

Next Friday, Mrs. Huston's room's closed door popped open as Carly approached it and an attendant emerged with a plastic bag of bed linens. Another attendant was making Mrs. Huston comfortable in her freshly made bed.

"Oh good, you're here," the attendant said. Mrs. Huston's head was turned away, looking out the window. As she walked past Carly and out of the room, the attendant whispered, "We had a little accident." Mrs. Huston turned her head toward Carly. Her eyes were red and wet.

"Should we watch the DVD?" Carly asked, not knowing what else to say. Mrs. Huston blinked as if she was confused or trying to remember something.

"The DV what."

"The opera?"

"Oh." She turned and looked out the window. "Sure. Why not. Yes.

Der Rosenkavalier. Of course."

Carly turned on the television and the DVD player and clicked on Act Two on the menu. The curtain opened on a different huge room with three story high French doors across the back. A woman, more beautiful than the other two sopranos, in a gorgeous, full-skirted dress, stood in the middle of the stage. She had platinum blond hair and beautiful eyes. She wore a huge string of pearls and matching pearl earrings, like the ones her mother wore on special occasions.

Carly's mother had come into her room on Monday night and closed the door behind her, which she never did.

"Have you been having sex with Don?"

Carly was not a liar, never mind a good one. She nodded and said, "Once."

"You haven't had your period this month?"

How did her mother know? Carly shook her head, and then nodded. Her mother held out a test thing like the one she and Sally Ann used on Friday and pointed toward the bathroom.

"Pee on this and then bring it back here."

The strip turned red like it had on Friday night. Carly's mother seemed as unsurprised as Carly.

"Don't tell anyone," she said, and left the room.

"That's Sophie." Mrs. Huston surprised Carly. She hadn't thought Mrs. Huston was watching. "The love interest. Very religious and humble. She considers marriage a sacrament. She wants to be good even though she'll be a baroness and thus entitled to behave badly."

Carly's mother had taken her to a clinic on Wednesday where a nurse had taken some blood and inspected her and confirmed she was pregnant. They scheduled her for an abortion. For the first time in days, instead of feeling like some sort of instant adult, Carly felt normal again, which had been calming.

"She's just out of convent school. Sophie's the 'sacred,' as opposed to the 'profane' of the characters, and action, in the first act."

The calmness hadn't lasted long. Carly's father called her school "the convent." Carly was now worrying pretty much all the time she'd be kicked out if they found out she'd gotten an abortion.

"She and her maid are excited because the Rosenkavalier is coming."

Mrs. Huston must have been feeling better. "They call him a messenger from God."

Then Don had shown up. They met in the alley behind the house. He was almost chatty. He wanted to know when the baby was going to be born. He said he'd always wanted to be a father. He asked whether it was a boy. "A boy, a son, would be nice. Are we getting married before, or after, he's born?" Carly waived her hands in front of her face, shook her head, and ran back into the house.

"Here's Octavian, rose in hand, beauty incarnate. Thin, young, and pure. The orchestra sounds like a church organ. But he's just spent the night with a married woman fourteen years older than he is. Things aren't always as they appear, are they?"

Had Mrs. Huston somehow figured everything out, like Carly's mother? Writing her paper on the relevance of things not always being as they appear in operas and in contemporary life probably wouldn't be a good idea.

"They are in love the moment their eyes meet."

Don had told her he loved her. He called all the time now.

"A beautiful aria now as Octavian delivers the rose."

He'd sent Carly some flowers, which she'd had to dispose of immediately in the alley.

"Beautiful singing, isn't it? He's saying it's a heavenly rose, not an earthly one, a rose from a sacred paradise. Sophie gets to sing the most beautiful music. She sings: 'The scent of the rose holds me as if I am caught in a trap.' Of course, she is. But she doesn't know it yet."

Carly felt trapped. How had Don known? The only person Carly had told was her father. He'd come into her room the night Don asked her when they were getting married and asked how she was. She burst into tears, which she never did. He put his arms around her and told her everything would be all right, which made her feel a little better, until he asked whether she wanted to have the baby. He told her he wouldn't mind having another kid in the family and wouldn't mind raising it, which just made Carly cry harder. Once she'd been able to talk, she asked whether he'd talked to her mother. He said he had and that he could take care of her.

"Are you sure?"

"Don't worry about it," he laughed, and left the room.

"Sophie sings this is a moment she will never forget as long as she lives."

Carly was confused. An engaged woman would fall in love at first sight with a messenger boy?

"She studies the nobility by reading books listing who's related to whom, what their titles mean, and what they own. She thinks being noble means you behave well, as in '*noblesse oblige.*'" Carly had heard the term. "She's an ingénue. She's naïve." Which was what Carly's mother called her when they disagreed. "She tells Octavian she likes him. She's direct rather than flirtatious, like the nobility."

Talking about the opera seemed to be calming Mrs. Huston. Talking to her father hadn't calmed Carly. She'd realized if her father had his way she'd have to have the baby and live with it the rest of her life as some sort of weird, super older sister. Plus, her senior year of high school would be wiped out. Maybe her mother was right.

"But things go downhill from here. You can hear it in the music. Ochs, the barnyard animal enters to this gorgeous, wedding cake of a woman." Ochs was looking all around the stage and up in the air.

When Carly told Sally Ann she was getting an abortion, Sally Ann whooped, "You're WHAT?" and threw herself back on the bed and laughed and laughed and laughed.

"YOU?" she finally blurted, "the patron saint of our class? Of the whole school?" before calming down. "Oh well, it happens all the time." Sally Ann shook her head before looking at Carly. "You've never told me what it was like? Was it great?" Carly frowned. "The S-E-X?"

Sally Ann was different than Carly. Sally Ann never worried about anything. Everybody in her big family went to Arizona State, even her parents and grandparents. Sally Ann had never given a thought to going back east, or to a good school in California, or doing any of the other things Carly was supposed to do.

"He's sizing up the palace, figuring out what it's worth. He surveys his fiancé as if he's buying a horse. He waggles her wrist. I'm surprised he doesn't check her teeth. But he's intrigued by Octavian, since he so strongly resembles the Marshalin's chambermaid he's interested in. Sophie's horrified. Her betrothed is fat and old." Ochs wasn't that fat but he was old. "Not exactly what Sophie's envisioned."

The day after the visit to the clinic, one of the mothers from school had called Carly's mother at work to say the other mothers didn't want Carly going to school with their daughters anymore. "Because she's pregnant, or because she's not going to have the baby?" Carly's mother said, and hung up the phone.

"Would they rather you were there and pregnant?" she asked Carly that night, as if she and Carly were on the same side, which was kind of nice. "Maybe they'd like that, huh? And what business is it of theirs anyway?" Her mother had a temper.

"In front of his soon-to-be father-in-law and fiancé, Ochs brags about sowing his wild oats. He's mocking romance." He was also just about feeling Sophie up. "He says everything's going like clockwork. He's going to get the father-in-law's money, his bride, and the chambermaid. All very smooth until…" Here Mrs. Huston raised her hand just as Sophie shouted.

"'Hands off!' Sophie screams. So much for everything going like clockwork."

Why hadn't Carly done anything to stop Don? Had she wanted it to happen, in such an unromantic way, with such a dud of a guy? If she was going to do it, why hadn't she done anything to keep herself from getting pregnant? Evidently nobody in opera or the seventeen hundreds worried about getting pregnant. Maybe it would be better if people still had stray kids lying around everywhere. It would sure make things easier for Carly. Her father hadn't come back to tell her they were going to adopt the baby, but she never really thought he'd get anywhere with her mother anyway.

"Ochs sings his waltz tune. Strauss is making fun of popular Viennese music. The words are 'with me, no night will be long enough for you.' Just like the opening act, but made crass. He's an awful guy."

If it was still the same in Europe, maybe Carly could go there and have the baby. She could be an exchange student. It would look great on her college application. No one would ever know for sure. Maybe her father would help her do that. She could fly on a regular airline flight. Her parents could afford that.

"Ochs calls Sophie an unbroken horse. Any boys you know call their girlfriend a horse?" Carly shook her head. "He's offering Sophie to his cousin Octavian as a plaything. Terrible."

Weren't operas supposed to be cultured? Did the nuns know Dr. Reed was having kids watch this kind of stuff?

"The barnyard soils beauty, romance and poetry. Ochs goes off to get the marriage contract finalized by the lawyers." Octavian and the new, pretty soprano Sophie, were left alone.

Sally Ann had been complaining about Dr. Reed and the summer assignment, which she hadn't started yet.

"Why did he make us watch operas? It's a humanities course, not a music course." Sally Ann was smart but she wasn't as disciplined as Carly.

"Many people consider opera the crowning artistic achievement of Western culture," Carly replied, which is what she remembered Dr. Reed saying.

"But couldn't we all at least have watched the same one?"

"Octavian apologizes to Sophie about Ochs. He explains they only met a day ago." All of a sudden, Ochs's servants started running through the beautiful palace, acting crazy and drunk, while the orchestra played all sorts of crazy music. Sophie stood in the middle like a damsel in distress until the servants all ran off the stage and she and Octavian were left alone again, which was weird.

"'You must be what you are,' Octavian tells Sophie. You have to figure out what you are and then you have to figure out how to be what you are. But Sophie thinks love, and beauty, and music are enough. She sings, 'When you hold me, nothing ugly can harm me and I want to stay in your arms forever.'"

How could this scene, this whole opera, be any more removed from Carly's situation? She didn't have a Prince Charming, or anyone else, holding her in her arms. She had Don bugging her all the time. It almost made her angry. The gossip mongers snuck onto the stage and watched.

"Beautiful moments don't last long. The gossip mongers catch the happy, young lovers making beautiful music."

Carly had to admit the singing was beautiful, but she'd never even had a beautiful moment to get ruined. Her moment had just been strange. And how could she, of all people, get pregnant from her one, and only, time?

"Here's Ochs again. Against all the rules of cultured society, Octavian tells Ochs the truth, that Sophie doesn't like him. Ochs cares even less than he cares whether his horse likes him. Ochs can't believe Octavian would say anything so preposterous. He asks, 'Is this some sort of cheap comedy?' And it is, a cheap comedy inside the highest comedy. Ochs says, 'Who pays attention to a young girl's talk?' Romance is just teenaged silliness. Ochs tells Octavian he's just a teenaged boy spouting nonsense. 'People in Vienna know who I am,' he says. He's important and Octavian's not. Octavian is obligated to defend Sophie's honor."

The situation with the mothers of other girls got worse the day after the call to her mom's work. At dinner, Carly's mother told her father the mother of the rich girl who'd had a baby without anyone talking about it, and certainly without Carly's mother knowing about it, was leading the group bugging Carly's mother.

"She's going to call the school and tell them they can't let Carly back in. Can she do that?"

Her father tilted his head and swallowed the food he'd been chewing.

"Her husband writes a check, the school gets a new building. We write a check, the school has to give us a few raffle tickets."

An unrealistic sword fight broke out. Ochs was nicked by Octavian's sword but acted as if he was about to die. His servant tore off part of a servant girl's petticoat to make him a bandage and a sling.

"The servant class's primary role is to provide bandages to preserve noble blood," Mrs. Huston said. Sophie's father came in. "He's outraged. He blames Octavian, even though Octavian's defending his daughter's honor. It's Octavian's fault his soon-to-be son-in-law is a jerk. Very nobly, Octavian apologizes. But having nobles wounded in your living room is not good for social climbing. Sophie's father says he's going to put her back into the convent 'for life, for all time.' Lots of discussion of time in this opera. Maybe you could write your paper about that."

Never mind writing her paper, what if the people running her school or the other mothers insisted Carly have the baby? How would Carly survive nine months of being pregnant? How could she lose a whole year of her life and her senior year? People only ever had one senior year in their life. Ochs went back to singing.

"End of Act Two," Mrs. Huston announced. "Ochs sings his obnoxious, low class, Viennese waltz. The equivalent of our pop music as far as Strauss was concerned. The gossip mongers bring Ochs a note from the supposed chambermaid, who's really Octavian."

Carly had begun throwing up in the mornings. What would that be like for months? She'd tried to hide it from her mother but she'd come into the bathroom like a missile the first morning it happened. Her mother was actually kind of nice. She explained it was what happened when you were pregnant and it didn't last for all nine months. Why had she told Carly that? Was her mother changing her mind?

"The note invites Ochs to have dinner and spend the night with the chamber maid. Ochs is ecstatic. He says everything is going 'like clockwork.' But instead of giving the gossip monger girl a tip for setting up the tryst, he kisses her hand. Then, because he probably can't write, he dictates his answer. Listen to the very low note he hits there. It's the low point of the opera. Aren't he, and that song, awful?"

Actually, Carly found the waltz almost pleasant and familiar, unlike most of the rest of the music everyone was singing. Where was Sophie's mother? The only parent in the opera was Sophie's father, who didn't seem all that great a dad.

Don had begun calling Carly's mother at work. He told her he wanted to have Carly have the baby and that he was going to hire a lawyer. Carly's father just said, "He can't afford one. And wouldn't he have a statutory rape problem?" He pointed his finger at Carly's mother. "Do not tell him that." So now Carly had to worry about her father having to handle a lawsuit against her or his father having Don thrown in jail, by surprise.

Carly stopped the DVD player. Mrs. Huston seemed tired. She waved Carly out of her room and rolled over to take a nap.

The following Friday, Mrs. Huston was sitting up in bed, all ready for Carly. The overture began as the curtain opened on a dark, ugly hall. People were running around opening and closing little doors that showed peoples' heads inside them.

"They're setting a trap for Ochs. Octavian's in his maid's outfit. The gossip mongers turned on Ochs because instead of him paying them their fee he wanted them to be satisfied with the money they could get the innkeeper to discount from what Ochs paid for renting the room. A lousy way to treat the servant class. So the rumor mongers are going to expose him." Ochs showed up and sat down to dinner with Octavian dressed as a maid. Octavian began singing.

"The maid sings about time and death. She acts as if she's obsessed with death instead of being obsessed with going to bed. Things are definitely not going like clockwork. The wine Ochs thought would get the maid into bed is depressing her. She decides to take a nap. The gossip mongers start with their tricks."

Carly's appointment at the clinic had been first thing Monday morning. She'd taken the whole day off from summer school and swimming and everything and her mother had taken the morning off from work. They took Carly into a room, had her change into a backwards gown, and lie on an inspection table with the stirrup things. They hooked her up to a bottle that dropped water into a needle they stuck into her arm after they took some blood. They gave her a shot they said would relax her. Then she and her mother just waited.

The orchestra started playing scary movie music while Ochs ran around the stage as if he was scared by the faces popping out of the little doors in the walls and the floor, which seemed kind of dumb to Carly. A woman showed up with a bunch of small children.

"It's the girl gossip monger saying she's mothered a bunch of Ochs's illegitimate children. Bigamy was a capital crime in Vienna. Ochs is at risk of being put to death." Ochs began singing loudly. "He sings 'order must be restored,' which is funny since he's the source of the disorder." A man in a uniform marched onto the stage.

A woman had come into the room. She said she was a physician's assistant and said she was just checking a few things. She had Carly spread her legs while she poked some things into her and felt around before saying, "Okay," and leaving Carly and her mother alone. After that, a male nurse came in and injected a needle into the tube going into Carly's arm.

"The chief of police arrives. Ochs thinks everything will go back to 'running like clockwork' now, but instead of throwing out the imposters posing as his wife and children, the police chief accuses Ochs of being a lecher, to which Ochs replies, 'I can't believe my eyes.' Which is all a little forced, but it's opera." Carly nodded. Sophie showed up.

"Sophie says all this bad behavior will disgrace her father. Ochs blames it on the maid trying to seduce him. It's always the girl's fault. He even calls her a slut."

The next thing Carly knew, she was in a different room and a nurse was asking her if she wanted anything to drink. Carly's mother was in the room, standing next to Carly's bed, holding Carly's clothes. Carly said she wanted some water and the nurse left.

"Are they done? Did they do it?" Carly asked.

"They didn't have to. They found out you've had a miscarriage. They aren't sure. Either that or the whole thing was a false pregnancy." Carly felt confused. Her mother put her hand on Carly's arm. "It's for the best."

The nurse came back in with a bottle of water for Carly saying, "You can get dressed, dear. Take it easy for the rest of the day, but you'll be fine."

Sophie left the stage just as the Marshalin entered wearing a fantastic dress and a beautiful, blond wig. She looked as beautiful as Sophie, who came back on stage just as Octavian came out of the bedroom wearing men's clothing.

Carly and her mother were quiet on the way home. It was bright and super-hot out. Maybe the drug made Carly feel the brightness and the heat more than usual. Carly went into the house and lay down on the couch. Her mother collected her work things and went to the office, touching Carly's arm and saying, "Everything's all right now." Carly drowsed and slept for most of the day. She woke up and began feeling normal as the sun was beginning to go down. It was disorienting waking up at the end of a day.

"Not exactly the intimate little rendezvous Ochs was planning for his bachelor party, eh? But watch, the Marshalin will waive her magic wand and bring matters to a close. She tells the police chief it's nothing more than a practical joke. And when she tells Ochs the chambermaid is in fact Octavian, he's not in the least embarrassed. He says, 'You see, there was nothing wrong with my eyes after all.' The Marshalin says it was just a masquerade, a party where everyone wears masks so they can cheat on their spouses without getting caught."

The next night, Sally Ann came over to Carly's house. She already knew everything and was mostly interested in giving Carly her own big news. She'd gone out on a date with Don.

"He called you?"

"I called him."

"He talked to you?" Carly was stunned. "What did he say, about me?"

"He knows you're not interested in him."

"Did he ask about the, you know?"

"He thinks you had a miscarriage, not that anyone else does. Boys are easy to fool about all kinds of stuff, particularly that kind of stuff."

"Ochs realizes the Marshalin and Octavian were sleeping together at the beginning of Act One, but the Marshalin tells Ochs she expects him to act like a gentleman and keep his mouth shut. Ochs is no gentleman, but he knows the Marshalin's powerful. He says he's a good sport, but he's actually a crybaby. He thinks he still gets to marry Sophie and inherit all her father's money. The Marshalin shouts at him, 'Can't you tell when it's over?' But it's also over between the Marshalin and Octavian." All sorts of people rushed onto the stage with their hands out, almost attacking Ochs, wanting to be paid. "The innkeeper, the musicians, the servants, the gossip mongers, the coach drivers, the guy who provided all the candles. But Ochs is broke, which is why he was getting married. It's the end of Ochs." Ochs ran off the stage ahead of everyone who wanted to get paid.

Wednesday night Carly's mother told her father she and Carly had to report to Sister Marie, the principal of Carly's school, the next morning.

"They want to know what's happened with Carly. It's no big deal."

"Well she didn't have an abortion. Isn't that sufficient?"

Her mother shook her head and then nodded. Her father frowned and looked at Carly and then back at her mother.

"You mean we're somehow supposed to, what, un-*do* the fact Carly … had sex?" Her mother had nothing to say. All her father said was, "Whatever happened to 'Let he who is without sin cast the first stone?'"

Carly was uncomfortable with talk of sin. She had to sit through religion classes with all the other kids at school, most of whom were real Catholics, but she wasn't an expert.

"Ironically, with a capital 'I,' Sophie wants the Marshalin's approval of her love of Octavian." The Marshalin and Octavian and Sophie all sang separate songs at the same time. "The Marshalin sings 'sooner or later she'd lose Octavian but she'll bear it with composure.' Octavian's telling Sophie 'All I see is your face.' The Marshalin tells Octavian 'don't talk so much. You're too pretty for that.' Octavian is telling the Marshalin she is 'so good.' The Marshalin is noble and good, a rare combination. This is a beautiful aria the Marshalin is singing. She says 'I promised to love him in the right way. But I didn't expect to have to let him go so soon. There are many things in this world we don't believe exist even when told about them. Only if it happens to you, then you'll believe it, without knowing why.' Beautiful poetry. The Marshalin says, 'with that woman Sophie, Octavian will find what men believe is happiness. So be it,' she says, 'Amen.'" Mrs. Huston and Carly listened for a while. "Beautiful singing, isn't it?" The Marshalin received a kiss from Octavian and left the stage.

Sister Marie had a second, private office up on the second floor. Carly had heard about it but had never been there. Carly's mother did all the talking.

"So, has Carly had an abortion?" Sister Marie asked after a little chit-chat.

"No. It was a false pregnancy." Carly looked at her mother. "Frankly, I'm not even sure Carly really had sex. Carly's father and I are pretty sure the whole incident was nothing more than a psychosomatic reaction to an unpleasant experience she had, with a boy." Sister Marie looked at Carly and then her mother and then back at Carly. Carly looked at her mother and then at Sister Marie, but she didn't say anything.

"That's the kiss the Marshalin failed to get at the end of act one. What she feared then has come to pass. Very sad. Fearing something is almost as bad as when it actually happens."

The next day, the office called Carly's mother to tell her Carly could register for her classes. Everything was fine. Carly might not even have ever been pregnant, may never have had sex, and she wasn't going to be kicked out of school.

"We've come full circle. Two lovers are alone as at the beginning of the opera. But now they're both young and genuinely in love. A very famous duet. 'Together, forever,' they sing. They're young and can talk about something lasting forever. 'I feel only your touch,' they say. No seeing age on their faces, no hearing time ticking, only touch." Mrs. Huston was quiet for a while. "They say, 'it's a dream and they're on the threshold of Heaven. The music reaches a harmonic resolution for the first time in the entire opera." They walked off together.

The strange, little, black-faced, supposedly Arab or Indian page came out, picked up somebody's handkerchief that must have fallen to the floor, and ran off the stage. The huge red curtain closed, and the audience clapped, and clapped, and clapped. All the singers took their bows. The audience clapped and clapped.

"I guess it's sad?" Carly ventured.

"Well, nobody dies. It's a comedy, it's not a tragedy. The social order is confirmed. Do we really need to feel sorry for a wealthy woman who wasn't lucky enough to be infatuated with a handsome young boy when she was young herself?" Mrs. Huston adjusted herself in her bed. "I don't feel well, sweetie. You'd better leave."

Carly felt a little sad the DVD watching was ended. Even though it was an assignment and part of having to volunteer, she'd kind of gotten to like it.

Carly had a nearly two-week break before school started. She was done with her junior college courses, and the swim team and choir were both on break. Even her piano teacher was on vacation. If she didn't practice, no one would know. Carly sat around the house, swam in the pool, played with the dog, took naps and relaxed. Her little brother was home too but he was still too young to get into any real trouble and he was getting old enough that he wasn't all that interested in bugging Carly all the time anymore.

Getting out of bed the second morning of what her father called her "sabbatical," Carly noticed the charm bracelet. It was the first time she'd seen it since Don had told Sally Ann to ask Carly to give it back so he could give it to Sally Ann.

"Or you can just give it to me," Sally Ann said. Since then, Sally Ann and Carly were no longer speaking.

Carly wasn't sure what she'd do with the charm bracelet. Maybe she'd keep it. Don hadn't been all that great, but it had been nice having a boyfriend, particularly an older one nobody really knew, or saw. The charm bracelet was all she had left. Like Sally Ann, Don wasn't even calling her anymore, which was kind of a relief. But still, it would be nice to have a boyfriend calling her.

Carly put on her bathing suit, wondering if she'd ever be able to put on a bathing suit without remembering the dumbest time she'd taken it off. She looked at her teddy bear. If she'd actually been pregnant and had a baby, it would probably have had a teddy bear.

Her grades from her summer school junior college courses came in the mail that day. She aced both classes, which was to be expected, but it was still a relief. She thought how close she'd come to having to stay in a community college or being poor and having to live on the Air Force base or something, rather than go off to a real college.

But she still had her opera report to do. She'd been thinking about it off and on and had concluded she'd just have to say opera had nothing at all to do with contemporary life. She might even add, "Or anything else, for that matter," but she didn't want to risk annoying Dr. Reed any more than she was probably going to already.

Although there just didn't seem to be any way around giving what could very well be the wrong answer, there probably wasn't that much risk. Any extra credit she might squeeze out would be better than none. You couldn't get hurt even getting an F on an extra credit assignment, so away she went.

Why Opera Is Not Relevant to Contemporary Life

Richard Strauss's opera "Der Rosenkavalier" is not at all relevant to contemporary life for a number of reasons, which I will lay out in this report.

First, the singing and the music are just a distraction. Why don't the characters just talk? And the style of the music is not that pretty. It just kind of wanders around too much. And the singing style is so stylized and unrelated to anything at all that it doesn't have anything to do with current life, which isn't all that surprising since the opera is about a hundred years old already and it's supposed to be about something that happened another one hundred and fifty or two hundred years before the opera was even written. So, it's certainly not contemporary, since it's really over two hundred or more years old.

The costumes are kind of interesting but they're pretty out of date and kind of frumpy. The people in the opera don't wear anything a person would wear today. Most of the women are kind of chubby and over-weight, which they evidently have to be to sing in that funny style in great big European concert halls without microphones or anything. Now we have good microphones so you don't have to sing that way, at least on TV. The men are mostly old. The actors and actresses just are not much to look at, at least by today's standards.

The plot is kind of dumb and not relevant to contemporary life. This really old, ugly guy wants to marry a rich young girl so he doesn't have to work. Actually, no one seems to work in the opera. They all seem rich, which can't be realistic and it's certainly not how things are these days. Everyone has to work now, even women. But the rich girl falls in love with this young guy instead of the old man. By the way, the young guy is going out with this really rich older woman when the opera starts. Which I suppose might be realistic but I doubt it happens that much in real life these days. Plus, the guy character is played by a woman singer, which is totally unrelated to anything in contemporary life. But the two young lovers come up with this weird plan to embarrass the old guy because he's trying to seduce a maid who is actually the young guy, which is pretty unbelievable, not to mention confusing. What kind of old guy would be fooled into thinking a young guy is a cute young girl? I don't think that would happen in modern times.

But they end up being successful. The young people get the old guy to run away rather than get in big trouble and the young guy and the young girl who have fallen in love at first sight, even though the young guy was madly in love with the older woman in the first act, get together and presumably get married and live happily ever after, not that we see that part because the opera has to end at some point. And the older lady seems kind of fine with it, which is a little strange.

And the music isn't that great either. It's not really classical sounding even though there are all these opera singers and a big orchestra. Except for one or two songs in the first act that actually sound nice, even though they're not supposed to, for some reason. There's only one cadence in the whole opera, which I think makes it kind of hard to listen to, musically.

So, in the end, everything kind of works out. The bad guy doesn't get away with anything much and the two love birds get together and the girl, or at least her father, has lots of money, so the love birds will be able to live happily ever after. And even the older woman seems kind of content to stay in an unhappy marriage. Which is all kind of interesting but I'm just not sure it has much to do with contemporary life or reality. I don't think people fall in love at first sight anymore and things don't seem to get tied up in neat bows at the end of anything.

What the big deal about opera is is probably beyond me. I'm sure it's hard to sing that way and memorize all the melodies and the rhythms and the words to the songs and the spoken parts, and I'm sure you need really good players in the orchestra, but other than that, I'm not sure what the point is. Plus, it's in German. Maybe you need to be German, or at least understand German to enjoy opera and find it relevant to contemporary life. Maybe life nowadays is just more complicated than it was over two hundred years ago.

But all the people in the audience in Austria must have been able to understand the German. They were all dressed up and seemed to be having a nice night out. Some people seem to really like opera which is obviously okay for them, but I guess I'm just not one of them.

In conclusion, because of the singing and the story and the costumes and the general oldness of it, I don't think opera is relevant to contemporary life.

Carly was going to add "Either that or I just don't get the point of it. Which may be true too." But she decided not to, even though she wasn't so sure. She submitted her paper and it was done. Maybe she'd get some extra credit after all. At least she wouldn't tick off Dr. Reed by not doing the paper at all. She felt relieved.

And she kept feeling better. She'd been thinking about it, and was getting used to the idea that maybe she hadn't really had sex with Don. It had been her first and only time. How was she supposed to know? It had been awfully quick, and it hadn't hurt like it was supposed to. Maybe she'd freaked out and somehow fooled her body into thinking she was pregnant.

A week later, when she was at school buying her books and registering for her classes, a couple of days before school was supposed to start, the secretaries told Carly Dr. Reed wouldn't be teaching AP Humanities. They said he'd "come into his inheritance" and was quitting teaching and "moving to San Francisco, or somewhere," which the secretaries seemed to think was hilarious. On her way to the bus, Carly ran into Dr. Reed in the faculty parking lot. She almost didn't recognize him. He was wearing a Hawaiian shirt, shorts and flip flops. His hair was all gelled up and he had sunglasses perched up on top of his head. Carly had never known Dr. Reed to wear anything other than a shirt and tie and, most times, a suit jacket.

"Carly! Hi!" he shouted and ran up to her and gave her a big hug, which he'd never done.

"You're leaving?" Carly almost complained.

"Yes. I am! I wasn't disinherited after all! Can you believe it? I can move back to civilization." Carly had never seen Dr. Reed so excited. "Your paper is very well argued. And you're absolutely right, opera is irrational, and exotic. But that's why we *love* it! Right? If I were staying, maybe I could change your mind."

"Mrs. Huston translated it for me and explained it to me." Carly felt a little defensive.

"A-hah! Dear old Nancy Huston. She can be a little literal, or maybe I should say literary. You didn't just click on the English subtitles option?" Dr. Reed gave Carly another hug, got into his car, which was a new convertible, waved and drove off.

With Dr. Reed gone, Carly wondered whether they'd need her to be the school pianist any more. Would the new AP Humanities teacher think she was smart? Would she get the good parts in the school plays and musicals? Would they even have school plays or musicals? Maybe she would need extra credit.

That night Sally Ann called to inform Carly that the word around school was Carly's mother had told Sister Marie Carly hadn't even had sex, never mind hadn't gotten pregnant and had an abortion.

"So now, everyone thinks either you're crazy or your mother's a liar. Or you're both."

The only word Carly could come up with for what she felt was panic. She didn't feel better like she'd begun to feel, she felt worse. What was it going to be like at school? Would she have any friends? Had she ever really had any friends, or did she just have people at school who hardly knew her but thought she was what, some kind of big deal, or admirable, or something? She felt as if she'd suddenly been dragged back into the nightmare of the last month. She hardly slept.

The next day, the last day before classes started, Carly mostly sat around worrying and dreading having to go back to school. She would have stayed home in her room all day if her mother hadn't insisted Carly go to the nursing home to say goodbye to the people there and to thank Mrs. Huston. When she got there, she went to Mrs. Huston's room, but it was empty. The bed had been stripped.

"Did Mrs. Huston get to move to her daughter's?" Carly asked one of the workers. "In Connecticut? Like she wanted to?"

"No, dear," the worker said, shaking her head. She paused before she finally said, "I'm afraid Mrs. Huston died."

"She did?" Carly gasped. Old people were supposed to die, but Carly felt like crying. "When?"

"Last night."

"Of what?"

"It's usually just one thing or a bunch of things. It's what happens. It's nature's way, sweetie. It's usually for the best."

Carly began crying and couldn't stop. She almost wailed. She was making a scene. Other nursing home people came running. She was supposed to be the smart one, the one who never made a scene or got in trouble or made a mistake. When was it going to end? She was supposed to be the one who learned from mistakes other people made. The nursing home people tried to calm her, but they weren't doing any good. Try as she might, she could not stop crying, and she couldn't figure out why.

Old Friends

"So how was your vacation?" Ralph asked before tilting his head to the side and squinting. "Wait. If you don't work, aren't you always on vacation?" He rubbed his chin and frowned. "You flew from Arizona to South Florida to, what, get a high school buddy to see a psychiatrist?"

Jim had mixed emotions about Ralph, the only lawyer he'd stayed in touch with after retiring. They enjoyed each other's company and still shared an admittedly sophomoric antipathy toward the practice of law and their fellow lawyers, which had gone a long way toward helping them survive what they called "their lot." But Ralph could be prickly during their lunch or cocktail hour visits.

"Didn't you say you should have been a psychologist, instead of a lawyer?" Ralph asked. Jim laughed.

"I should have been any number of other things. My mother wanted me to be a priest." Ralph feigned shock, sitting up straight and enlarging his eyes. "I made him an appointment, and he said he would be there, but he disappeared." Ralph turned his head to the side, narrowed his eyes and made his mouth and lips into a thin, straight line, his David Letterman "I told you so" look. "But I had my audience with the judge, my buddy from grade school, the Federal District Court judge," which didn't seem to register with Ralph. "So how are Linda and the kids?" Linda was Ralph's first wife with whom Ralph had two children. "And Stephanie?" Stephanie was Ralph's current wife.

"Oh, your buddy from grade school. Everybody's fine." Ralph looked around for the waitress. "You ask him what it's like getting full pay for the rest of his life?"

"He's the senior judge now."

"He can make all the other judges miserable."

"He does seem pretty content." Ralph tilted his head and almost guffawed.

"I bet."

"I visited him at his office. He rocked in his big, black, executive chair wearing his robe and held his hands under his nose with his fingertips touching." Jim placed his fingertips together and compressed his hands together like bellows. "Remember that joke, 'What's this?'"

"A spider doing pushups on a mirror."

"He did that most of the time."

"When they retire they get an office and a secretary for as long as they want." Ralph kept looking around. "They can even hear cases." There didn't seem to be a waitress anywhere on the floor of the busy lunch room, one of Ralph's preferred locations. Whenever they tried to get together, Ralph invariably had meetings scheduled for nearly every upcoming breakfast, lunch and cocktail hour, probably a hangover from their big firm days. They'd been in a senior partner's office for a conference call with a client, at the end of which the client asked the partner whether they could meet to discuss another matter. "Let me see what my calendar looks like," the partner said, lifting his appointment calendar off his credenza for Jim and Ralph to see before winking broadly. The calendar was blank for most of the month. He winked again and said in a kind of bravura voice, "I think I can fit you in. How about next Wednesday, around 4:30?" But Ralph seemed to be genuinely booked most of the time. He was flourishing on his own with a few large, loyal clients, making preposterous amounts of money by billing his time at a rate higher than lawyers in even the largest Phoenix firms. Plus, he kept his overhead low.

"He probably used that spider joke when we were in fourth grade. He had an older brother and sisters and brought a lot of jokes to school. There were seven kids in his family." Ralph looked at Jim.

"Mormons?" Jim and Ralph had worked with a number of Mormon lawyers, including a tax lawyer friend who was manic depressive, obsessive compulsive, and probably suffered from hyperactivity and attention deficit disorder. When at his desk, he'd play two or three hands of internet poker on his computer while advising clients over the speakerphone. But he was rarely at his desk, and once cell phones came in he was gone. Driving was his primary mania. Jim and Ralph thought he could drive around in an R.V., pick up his secretary and paralegal in the morning, have them man phones and work stations in the back while he'd drive and dispense advice over the phone through his headset. He could pick up clients who'd sit in the R.V.'s living room while he'd drive. He could put an air horn on the R.V. and blow it at all the other drivers on the road who, according to him, were — just like other lawyers — idiots and always doing something stupid.

Ironically, Ralph had implemented this M.O. but on a lesser scale. Although purporting to work in a friend's firm's offices, and although the firm's receptionist took messages for him, Ralph drove around town most of the day meeting clients at their offices or at a restaurant for a meal, coffee, or drinks. As had Jim, Ralph disliked sitting behind a desk like a metal duck in a county fair shooting gallery, targeted by an armed mob of opposing counsel, judges, bar officials, impatient clients, and, perhaps worst of all, disgruntled partners and employees.

"No Mormons in Miami. At least not back then. Catholics. I remember him, in fourth grade, saying of a girl in our class, 'I wouldn't kick her out of bed for eating crackers.' I had no idea what he was talking about."

"I eat crackers before going to bed," Ralph deadpanned. Jim laughed. Ralph had a large appetite and didn't object to Jim's calling him "Falstaffian." Ralph looked around the restaurant. "Do you suppose they've fired the wait staff and gone to self-serve?" One of Ralph's clients owned most of the retail and commercial buildings in old, downtown Scottsdale. It was a family operation begun by the now very elderly father and run by the less old but near retirement age son who'd wanted to be a minister rather than the landlord of dozens of tenants in the buildings his father had accumulated, which now generated piles of rent. Ralph was scanning the room as if totaling customers and calculating percentage rents. Perhaps Ralph had struck a deal to check on his client's properties by eating at the tenants' restaurants. Ralph tended to wander off at times.

"The judge's father was a World War II Marine pilot. A big, silver-haired guy. Flew at Midway."

"And thus, ending the war in the Pacific before it started," Ralph intoned in his Walter Cronkite impersonation.

"The pastor of our church had been his chaplain and buddy during the war. I'm pretty sure he got him the job." Ralph tuned back in.

"My old man spent the war in the Pacific being moved from base to base, then waiting for his orders to catch up to him. When he asked a guy whether he should do anything, the guy said, 'You wanna get killed? Keep your mouth shut.' He played cards a lot." Ralph opened the menu and scanned it. "My dad's a wise guy," Ralph chuckled, "and a Ford guy. He went on a camping trip with my Boy Scout troop and some of the other dads. The other dads pitched tents and slept on the ground like us kids. My father slept on a mattress in the back of our station wagon. It was raining the next morning and the other dads tried to start a fire on the ground, with wet wood. My dad pulls his big Coleman stove onto the tailgate of the station wagon and fixes a pot of coffee. He stands there in his mail carrier rain suit, under his umbrella, sipping his coffee, while the other fathers keep trying to light their regulation Boy Scout fire. 'You want some?' he asks them, 'it's goooood.'" Jim laughed.

"The judge's family had a Mercedes sedan, way before people even knew about them. Once we were in high school, they moved to a big house on an acre in a better part of town. He was a downtown banker, wore a suit, never did a thing around the house. Classic T.V. show dad. There were five girls and just two boys. The oldest girl was a really good-looking stewardess, made up like a doll, surprisingly sexy for a Catholic girl."

"Cain't judge a book by its dang cover, Jim." Ralph said in his Chill Wills-Slim Pickens-T.V. western character actor voice and pulled a toothpick out of the holder in the middle of the table. "No sir." Then he chuckled. "You missed something not growing up around them Mormon gals. Before they settle down, they can be more fun than a barrel of monkeys." Ralph picked his teeth then laughed. "Where did that expression come from?" before laughing again. "So, the judge was 'to the manor born.'" Ralph tilted his head and frowned. "Is it 'M-A-N-O-R' or 'M-A-N-N-E-R?' I've never really known."

"'E-R.' Shakespeare. 'Hamlet.'" Ralph shrugged, put down the toothpick and opened a cellophane-wrapped bread stick and began munching it.

"So, where'd your old man spend the war?"

"A tuberculosis sanatorium." Ralph nearly choked on his bread stick. Jim chuckled. "Got put in when he was sixteen and was thirty-three by the time he got out, at which point the war was almost over. Even then, he wasn't the picture of health. He wasn't a war hero. He kind of crouched when he walked, as if a safe was about to fall on him, probably because he'd had a lung removed. When he got home from work, he'd just eat dinner, read the newspaper in his La-Z-Boy, and head to bed. But he out-lived everybody in his generation. The judge's dad died of a heart attack in his fifties. His mother died of a broken heart a year later."

"That really happens?"

"She tried to jump into the coffin with the father when he died." Ralph's eyes got big.

"No kidding."

"That's what they said." Ralph did his Johnny Carson impersonation, tapping his fingers on the table and saying, "Hmmm."

A waitress appeared, set glasses of water on the table and pulled out a pen and her order book. Although she was a young, natural beauty, she had a quarter inch ring through one eyebrow, a pointy stud through one of her nostrils and a tattoo of a dragon climbing up her slender left arm and wrapping around her long, lovely neck.

"May I take your order?" she asked politely. Ralph looked at the tattoo and rubbed his chin.

"You know they use automotive paints in those?" The waitress cocked her head.

"I beg your pardon?"

"I said, I hear they inject automotive paints into people's skin to make tattoos."

"My fiancé does all mine." Ralph did a full Carson double take.

"You're marrying a guy who tattoos people? For a living? Is that a good idea?" The waitress, clearly flustered, blinked and looked at Jim and asked him what he'd like to have. Jim ordered a Cobb salad and a lemonade. She turned to Ralph who ordered a bacon cheeseburger with fries and an iced tea. The waitress thanked them, took their menus and walked away as if Ralph hadn't said anything out of the ordinary.

"Man, I hate tattoos, particularly on girls," Ralph muttered, shaking his head.

"Wasn't that a little harsh?"

"I got it from my old man." Ralph shrugged his shoulders and tilted his head. "He always annoys young people. When a Jehovah's Witness kid comes to the door or someone makes a cold call on the phone, he challenges them: 'Why aren't you in school? You need a college degree. You're selling yourself short.' He can be a bit of jerk about it."

"She's really good looking. Youth is wasted on the young." Ralph laughed and shook his head.

"I bet her fiancé" Ralph made quotation marks with his hands "is banging the hell out of her." Jim laughed but shook his head.

"Sometimes I wonder whether women crave sex as much as guys do, or at all."

"Really?" Ralph seemed genuinely stunned.

"I wonder whether they just indulge us and tolerate it."

"I guess I never thought of that!" Ralph exclaimed.

Ralph actually meant he thought Jim's comment was idiotic. Years ago, on a trip to meet with a client on the Texas-New Mexico border, they'd been driven through the oil patch by the client's gofer, Robert. As usual, Ralph chatted up Robert who, surprisingly, had a sister who was a partner in a massive, Houston-based, international law firm. "How old's your sister?" Ralph asked, to which Robert replied, "When I was ten she was fourteen." "So, she's still four years older than you?" Ralph volunteered, to which Robert eventually replied, "I guess I never thought of that." Another of their preferred shorthand phrases for skepticism or downright ridicule dated to their attending a bar luncheon where a blowhard they'd worked with at their big firm had asked a long, overly involved question of the guest speaker judge in an obvious attempt to impress the judge and the assembled lawyers. Once the question ended, the judge paused, looked down from the dais, pointed at the questioner's banquet lunch salad, and asked, "Did you already get salad dressing?" before pointing to another questioner.

The lunch with Ralph was going about as uncomfortably as it could. Which reminded Jim of another of his and Ralph's shorthand expressions. They'd strategized at great length once on how to present some bad news to a client during a conference call, at the end of which the client snarled and hung up, whereupon Ralph had said, "Well, that went about as badly as it could have."

"Another joke of his was to say to a girl, 'If I told you you have a beautiful body, would you hold it against me?' At least I understood that one." Ralph didn't react. "I think he also told me, when he was working as an assistant U.S. Attorney and I was about to go to law school, 'What do they call the first guy and the last guy in a medical school graduating class?'"

"'Doctor,'" Ralph responded, as if answering a question on a game show. "I heard the same line from a guy during our first week of law school. He ended up first in our class."

"I'm pretty sure the judge was close to last in his class." Ralph moved in his seat and became animated.

"So, what did he say when you asked him about the girl?"

Ralph had a nearly photographic memory. At their last lunch weeks before, Jim had mentioned the judge's grade school and high school girl-friend, who'd lived in Tucson for years and had never forgiven him for not marrying her after she'd had sex with him in high school upon his, at least as far as she was concerned, promising to marry her. She was still livid. Ralph read car magazines and memorized the specification sheets for the reviewed cars. Like most lawyers, Ralph enjoyed showing off his intellect, or at least his capacity for recalling and marshalling details. Jim had realized too late most lawyers are essentially, and excessively, competitive. Ralph had played football in high school as an undersized linebacker who'd enjoyed administering hits. He'd tried to walk on to the football team at Cal and lasted a few days until one of the coaches convinced him he could get seriously hurt by the bigger, faster, and stronger scholarship players, some of whom went on to have decorated professional careers. Which was a story Ralph loved to tell.

Jim had been sort of a jock as a kid himself. He'd played organized basketball in grade school and then high school until he'd realized he wasn't tall, quick, or athletic enough to be particularly good at that level, never mind play in college. So, to a certain extent, Jim and Ralph were both jocks, or worse, ex-jocks. But they weren't as bad as most lawyers, particularly the litigation partner at their big firm who wore cleats to the firm's no sliding lawyer league softball games and spiked opposing players. Their athletic and competitive days were a long-ago time in distant, prior lives.

Jim had also noticed lawyers love being better than other lawyers, primarily by pointing out that other lawyers are not good lawyers, or are wrong about something, or have made a mistake. Whenever Jim and Ralph's Mormon lawyer friend spoke of another lawyer, he'd invariably conclude by saying, "He's not a good lawyer." In his first year at his big firm, an old, very senior partner who twitched and stuttered had reviewed a stack of closing documents Jim had prepared and called Jim in. Jim sat down with the documents in a tall pile on the desk between him and the senior partner. The partner almost screamed. "There's a t-t-typo! R-r-right –" and peeled off half the documents and jammed his finger at a word in the middle of the exposed page, "HERE!" Mercifully, certainly for Jim, the partner died of a stroke a year later.

But one story Ralph told didn't fit the profile. He'd missed a hearing early in his career and was crestfallen. He went into the supervising partner's office and began with "Bert, I screwed–," but before Ralph could get any further, Bert held up his hand like a traffic cop, leaned over, pulled a beanie out of his desk's bottom drawer, put on the beanie and spun its propeller before saying, "Okay, go ahead." Although a very highly respected lawyer, Bert carried no weight in the firm. He'd been passed over thirteen years in a row before making partner.

Jim got on with the story, not wanting to lose Ralph's attention when he had it.

"He said he was in Tucson once at a judicial conference, years ago."

"Federal judges get flown to lavish resorts for conferences at least twice a year," Ralph explained, taking a sip of water.

"He looked her up in the phone book and almost called her, but then he didn't." Ralph almost spit out his water and erupted into a near guffaw before regaining his composure.

"Clearly," Ralph laughed, "he's judicious."

"'What would have been the point?' the judge said. Then he said, 'So you've figured women out?' I said, 'Maybe enough to know you don't tell them you'll marry them just to get them to have sex.'" Ralph tilted his head, grimaced, and shifted his eyes from side to side, mimicking

Danny DeVito feigning guilt. Then he laughed.

"You don't?" Both Jim and Ralph laughed.

"Then he did that spider thing and said, 'Last I heard, years ago, after we graduated from college, she was living in Taos, New Mexico, smoking dope and going down like a democratic drawbridge.'"

"*The Lion in Winter*. Peter O'Toole. Katherine Hepburn." Except for car magazines, Ralph hated to read to the extent Jim suspected Ralph was at least mildly dyslexic. He watched movies. He'd wanted to be an actor. "He really used that line?" Ralph asked. Jim nodded. "So, he dodged a bullet."

"She's as nice as can be and smart, but I'm pretty sure she's clinically depressed. Runs in her family. But she manages it. Married and divorced, twice." Ralph opened another cellophane breadstick and took a bite.

"So that's why he dumped her?"

"Maybe more the result than a justification."

"Clinical depression?" Ralph did a Johnny Carson, wide-eyed double take and sat up straight. Jim expected Ralph to tap the breadstick on the table like Carson did with his pencil, or do his "Casablanca" "I'm shocked, shocked I tell you!" thing, but he seemed genuine. Then again, one of Jim's favorite lines was Louis Mayer's (or whoever's) "When you can fake sincerity you've got something" line. "You really think," Ralph almost gasped, bug-eyed, "being dumped induces mental illness? In women?"

"The judge said the same thing." Ralph tilted his head to the side. "You don't think being mistreated by guys can make girls licentious?"

"Sometimes you do stupid things when you're in love."

"You were in love with the girls you dumped?" Ralph shook his head.

"It's from a Bob Dylan documentary. He said that when they asked him why he'd publicly humiliated Joan Baez. You're saying the judge should have married her just because he had sex with her? I thought depression ran in the family." The waitress showed up with set ups and the lemonade and iced tea and put them in front of Ralph and Jim.

"Let's avail ourselves of an expert," Ralph announced, turning to the waitress and gazing up to her pleasantly. "If you had sex with a guy who'd promised to marry you, then he changed his mind and didn't marry you, would you be angry with him for, oh, say, the next thirty or forty years?" The waitress was taken aback and nearly glared. Ralph looked at her benignly, batting his eyes.

"What's having sex got to do with getting married?" she scoffed before walking away. A huge grin on his face, Ralph leaned over and touched Jim on his fore arm.

"There!"

"Oh, come on, Ralph, she lives in a different world than we grew up in." Ralph laughed. "Nobody other than guys in the navy and mechanics got tattoos when we were kids."

"But it's what guys did. Was she entitled to rely on anything a high school kid would say? In that dire a situation?" Which was essentially the argument Jim would make if he had wanted to press the point with her. "All she had to do was wait until they were married." Ralph took the paper napkin, unfolded it, and tucked it into his collar. He could be fastidious about certain things. "What else did the judge say?"

"He said he didn't recall promising her anything. It was his first time too. And it wasn't all that great." Ralph shrugged.

"It takes practice. So, how'd he dump her?"

"Just stopped calling her and avoided her." Ralph wiggled in his chair and leaned forward.

"I'd tell them something vague like I wouldn't be seeing them anymore." Jim had heard this story before, but it was funny. "They'd usually blurt out, 'It's my ankles, isn't it!' or 'It's my hips!' I'd act non-committal, they'd burst into tears, and, presto change-o, that would be that." Ralph sat back in his seat. "But, you know, there was this one girl. I told her I wouldn't be seeing her anymore and she said, 'Why?' I acted non-committal, but she kept pushing for an explanation." Ralph paused, then shrugged. "But other than that one time, it worked great."

Jim couldn't be certain which of Ralph's tales were made up, but common acquaintances who'd known Ralph in high school or college or law school verified many of his exploits. Jim continued.

"I asked him if he felt guilty and he said, 'She thought I was serious?' Then he did the spider thing and said, 'Wasn't it just a game?' He wears those Ben Franklin reading glasses down on his nose and looks over them." The managing partner at Jim and Ralph's big firm, like lots of other big-shot trial lawyers, affect the same intimidating look.

Ralph laughed.

"He may be right. A guy next door to us smoked like a chimney. His wife wouldn't let him smoke inside so he was always out in his carport, even when it was over a hundred. He'd tell stories to anybody, even us little kids. He'd almost always mention how he was engaged to this woman or that woman. One day I asked him why he'd been engaged to so many women. He coughed out some cigarette smoke and said, 'How do you get women to have sex?' I was about twelve. Great guy. Toward the end he'd sit there with oxygen tubes in his nose while he smoked. Surprised he never blew himself up." Ralph wandered off topic when he was bored.

"I asked him, 'Are you going to apologize to her?'" Ralph wagged his finger.

"Never admit a mistake and never apologize." Which was how Ralph and Jim had been sternly admonished by the schoolmarm-ish senior associate they'd trained under.

"He said, 'What good would that do?' So, I asked him about Silvio Sebastiani, and he said, 'Silvio who?'"

"Who?"

"The main thing I wanted to ask him about." Ralph stared blankly. "The gay kid in sixth grade I told you about. I reminded him how we'd followed him home shouting at him and then we spat on him, right in front of his mother when she opened the door to let him in. He said, 'What happened to us?' 'Nothing,' I said. Nobody ever said a word. His mother must have complained to the school, but no one said a word, none of the teachers, not the principal, not the pastor, his dad's buddy, nobody. 'Hm. So what happened to the guy?' he asked.

"'Gone the next day. Never came back,' I said. He sat there rocking. 'We were bullies,' I said. 'You think so?' he said. 'We spit on him,' I said. 'Whose idea was that?' he asked. 'Yours,' I said. 'You started it. I joined in. I'm not sure which is worse.' 'I might remember him,' he said, finally. 'Walked like a girl, wiggled his butt. Had his hair all, what, pomaded? Is that the right term? Looked as if he was wearing lipstick and rouge. Definitely light in the loafers.' 'So? We terrorized the guy,' I said.

"'You're sure it was me,' he said, turning around in his chair to look out the window. 'Of course, it was you,' I said. He turned back around, reached in his desk and took out a toothpick and picked his front teeth, like ol' George?" Jim and Ralph both laughed. Years ago, Ralph had recounted interning in Congress and seeing then Vice President George H. W. Bush exit his motorcade and spryly scamper up the Capitol building steps three at a time. Reaching the top of the steps, he paused, pulled his toothpick out of his mouth to give the bystanders a jaunty salute, placed his toothpick back in his mouth and disappeared inside to preside over a joint session of Congress, a job certainly Ralph, and likely George Bush, Sr. himself, considered the world's least demanding but most prestigious, an unbeatable Quinella.

"'And nothing ever happened to us?' he asked. 'He must have had to move out of the parish,' I said. He rocked his chair a little and said, 'The experts say until they're civilized, kids can be pretty savage.' He turned back and put the toothpick down and leaned forward with both his arms on his desk and folded his hands with his fingers interlocked like a kid praying at his desk. 'Not that I'm saying we did anything, but maybe we were doing what was expected of us.' I said, 'You're supposed to enforce anti-discrimination laws?'"

"You said that?" Ralph asked. Jim nodded.

"He said, 'Prosecutors enforce laws, judges just referee.'" Ralph nodded.

"Justice Roberts' line."

"Then he got almost chatty. 'We were just bit players,' he said. 'The important people were guys like Kennedy and Castro. All those Hispanic kids washing up on our shore and into our lives. We were what, eleven or twelve?' I said, 'He wasn't Cuban, he was Colombian.'"

"How do you remember all this stuff?" Ralph asked.

"There were people from throughout Central and South America in Miami before the Castros came to power. The judge didn't slow down. 'It was a different time,' he said. 'Homosexuals were considered a threat to society. The Church still considers homosexual activity sinful.' Then he paused. 'So, we should have been thrown in juvenile detention for assault?' I said, 'Something should have happened. Certainly not nothing.' He said, 'Maybe the adults thought we were doing the right thing.' 'We were sixth grade vigilantes?' I said. 'Maybe the adults didn't know any more what to make of the kid than we did. Didn't he look like he was wearing makeup?' He looked out his window. 'Times change,' he said, after a pause. 'But it was incredibly cruel.' I said. All he did was shrug his shoulders. Eventually, he spun back toward me.

"'She's clinically depressed?' he asked. 'It's supposed to be treatable with medicine and therapy,' he said. 'Something must have warned me away from her.' I said, 'But it was a pretty rotten thing to do. She's certainly taken it hard all these years.' And then, get this, he turns away and looks out his window and says, 'I believe in the forgiveness of sin.'"

"He said what?" Ralph's eyes had been wandering the room. Jim was a little surprised Ralph was even paying attention. The waitress brought their food without incident. Ralph dug in.

"It's from 'The Credo,' a prayer, Latin for 'I believe.' It lists the things Catholics are supposed to believe. One of the main things listed is 'I believe in the forgiveness of sin.'"

"Humph," Ralph managed.

"'So, you've confessed it?' I asked him. 'It?' he said. 'The Silvio whatever-his-name-was thing? I don't remember it. We were just kids.' I said, 'But what about the age of reason?'"

"The Eighteenth Century," Ralph volunteered despite having a mouth full of food. "Or was that the Age of Enlightenment?"

"In Catholicism, before you're seven, you can't commit a sin. After seven, you're on the hook. It's the age of reason." Ralph chewed, then swallowed.

"First grade?" he asked. Jim nodded.

"I asked him if he felt any guilt about either the girl or the gay kid and he said, 'Guess I'll have to confess them when I go to confession.'" Ralph swallowed.

"What is that, exactly, that confession thing?"

"It's a sacrament."

"What's that?" Ralph asked before taking another bite of his burger.

"A Ritual. There's a bunch of them, not just baptism. They're what makes Catholicism different from Protestantism. Well, that and Mass and saints and statues." Ralph wiped his mouth with his napkin and sat back.

"Tell me how this confession thing works." Misdirection and distraction were negotiating techniques Ralph and Jim had learned from one of the partners at their big firm, but Ralph could also focus unexpectedly. "In our church, there was a lot of 'repent for this and repent for that,' and 'the wages of sin are death.' What does that even mean? But nobody ever admitted to doing any specific thing wrong."

"It's confidential. You go to a priest and tell him the sins you've committed and he waves his hand so when you die you go to Heaven. If you've committed certain sins and haven't confessed them, you go to hell. Those are 'mortal sins.'"

"Like what?"

"Murder, theft, sexual offenses, infidelity." Ralph raised his eyebrows.

"You believe in this stuff?" Jim waived his free hand.

"I haven't been to church since I got my driver's license. I'd disappear on Sunday morning, and my parents would assume I was going to church, or at least I assumed they did."

"But the judge still believes in this stuff?"

"Evidently. He says he does."

"And this confession thing, it works for everything?"

"They take confessions of guys they're about to execute, at least in movies."

"So that's what that's all about."

The waitress appeared and asked whether everything was all right.

"Well, Darlin' that depends now, don't it?" Ralph said, wiping his mouth with his napkin before putting his hands on the table and looking up into the waitress's face. "Are you going to school?" The waitress frowned questioningly. "Well, then things aren't all right. You need to get an education. You can't support a family without an education."

"I have a daughter. I don't have time to work and go to school."

"Then you need to quit working, so you can go to school." The waitress frowned again.

"That's easy for you to say."

"Yes, it is," Ralph said, laughing, "I did just say that, didn't I? But that doesn't make it any less true." The waitress turned and walked into the kitchen. Ralph picked up his burger. "So, if you screw up, you just do this confession thing and it's as if it didn't happen?"

"It's a little more complicated than that, theologically. You have to believe in God and an afterlife, for example." Ralph chewed on a bite of his burger, then washed it down with some iced tea before shaking his head.

"I'm not sure my old man believed any of the stuff he went on about. I think he just liked telling people what to do. Was your father religious?" Jim shook his head.

"He helped around the parish, but never attended church. He'd been brought up going to church, but I think he felt too guilty to go to church as an adult."

"Guilty of what?" Ralph said before taking another sip of tea.

"Fratricide." Ralph almost spit out his tea. Jim laughed before continuing. "When he was eleven, he told his father a bolt was loose on the big Snidely Whiplash buzz saw they were using to cut up firewood. But he didn't insist his father tighten it, and he didn't tighten it himself. Pretty soon the bolt came completely loose and the shaft of the saw, which they were running off a belt from a tractor, pops out of its bracket. The saw jumps up, and gashes his father in the face, and takes out one of his eyes."

"Jesus."

"But he survives. They take him to the hospital and stitch him up. He's there for a week or so before they drove him home in an open car. This is in the early nineteen twenties. The wound gets infected, and in a few days, he dies, leaving my father and his little sister, who had already lost their mother to tuberculosis, orphans." Ralph shook his head. "He never talked about it. They had to sell the farm. Literally. Then, his last year in high school he contracts tuberculosis and, like I said, he spends the next seventeen years in the sanatorium. They took out one of his lungs and a bunch of ribs. I figure he thought he was the last person on earth who should be hanging around a church. He must have considered himself a murderer." Ralph shook his head and raised his index finger.

"Every Sunday morning my old man drove us into the rising sun to the other side of Globe, so he could drive a school bus around the reservation, picking up all the women. Ever seen the reservation outside Globe?" Jim nodded. "Makes Mexico look like Sweden. While the men were sleeping off their Saturday night benders, the women were more than happy to ride on a bus and sit through a couple of hours of bible study. Then my mother and my brothers and I would serve them a lunch my mother would prepare while my Dad was lecturing the women. Then they'd pile back on the bus and my father would drop them all off at their houses, such as they were. We'd get back in the station wagon and drive home into the setting sun. I'd do math problems in my head to pass the time during his services. The Navajo women just sat with their eyes closed, nodding. Maybe they were doing math problems in their heads."

"What was your Dad atoning for?"

"My old man? Never made a mistake in his life. Completely risk averse. One Sunday he just stopped doing the mission thing. Hasn't been inside a church since. I have no idea whether he believed any of that stuff."

"Late in life, my father converted to Catholicism and started going to Mass. Maybe he forgave himself. Maybe he confessed it and was forgiven." Jim took a sip of his lemonade. "What do you do about screw-ups you've been involved in?"

"Me?"

"You've never done anything you shouldn't have done, anything you've regretted?" Ralph had told Jim lots of stories of his younger, bolder days, most involving fisticuffs or sexual conquests. Ralph squinted and then cleared his throat.

"So, this confession thing. How do you do it, exactly?"

"You go into this closet and kneel down so your mouth's at the level of a screen you can talk through but can't see through and the priest sits in the closet next door. You say, 'Bless me Father, for I have sinned.'"

"Your father?"

"It's what you call a priest.

"Oh. Like guys in westerns calling priests 'Padre.'"

"Then you say, 'It has been X number of days, or weeks, since my last confession.' Then you list off all the sins you've committed."

"What happens if you haven't sinned?"

"There's always something to confess when you're Catholic."

"Then what?"

"The priest recites some boiler plate and tells you to say some prayers as penance. Then he blesses you by moving his hand around and says, 'Go and sin no more.'" Ralph grinned and rubbed his hands together.

"Let's give it a try. I'll be Padre Ralph. You confess your sins to me, and I'll forgive them."

"It won't be anonymous." Ralph spread his hands out, held them upright and broke into his stock football coach impersonation.

"It's just me, your ol' Padre Ralph, son." Jim laughed.

"When I was in law school, a harried lawyer from downtown warned me in passing that if I ever made a mistake, another lawyer would put his foot on my neck and never let me up. Not a happy guy. I assumed he'd just had some bad luck, or wasn't smart enough. You know the difference between practicing law and practicing medicine?"

"When you're a surgeon, there's not another doctor in the operating room trying to kill the patient." So, Ralph had already heard that line. Maybe he'd told it to Jim.

"When they taught us how to go to confession, the nuns said we should make up three sins for the practice confession they heard. I used those same three sins for every confession I made for the next five or so years. They were, 'I was angry, I used profanity,' and one other."

"So, you didn't confess the thing with the gay kid?"

"Never occurred to me. I only started thinking about it a few years ago, when bullying became a thing."

"And you never dumped any girls?"

"I never thought of that." They both laughed. "Maybe I didn't pursue things with girls who had hoped I would, but no, I never dumped any of the very few girls I was in a relationship with, or hoped I was. But my college roommate mentioned how embarrassed he was that he'd dumped his college girlfriend long distance by leaving her a message on her answering machine."

"I never thought of that," Ralph said. Jim laughed.

"Did any girls ever dump you?" Jim asked.

"No."

"Didn't Linda cheat on you during your divorce?" Ralph stopped with his tea half way to his mouth and looked right at Jim.

"That's different," he said, taking a sip.

"And you never forgave her."

"Not really," Ralph said, shaking his head before almost chuckling. "No."

"You don't believe in the forgiveness of sin." Ralph laughed.

"So, all you have to do in this confession thing is tell a guy what you've screwed up, and you're good to go?" Jim nodded. "Makes no sense."

"Makes sense if you believe it. We were pickled in all that stuff."

"But what if you don't believe in guilt, or even sin." Ralph had cleaned his plate and pulled a fresh toothpick out of the little holder in the center of the table and unwrapped it. "Seems pretty simple to me," he said, popping the toothpick into his mouth. "When you're dead, you're dead. All the stuff about an afterlife and souls and so forth just seems to get in the way." He picked his teeth a little before continuing. "Why'd you get out of the practice of law?"

"I was tired."

"I'm tired, but I doubt I'll ever be able to re-tire."

"I didn't trust myself. Plus, I made mistakes I didn't even know were mistakes."

"Like what?"

"I'm not going to tell you," Jim blurted before regaining his composure. "Let's put it this way, I worried about screwing up."

"That's what malpractice insurance is for." Ralph resumed his coach impersonation, talking with the toothpick in the corner of his mouth. "Come on now, son, it'll do you good to get it off your chest. Just give me the details." Ralph reached over and patted Jim's hand.

"You'd make a good interrogator for the cops."

"Yes, I would," Ralph belly laughed.

"I asked Ray Hunter once if he worried about screwing up." Ray was a Harvard Law grad Jim and Ralph had worked with. "He was astounded. Said he'd never considered the possibility he'd ever made a mistake."

"Ray's been sued for malpractice and the bar's had to investigate him for complaints. There's got to be a statute of limitations on the sort of things you're talking about. Witnesses die, memories fade."

"There's no statute of limitation on sins that I know of. Maybe I wasn't smart enough to be a lawyer. I got snookered by clients a few times."

"Is that a sin?" Jim knew that was a good question. "The public holds us in contempt, but lawyers act as if they're each more ethical than the other and we're all as pure as the driven snow. People don't understand, we're hired assholes." Jim laughed and Ralph continued. "So, you argued with the priest during your confessions?" Ralph slipped back into Padre Ralph the football coach, scratching his chin. "So, son, were you ever sued for that there whatchyamacallit… malpractice?"

"Once, but not for anything I'd done, or not done. Another guy in the firm had supervised a paralegal who'd done some research and sent it to the client. The client ignored it, got into trouble, then sued for bad advice. I'd done a bunch of subsequent work for the client and they'd come to think of me as their lawyer. By the time they'd sued, I'd left the firm, so the firm tried to pin it on me. Eventually, they stopped rattling my cage and even settled with the client. They shouldn't have, but the lawyer defending them was one of those guys who just settles." Ralph wagged his finger at Jim.

"You're trying to distract Ol' Padre Ralph, son. Maybe you need to forgive yourself like they say on them talk shows on the Tee-Vee. You're more than your mistakes." Ralph chuckled and came out of character. "That's a pretty good line. I coulda' been somethin'. I coulda been a priest!"

"For an effective confession, you're supposed to do all you can to redress your wrong. But undoing a mistake usually has an adverse impact on a client, or your insurance carrier. Did you ever–"

"I'm the priest here, son. I'm not confessing, you are." As was Jim, Ralph seemed to be getting a little irritated. "Not disclosing a mistake would be fraud." They looked at each other for a while and Jim took a sip of water. Ralph was the first to speak.

"Sometimes you make an inadvertent mistake. No one admits it, but it's the truth." Jim couldn't tell whether Ralph was playing a character. "Anyone ever told you you think too much, son?"

"Maybe it's just better I'm not a lawyer anymore," Jim said. "Maybe it's my penance. At least financially." Ralph shrugged and tilted his head. Jim continued. "My piano teacher always told me everybody makes mistakes and I should make my mistakes with conviction."

"Practicin' law and playin' the piano is differnt, son."

"Yeah," Jim chuckled, "I've never really understood that one."

"What do they say about stock car racing? If you ain't cheatin' you ain't tryin'? Reading the cases in the bar magazine, it seems the only two things bar associations care about are if you steal a client's money, actual cash on hand, or you don't return clients' calls because you're on a bender."

"What about Denny Fox?" Denny was a partner at Jim and Ralph's big firm who'd withheld key evidence in a case and been kicked out of the firm.

"Had breakfast with Denny. He said he knew he was taking one for the team when he did it and they'd throw him under the bus, but he was okay with it since he knew he'd get run off sooner or later for wanting a fair draw. Plus, they tossed him a bone. He died last year. Heart attack." Ralph took a drink of water before continuing. "So how long you been retired now?"

"Fifteen years."

"How's the writing going?"

"Slow."

"Sold anything?" Jim shook his head. "Finish anything?"

"Sort of."

"Did I ever tell you what my Chinese roommate at Cal said to us when a bunch of us were sitting around talking about how famous we were going to be in Hollywood while he was doing his engineering homework?"

"'If you not a genius by the time you twenty, you never be a genius.'"

"Told you that one." They laughed. "What was it your high school girl friend said when you told her you wanted to be a writer?" Ralph asked.

"'Why would anyone want to do something that will only make you famous once you're dead.'" They both laughed. "Woody Allen wants to become immortal by living forever." Wanting to get things back on topic, Jim continued. "At a loan closing we were sitting around telling stories while waiting for word from the title company the documents had recorded. The lender's lawyer, Bill Avon, told everyone, including his lender client, how when he was young and running a closing, he was gathering up the loan documents and noticed one of the borrowers hadn't signed something. Of course, that particular borrower had already left for the airport. This was before cell phones. The other borrowers all acted concerned and asked Bill whether he couldn't give them a minute alone to discuss the situation. He said 'sure' and stepped outside the conference room. After a few minutes, they let him back in and, 'lo and behold,' those were his exact words, the document had been signed after all. Everyone was delighted, particularly Bill, and he proceeded to close the loan." Jim shook his head and Ralph chuckled. "And he told this to other lawyers and title people, even his lender client!" Ralph waived his hand.

"I missed filing for a deficiency against a guy I'd foreclosed on for the bank. I was really sweating it. I go see the collections guy at the bank and say I screwed up. He says, 'Ah, he probably isn't good for it anyway. How's Linda?'" Jim shook his finger.

"My old piano tuner gets called to a Catholic boys' high school when he lived back in New Jersey. They had an old, but really good make of grand piano in the gym, of all places. It was a little beat up on the outside but he opens it up and it's not in bad shape. Perfect for a rebuild, but there's a crack in the soundboard. He sighs, shakes his head and looks at the priest. 'Is it bad?' the priest asks. A cracked soundboard sounds like a car having a blown engine, but it's not really a big deal, particularly if a piano's going to be rebuilt anyway. 'It's bad, Father,' the tuner says as if he's a surgeon who's found cancer and is about to sew the patient back up. 'The soundboard's cracked.' The priest gasps. 'Is there anything we can do?' 'I can have somebody haul it away for you,' the tuner offers. 'That would be great! How much will it cost?' 'I'll take care of it, Father.' 'God bless you, my son.' He sold the piano to a rebuilder later that day for seventy-five hundred bucks. And this guy was a nice Catholic boy. High strung though, smoked like a chimney. Died of a stroke in his forties. Why would he tell a story like that on himself?

"And then there was our handyman. He gave me a deal on cutting down a dead mesquite in our yard thinking he could take the trunk to a sawmill and more than make up the difference. He cuts down the tree and hauls a big log down to the sawmill in his pickup. He wheels into the mill yard and asks the guy what he'll give him for it. The mill guy shakes his head and says, 'Can't use it.' 'You can't?' 'Nope. It's a velvet mesquite.' My guy's disappointed but the mill guy says, 'But you can leave it here.' And he did and was happy enough to tell me about it."

Once they both stopped laughing, Ralph started in again.

"So how would it go? You'd say, 'Bless me Padre Ralph,' or just 'Father,' for I have sinned. It has been,' what, 'fifty years since my last confession?'"

"There's also the concept of mercy. They say, 'Lord have mercy,' right in the mass. It's the Kyrie, which is Greek, for some reason. The rest of the mass is in Latin. They say, 'Lord have mercy, Christ have mercy, Lord have mercy.' I'm not sure what the difference is between 'Lord' and 'Christ.' It's part of all the big masses. Mozart, Beethoven, Bach." Ralph frowned.

"If God is supposed to have mercy on you, why do you have to confess your sins?"

"You have to acknowledge your sins before they can be forgiven." Ralph grimaced and drummed his fingers.

"God doesn't know people screw up?" Jim laughed but Ralph didn't.

"He's all-knowing."

"Must be comforting," Ralph said, "believing there's a God who's looking over everything, helping you score a touchdown, or waiting for you to die so you can live happily ever after with him some place nice." Ralph shook his head before continuing. "I hear Mormons believe every guy gets his own planet when he dies."

"We memorized all sorts of Latin as altar boys," Jim said, "responses to what the priest would say. I suppose we had some idea what we were saying. I think it was translated on the cards they gave us to memorize from, or to use as cheat sheets if we forgot. But that was frowned upon. Occasionally a priest would call out somebody for just mumbling and slurring, but we didn't have to know what it meant. It wasn't until after I'd quit going to church regularly that they switched to English, and the stuff sounded pretty dumb when you heard the actual meaning. And we make fun of the Islamic schools for making kids memorize the Koran rather than learning how to read or write or do math." Jim laughed. "Maybe it's the comfort of repetition, or just saying something out loud. The words were antiphonal responses, not just memory exercises. It was part of a ceremony. I guess there's something calming and re-assuring about a ceremony. I'm sure Joseph Campbell had some sort of profound comment on that. Probably psychically beneficial. Good for you. Contemplative, meditative. The comfort of just saying things out loud, over and over again. Telling the same stories over and over again."

"Joseph Campbell?" Ralph asked and frowned.

"I went by my old church when I was there in Miami. It's a former military chapel from the World War Two air base in Sebring, where they run the twelve-hour car race every year. The government threw it up during the war. The Catholic diocese had it disassembled and hauled down to Miami and reassembled there. Probably paid a dollar for it. My father actually hauled the furnace down on a truck he borrowed from his work, which was considered an almost mythically heroic act in the founding of the parish. I never saw the furnace. Why they thought they'd need a furnace for a church in Miami, or even Sebring, is beyond me. It must have been built to some sort of standard Pentagon specification. Might have even had a basement in Sebring. A mystery, I guess. It's a childcare facility now. They built a new church in front of it about the time the judge and I went off to separate high schools. When we were kids, they used it for the only Polish mass in the diocese. All the Poles who'd been displaced during the war and were living in Miami would come. We'd serve their masses, as altar boys. Latin for the Mass and then the sermon and announcements in Polish. The entire hour was incomprehensible. We always had at least one Polish priest on staff. They could hardly talk to us but we got by. One of them would use his little finger to make sure we poured all the wine into the chalice." Ralph didn't seem to think this was as funny as Jim did. "Did I ever tell you about the Polish kid I had when I taught ninth grade English? He brought in snap shots his family had of corpses at Dachau or Auschwitz. He shows them to me and says, 'Kind of makes you glad we're Catholic, huh?'" Jim laughed but Ralph didn't.

"And you believed that stuff?" Ralph asked, exasperated. Jim held up his hand and began reciting.

"I believe in one God, the Father almighty, creator of heaven and earth, in Jesus Christ, his only Son, conceived by the Holy Spirit, born of the Virgin Mary, who under Pontius Pilate was crucified, died and was buried. He descended into hell and on the third day rose again from the dead. He ascended into heaven and is seated at the right hand of the Father. He will come again to judge the living and the dead. I believe in the Holy Ghost, the holy Catholic Church, the communion of saints, the forgiveness of sins, the resurrection of the body, and life everlasting." Jim even added an "Amen."

"What was that?"

"The Credo thing I told you about. Latin for 'I believe.' We learned it in school." Ralph frowned.

"And you still remember it?" Jim nodded, a little surprised himself. "From what, half a century ago?" Jim nodded and chuckled.

The manager, who Ralph knew, approached the table with the check. "I think I owe you from last time," Ralph said to Jim. "I'll pay for both of us."

"Hello, Mr. Cavelo," the manager said to Ralph, laying the bill on the table. "How was everything today?"

"Fine, Timmy. But what happened to our waitress? She disappeared on us. Which isn't necessarily a bad thing, but some people might need something."

"I think she quit," Timmy said. Ralph feigned surprise. "Took off her apron and walked out the back door. Didn't say a word."

"Huh," Ralph said, looking at the bill and pulling out some twenties and placing them on the bill. "You've gone back to school, right?"

"Soon," Timmy admitted.

"That's not good enough, Tim. You don't want to be wrangling waitresses, cooks and dishwashers your entire life, do you?"

"Right, Mr. Cavelo," Timmy said with a smile and a nod before picking up the bill and the twenties and walking away. Ralph looked at Jim, who began again.

"Anyway, the day I was reminded of was cold, for Miami, like it can be cold in the winters here. The sky was that pale, clear, endless blue. I'd been serving a funeral mass. We'd usually get to ride out to the cemetery for the interment so we'd be out of class for almost the whole morning. Sometimes we'd even get tips. After spending the whole morning around a casket and undertakers and hearses and mourners in a dark, cold church, hearing about death and judgement and eternal life accompanied by all sorts of sobbing – it was absolutely Dickensian and I was pretty young and impressionable – I remember coming back from the cemetery and heading back to school and looking up at that sky and thinking I could see Heaven, and God, and all the saints, right there." Jim paused and Ralph just looked at him. "The conversation ground to a halt," Jim would have written in one of his stories. Or perhaps, "There was a prolonged silence."

"So," Ralph eventually said, grimacing, "you're not going to confess your sins so your Ol' Padre Ralph can forgive them and wipe your slate clean?" Jim shook his head. "Even though you know everything about me." There was another prolonged silence as they looked right at each other. Finally, as he stood up to leave Ralph pointed at Jim's salad.

"Did you already get salad dressing?"

Jim looked at his salad, which he hadn't really eaten very much of because he'd been talking so much, then looked at Ralph. They stared at each other some more before it was Jim's turn.

"Well, I guess this lunch went about as badly as it could have."

After another painfully long pause, they both broke into a good, long laugh. After shaking Jim's hand, Ralph headed out the door to his car and Jim finally focused on his salad.

Juvenilia

The author, New Haven, Connecticut, Labor Day Weekend, 1973.
Photograph- Alan R. Freidman, Esq.

Portrait of the Artist as a Young Jerk

Louise had been battling symbolic representations of Quentin's decline all day. Washing dishes, she'd envisioned her younger son as a piece of silverware approaching irreparable damage in the garbage disposal. Typing, he was a word extending beyond the margin, past the edge of the paper, onto the roller, and into oblivion. Although she could admit he was a disappointment, she held off concluding he was "going down the drain" or "over the edge." But as he failed to appear and the day progressed, her optimism had waned. By the time he arrived, in a cab of all things (What an extravagance. Why hadn't he just called for them to pick him up?) she went into the living room expecting the worst.

All she could think was he was a mess. His hair was oily and hung well over his collar. His beard was unkempt. He seemed as wild-eyed as ever. She gave herself credit for being able to see past appearances but, as she had feared she would, she found what Quentin was saying more objectionable than his appearance. He was lecturing his father about everything a person could learn about a nation by looking at it from thirty-five thousand feet in an airplane going six hundred miles an hour.

"Whitman would have given his eyeteeth for a chance to do that!"

She'd learned there was no point in contradicting Quentin well before he'd gone to college. She let him ramble on, confining his remarks to geography and poetry until he concluded with his first display of discontent. "It was clear, absolutely clear, until we began our descent into Phoenix. As soon as I get close to home, BOOM! Dust storms are building up!"

He looked at her for the first time. Ignoring Quentin's outstretched hand, Louise planted a kiss on his fuzzy cheek. She knew he had an aversion to being home. He'd only been home twice during his year away, which she'd expected but had found harder to take than she'd anticipated. His leaving the nest didn't bother her as much as did his use of innuendo. He could very well not come home often if only he didn't resent every minute he was home, and take every opportunity to impress upon his parents the fact he'd rather be someplace else. If he would be honest, she could take it.

But there was also his muddle-headedness. Despite his loquaciousness, he rarely seemed to know what he wanted to say. Before thinking any further, she said "We've had a good monsoon season this year."

"But Mom, it's about to dust storm. It looks dry as a bone. As usual." She'd said the wrong thing.

"Sometimes there's more to things than meets the eye, Quentin." This was not the correct response. Quentin's father, Lon, less a visionary than his son, and less attuned to his precarious state, redirected the conversation in an even less promising direction.

"How much did it cost, your plane ride?"

This topic was much more prickly than the weather. To date, Quentin had shown little grace in his dealings with money. He insisted on making it into more than it was. He'd made a fuss when he left for college about how much he should get for spending money and there had been tenderness ever since.

"I paid for it by check."

"That doesn't tell me how much it cost."

After Quentin's Easter vacation visit, Louise had asked Lon whether he noticed how often money came up in their conversations with Quentin. "What else is there to talk about?" he'd replied. "I don't want to talk about the weather and he's not interested in hearing about anyone in the family. He knows too damned much more than I do about what he knows. Finding out if he has enough money is the only thing I can ask him." As far as Louise was concerned, there was little to be said to Quentin about money.

"Your Aunt Hattie's coming home today." Upon saying this, Louise realized the subject was potentially as volatile as money.

"Where's she been?"

Louise had hit upon another sore spot. Upon graduating from high school, Quentin had decided he was ready for extensive travel. He'd wanted to "expatriate." The idea had been vetoed with little debate, with Louise saying if Quentin got through a year of college, they would gladly finance any summer semester abroad his college sponsored. Quentin never brought it up again and had spent the summer writing in a dormitory and painting houses, or something. Louise also didn't like Quentin's attitude toward his aunt. In fourth grade, without explanation, he'd named his pet guinea pig "Hattie."

"Camping in Northern Minnesota. The Thousand Lakes."

"How's she like it?"

"She doesn't care much for the mosquitos." Louise and Lon had received a postcard reading: "Mosquitos numerous and the size of WWII bombers. Accommodations rustic. Cold in morning, mid-day heat wilts everything. Cigarettes expensive." Louise didn't feel like giving Quentin any more grist for his mocking mill.

"She's surprisingly spunky, that Hattie. She must have saved money by camping."

"The camping cost an extra two hundred dollars compared to just staying in a cabin." This of course from her husband.

"You two should do things like that."

Did Quentin mean they should travel? She'd been waiting for a year for that topic to come up. Did he mean they should spend more money? On themselves, or on him? Did he mean they should make themselves ludicrous by doing something like camping in the northern woods?

"I've got to mail this last insurance letter," Lon announced, signaling the end of the conversation. Lon had spent most of the day puttering around with the letter, which concluded months of negotiations with the parties involved in the destruction of the family car the day after Quentin left for college, an incident which held a great deal of truth in a readily discernable format, at least as far as her husband was concerned.

In the last sale Lon had made before retiring, he'd sold twenty Trash Removal Units, i.e., garbage trucks, to the City of Phoenix with the understanding the operators would be specially trained to achieve the maximum efficiency and safety that would justify the additional cost of the expensive and sophisticated machinery. The city promptly ignored Lon's directive and cut corners with the result that on the first day of use, an ill-trained operator lost control of his Unit and ended up lifting the salesman's pride and joy, purchased with the commission on the garbage trucks, instead of a city provided trash receptacle, onto the truck, destroying the car and damaging the truck.

During Quentin's Christmas visit, Lon had tried relating the main themes of the incident to his son. Quentin had squirmed through about half the story then left the room proclaiming, "Possessions should be owned by their owner, and not own their owner." For her part, Louise had never fully disassociated the random and violent destruction of the family car from the beginning of her son's college career.

Quentin let the mention of the destroyed car fiasco pass uncommented upon. Lon went out to mail the letter. Louise retreated into the kitchen thinking her chances at conversation might be better if attempted from a safer distance.

Reaching the kitchen, Louise realized by retreating she'd consigned herself to a defensive holding position. Maybe she had to just stop talking about subjects that created conflict. But this was difficult considering Quentin's predilections and her husband's limited arsenal of topics. But mostly, she was annoyed by having to strategize. Louise liked to talk. She didn't mind if her son didn't want to talk so long as he wasn't so darned emphatic about silence. He acted as if there was something inherently wrong with talking. Unfortunately, Lon expressed a similar attitude, saying any time he had the chance: "If you keep your mouth shut, people might think you're not a fool. If you open your mouth, you're likely to remove all doubt."

What Quentin really needed was something to do. She was sure he was sitting there with the nonchalance, and self-righteousness, of a pile of freshly laundered clothes. He lacked something. It was as if he'd been washed and dried but had yet to be starched and ironed. On the other hand, her older son had perhaps been over-starched. The military hadn't agreed completely with him as far as Louise was concerned. He'd been disciplined to the point of apathy. But then again, Quentin could be stiff and silent, and then warm up to the most unexpected topics.

Relieved of his parents' overbearing presence and left pleasantly alone in the living room, Quentin sank into the couch. After he'd left for school, the couch he'd grown up with had been replaced with the new one.

New furniture was problematic. Although better looking than the old one, the new couch had yet to prove its reliability. Furniture was a not insignificant factor in Quentin's decision to come home for a while before classes started up again. His feelings about his generation's preference for minimal furniture were mixed. To his generation, "furniture" seemed to mean "mattress," serving as chairs, sofas, dinettes, recreation areas, and beds. Enjoying a real couch, Quentin reflected upon the fact good furniture made thinking easier. But sinking deeper into his thoughts, other factors came into play regarding furniture's effects on consciousness.

Quentin hypothesized a directly proportional relation between the amount of pressure taken off the sitter by the furniture and the amount of pressure exerted upon the sitter by the furniture. Because the more comfortable the chair, the greater its cost, as the sitter savors the chair's comfort, he can't help thinking about the money required to pay for it. Thus, furniture lulls one into thinking about money, and, by extension, its opposite, security. Quentin shook his head. The insidiousness of the capitalist economic structure never failed to amaze him.

Further, his contextualization of furniture, when related to the change in furniture, shed light upon the workings of the family: old furniture and its absence pointed to the false security the notion of "family" instills in its victims. The family creates false security and, its inevitable consequence, neuroticism. It was because of the deleterious aspects of "family" that Quentin was upset about the new sofa. And even further, he realized furniture served a dual function in the family. Although furniture was intended to aid thought, more importantly, it sought to shape the very nature of that thought. The family purported to give you security, then demanded an unnatural loyalty to that security. So with furniture.

The extreme example of all this was the furniture in some people's homes that was swathed in clear plastic, as if awaiting the perfection of the self-cleaning guest. Plastic conceptualized furniture. With plastic inserted between furniture and sitter, furniture becomes completely non-functional and works only as an expression of money.

Which was all very interesting. Quentin untied his hiking boots, kicked them onto the floor, and stretched out on the couch while his mother banged around pots and pans in the kitchen with, he noted, the cacophonous conviction of a martyr. He should write that line down. Soon, he found himself physically at ease despite the intellectual discomfort of being ensconced in a graphic representation of the corrosive economic foundation of the family, and modern American society as a whole.

Surveying the living room in the light of this new context, a familiar face caught Quentin's eye. A recent picture of Quentin was propped up in what he called "the portrait corner," next to his brother's West Point graduation picture. The proximity of the photos was not a coincidence. There was actually a third photo in the constellation. Quentin knew his corny high school graduation picture (goofy mortar board on his head above his clean-shaven face, shirt and tie and rented gown, gold embossed "Class of '69" in the corner, and all) had been relegated to the opposite side of his more recent, hairier picture. This crafty staging of pictures, as did the furniture, cluttered the room with ramifications. The juxtaposition of the military and anti-military portraits was clearly an indictment of the obviously shaggier subject. The contrast was meant to so inspire the shaggy Quentin that he would straighten himself out and follow in his brother's footsteps. The two sides of Quentin's portrait functioned on two levels. On the social level, his mother could simply turn the high school picture out when guests or relatives were in the room. On the psychological level, the contrast between the two Quentin portraits was as an overt attempt by the family to induce schizophrenia and have him view his present self as nothing more than a perverted devolution of what he had been, and had been intended to, become.

Obviously, if Quentin could be made to see his present self as an aberration, he'd promptly revert to his old ways and regain his consistency. His family had been founded on consistency being the spice of life. Ironically, Quentin considered himself a completely different person than the one he'd been in high school. He'd made a new person of himself, which far from unnatural, Quentin considered his greatest achievement. He'd taken his life into his own hands, cut the restraining influences of things around him and made himself what he should be. Unfortunately, all he could do was consider it all very ironic, noting however that the powers of the family were real and awesome. As if a physical manifestation of his thoughts, Quentin's mother shouted from the kitchen.

"Your brother is getting married."

Which was more blatant than anything Quentin could have anticipated.

"Really? To whom?"

"Joan Louise."

"Joan Louise Who?" There was a crashing of pots and pans.

"That's her last name. She said you've met."

Quentin remembered his brother bringing an unspecified female by the house briefly when they'd all been home over Christmas.

"Oh, her. I'm surprised. When are they getting married?"

"December."

"Why don't they wait until June? Isn't everyone supposed to want to have a June wedding?"

The din in the kitchen increased, conversation ceased. His mother had evidently lost interest in the topic.

Although unexpected, the marriage thing was a logical extension of the sort of family mentality that had placed the two sons' portraits next to each other. Quentin was old enough to be forced into smothering security by being lured into marrying and starting a family of his own. Self-perpetuation was the crux of the family problem: as soon as people grow out of their nuclear family, their fear they cannot function outside a family forces them into marrying and establishing their own family. Fortunately, because Quentin was hip to the scam, it posed no threat to him.

However, his brother's impending marriage did provide Quentin food for thought. As a boy, Quentin had worshipped his brother, but as he'd matured Quentin had concluded his brother was virtually incapable of interpersonal relationships. His brother was doubtless marrying in response to, as noted above, the pressure to remain in a family. Ironically, December was perfectly apt for his brother's wedding; his brother was

December incarnate.

Quentin's father, or as Quentin preferred to think of him, "Lon," came back in from wherever he'd been.

"So, you had enough in your account to write a check?" Lon said as if the two of them had been having an imaginary conversation while he was gone.

More direct than Louise, Lon could be just as subtle. His blatant salvo was clearly an indictment of what he perceived to be Quentin's monetary laxity, which had inadvertently resulted in one of his checks bouncing. At least that's what Lon thought had happened. In fact, Quentin had underwritten a summer acquaintance's illegal trafficking in some marijuana and had overdrawn his checking account during the term of the loan. The bank ratted Quentin out to his father, but Quentin deposited the proceeds of the transaction during the interim. When Lon phoned him asking what the problem was, Quentin merely informed him the bank had made an accounting error.

"Accounting can be pretty exacting work on a large scale," Lon had replied. "I'm surprised the people at the bank didn't send you an apology, or at least a written explanation."

"I'm sure they're pretty busy," Quentin replied, trying to imagine what being an accountant must do to a person. An accountant could very well become totally pre-occupied with money. Money could absolutely pervade both a person's public and private lives. What a depressing thought. "Think of all the accountants in the world leading lives of quiet desperation," he said to his father, ending the phone conversation. Back in the present, Lon was on to something else.

"Heard on the car radio, how women are advised against going downtown unescorted." Lon's father jerked his thumb over his shoulder, which meant anywhere between the front porch and Baja California or South America, both being in the same direction and of equal importance in so far as they were both outside the house. Again, Quentin was struck by what a small portion of existence penetrated the house and the family. The living room was a microcosm. Home and family breed pervasive provincialism.

"So, why are women not supposed to go downtown 'unescorted?'" Not that Quentin saw any point in ever going to Phoenix's downtown, which had gotten pretty seedy during his childhood and nearly rendered obsolete by newer shopping malls on the edges of town.

Lon had seated himself in his designated chair, a.k.a, "The Throne," but had yet to untie his shoes. He leaned back in the chair, stretched out his legs, clasped his hands on his lap and stared out the window.

"There's a … uh, a…."

Quentin had forgotten how small his childhood home was: two bedrooms, one bathroom, kitchen and living room and, quaintly, the Arizona room off the living room. With everyone in the living room at the same time, there was little room to think or work, certainly not when someone was talking. Coming home, Quentin had promised himself at least one short story before returning to school, but the likelihood of his being creative in such an oppressive environment seemed remote.

"… there's a NUT loose."

Lon had concluded his suspended sentence and continued looking out the window with a grimace. He scratched the inside of his right leg with his left foot as if an itch had made him grimace. The grimace began to fade as the corners of his mouth turned up slightly. Quentin began to give up hope his father would retire to the bedroom and take a nap. Quentin responded with his usual tactic of making the most of whatever his parents happened to be discussing.

"There are a lot of nuts loose in an army during a war."

There came a clanging from the kitchen, but Lon continued, undeterred.

"There's been four attacks," Lon said, before pulling out his handkerchief and wiping his nose.

"Attacks? In the daylight?" Quentin was dubious.

"Yes, in the daylight. In parking lots," Lon said, leaning over and preparing to untie his shoes.

Quentin was amazed. First, discussion of blatant sexuality in the family ran directly counter to the family as a concept. As the legitimizer of sex, the family could ill-afford to countenance illicit sexual behavior. Rape was "out there," somewhere between the front porch and South America. But perhaps, for the very reason illicit sex was so far removed from the confines of the family, it could actually be discussed without posing a threat? No, Louise would never come to such a radical conclusion. And certainly, Lon had never thought through anything even remotely of this nature.

Second, in and of itself, the rape impressed Quentin. The thought of some guy running around in broad daylight raping people was spectacular. What must it be like to be that depressed? Even though imagination was his stock in trade, Quentin could not imagine his existence being so meaningless that the only way he could communicate his frustrations was by raping people. What kind of environment did that guy come from? What had his home life done to him? He must be black. Quentin knew what Phoenix was like for blacks, and Mexicans, and Chinese, and other minorities.

"What do you think of a society that produces people like that?" he asked Lon.

"They said on the radio they think he's crazy."

"But the whole society is insane."

"Ah, nuts," was the best Lon could muster.

His father's limited vocabulary was another thing that bothered Quentin. Was he providing the answer to "What do you screw onto the end of a bolt?" Could he mean "Phooey," as if to say "I, for one, don't think he, the rapist, is mentally deranged?" Perhaps Lon did think the rapist was mentally deranged. Most likely, he meant, "Damn the whole thing." But he didn't seem hot enough under the collar to mean that. Essentially, Lon was impervious to Quentin's thought processes.

"Hell," Lon erupted unexpectedly. "That boy's only problem is a warm bomb."

Quentin could not decipher any anatomical reference in Lon's original utterance. The phone rang before any of this could be taken further.

"I'll get it," Louise shouted as if the desire for conversation among the members of the family was such that she needed to claim the right to say "hello" over the phone before anyone else had. Shrugging his shoulders and seeming a little disappointed, Lon finally leaned over and untied his shoes.

By the time the phone rang, although she'd calmed down, or at least realized she was excited and should calm down, Louise was glad for a chance to break up the talk about the situation downtown. There was something frightening about a rapist roaming around Phoenix that was not to be made light of. Besides, things were complicated enough without introducing a topic like rape into the conversation.

"Hello?"

"Louise?" Her sister Hattie was going deaf and her voice was loud enough to be heard throughout the house. Hattie was another source of anxiety for Louise. Since her retirement as a school librarian the summer Quentin had left for college, Hattie had been traveling with a vengeance. It was almost as if she'd had a change of personality and wanted to have nothing to do with her prior life. She was easily offended when she was home, and would take off on another trip at the drop of a hat. Louise also worried about the effect Hattie's presence would have on Quentin. Whenever his aunt was around, Quentin said things like his aunt was "absurd," "arbitrary familial relationships were detrimental to a person's sanity," the family accounted for "more mental patients than any other cause," and "the family was dead."

"Hattie! Where are you?"

"The airport."

Someone would have to pick up Hattie at the airport. Given that Lon was due for his nap and Louise had things to do, that someone would have to be Quentin.

"Where are you going next?"

"I'm not going anywhere. I'm staying home. If I were going somewhere else wouldn't I be content to be at the airport?"

"That's nice. I hope you like it here."

"I think I've scratched my travel itch."

"That's nice. Someone will be out to pick you up."

Surprisingly, Quentin volunteered.

"I'll go, Mom."

"You need any money for parking or anything?" Lon asked without opening his eyes. He had pushed back his recliner and was drowsing.

"I've got plenty, more than enough," Quentin said, extricating himself from the couch.

Since Quentin would be hard pressed to get anything thought out in a house whose atmosphere was neither creative nor intellectual, he'd probably have to stay outside to get anything done. Plus, he could hit one of the bookshops at the airport and pick up something to read. Getting some reading done might improve his frame of mind.

Happily behind the wheel, Quentin reveled in motion as opposed to the oppressive stagnancy of the so-called "living room." Boy, was that ever an ironic term. Quentin had a good working relationship with cars. He knew little about them, such as how they actually worked, but he could drive well and had an optimistic outlook. He was lucky with cars, they rarely gave him trouble. But he'd run into increasing difficulty coming to grips with them conceptually.

Of course, the whole social thing needed to be considered. What do cars mean to people in a society of conspicuous consumption? There was also the question of cars as symbolism. What is really at work with a car? What do they really mean? What is their place in the subconscious?

As his mind turned over and started to sleep, Lon heard the tires screech as his son backed the car out the driveway and onto the street. He fell asleep before deciding whether or not he was surprised how little common sense his son had shown in over-revving the engine before giving the oil pump sufficient time to do its job, never mind dropping the car into gear and spinning the tires, stressing both the transmission and the tires.

For Quentin, his Aunt Hattie was acceptable in theory, but difficult in practice. As best he could determine, she'd had an essentially unsuccessful life. She'd never married and had done nothing more than taught school and then been a librarian. Quentin had borne the brunt of her copious repressed, or frustrated, maternal instincts. She smothered him with gifts and kisses. Fortunately, he realized that in so far as she was a product of the pressures of the family, she had a lot of pent-up aggression and frustration with which he could sympathize. He also had to admire her for travelling all the time. Why would anyone want to stay in a cow town like Phoenix, long term? His parents had both moved there as kids because they'd come down with tuberculosis and the climate was supposed to be good for them. But for that, Quentin would have been from a real place instead of the city that air conditioners built.

Maybe he could distract his aunt by getting her to go into the terminal and get him a book. He wasn't sure what he wanted, but he'd gotten into suicide recently, and a girl who took sociology had told him of a book on the topic. Another girl he knew was really into a poet who'd made herself important by putting her head in an oven and breathing the gas to kill herself. He'd even written a story about a guy who'd committed suicide, but he didn't consider it his best effort. He wanted to try again and thought it might help if he knew, in general, more about the topic.

The airport parking lot was packed. Before finally finding an empty space, Quentin was on the verge of giving up on trying to live in a mass society. Then, to his complete annoyance, just as he pulled into the space, he saw a policeman putting a "No Parking" sign over the space's meter. Quentin didn't know which he resented more – the loss of his parking space or the cop's appearance. The guy was your definitive pig: mirrored sunglasses, paunch, shiny boots, the whole deal. Next thing you knew, he'd say something in pure, Arizona Okie, like, "Well hey there, fella, or is it Miss, with that hair?" Before Quentin had a chance to say or do anything, the policeman walked to the driver's side window of the car.

"I'm sorry sir. I'm afraid you can't park here." Quentin recognized the voice as that of one of his brother's grade school and high school classmates. It was incredible how someone who'd been young only a few years before could be so middle-aged and look as if he'd just stepped out of a documentary on racism. "I think there are some empty parking spaces off in –"

"Beau!" Quentin complained, "Don't you remember me?"

Beau thought for a second, lowering his sunglasses as if he couldn't recognize Quentin.

"Quentin? I didn't recognize you, under that mask."

"Oh, come on, man, it's just a beard."

"You look pretty wild. How's Gene?" Quentin wasn't buying Beau's faux pleasantries.

"What's this shit about my not parking here? You got something against 'hippies?'" Quentin made little quotation marks with his fingers.

"I hear Gene's getting married."

Quentin realized there was nothing to say to people who could not accept the fact he'd changed. Even though he'd never thought people in his generation would turn into old people, authority figures in particular, he also realized he'd missed seeing what a perfect cop Beau would make until he'd actually seen him dressed up like one.

"I can't believe this shit you're handing me. You're really going to make me find another place? I mean, come on, man, that's fucking... absurd."

Beau pushed his glasses back up his nose, adjusted his helmet and shifted his weight.

"I'm afraid you're going to have to move your dad's car on out of here."

"Look Beau, I'm in a hurry, man. You've got to be joking."

"You see the sign, don't you?"

"What sort of game is this? This doesn't make any sense at all. I mean, there are all these fucking cars here and you are trying to tell me for no reason at all I can't park here?"

"Affirmative."

"If you weren't so set in your God damned ways, you'd see what a joke this is."

"Listen, Quentin, you can change the world all you want as long as your car isn't parked here while you do it."

Quentin had about had enough.

"Okay, pig. You win. This time. Peace."

Beau the Cop straightened up, Quentin backed the car out of the space, stepped on the gas, and forgot about the whole thing. He knew better than to let people like that asshole Beau bring him down.

Quentin parked in the terminal driveway's passenger pickup zone within sight of his Aunt Hattie. Oblivious to Quentin's approach, she was standing next to her suitcase looking in the wrong direction, smoking a cigarette. She looked as if she was ready to be transported to the next airline over and depart for somewhere else. As he neared her, she turned, puffed billowously, as if her cigarette was shocked by his appearance.

"There you are!" she shouted, taking her cigarette from her mouth and looking demurely over his left shoulder exposing her right cheek to the anticipated kiss. Quentin extended his hand warmly. His aunt blinked and turned her head back toward Quentin. Seeing the outstretched hand, she put her cigarette back in her mouth and shook hands, muttering, "Have it your way then."

"How was your flight?"

"It was nice but there was a little turbulence after lunch."

"My plane didn't come through any."

"A man spilled his lunch trying to pinch a stewardess. She slapped him. It was a mess."

Quentin's curiosity and his desire for conversation with his aunt, neither too great, were both quickly satisfied.

"Is this all your luggage?"

"No!" she shouted. "They can't find my other suitcase. I've got one of the colored boys looking for it." Quentin wondered whether his aunt's next trip shouldn't be to the South Pole. It would be far enough south for her and completely white. There probably wouldn't be any Mexicans, either. "It's annoying. I'm getting a little tired of traveling. Maybe I'll stay home for a while."

The "colored boy" appeared with her other bag, which had evidently been delivered from the threatening hands of all sorts of weirdos in constant cahoots to deprive Hattie of her luggage and a fresh change of clothes. She handed the "colored boy" what to her, and possibly the porter, was a generous tip. The concept of tipping – nothing more than a thinly disguised assertion of the supposed inferiority of the servant class – revolted Quentin. Phoenix was such a racist town. And don't get him started on how Mexicans and Chinese are treated. The porter nodded in thanks and touched his index finger to the bill of his cap. Quentin winked and stretched his mouth at the corners in what he thought was a knowing grin. The porter looked at Quentin inquisitively before turning and strolling off. Unlike the rest of the family, Quentin understood people not like himself. He wouldn't make their racial mistakes. His aunt lit another cigarette from the end of the previous one and began talking.

"We had an interesting time on our lake in Canada."

"Have you ever been to the South Pole?"

"We had an outdoor privy that we shared with the boys next door over."

"I was just thinking what a great place it would be for you to visit."

"We'd get up early so we could use it first." Quentin considered himself the last in a long line of inveterate story tellers. Each story was told to the family, with its little moral, over and over, until everyone knew the story by heart and was thoroughly bored. "The paths down to the john from each of our cabins met about twenty feet or so from our cabins." She stopped to pull on her eternal cigarette.

"I'm going to get a book in the bookstore in the terminal, Hattie. You get in the car and I'll be back down in a second. Maybe you can get a porter to load your bags in the car."

"If you'll tell me what book you want, I can get it for you, at a discount. I still get the teachers' discount."

"No. I'll just run in and be right back." His aunt shrugged and puffed on her cigarette. Quentin avoided using his aunt as a book buyer. He'd asked her once to get "On the Road," or some other Jack Kerouac stuff. She'd gone off thrilled to have a mission and came back saying they didn't have any "Cairo-ack" in stock, but she'd gotten some other travel books. He still had them in a box somewhere: "The Adventures of Humphrey Clinker," and "Pickwick Papers." They were both, without a doubt, the worst books he'd ever started.

The bookstore didn't have the book Quentin wanted about suicide. He looked at a book about apocalyptic literature, which he thought might be of some use. But he hadn't read any of the books it talked about, and he wasn't too gone on criticism anyway. Drifting around the store, he came upon a display of books by a poet who'd recently killed herself. He settled on buying the book, whose back cover blurb called it the poet's "best:" "Vibrant, vital … sparkling with death in every word." Returning to the passenger pickup area where he'd left the car, Quentin found his aunt planted in the front seat, smoking resolutely. She began talking before Quentin had even gotten into the car.

"So, on mornings, we'd sometimes meet these men on their way down to the commode, as we came back up." Quentin noticed what appeared to be a parking ticket on the windshield.

"God damn it, Hattie! How did this get here?"

"We usually tried to have something nice to say to them so they wouldn't feel ill at ease."

"Hattie!" Quentin was shouting. He knew he could be obnoxious with his aunt and get away with it. He could also call her by her first name with impunity. She was not of sufficient family rank to warrant serious consideration. Quentin derived a certain satisfaction from cursing in front of her, but he was also mad. "Why didn't you do something?"

She just sat there.

"Why didn't you move the car?"

"I doubt your father would want me touching his car in any capacity other than that of passenger."

"But I left you here to move the car if this happened!" Which was true only in retrospect. His aunt sat firm and puffed.

"The policeman told me not to worry, that it was a joke, and to tell you, when you came back, that the whole thing was absurd." Quentin glared. "He said he was a friend of yours."

As she concluded her story on the way out of the airport, Hattie noticed how wild a driver Quentin could be.

"So, we'd said a few things to them, and then one day, it rained and was very cool the following morning. We met them on the way back while they were on their way to the outdoor plumbing. Upon their asking us what we thought of the weather, I just said it was very nice, but Marge, one of the girls, who insisted on being a little more specific, I guess, said, 'On the whole, it's rather cold.'"

Quentin took his aunt directly to her apartment. The last thing he wanted in the house was more bourgeois distraction.

"Why are you taking me here? My car is at your house."

"Mom told me to bring you right home because you would be tired."

"I have a bridge game tonight and I need the car."

"You need a rest."

When Quentin got home, his mother was at the door.

"Where's Hattie? Why didn't you bring her here? I told you to bring her here." Quentin knew this was not exactly true, but then again, she hadn't told him to take Hattie to her place either.

"I forgot."

Napping in his eponymous La Z Boy, Lon spoke without opening his eyes.

"Pipe down and go get your brother's fiancé."

"How am I supposed to know where she lives?"

"You're supposed to look at the address on the piece of paper on the table there."

His mother was on the phone to his aunt.

"No, Hattie. I wanted him to bring you here. I don't know why he didn't. There must have been some sort of misunderstanding. Are you sure you want to leave town so soon? Of course, you can if you want. No, we can't stop you. Yes, I'll bring the car right over. But you have to promise not to go downtown to get the tickets today.... Because there's a fellow fooling around down there. No, it's not safe, he's fooling around."

"Fooling around hell," Quentin interjected, *a la* Lon. "He's raping people!"

"Shush. We can pick up the tickets for you tomorrow, Hattie, when Lon and I have to be downtown."

"I will not shush. I'm not like Dad who only says anything when he wants something practical done or he wants someone to be quiet."

"No, Hattie, that's not true. We'll get the tickets for you."

"Well, just about."

"Won't you have dinner with us?"

"If we don't get a little honesty around here, this place is going to explode. This whole house is nothing but a euphemism. What we need around here is more truth!"

"You can get a ride to bridge club. I wish you weren't leaving so soon. Yes, I understand."

Having let off all his steam, Quentin exited the scene before his mother could reprimand him and, without further discussion, went to pick up his evidently soon-to-be sister-in-law. Once she was in the car, his passenger struck Quentin as a decidedly low-risk item. Joan was a little on the big side, but other than her general blandness and the fact she was wearing tennis shoes, she was just about what Quentin had remembered. She was the type who wouldn't do, or say, anything you couldn't predict well before she did. She was a passive rider and displayed little interest in talking to him. While playing chauffeur, Quentin hit upon the idea of writing a story about a rapist who commits suicide, which kept him occupied and, coupled with her silence, kept conversation at a minimum. Quentin worked on his story through dinner and even grew slightly suspicious of Joan's silence.

Watching the food disappear from the dinner plates, Louise felt disburdened of her vision of Quentin going down the drain. She'd shed the overwhelming sense of irreparable decline and only found herself aggravated by what her son did.

Quentin hadn't said much during dinner, which was a common tactic. The times he did open his mouth, he spoke only to annoy her. Criticism of her cooking was something Louise had gladly gone without during Quentin's absence. Even as a child, Quentin had considered himself the resident restaurant critic, tasked with coming down hard on any dishes he considered remarkable. Experimental, or even new, dishes were greeted with disdain. Quentin was a stickler for regulated variety, within the confines of his strict, but vaguely defined, demands for excellence.

As a young child, variety or redundancy (take your pick), were objected to by an abstinence fortified by sneaking cookies from the cookie jar before and after dinner. Growing older, Quentin had added innuendo to his arsenal, which had little effect on his target, but provoked more spectacular reactions on the part of his audience, actually being spanked by his father at age fourteen for likening a variation of hamburgers topped with powdered cheese to "dung patties covered with lime."

More recently, his criticisms had expressed themselves in snideness. He made puns on food ("The corn's poné 'n' so are we.") or made a general nuisance of himself because he didn't like white sauce on his broccoli or mushrooms in his eggs.

Louise had hoped college would sound the death knell of his craft. Surely the college cook didn't eat with the students, and like so many of his generation, Quentin would find institutions unresponsive to the demands of the individual. Surprisingly, since he'd been away, his critical perspective seemed to have simply spun a hundred and eighty degrees. Now, when he complained, he cited her conservative, totally predictable menu: her food was "not imaginative, too plain."

Dinner had been traditional: roast beef, green beans and mashed potatoes. When she served apple pie for dessert, Quentin began to complain. She should have been glad to hear him wanting more interesting food, but it irritated her instead. She could have said a regular diet was healthy and radical eating habits were dangerous, but she didn't really think that.

While thinking about rape for his short story Quentin had arrived at a working theory concerning deviant behavior in society: criminals are invariably victims rather than victimizers. As such, criminals are manifestations of the aberrations inherent in the society itself. Society, not criminals, is at fault.

His mother's criticism of his theory came in the form of her relating an episode from her childhood to the evening's guest who was, as yet, uninitiated into the official family mythology. Louise's father had owned a movie house in Iowa City, which was only remarkable because its brand new and long saved-for "Silva-Screen" had been slashed by vandals on the first night of its short-lived career. Perhaps his sympathy for his mother and her father had prevented Quentin from properly sympathizing with the vandals. Putting them into their proper context, he'd made an important realization that had eluded him: Previously, he'd condemned the vandals for the irrationality of their act. Mistakenly dwelling on the pain purportedly incurred by his mother's father (in her words, it had "broken his heart"), Quentin had missed seeing the criminal act was, in its very illogicality, an expression of the irrationality of the society as a whole!

In so far as his ideas were developing sufficiently in conjunction with the ongoing conversation, Quentin said nothing until he felt the main threads of the conversation were being lost in a discussion of his brother's traits and habits. With the arrival of dessert, Quentin was afforded a topic of conversation that would allow him to flesh out his thoughts without tipping his hand completely. He jumped in with both feet.

"This apple pie is sweeter than you usually make it."

"Yes, it's a different recipe I'm trying."

Quentin had successfully engaged his mother's attention.

"Are they old apples from last season, or early apples?"

His father interrupted here.

"You don't find many good eating apples this time of year."

"I'd say they're refrigerated from last fall," his mother added. The conversation was going in Quentin's desired direction.

"Someone was telling me that old apples are all right for making sweet pies," Quentin continued. "I was told never to cut out soft spots of apples because they were the best part to bake."

"I think that's bananas." Quentin surprised his mother would use such a colloquialism. "You use soft bananas for making banana bread." His mother's objection was not to the point.

"But isn't it interesting that a bad apple should be good for an apple pie?"

"But a bruise is not really a bad part." His mother was trying to deny him his premise.

"But some people won't eat a bad part." Quentin was not afraid of appealing to subjectivism to justify his arguments. He didn't believe in objectivity, anyway.

"Then those people just don't know better." Since his father interrupted again, Quentin felt compelled to pursue a more obvious course.

"But what about rotten apples?"

"Your mother doesn't usually serve rotten apples to her guests, or her regular customers, for that matter." Quentin proceeded to the crux of this thesis.

"Can a bruise rot an apple?"

"No. A bruise is just a bump. You cut it off and use the rest."

"But aren't rotten apples of use?"

"You cut off what you can't use and use the rest." His mother was surprisingly utilitarian.

"What about 'a rotten apple spoils the bunch?' Isn't it actually undue pressure exerted by the apples surrounding a weakened apple that results in the weakened apple getting further damaged?" Quentin was intent upon showing that the cause and effect between society and deviant behavior ran opposite to the commonly believed direction. Rather than a protection from deviant behavior, society was its cause. His mother seemed baffled.

"I don't know if that's true in the case of apples. Apples go bad at the same time, but—"

"All right. But what about an apple either bruised or rotten in spots?"

"Like I said, unless you're making banana bread, and I don't mean to mix apples and oranges, or bananas, you cut—"

"But what if you wanted to use it for something and you couldn't just cut out the bad part?"

"Then you'd get a suitable apple—"

"But what about the one that's 'not suitable?' *That's* the important apple. *That's* the one with which we have to contend. It's the bad apple that poses the threat. What do we do with the bad apple?"

Lon finished his piece of pie, drained his milk and wiped his mouth before attempting to end the conversation that had so interested his son, confused and upset his wife, and apparently mystified, or bored, he wasn't sure which, his future daughter-in-law.

"You eat it."

Lon's comment struck Louise as apt, but did little to help her understand what was bugging her son, beyond his distaste for anything but tart apple pie. Perhaps he'd joined in the fad for health foods. Sugar had fallen into ill-repute. Maybe Quentin believed anything sour was better for you than something more palatable.

Perhaps because he'd been raised on the theory that getting up from the table before you'd finished everything on your plate was forbidden, Quentin assumed any topic brought up during dinner had to be entirely disposed of before anyone left the table.

"How do you know that's what you do with it?"

"What else is there to do with it?" Clearly unaware of the epistemological implications of his assertion, his father folded his napkin in two and wiped his mouth as if he were preparing to make a significant defense of his position, but only said, "I've been doing it since I was a boy."

The talk of apples and spoilage reminded Louise of an old family story.

"Lon's sister tells this story. Quentin's grandfather used to buy a barrel of apples every fall and put them in the basement. He denies it but I can believe it. By January, because there were too many apples to be eaten by the family, some of the apples on the top would start to go bad. Whenever they wanted an apple, they'd pick out one that was going bad and eat around the bad spots. So, expending all their time and appetites rescuing bad apples, they never got to the good apples until they too had gone bad. As Lon's sister said, the whole family spent the entire winter slightly sick to their stomachs and one step behind the decaying apples, but sure they were doing the right thing!"

Even though Louise delivered the last line of the story as if it were a punchline to a joke, which was pretty much what she considered it to be, no one said anything until her future daughter-in-law piped up.

"Gosh, you'd think they would have thrown out a few of the bad ones so they could have eaten the good apples."

Silence. Rather than have Quentin jump in with more about rotten apples, Louise defaulted to another anecdote.

"There's no chance of that. Once, when Lon's sister was visiting, I was fixing a Waldorf salad and pitting some grapes. She sees the pits in the pile of peelings, picks them out, and pops them in her mouth. I said, 'June, what are you doing?' and she said I shouldn't throw out the pits until I'd first gotten everything off them."

"Aw, they weren't grape pits," Lon protested, "They were dates, or maybe even peach pits. I'd have done the same thing." Maybe they had been.

"You see what I mean?" Louise asked. "My father was only making ten dollars a week during the Depression, but he didn't go over the food preparation scraps as closely as Lon's side of the family does. He picks over an apple core once I'm done with it."

"I'd be a fool not to."

Attempting to ease her past some of the family's, if not seamy, at least boring aspects, Quentin grimaced at his future sister-in-law. After ending his doomed attempt at placing the conversation within a meaningful intellectual context, Quentin had lost his mother's point, despaired of seeing what eating had to do with apples, and gave up any hope of facilitating any worthwhile discussion. As per usual, the familial "furniture" was exerting its pressure and stifling any original thought. Even if something intelligent could be discussed, his ideas would surely be ignored and, unwept and unsung, buried beneath a mound of family anecdotes.

The confusing dinner conversation had forced Joan to really concentrate. As she usually was around her fiancé's family, she was cautious about what she said to the point of only speaking when spoken to. She'd avoided attempting to make any conversation during the car ride to the house because her fiancé's brother had been in a bad mood and seemed irritated by having to drive her. The conversation having come to a halt, not wanting to appear bored, or disinterested, Joan thought it as good a time as any to say something.

"I've just started with a new piano teacher, and I'm really enjoying it."

"I really like music," Quentin responded, surprisingly. Everything said at dinner seemed to have hidden significance. She missed her fiancé's presence but surmised her next move could be made with minimal risk.

"Do you play?"

"No. He doesn't," her future mother-in-law replied frostily. Joan had evidently struck another nerve.

"What I think is that most of us shouldn't be dilettantes and try to be musicians."

About the time Quentin began filching cookies to fuel his criticism of her cooking, Louise had let him quit taking piano lessons. After four years of instruction and relative success, he'd simply refused to go any further. His teacher said he'd learned his scales faster than any other student. But unbeknownst to his teacher, those scales had been learned only after a great deal of wailing and gnashing of teeth, most of which had been done by Louise. His teacher had been kept blissfully unaware of the difficulties as a result of Quentin's always being practiced enough at his assignment by the next lesson. But the effort required eventually took its toll, and Louise finally acceded to her son's wishes.

Upon being informed her pupil was being consigned to the illimitable mass of children who didn't study piano, Quentin's teacher tightened at the waist of her raw silk dress, threw back her teased hair from the jolt of her constricting stomach muscles, and nearly hissed, "Some mothers ... my dear ... have ... FORTITUDE!" Lon insisted the teacher's interest was less artistic than economic, scolded Louise for having only enough self-possession not to change her mind and give in to the teacher's attack, and upon her asking him what she should have said, replied, "Some music teachers … my dear … have MORE STUDENTS!" Quentin talked on.

"I don't think another second, or third-rate amateur pianist is at all necessary. We need good listeners." Louise wasn't sure whether she was bothered by having allowed her son to quit piano or his cocky attitude toward amateur musicians. Her wanting Quentin to take lessons had been based on her belief that doing something was the best way to learn about it, music providing the best example. She began clearing the table. "Any art form needs audiences as well as artists. I have a good dancer friend who says he's not a consumer of dance. Personally, I find it easier to understand what a composer is saying when I'm listening, than I ever could if I were butchering a piece myself."

Joan felt trapped in the middle of a minefield. She was sure Quentin had never heard her play, but she was beginning to wonder.

"Music gives the mind the greatest amount of freedom, in the arts, or, for that matter, life. It's pure and appeals directly to the emotions. Music is the only place where you can be free. That's what music is all about. People in the world can never be free but when, say, you hear the end of a symphony with that 'Bump, Pump, baBuuuummm,' everything is let loose, as it were, freed. And music is a universal language. It transcends all nationality and race. Take Beethoven, for instance. Anyone can relate to his music. It's universal."

"It's Germanic."

Louise, who Joan thought was the noisiest table clearer ever, seemed to have it in for Quentin, but he seemed oblivious.

"You see, for Beethoven freedom was the main concept. It's essential to music to begin with. In an opera he wrote, the chorus gets let out of prison at the end. It's as if freedom is made possible for us by music and, what's more, it shows that freedom is possible in real life."

Ideas were blossoming furiously in Quentin's mind. He was making connections and breakthroughs he'd never made before. He made a mental note to make the rapist in his story a musician.

"Beethoven is showing us that we should go out and work for man's freedom. It's like with the apples. That man's music is immortal."

"It's Romantic," Louise protested with a note of disdain, which she regretted immediately. "Why don't we move to more comfortable chairs?"

"No reason not to," Lon replied.

Joan nodded in agreement, bolted to her purse, took out a cigarette, lit it and felt much better by the time she'd had a few puffs. Her fiancé's family relocated themselves less frantically.

"Well, that's what I believe about it, anyway."

Quentin was finished but Louise made the mistake of not letting things drop.

"I'm just not so sure there isn't anything to be learned about music from practicing an instrument. Would you care for some coffee, Joan? The boys don't care for it but you're welcome to have some."

Finding the path unusually free of complication, Joan nodded vigorously.

Upon departing the table, the conversation became so vague and unstructured that participating in it struck Quentin as pointless. Metaphors and similes were introduced with no concern for the implications they held for the ideas he was working on. Finally, a prolonged silence was punctuated by his father's burp. His mother's expressed displeasure with her husband's demeanor, as much as his digestive gesture, signaled the conclusion of the evening's festivities. His parents were totally predictable. Lon would now retreat to his and Louise's bedroom, turning lights out along the way, change into his pajamas and pad between the bathroom and their bedroom a few times to perform his ablutions, before finally going to bed. Although Quentin didn't wear a wrist watch, because he didn't believe in giving in to time constraints, if he did wear one, he could have set it by his parents' habits.

Tiring as the dinner party wore on, Louise was upset by Quentin's behavior but there didn't seem to be anything she could do to make things better. Once Lon went to bed, she withdrew to the kitchen, leaving Joan and Quentin to themselves. When everything was done in the kitchen, she was ready for bed. The last thing she heard before falling asleep was Quentin and Joan leaving the house.

His parents' departure provided Quentin an opportunity to pursue some ideas he'd just hit upon. Identifying the rapist as a symbol of deviant behavior impressed upon Quentin the importance of the sexual aspects of the rapist as symbol. To the extent the rapist manifested how societal pressures affect individuals, the nature of his response, i.e., the act of rape, was itself a challenge to the status quo. The frustrated individual embodied the failure of interpersonal relationships in society and the rapist's response attacked both the premise of interpersonal relationships and the entire concept of "society." Further, the act of rape brought into doubt the bourgeois concept of sex, another cornerstone of society.

Quentin's pleasure at being left alone with the guest and his thoughts was enhanced by two things he'd noticed about the guest. First, he was impressed by the spunkiness she'd shown in blatantly lighting up a cigarette in front of his aggressively non-smoking parents. She seemed pretty rebellious for someone engaged to his brother. She might be interested in hearing what he was thinking about, and might even share some of his sentiments. His second observation concerned Joan's physical rather than emotional aspects. In brief, she was big, and well-built, and had a pretty face.

All of which struck Quentin as incongruous with the necessarily docile, stiff nature of anyone his brother would be interested in dating, never mind marrying. Considering both her rebelliousness and latent sexuality, Quentin concluded Joan might be a legitimate prospect to continue pursuing his exploration of rotten apples and rape. Surprisingly, she initiated the conversation.

"Gene tells me you're a poet."

"Oh, does he?"

What Joan had assumed to be a safe but sure-fire conversation starter had fizzled. Her next question was to have been, "Do you major in English?" Maybe Gene was wrong. Before she could become too alarmed, strange Quentin began talking, which was all she'd wanted.

"I have written some poetry, but I'm not a poet. I'm not very good at it. I guess I'm not your standard poetic type." Joan nodded while she rifled through her purse to find another match, considering Quentin the kind of conversationalist who could talk uninterrupted for great lengths of time. Gene had remarked in passing that his brother could talk for great amounts of time without ever actually saying anything. "There are too many people writing poetry who should be doing something with their hands, or something. No. I'm not very good at it, but it's good for a person to know what they're not good at."

"Oh really?"

Joan clearly had the habitual smoker's inability to hear what was being said until their cigarette is lit. Quentin waited knowingly until she had puffed once and focused her eyes through the ensuing fog.

"Would you like a beer?" he asked once the smoke had caused all the appropriate visual, aural and oral circuits to be engaged.

"Yes, I would."

"In that case, I'll be right back." Quentin headed to the kitchen for provisions and to re-group. He was not really all that interested in talking about his writing. He was hot on the implications of rebellion against the status quo and interpersonal relationships in society. If society insisted on people relating to people in specific ways, acting toward other people in an opposite or even anarchic way made an explicit comment upon society. He took two beers out of the fridge. He was excited at the prospects his ideas presented. He was skimming from one intellectual summit to another, making interconnections at every brief stop along the way.

Joan seemed interested and willing to follow what he had to say. Although he wasn't interested in talking about his writing, he probably expressed himself best when he was talking about his writing, considering it, as he did, a metaphor for communication. He returned to the living room with the two beers, bubbling with possibilities.

"Actually, what I write is fiction, you know, short stories."

"That's right, Gene said you were working on a novel. How is it going?" Quentin had concluded that novel and another since he'd last seen his brother. He let this pass to save time.

"Fine. I'm working on some short stories at the moment. But it's dry as a bone down here, literally, and figuratively. Or should I say literarily? Does Gene still go to church?"

Joan exhaled as if she was surprised.

"Yes. He's very religious."

"Actually, I'd say he's a virtual Puritan."

Joan had anticipated this sort of comment. Gene had described his brother as "a Bohemian." She wanted to avoid arguments at all costs.

"He's very religious."

Quentin was impressed by Joan's respect for religiosity in others despite her apparent lack of belief.

"I've given up religion, or rather, renounced it. Indefinitely. I went to mass not too long ago as kind of an investigation. It struck me as sort of voodoo. I mean there was a 'priest' in special, magic clothes mumbling magic incantations, while this big clump of near savages mumbled back at him."

"I'll probably convert."

"Become a Catholic? Really?" Quentin was surprised but perhaps Joan's lax attitude toward religion had significant implications. Insofar as religion was a primary pillar of the status quo, when religion was finally expunged, things would start hopping. Joan still had something to say.

"I've never really been anything, religion-wise, but I think of all the religions, Catholic isn't too bad. And your family is religious. Isn't your father a convert?"

"Now he's retired, he has time to be religious, I guess. But you're right about my mother. If she's anything, she's religious."

"What do you write about?" Joan asked, wanting to switch to a less controversial subject. She lit another cigarette.

"What do I write about? Many things, but I guess I would have to say 'change' is my primary concern."

"I'd think that would be difficult," Joan said, exhaling a cloud of smoke. She'd begun regretting having asked a question. Gene was too quiet and Quentin provided a refreshing contrast, but the contrast's attraction was fading.

"How people relate to change determines their lives. It's the real differentiator between people, and between generations. When you're young, you want everything to be always new. So, if you don't want to grow old, you keep seeking out new things and experiences. You see, things are always changing."

"Really?"

"Oh yes, that is what the young know: experience isn't as important as everybody says since nothing happens twice."

During the abortive excursion into religion, Quentin had jumped a few intellectual mountain ranges over and even he was having difficulty seeing how what he was saying related to what he meant. Undaunted, he forged ahead.

"You have to be open to new possibilities and relationships. We have no right to be closed to anything, or anyone. That's why there are no rules, if you realize everything is change. It all ties together. It's really something and you have to see this."

Joan nodded. She hadn't paid attention and nodded too emphatically. It was getting late. It had been dark for some time and the whole thing was getting to be too much.

"Don't you agree?" Quentin insisted.

"Oh yes, of course. I suppose it's like when my mother used to tell me 'you can't cry over spilt milk.'"

"Well, yes, I suppose, but that's not the same. Well, we know things our parents don't know. But anyway, my stories are about people like us who are trying to act now. The past has no relevance, and what we do tonight will have no effect tomorrow."

"Would you like to take me home?"

"I'd love to."

For the most part, the ride to Joan's house was silent. Perhaps because of the beer Quentin had had in the living room and the one he'd chugged getting from the house to the car, Quentin felt the need for a cigarette, negotiations for which had provided the only conversation.

Quentin seemed concerned with something weighty enough to wrinkle his brow, but Joan was too tired to attempt any conversation. Self-consciousness seemed to be Quentin's primary characteristic. Gene was often mysteriously quiet, but being quiet seemed unnatural in his chatty, younger brother.

Arriving at her house, Joan explained that her parents were out of town and thus the darkened house. Quentin turned off the car and looked resolutely at the vacant house. He asked if he could come in. Joan said "no," thought to say something more, then went inside without saying "good night."

Louise woke up feeling as if she'd been awake all night. She'd dreamt a great deal but could only remember one dream. The family had been in the car and Quentin (aged four) had to go to the bathroom constantly. He kept missing the Planter's Peanut can provided for such emergencies, and even when he succeeded in peeing into the can, he insisted on being helpful by dumping his handiwork out the window himself. By the time they got to wherever they were going, the entire rear half of the car was yellow rather than green.

Louise's resolve in dealing with Quentin had also weakened. He was headed in the wrong direction, but all challenging him did was generate friction and sparks. A conflagration was the only likely result. Short of open warfare the only option was barely peaceful co-existence, all of which she'd concluded between waking up and actually getting out of bed.

Up and around for a few minutes, Louise began to reconsider her initial conclusion. There were certainly things she and Quentin were going to disagree about, and it was simply wrong for her to agree with any and every thing he said or thought. She'd just have to continue to react to him honestly. This was her best bet.

She cooked breakfast for herself and Lon who was already up and reading the paper. As the morning progressed, she took comfort in moving into her extramural activities, phoning and typing for her church organizations, and generally getting things done.

Quentin had gone to bed at one in the morning with the intention of getting up at eight and writing. He'd elaborated on the ideas for his story about the rapist and was anxious to begin. His plan for the story had caught up to the breakthroughs he'd made in his thinking. Having been promoted to social critic (his act, rape, brings the entire social fabric under scrutiny), the rapist had gone from victim to hero. Making the required alterations to his plan for the projected story had taken a lot of effort. As a result, Quentin was not awake until ten and even then, only because his mother was making her phone calls right outside his bedroom door. He was finally in the kitchen for breakfast by eleven-thirty.

As Louise's day settled into its usual rhythm, her plan to simply indulge Quentin grew less viable. Although she knew Quentin preferred late hours, she couldn't help attaching a moral laxity to his sleeping late. The later he slept, the more evident his decline became. By the time Quentin was ready for breakfast, Louise was ready for a confrontation.

Awaiting his bacon and eggs, Quentin thumbed through the morning paper his early bird father had already manhandled. There wasn't much happening in the news. The only article of interest was about the rapist. It was small and enclosed in lines for emphasis at the bottom of the front page. There was little mention of the character of the rapist or his motives and there was no editorializing. The emphasis was on women not going down town "unescorted." The article looked like a formal invitation and struck Quentin as quaint. His breakfast prepared and delivered, Quentin felt obligated to converse.

"Did you know Joan is thinking of converting?"

"No. I did not. I'll pray for her."

"I don't believe in prayer." Now that he thought about it, Quentin realized prayer was part of the social order. As a means of correcting something wrong in society, prayer was as bogus as the society as a whole. His mother seemed cool to the idea.

"Well, some things have a way of happening."

Quentin didn't want to pursue the matter any further. He was preparing to batten down his intellectual hatches preparatory to beginning writing. If his ideas became too extensive they would over-reach his creative energies and the whole story would go up in smoke before he could start. Although he was gladly taking advantage of the benefits of being home (food), he was disturbed by home's greatest drawback (mundane distractions). First his mother asked him if he wanted to go to church. He hadn't been in quite some time and it was a Holy Day, so called. He ignored this altogether. Then his father barged into the kitchen, adding to the general annoyance.

"Where are my glasses?" Lon rumbled through the kitchen with the intensity of a monomaniac. His mother, as if in another world, pursued her own line of questioning.

"Are you ready to go?"

"I can't find my glasses."

"I told the girls I'd be down there by twelve-thirty."

"I had them to read the paper a while ago."

"We'll have to park around the block, so we'll have to allow time for that."

Quentin's father was looking under everything in the kitchen while his mother tidied up the counters. Despite the antics, Quentin had concluded that his mother was going downtown and, due to the rape warnings still flying, his father was going along.

"I'm ready to go now," Lon said, scratching his head.

"Good. Your glasses are on the dresser. I've got Hattie's ticket info and we can pick up her tickets at her travel agency on the way home." Quentin had finished his breakfast and pushed his plate away.

"Are you 'escorting' Mom downtown, Dad?"

"I'm going to church." His father turned toward the hall in the direction of the dresser and his glasses.

"Oh, c'mon Dad, you're going downtown because of the rapist."

"You can believe what you want."

"You don't really believe that, do you?" Quentin's question was three-pronged. Did Lon consider the rapist a threat? Did he really think he was going downtown to go to church rather than escort his wife? Did he believe in the efficacy of Mass. Although the nature of his question only struck Quentin after it had been asked, it was brilliant nonetheless.

"What kind of question is that?" Lon parried.

"A crucial one."

Acting confused, Lon shrugged his shoulders and headed down the hallway.

On the ride downtown, Louise wondered whether Quentin was going insane. She knew there were drugs at colleges. Perhaps Quentin had suffered some sort of brain damage. Even if he'd been affected by drugs, she'd still have to straighten him out, wouldn't she? She'd come full circle, back to where she was when he'd arrived. Her early morning detachment had collapsed. The spoon was still moving inexorably toward the drain and there was nothing to be done about its impending demise.

Quentin preoccupied Louise throughout her meeting such that she was not her usual incisive self. Nothing much was accomplished. Rather than wait for her husband to meet her with the car as had been planned, she went to the parking lot with the intention of getting the car and meeting her husband in front of the church. There were no rapists in sight, but as she explained to herself afterwards, she'd had too much on her mind to notice much of anything.

While exiting the parking lot, she pulled up too far from the attendant's booth to simply hand over the ticket and the money. She got out of the car, stepped to the window and was receiving her change when the attendant looked up and past her right shoulder, wide-eyed. She turned around in time to see her husband's white car moving slowly, but resolutely, out of the parking lot and into the street. She watched helplessly as the car slipped between two cars that swerved to avoid it as if the car, by simply looking as if it knew what it was doing, had more right to be there than any cars that were under control. After intimidating all the legal traffic, the car climbed over a curb on the far side of the street and, as if intent upon blinding itself, ran directly into a concrete wall, accompanied by breaking of glass, a little crunching of metal, and a single "toot" of the horn. The car stalled and the open drivers' side door, signaling the conclusion of the scene, snapped firmly shut.

By the time Louise got across the street, there was a small crowd, including her husband, gathered around the car.

"I wouldn't have believed it if I hadn't seen it with my own eyes," Lon observed.

"There was nothing I could do!"

After Louise and Lon left, Quentin set up his typewriter on the kitchen table then went into the living room and looked through old magazines. Quentin worked on what he considered the "worry-inspiration method," which involved doing something worthless until he was inspired. After fifteen minutes in the living room, he jumped up and ran into the kitchen. He pounded away, then looked to see what had inspired him.

> I came to this town here in the north to get rid of all my problems, but here I am in this unpaid for apartment and my name is being broadcast over the radio.

Seeing his work on the paper, Quentin recognized there were changes that needed to be made. He took out his blue pencil and changed "apartment" to "flat," then changed it to just "room." He changed "name" to "description" and "radio" to "newspaper." His hero could afford neither an entire apartment nor a radio. Nor could he have his name known if he was to stay free long enough for another rape to be included in the story. Being only minor in scope, these problems were quickly dealt with.

But upon seeing the first sentence, Quentin realized his conception of the rapist, and the story as a whole, had changed since he'd first taken an interest in the topic. He'd written what he'd been thinking yesterday. Now, the nature of the rape, and its implications, and therefore, the rapist, had taken on greater meaning. Quentin no longer saw the rapist as a minority member and representative of deviant behavior caused by the pressures applied on creative individuals by a mass society. No longer shaped by forces outside himself, his protagonist needed to be self-defining and fully conscious of the import of his act.

Quentin's rapist would now be a white, moderately wealthy, educated, young person convinced of the import of his activities, which would necessitate a completely different atmosphere, setting and character. Quentin removed the first sheet from the typewriter.

The rapist would be seen in his chambers after his friends, whom he'd had over to dinner, had just left. After dinner, they'd discussed "life in society" and all agreed that sex was the big hang up. But they also all agreed there was little to be done about it. All, that is, other than Quentin's hero. The prospective rapist had not fully committed himself, but was an advocate of revolutionary activity. This was another element of the message of the story: the hero would be an intellectual willing to act upon his ideas, he'd convert his thought into action.

Quentin paced around in the living room for five minutes before returning to his typewriter in the nick of time.

> Fists firmly clenched, the young full professor forced his aesthetic weapon into her reverent scabbard.

Quentin liked it. It would make a good beginning. It summed up his lead character's projection of what his act would be, and mean. Quentin considered changing the professor part, but the educational aspect of the hero's act was essential to the story.

It was a good start. Next, he would go into the professor-rapist's background. Hemingway never stopped writing until he knew what he was going to do next. The following paragraphs would lay out how his hero had achieved his personal freedom from society.

"Well begun is half done" being one of his mother's favorite sayings, Quentin proceeded into the living room to relax. After a few minutes stretched on the couch, he fell asleep with his thoughts all pleasantly a-jumble. The telephone woke him. It was his father.

"I called to tell you we'll be a little late getting home. There's been an accident down here, at the parking lot."

"That's all right, you didn't have to call." Quentin could be grouchy when he woke up. "You're both old enough to take care of yourselves."

"Your mother's a little shaken up, but it's nothing serious. I should have stayed with the her."

"Okay. I'll see you."

By the time he'd hung up, Quentin began to remember what his father had said. There'd been an "accident" involving his mother in a parking lot. The car was not mentioned, so "accident" must have been, so typical for the family, a euphemism. Clearly, his mother had been raped.

Picturing the "accident," Quentin was disturbed by the force and ugliness of the act. It must have been terrible. He had to do something. He looked at the list next to the phone of numbers to call in emergencies. Obviously, the police had already been informed. There was no need for the fire department or an ambulance. The only remaining options were a priest or Dial-A-Prayer. Quentin called the number of the parish rectory but the line was busy. He slammed down the phone and stomped around the living room. He thought of the terror, skinned flesh and bruises of being raped. Getting better control of himself, he went to the phone and called his aunt. He waited for her to answer and told himself to settle down. Nothing could be so bad that he'd want to call a priest about it.

"Hello? Hattie? Mom's been in an accident."

"What hospital is she in?"

"She's not in a hospital."

"What kind of accident is it that you don't go to a hospital?"

"It wasn't that kind of accident."

"Was it her fault? Is she in jail?"

"She was raped! Goodbye."

Hattie's matter of fact attitude snapped Quentin back to his senses. Calling his aunt was clearly symptomatic of some sort of stunning irrationality on his part. He sat down at the kitchen table to think. The physical aspects of the rape were receding. It was common knowledge that the mind blots out the memory of painful experiences. And even if the rape was a terrible thing, what could be done about it? Were "bad" experiences less important or less legitimate than "good" ones? Didn't his mother have to come to terms with the experience despite its nature? Was empathy a useful emotion? There was no reason to reject rape as an unimportant experience. There was a great deal to be learned from anything, a great deal of growth.

The real question was whether his mother was alive enough to learn and grow from the experience. The answer had to be "yes." Organisms either grow or die. Stasis is decay. Quentin began to relish the prospect of seeing his mother gain from her experience. She'd been presented with a tremendous opportunity to learn a great deal. He was more than willing to do all he could to help. With the proper encouragement, her experience could be made into an epiphany.

Quentin's freshening outlook had made him forget about his aunt. Hattie's arrival interrupted his thoughts. He wondered whether her presence might be a bad influence, but there was evidently nothing he could do to remedy the situation.

The accident took surprisingly little time to straighten out. There was only damage to the lights, bumper and grill. The car ran fine. The police officer who showed up turned out to be an old friend of Gene's from high school who had seen Quentin at the airport the day before and asked Louise to be sure to say hello to Gene for him. He didn't give Louise a ticket, saying she seemed upset enough and no harm had been done. Louise thought it nice Phoenix was still small enough people could know a policeman as a friend. So, aside from the expense, there was no problem.

On the way home, Louise thought about Quentin and her trouble with him, but found that situation hard to get excited about. One way or another, it would take care of itself, regardless of what she thought the outcome should be. She shouldn't worry about something bad happening until it did. For the first time in two days she could relax without having to block Quentin out of her mind.

Louise's moment of peace came to an abrupt end as soon as they turned into the driveway at home. Hattie jumped out of the lawn chair on the front porch, bolted to the front door as if she'd been keeping lookout and yelled something. Quentin walked out the door as if to calm his excited aunt and strolled toward the car with a concerned look on his face.

"The car's a wreck too!" Hattie exclaimed. "Louise, how are you?"

"I'm fine. It's the car that's a little worse for the wear."

"You can walk? But what about the, uh, accident?" Hattie seemed to have something on her mind.

"It wasn't really an accident, it was just absentmindedness on my part."

"Absentmindedness? Didn't it upset you?"

"I was scared while it was out of control but when it finally bumped up against the wall and stopped, I was relieved."

Everyone but Aunt Hattie was looking at the damage done to the front of the car. It was evident to Quentin he'd been mistaken about the nature of the accident. His Aunt was on the verge of making the same discovery.

"You didn't get raped?" His Aunt gasped. Her eyes were lighting up. She pointed at the damaged car. "That's," she paused for emphasis, "the 'ACCIDENT?'"

Louise wasn't sure what all the commotion was about, but she wanted to try to keep Hattie from flying off on another trip so soon.

"I'm afraid Lon and I forgot to pick up your airline tickets. Stay home for a while, Hattie."

Concluding nothing significant was going on, Quentin headed back inside to work on his story, disappointed the whole thing had turned out to be so typically, for the family, mundane and unenlightening. His aunt was shaking her finger at his father.

"Lon, you rascal, playing a joke on your son like that. It's scandalous. I never in a million years expected that. But it was very good!"

Louise gave up trying to understand what was going on and headed inside smiling, leaving the "joke" to her sister's enjoyment, as it seemed to please her to no end.

What Did You Do in the War, Daddy?

Three twenty-seven, the displacement in cubic inches
of a Chevy Corvette V-8, right there in the afternoon paper,
right next to my birthday.

I'd never be drafted. Never swelter in a jungle infested with
insects and land mines. Never fly in a helicopter being shot at.
Never wear soaking, Army green, canvas boots. Not have to exile
myself to Canada. Not have to convince myself I was morally
opposed to war, or a Quaker, like, of all people, Richard Nixon.

To celebrate, we drank gin and tonics on our college's deserted
summer campus while the tall, leafy trees grew darker and the sky
grew translucent. We listened to a Detroit Tigers baseball game
in which Denny McLain, then and still, the last thirty game winner
in years, pitched his first game back from an injury, or a suspension,
or something. In any event, it was a momentous occasion
for my friend, a Detroit area native and Tigers fan.

We drank, and got bombed. Likewise, Denny McLain got
shelled and was gone after two and a third innings. And
the color drained from the sky until we could no longer have
seen the canopy of trees even if we'd been able, or cared, to.

About the Author

Born in Miami, Florida in 1951, Bill Fearnow obtained his B.A. in English from Hamilton College in 1973, then worked odd jobs and taught grade school and high school before obtaining his J.D. from the University of Notre Dame Law School in 1981, where he served as articles editor of *The Notre Dame Lawyer*. Long retired after practicing law for twenty years in Phoenix, Arizona, he splits his time between Paradise Valley and Tubac, Arizona with his wonderful wife of forty-five years, within easy visiting distance of their three grandchildren, two children, and their respective spouses.